AR... I'M GOING TO DO IT. I'M GOIN...
EIR I HAVE TO, BECAU...
HAVE
PUT YOUR PAIN TO PAPER
A LAKE FORTUNE NOVEL
HIS
to
SAVE
...HOPE. NOW
...SOMEONE... TO F...
NOT
KICKING AND
LK FARLOW

DEDICATION

To my Phoobs, you might not know it, but you absolutely rescued me.

CONTENT WARNING

This book contains content that may be triggering for some readers. Please see my website for a full list.

PROLOGUE
Grace

"He's a charmer, that's for sure. A silver-tongued devil with twinkling eyes," I mutter to myself as I rummage through my filing cabinet, searching for his folder.

My receptionist has been on me for years to digitize, but I much prefer to write all my notes by hand. It's more...*personal*.

I've been seeing Rand—*I mean treating Mr. Wallace*—for almost a year now, trying to help him navigate life as a single father after the tragic loss of his wife. It's been nearly six years since she passed, and he's still the textbook model of grief.

From denial to anger, bargaining to depression, and finally acceptance, I've helped him through it all. I've seen him at his worst, lost in the depths of his despair, and at his best, full of charm and easy smiles as he tries his best to get me to agree to a date.

I always turn him down, though, because as long as he's my patient, I can't ethically see him. But my goodness, as much as I don't want to admit it, the temptation is there.

In a way, he reminds me of my Jim, of the love I've lost. Which is absurd; they couldn't be more different.

Night and day, those two, truly.

Where Jim was a giver, kind and caring and always quick to smile, Rand is mercurial and compelling, with sharp wit and an even sharper tongue. We are the sun and the moon, and yet for reasons I don't fully comprehend, I'm drawn to him.

My chest pinches tight, making it impossible to draw in a full breath as traitorous thoughts of my patient slip out of the padlocked box I keep them in.

I shouldn't feel like this about him. About any man. *My God, what kind of monster am I?* My Jim's only been gone four months.

Moisture gathers along my lashes, but I refuse to let the tears fall. I'm a professional, and my patients deserve nothing but the best, even if sometimes it feels as if Rand sees into the depths of my very soul, making it hard to tell who's helping who.

"Get it together, Grace," I admonish myself as I read over my notes from his last session. "Get. It. Together."

It doesn't matter how pretty his words are or how inviting his smile is—he's off-limits. Giving into him would mean giving up the life I've worked so hard to build.

Becoming romantically involved with a patient is one of the worst offenses someone in my profession can commit. It's career suicide, seeing as it would mean the loss of my license. No psychiatrist worth their salt would ever cross that line.

I've told Rand this before too, that it's inappropriate—*forbidden.* The sly dog just smiles and says the best things in life always are.

"You are strong and capable." I speak the words out loud as I take a seat behind my desk, shielding myself behind the wooden monstrosity. Usually, we both sit in my armchairs, knees nearly touching as we bow our heads together and share our pain. But something—mostly my weakening resolve—tells me distance is needed if I'm to keep my head on straight.

The intercom on my phone buzzes, and then my receptionist's voice filters through. "Your eleven is here."

I suck in a deep breath and hold it before slowly exhaling. "Great, send him back."

My heart thunders in my chest as the seconds creep by. I swore to love Jim, and while our vows stated "till death," I never in a million years thought I'd lose him so soon.

We were high school sweethearts, and it's only been four months since he died. A mere blink compared to the eternity we promised one another.

Toward the end, Jim told me he wanted me to move on, to find happiness with another person again. *It's too soon.*

My breaths come quicker now, sweat beading along my hairline.

But then, the door opens and Rand walks in, his lips turned up in a knowing grin—and just like that, my rising panic ebbs.

"It's been too long, Gracie," he murmurs, his dark stare boring into me as he crosses the room to claim his usual seat.

"It's Dr. Morgan," I correct him softly, my cheeks burning with equal parts desire and shame. I don't know what it is about him, that he's able to stir such conflicting emotions within me.

Every minute in his presence feels like a full-on war; I'm enchanted by his sweet words, enticed by his physique, horrified by my weak resolve, mortified by my ever-slipping professionalism, and ashamed for thinking of any man other than my Jim in such a way.

"Come on now, doll." He leans back in the chair, a devilish smile twisting his lips as he spreads his legs wide. "We both know we're past that."

The deep drawl of his voice causes my nipples to pebble, making me extra thankful for the bulk of my sweater. "That's…" I swallow roughly, counting down from five in my head before trying again. "That's not appropriate, Mr. Wallace."

He stands from his chair and prowls toward me. My heart thunders in my chest as he rounds my desk, planting himself on the edge, right in front of where I'm seated.

"Um, Rand—Mr. Wallace, uh…" My words trail off as my heart shoots into my esophagus as he drags my chair closer, leaning into my space. "You… We can't!"

"We can." He presses his index and middle fingers to my temple, massaging lightly. "And we will, Gracie. You've spent too long denying this thing between us, and you can keep trying to pretend it isn't happening, that *we* aren't happening, but I assure you, we are."

The war inside of me rages on, as wanton desire goes head-to-head with wrenching guilt.

I gasp for air, my breaths coming in sharp pants as my vision pinpricks. I can't decide if I'm floating or falling—either way, my landing's going to hurt.

"It's okay, Gracie," he murmurs, trailing his fingers down from my temple, following my jawline. "Everything's going to be okay."

"No!" I try to shake my head, but he glides his palm across my cheek and tunnels his fingers into my hair, before curling them to hold me still.

Tears dot my lashes as I stare up at Rand. Nothing about him reflects the worry barreling through me. He's cool, calm, and collected, like he truly believes being together is the right thing—the only thing. As far as he's concerned, we're a foregone conclusion.

I should have seen this coming. For months now, he's been laying the groundwork for this, but I foolishly brushed it off as some kind of strange form of transference.

But now, I don't know... He seems so sure.

His eyes soften as he looks down at me, his palm still warm against my cheek. "Rand, I—"

He leans all the way in and silences me with a kiss.

My entire body jolts at the feel of his lips moving against mine. Firm, yet soft. Teasing, yet serious. Forbidden, yet indulgent. *Wrong, but so, so right.*

"Open for me, Gracie," he growls against my lips, causing me to gasp. This man is an apex predator in a button-down shirt, and I'm nothing more than the lamb he's about to slaughter.

Rand doesn't waste a single second, deepening our kiss. Before I know it, we're a frenzy of desire, using our lips, teeth, tongue, and hands. Time slows as we greedily explore one another.

I tug him closer, needing to feel the weight of his strong body against mine. Luckily, Rand can read me like a book and hooks his hands beneath my thighs, lifting me while somehow maneuvering us so that he's in my chair and I'm straddling him.

But the feeling of his erection pressing into my core breaks the moment, and I shove out of his lap as guilt and regret rain down on me, drowning me in a tsunami of shame.

"Rand—" My lower lip wobbles and hot tears fill my eyes, falling unchecked.

"Now, Gracie, don't cry." He leans in and kisses away my tears, groaning softly, almost as if he's savoring the taste.

"We...we—" I try again, but I can't seem to get my brain and mouth on the same page.

"We got a little carried away, that's all." He kisses my lips once more before standing and heading toward the door.

"And don't you dare say it was a mistake," he murmurs, his hand hovering over the knob, "because what we just did wasn't a mistake, and I damn sure don't regret it. You're like pure sunshine, Gracie, and I...I need your light."

He sounds so sincere. Maybe he's right. Maybe us being together is a good thing. Maybe we can heal all of the broken parts of each other.

"Tell me you agree, that you don't regret what just happened."

I take a few steadying breaths as I formulate my reply. "I don't regret it, but I also need time to think, Rand."

For a split second, something like anger flashes in his dark gaze, but it's gone so fast, I almost wonder if I imagined it. "Take all the time you need, Gracie," he says as he opens the door.

I breathe a sigh of relief, at both his reply and his retreat.

"But I need you to understand something, Gracie. *You're already mine.*"

ONE

Atlas

"You've reached the voicemail of Randall Wallace, please leave a message after—"

I jab the *end call* button and toss my phone down onto my passenger seat as my frustration reaches an all-time high.

This is the fourth call my dad hasn't answered this week, and while that's not necessarily cause for concern, he's been acting squirrely as hell here lately—enough so that I'm tempted to ask Ellis to do a wellness check on his next shift. Perks of having a cop for a best friend, I suppose.

Dad's always been a little closed off and cold, but since his latest wife—my stepmom—died, he's been worse than usual. Defensive, blunt, secretive... paranoid.

The same way he acted after your mom died, a sinister voice whispers in the back of my mind, hinting at something I've always wondered. I mean, what are the chances of a man losing *two* wives, both to mysterious illnesses?

Add in that he's now the sole caregiver for a teenage girl, and yeah, I'm fucking worried.

The trees surrounding the cabin I share with Ellis pass in a blur as I near our property. Maybe I'll call him again after dinner. Hell, maybe I'll just go by there, catch him unaware and force him to show me he's okay.

I make a quick pitstop at the mailbox to grab the mail, tossing it in the passenger seat before turning down our long, winding driveway.

"Should've stopped for a burger," I mutter under my breath, thinking of our empty fridge and bare-as-fuck pantry as I throw my truck into park and cut the engine. "A big, juicy burger."

I'm debating heading back into town to get one when a flash of orange in the passenger seat catches my eye.

I grab for it, surprised to find a very familiar-looking notebook tucked in the middle of my mail pile.

Why is Nora's—

My line of thinking smashes into a brick wall when I turn it over and find a neon-yellow sticky note pressed to the front with the words *please read me* scrawled sloppily across it.

"What in the actual fuck?" I ask out loud, despite there being no one to answer me. "I need a drink to deal with this shit."

Decision made, I grab the mail—and the notebook—and head into the house, ready to get to the bottom of this. Dinner's going to have to wait.

DIARY ENTRY, AGE 13

Dear Diary,

You don't know me yet, but you will. Mama says we'll be good friends. Seems weird since you're just a fancy notebook, but I'm willing to try anything at least once… Mama says I take after my dad in that way.

I keep expecting him to walk through the front door any minute, with a bouquet of daisies for Mama and a new book for me, but he's not going to. Not tonight, or ever again, because he died yesterday at exactly nine-oh-two in the morning. A pretty stupid time of day to die, if you ask me-even if I can't think of a better one. It sounds silly, but I guess I always thought he was unbeatable, like a superhero…

Only the villain that took him out was his own body-glioblastoma, whatever that is.

I haven't cried yet. Mama's worried. She keeps telling me it's okay to cry, but I'm not sure if she's saying it because I'm not or because she can't stop. It's not that I'm not sad, because I am. My dad was the best man to ever live, but I know crying won't bring him back. I can cry enough tears to fill an ocean, and he'll still be gone.

But Mama doesn't get it. She thinks I'm "internalizing" or something. She says it's not healthy to hold it all in, and I guess she'd know, seeing as she's a shrink. So, she got me you, and told me to put my pain to paper, so here we go.

I'm not entirely sure it'll work, but like I said, I'm willing to try

Skeptically, Nora

"Are you ready to go?" Scarlet, my on-and-off girlfriend, asks. The hint of irritation tinging her tone tells me I've either forgotten something important or it's not the first time she's asked. Probably both, if I'm being honest.

Rolling my shoulders, I suck in a steadying breath and force my gaze away from Nora's diary.

She never lets the leather-bound notebook out of her sight, and I truly mean never, which makes finding it between my water bill and a stack of junk mail pretty damn strange.

Under normal circumstances, I wouldn't give one single fuck about the contents of an eighteen-year-old girl's diary, but given everything that's happened recently, let's just say my interest is piqued.

I can't explain it, but something deep in my gut is telling me I need to read it, though given the first entry, I can't possibly fathom why. So far, the only thing Nora and I have in common is that we're both members of the dead parent club. Who knows— maybe this is her weird way of trauma-bonding?

In the last few months, she's really drawn into herself. Well, *more* into herself, I should say. She's always been quiet and reserved, the kind of kid who prefers the company of characters in a book than her peers. But the few times I've seen her since Grace passed, she's almost become a shadow of herself—like she's slowly fading away to nothing at all.

Dad says she's trouble, but I find it hard to believe. She seems so soft; fragile even. Not just emotionally but physically, too. A strong wind could probably knock her on her ass.

In fact, the first time we met, one nearly did...

I glance at my clock and wince as I turn down Dad's driveway. He told me to be here at six, said he wanted me to meet someone, but now it's six-twenty and I have three missed calls.

I'm sure he thinks the worst, that I'm showing up late just to spite him. And hell, maybe part of me is. I could have clocked out on time, but when Lane asked me to help clear a fallen tree from the main hiking trail, I agreed.

And now, there will most likely be hell to pay. No good deed goes unpunished, and all that shit.

By the time I make it to his house, which is set way back on a heavily wooded plot of land, he's on the front porch, pacing. Fuck.

I park and hop out, my hands in the air like I'm trying to placate a rabid dog. "Atlas!" he growls, and I realize that's exactly what I'm trying to do.

"Sorry, Dad, got stuck at work. The storm earlier today knocked a tree down, and we had to get it off the trail."

He continues glaring, and for a second, I worry he isn't going to let it go.

So, I deflect. "You said you wanted me to meet someone?"

"Grace," he murmurs, his features soften momentarily before going hard all over again. "They're running late, too. But her kid doesn't have a damn storm to blame."

I had a feeling I was here to meet the woman who's been occupying all of his free time, but the fact that she has a kid is news. Very surprising news, at that.

Dad barely likes me, and I'm his flesh and blood, so I can't really imagine him playing house with someone else's kid.

Guess love makes us do crazy things...

The sound of tires spinning on the gravel jerks both of our eyes back to the driveway. An older gray sedan makes its way toward us.

I squint, trying to make out the driver, but they're too far away.

"You best be on your best behavior tonight," Dad says without

ever looking my way.

His warning is useless, though; aside from being a grown-ass man that knows how to act right, I learned a long time ago not to piss him off if I can help it. The consequences are rarely worth it.

Finally, the car comes to a stop in front of the house. Dad's down the steps and at the driver's side before the engine's even off, pulling the door open.

I'm not sure what I'm expecting, but when a short, slightly plump woman in her mid-forties steps out, well—let's just say I'm surprised.

Maybe it's all of the shit Ellis watches on TV, but for some reason, I was half-expecting a young bombshell behind the wheel.

I watch with bated breath as Dad leans in and whispers something in her ear. Is he berating her for being late, as well? Will he punish her? I flex my fists at my sides, ready to spring into action if need be. But it seems like whatever he's saying makes her smile, which eases some of the weight pressing against my breastbone.

Maybe he's different with her...nicer.

"Come meet Grace," he calls as he leads her around the front of the car.

I take the porch steps two at a time, making it to them right as the back door swings open and a wisp of a girl climbs out.

"Grace, this is my son Atlas," he says, gently propelling her forward. "Atlas, this is Grace."

"I've heard so much about you," she says with a kind smile, her dull auburn hair sparkling with hints of silver in the evening light.

It's a fight to keep my face blank because this is damn sure the first I've ever heard of her. "It's a pleasure to meet you."

I turn my focus back to the kid. She's small, five feet if I'm being generous, with a shock of red hair and a frown that could rival the grumpiest of old men. It's hard to tell how old she is, other than a hell-of-a-lot younger than me.

"This is Nora," Grace says, nudging her daughter forward.

Dad goes to shake her hand, but she steps back, clutching an orange-covered book to her chest.

I guess this is their first-time meeting, too. Interesting.

The tips of his ears go red, and for a second, I worry he's about to go off, but instead he smiles. It's the fakest smile I've ever seen, but it's better than yelling, so I'll take it.

"Well, let's head inside before the sky falls," Dad says, guiding Grace away from her daughter and up the steps.

Nora glares after them with all the rage of a newborn feral kitten.

Despite the wind starting to pick up, she makes no move to head inside.

"You coming, Pip?" The nickname slips out unbidden, but somehow, it fits.

"What did you just say?" She turns her icy glare on me.

I don't know why, but I grin. "Pip—you know, like pipsqueak."

She bares her teeth at me. "My name is Nora!"

"Right." I glance down at my well-worn boots to hide my smile. "Well, you coming inside, Nora? I know you don't wanna be here—and I'll tell you a secret: I don't either—but at least inside there's food and no rain."

"It's not raining out here either..." She trails off, the unspoken yet hanging between us.

"Suit yourself, then." I turn toward the house, feeling some kind of way about leaving someone so small outside when it's about to storm. I know firsthand the kind of damage storms like these can bring.

But before I can ask her again, a huge crack of thunder booms overhead, and I hear a squeak followed by the sound of her shoes on the gravel as she bolts toward me, only before she can make it to the first step, the wind starts to howl, and she must be smaller than I thought because the gust sends her flying my way.

She windmills her arms, trying to keep herself upright, but it's no use. The kid's going down.

I reach out and steady her before she can hit the ground. "You good?" I ask, making sure she's steady before releasing my hold on her shoulders.

"Fine," she mutters, like the single syllable hurts her to give up, darting up the steps and into the house.

I always chalked Nora's oddness up to grief and a healthy dose of teenage angst. The kid lost both of her parents in less than five years of each other, and now the only family she has left is me and Dad. The fact that I never really made an effort to get to know her sort of has me feeling like shit now.

Still, I read over the first passage a few times, thinking maybe there was a hidden meaning, but I've got nothing.

I guess I'll have to keep going and see what I find, if anything.

"Atlas!" Scarlet snaps her fingers and I shut the diary, shoving it under my pillow, focusing all of my attention on her.

She's dressed in a short little black number that hugs her curves like she was sewn into it as she leans against my door frame in a way I'm sure is meant to be seductive.

And yet, in this moment, even with her toned legs and ample cleavage on display, my dick stays soft.

I'm pretty sure we're headed toward being *off* again in the near future, because while she's certainly a looker, my libido seems to be on an extended vacation.

"Sorry, what?"

"Atlas." She sighs, sauntering my way. "We have plans tonight, don't you remember?"

"Remind me?" I give her my best grin, and she melts, running her fingers through my hair.

"Dinner and dancing ring a bell?"

I could lie and say I remember but honestly, I don't, and I'm sure the look on my face is a dead giveaway. "Not even a little."

Guess it's a good thing I didn't get that burger...

"Ellis's new flavor of the month—" I don't miss the way her lip curls at the mention of Carrie—or maybe her name's Kelsey? "—wants to check out some rock band, and he so kindly volunteered us to tag along."

Spending hours in a crowded bar sounds like fucking torture, but even so, I find myself nodding along. Sometimes giving in to her is less of a headache than arguing. "Give me fifteen to shower and change."

"Or..." Scarlet leans down, thrusting her tits into my face as she licks her red-slicked lips. "I could join you and we can make it twenty."

You'd think I'd be all over it; she's hot as sin and a sure thing, but still, nothing. Maybe a night out isn't such a bad thing. Hell, after a few drinks, I'm betting I'll be begging her to sneak away to the bathroom or my truck for a little fun.

But here and now, it's not happening. "Don't wanna keep Ellis waiting, right?" I stand from the bed and press my lips to hers, hoping the kiss softens my refusal.

Sure enough, she melts under my touch and pads back out to the living room to wait.

I make quick work of showering and dressing in a pair of

well-worn jeans and a button-down shirt. A quick glance at my phone tells me I have five minutes to spare.

Logically, I know I should just head on out to the living room so we can get on the road, but instead, I find myself reaching for Nora's diary. I'm not sure why, but I feel—*Fuck, I don't know,* compelled?—to read it or something. It's like this itch under my skin, and the only way to scratch it is to get to the bottom of why she left it for me, and so, with sure fingers, I flip to the next entry, and let myself fall into her words.

DIARY ENTRY, AGE 13

Dear Diary,

Today was weird. Carson Childress told me I was pretty and asked me to sit with him in the cafeteria while we were studying in the library, but then at lunch when I approached his table, he said I had to give him a kiss to sit down.

I don't want to kiss Carson. I barely even know him. Mama says he's probably trying to show off or impress me, which makes it double dumb. There's nothing impressive about forcing a girl to kiss you.

Even worse, Kelsey and Eliza laughed at me instead of having my back, and they're supposed to be my best friends. After lunch, they told me I couldn't sit with them anymore because their table was for couples only. No one told me getting a boyfriend changes your personality. I don't really get it, but a part of me can't help but wonder if I'm missing out. Then again, if Carson Childress is my only choice, maybe I'm better off alone.

Mama says it's called peer pressure and that if I don't like Carson, I should stand my ground. But I don't know which sounds worse: having a boyfriend who's a jerk or sitting all alone.

I guess since it's Friday, I have the weekend to think about it.

Doubtfully, Nora

Dear Diary,

After two days of Carson pestering me during our shared classes and eating all alone at lunch while my so-called friends pointed and laughed, I gave in and told Carson I'd be his girlfriend.

That good-for-nothing snake said he'd only date me for a kiss and a boob squeeze. I told him to kick rocks and then he called me a Goody-Two-Shoes fire crotch.

Mama says I hurt his "masculine pride" by turning him down. But if he's that dang fragile then I'm definitely not interested.

But the whole thing got me thinking about what I want in a boyfriend. So, here's a list:

-Smart

-Funny

-Kind

It seems like a short list, but Dad was all of those things, and he made Mama happier than anyone else on the planet.

He's been gone for three months now, and she's still so sad. I wish I could do something to help, but the only thing that would make her better is him not being dead.

But he is, and I haven't seen Mama smile since. I miss her smile. It was wide and toothy, and just the sight of it felt like the best kind of hug.

This got off track pretty quick, huh, diary? I don't know. I guess I just needed to vent.

Annoyed, Nora

TWO
Atlas

"Please don't be mad," I murmur, reaching across the center console for Scarlet's hand.

Much to my surprise, she allows me to interlace our fingers. She's been giving me the silent treatment and glaring like a pissed-off alley cat ever since she came back to my room to find me with my nose buried in Nora's diary, instead of coming straight out to her after getting ready.

"I just don't get it, Atlas." She strokes her thumb over my knuckle. "First you forgot we even had plans, and then after being reminded, you still blew me off to read your sister's diary."

Not my fucking sister, I think to myself, knowing better than to say it out loud. I'm trying to shove the worms back into the damn can, not open it from both ends.

"I'm not trying to be rude," she continues, "but like, it's kind of weird, don't you think?"

"Weird how?" I ask, turning into The Creek's parking lot. Although, if I'm being honest, I'm not entirely sure I want to hear her answer.

"Seriously?" She yanks her hand out of my grip. "You don't see anything weird or creepy about a grown-ass man reading his little sister's diary?"

I heave out a breath and throw my truck into park. "First of all, Nora's not my sister. My dad married her mom—"

"Fine, she's your *stepsister*," Scarlet growls, cutting me off. "That's still family."

Anger simmers beneath my ribs, but I swallow down the urge to lash out, and continue evenly. "Second, I barely even know Nora. Hell, I've probably only been around her a handful of times in the *years* our parents were married. Third, it's not that I care about what's in her diary, it's that she left it for me, with a note *begging* me to read it. Begging me, Scar. You're over here making me out to be some kind of fucking pedophile, and that's fucked up, big time fucked up. Not to mention, you know Dad's been MIA and I'm worried about *both* of them. So, excuse-the-fuck-out-of-me for latching onto any clue I can."

"You're right, I'm sorry." Scarlet looks away, shame coloring her cheeks. "I guess I was just jealous you forgot about me."

Leaning over the console, I run my knuckles under her chin, drawing her gaze back my way. "No need to be jealous, Scar. You know you're my girl."

The words sour on my tongue the second I form them, because Scarlet and I both know she's *not* my girl a hell of a lot more than she is. I mean, shit, it wasn't even an hour ago that I was thinking we should take a break again.

"You mean it?" she asks, blinking up at me through thick, sooty lashes.

I really don't...

The realization smacks me across the face with the force of a two-by-four, but I'm not trying to spend the night fighting, so instead I force my lips up into a grin and nod. "You know it. Now let's go find Ellis and order some drinks."

We both open our doors at the same time—I used to try to open Scarlet's for her, but after about the second or third time, she let me know she could get her own damn door—and meet in front of my truck.

"Are you actually gonna dance with me?" Scarlet asks, stepping ahead of me to get to the door.

I ball my hands into fists at my sides and let her hold it open for me. It's not that I'm against women doing things for themselves, it's just one of the many things my mama ingrained in me before she passed away.

Swear to God, some days, I can still hear her voice as clear as day telling me *hold that door* or *a gentleman walks on the outside of the sidewalk to place himself between his companion and harm.*

But Scarlet's as headstrong as an ox, and I know damn well I'm better off respecting her feelings than pushing my own on her.

The second we enter the dimly lit bar Scarlet's hips begin to sway in perfect time with the music pulsing through the speakers. I follow behind her as she weaves her way through the crowd in search of Ellis.

I'm not sure who's playing tonight, but whoever they are, they have a hell of a following, because there are people wall to fucking wall in here.

I scan the bar and by sheer luck I spot him and his date cozied up together in a booth on the far wall. With the way he's leaning in close and whispering in her ear, I'm half-tempted to leave them to it.

But Scarlet spots them, too, and takes off in their direction before I can suggest giving them some space.

"Well, well, well," Scarlet chides as she approaches their table. "Isn't this... *intimate.*" She's always been a bit weird whenever Ellis dates, and maybe that should bother me, but it doesn't.

You're not invested enough to care...

Revelations are hitting me left and right tonight, or maybe I'm finally admitting what I've always known. Either way, I'm going to need a drink or two to survive the night.

Ellis straightens in the booth, wrapping a protective arm around his date in the process.

"'Sup, man?" He lifts his chin in greeting as I slide into the opposite side of the booth.

"Not a whole lot," I say, causing Scarlet to scoff. Girl holds a grudge like no one else I've ever known—except for my dad, maybe—but if I start thinking about him, I'm going to start thinking about Nora, and then the night will for sure end in a fight.

Ellis's eyes flit between us, but with a subtle shake of my head, he lets it go. "I'd like y'all to meet Callie. Cal, this is my roommate, Atlas, and his girl Scarlet."

"It's nice to meet you. Heard a lot about you," I tell her while Scarlet plays on her phone, ignoring all of us.

Callie's cheeks turn a deep shade of pink. "It's nice to meet y'all, too."

I nudge Scarlet with my elbow, not even trying to keep up

with her mood swings. If I didn't know better, I'd think my girlfriend had a thing for my best friend. But she can barely stand him most days. Still, no reason for her to be rude, especially when she's the one who dragged us out here for a double date.

For a second, I worry she's not going to put her phone away, but after she finishes typing something out, she sighs and locks the screen before sliding the slim device back into her purse.

"Sorry about that," she says, not sounding the least bit sorry. "So, tell me, Sarah, how did y'all meet?"

"Her name's Callie," Ellis and I correct her in tandem, but Scarlet just smiles and murmurs another feigned apology.

"Well, it's actually a pretty funny story." Callie smiles up at my best friend, and I've got to admit, the way she doesn't even falter a little in the face of Scarlet's cattiness impresses me. "I was driving down the older part of Driftwood Way—you know, where it's only a single lane of traffic?—and he was coming from the other way, so I tried moving over to make room for his beast of a truck and I got stuck in the mud!"

Ellis laughs. "My beast came in handy, though, didn't it?"

"Your winch did, anyway," she quips, reaching for her drink.

"Isn't that charming." The strain in Scarlet's voice steals my focus away from the happy couple. She's usually pretty pleasant—even around Ellis—but tonight she's all poison, and I'm not really sure why.

"Why don't you go and grab us a pitcher and ask for them to start us a tab?" I ask, trying to get this night back on track.

"I could definitely use a damn drink." She stands from the table and stalks off toward the bar without so much as a backward glance.

"Who in the hell pissed in her Cheerios?" Ellis asks as soon as she's gone.

"I think I did," I admit, running my hands through my hair.

"I know she's a spitfire, but tonight she's more like a fucking bonfire doused in gasoline."

Callie props her elbows on the table, balancing her chin on her fists. "I just figured she didn't like me."

Ellis laughs. "I don't think Scar likes anyone."

I nearly laugh, but swallow the sound back before it can escape. I'm already on thin ice with her, and despite being unsure about the future of our relationship, I can't stand by and let him talk shit. "She's not that bad. Honestly. Scarlet's typically pretty nice, if a little high-strung. Our night got off to a bad start because I forgot we had plans."

"In the doghouse, huh?" Ellis laughs, his eyes crinkling in the corners. "Woof!"

My best friend is a complete and total jackass.

"Shut up."

"No, seriously, what'd you do?"

"Well..." I glance toward the bar and see there's still a few patrons ahead of Scarlet. "I found Nora's diary in our mailbox, and—"

"I'm sorry, what?" Ellis cuts me off. "Why in the hell would your little sister's diary be in our mailbox?"

"She's not my sister," I mutter, pinching the bridge of my nose. "And I haven't figured out the why yet, but she left a sticky note on it asking me to please read it."

"And you're actually doing it?" Ellis's whole face screws up. "Like, you're reading all about her little teenage crushes and shit?"

Callie cuts her eyes at Ellis and then to me. "Yes, because that's all girls are capable of, right?"

"Hey, whoa!" He holds his hands up, backtracking. "I didn't mean anything by it. It's just… weird."

"Yeah, well, Scar thinks so, too." I shift my shoulders, trying to shake off my growing frustrations. "But with how Dad's been acting, I need all the help I can get."

Ellis looks thoughtful as he takes a sip of his drink. "Still haven't heard from him?" he asks, after he swallows.

"Nope. He's been *off* since Grace died, like more so than usual, and now…" I trail off as I try to find the right words. "He's not exactly a warm guy on the best of days, and on the worst, he's an outright asshole, and Nora's so small and her mom was all she had, and I guess I'm just… *fuck.*" I sigh, unable to articulate my concern.

"You're worried, man, and that's okay."

"Yeah, I am. I just can't shake the feeling that something's wrong. I was actually going to ask if you could do a welfare check?"

"Yeah, of course."

His easy agreeance instantly has me feeling ten pounds lighter.

"Thanks, man." I hold my fist out toward him, and he bumps his knuckles to mine.

"It's what friends are for."

I turn to Callie, feeling slightly embarrassed, having just spilled all of that in front of a virtual stranger. "Sorry about that…"

She smiles and knocks her shoulder into Ellis's. "No apology needed. Promise."

Ellis quirks his brows at me and then leans down to press a kiss to Callie's temple. "She's a good one, man."

"Seems like it."

"Aw, am I interrupting a moment?" Scarlet asks, thrusting the pitcher down onto the table. A little beer splashes over the side, but Callie grabs a napkin and sops it up before I can.

"Just catching up," I tell her, pouring myself a glass.

"Catching up?" She blinks and then laughs humorlessly. "You live together, what is there to catch up on?"

"Scarlet—" I start, but the sound of a loud guitar riff cuts me off, stopping our fight before it can even start as the band takes the stage.

"I'm so excited!" Callie shimmies in her seat. "I've heard they're so good. C'mon, El, let's dance."

He slides out of the booth and extends a hand to her, which she readily grabs, and together they head out onto the packed dance floor.

Scarlet still looks sour, but maybe once the music starts and she's had a few drinks, she'll forget all about being upset with me.

I top off her drink as the band's frontman addresses the crowd. "What's up, Fortune, Georgia? We're Iron Resurrection, and we're fucking stoked to be here tonight!"

The bar erupts into cheers, as the drummer counts them off, launching straight into their first song.

"Don't be mad, Scar." I damn near have to shout for her to hear me.

She turns to face me, hurt and fury all over her face. "I heard you, you know?"

"Heard me what?" I rack my brain trying to think of what she could be talking about, because unless she can hear my innermost thoughts, I can't imagine what she could have heard to have her this pissed off.

I swear, this whole fucking night feels like one step forward and two back.

"Talking about Nora and how worried you are about her

because she's so soft and delicate."

"What?" I cock my head to the side, trying and failing to get a good read on the situation. "You're mad that I'm worried about my stepsister?"

"I just think it's interesting that she's all you've been able to think about tonight. Like, what the fuck, Atlas?"

I down the rest of my beer, trying like hell to keep my cool. But Scarlet almost seems hungry for a fight. "I'm struggling here, Scar. Help me out."

"If we fucked tonight, would you think about her then too? Would you call her name out when you came?"

"What in the actual hell is wrong with you?" I ask, horrified by what she's implying.

"I'm just saying you seem a little *too* concerned."

"Get up," I growl, already moving forward.

Scarlet scrambles out of the booth and I stalk past her, heading toward the bar without sparing her so much as a second glance.

"Atlas! Wait!" she hollers after me, but I keep on, determined to settle our tab and leave. This whole night has been a dumpster fire, start to finish.

"Another round?" the bartender asks.

"Cash me out." I pull out my wallet and pass him my card.

I feel someone tug on my shirt as I sign the bill, and I turn to find Scarlet behind me, her eyes wet with tears.

"Please, Atlas, I didn't mean—"

"Mean it or not, you said it. You've been itching for a fight all night, so you went low to get a reaction out of me."

She sucks her wobbling lower lip between her teeth and glances down at the sticky bar floor.

"I can give you a ride home or you can call an Uber. Either

way, I'm out."

"You don't mean that," she whispers, looking up at me from beneath damp lashes.

"I really do." I slide my phone out of my pocket, tap open the rideshare app, and tilt my screen toward her. "Now, what'll it be?"

Right before my eyes, her melancholy and regret morphs into anger. "You're a real piece of work, Atlas Wallace!" she shouts, garnering us more than a few stares before turning and storming off.

"Guess she'll find her own way home," I mutter, closing out of the app and opening my text thread with Ellis.

Me:
Heading home. Pissed Scarlet off,
nuclear level. Keep an eye out?

Miraculously, he texts me back instantly.

Ellis:
10-4. Eyes on her now at the table.
Drive safe.

With that settled, I slide my phone back into my pocket and head for my truck. This whole night's been shit, and the only thing that sounds remotely appealing is climbing into my bed and conking out until morning.

The drive home feels longer than usual, and by the time I make it through the front door and into my room, I'm exhausted.

After brushing my teeth, I strip down to my boxers and all but collapse onto my bed. My eyelids are already heavy as I slip beneath the covers, but as I slide my arm beneath my pillow for support, my fingers brush against something hard.

Nora's diary.

And just like that, I'm wide awake and flipping to where I

left off.

DIARY ENTRY, AGE 13

Dear Diary,

It's almost my birthday, and Mama keeps asking me what I want and I keep telling her I don't know and she keeps getting frustrated and saying they don't sell that at the store. But, Diary, the problem is, they don't sell what I want...

Unless you can bring people back from the dead for real and I just don't know it.

My best friends-well, former best friends-told me I needed to get over my dad dying because no one likes sad girls. But how? How am I supposed to just get over it? It's only been six months since he passed. Six months that somehow feel like the blink of an eye and an eternity all at the same time.

But I can't just tell Mama all of that, because she's been smiling recently. And for a while there, I didn't think I'd ever see her smile again. So, I'll just keep my mouth shut and make up something that I want so that she can feel like things are the way they should be. And so she'll think I'm "healing."

Because I know she feels guilty. Which is kind of dumb because she didn't do anything. It's not like she killed him. But like Ms. Maggie (that's my therapist) says, grief isn't always logical.

In fact, she says that sometimes grief is downright sneaky. That you can be fine and then all of a sudden sobbing and then raging at the unfairness of it all in a single breath. I guess she's right, too, because I've done just that.

Like, even silly little things will make me so mad that I just blow up. I know it worries Mama (clearly, since I'm seeing a shrink every week-luckily, she doesn't work for the same place Mama does, because that would be weird) but she mostly just tells me to write down how I'm feeling.

Over and over, she tells me to put my pain to paper and to give it away.

But sometimes I worry that if I keep writing it all down that I'll forget. Not my dad—I'll always remember him, Diary, because he's the best man I've ever known. No, I worry I'll forget how sad I am without him. I worry that one day I'll smile like nothing ever happened...like he was never here.

Deep down, I know he would want me to be happy and to smile, but here's that illogical grief creeping in again, like it always does, wrapping itself around me like a heavy blanket, making sure I stay a sad girl—the kind of girl Kelsey and Eliza say no one likes.

But maybe that's my lot in life. To be the sad girl without a dad who dreads her birthday and smiling. Or maybe today was just a lot and I needed to vent.

Who knows. I guess time will tell.

Sadly, Nora

DIARY ENTRY, AGE 14

Dear Diary,

Today's the big day. As of 4:45 this afternoon, I'm officially fourteen. Mom started the day with waffles and bacon, like always, but where Dad always made perfect bacon, hers was burned. I mean it, too—it literally looked like strips of a tire. But I ate every charred bite with a fake smile on my face because she's been sad again.

We're both sad girls now, except today I have to pretend to be happy. Which sucks, because I'm anything but.

Mama insisted on throwing me a party last night, and she double insisted on me inviting pretty much my whole grade. She said fourteen was a special year (I don't know what's so special about it) and so she booked the skating rink and bought a bunch of pizzas and cake.

Surprise, surprise... No one came.

Mama kept asking if I handed the invites out (I did) and I kept asking if she had the date and time right (she did), which really sucks because it means Kelsey and Eliza were right after all. No one likes sad girls.

No one likes me.

I somehow went from being in the cool crowd to the weird loner who eats lunch in the library. I guess this is what Mama meant when she said teenagers were fickle. Although, I'm pretty sure that's just a nice way of saying shallow assholes.

Then again, I barely like me at this point, so maybe Kelsey and Eliza are actually onto something. All I do is cry and read and listen to all of Dad's favorite songs. Mama says I'm suffering from depression, and Ms. Maggie agrees. They think I need to be medicated, like some freaking happy pill can take away the ache of losing him.

But the thought of the pain ever really easing only makes me hold onto it that much more, because won't being happy again mean that I've forgotten him?

Mama says it's not healthy to carry around this kind of hurt, but I say she's a hypocrite because she carries it around, too. She just hides it with concealer, lipstick, and brittle smiles.

I guess I should tell you about my birthday gift. I ended up telling Mama I wanted a gift card to the local bookstore. She bought me and loaded it with a hundred dollars. She also bought me some nice pens (I'm using one now) and a framed picture of Dad and me from my thirteenth birthday. We're both making silly faces in the picture, and I cried like a baby when I saw it.

So, even though I'm apparently a giant loser with no friends, it was still a pretty good birthday...as good as it could be, anyway.

Numbly, Nora

THREE

Atlas

"You leave any coffee for me?" I ask Ellis the following morning as I drag my tired ass into the kitchen.

"I can make more," he says, far too chipper for the early hour; the sun's not even out but he's bright-eyed and bushy-tailed.

Meanwhile, it's my damn off day, and I'm *still* up with the birds.

I let his happy-go-lucky-morning-person shit slide since he's already dumping the grounds into the trash and starting a fresh pot. "You go somewhere else after you left last night?" he asks, smirking, "You look like shit."

A sound—something between a low laugh and a growl—slips out of me before I can stop it. I fucking wish I could blame my haggard appearance on a hangover. "Stayed up for a while reading, but my dreams were crazy and I kept waking up."

His lips quirk up into a wry grin. "Let me guess, the diary?" He presses the button on the coffee maker, and it gurgles to life.

I slump down onto a barstool and rest my head against the cool granite of the island. "Yeah, man. I don't know why, but I can't stop reading it."

"Huh." He grabs a mug and pours it full, knowing I like it black. "Find anything useful?"

"No," I mumble, tracking his movements as he slides the mug my way. "Not really."

"Then why keep reading?" He rounds the island and sits down on the stool next to me.

"I—don't even know how to explain it. I just have to know, you know? Like I'm *compelled* to finish it."

"Is it even remotely interesting?" He scratches his chin thoughtfully. "I can't imagine reading the innermost thoughts of a teenage girl would be, but—"

"Liar." I cut him off, and we both start to grin. We're two sides of the same coin, and he already knows exactly what I'm going to say. "Your ass loves all of those bullshit high-drama teen shows. What did you just finish rewatching... *Gossip Girl*?"

"Listen, asshole," he starts, his lips quivering as he tries not to laugh. "There's just something about the Upper East Side that does it for me."

"More like the brunette chick does it for you."

"Blair?" he groans. "Fuck yeah, she does. There's just something about that bitchy attitude of hers... *mmm*."

The fact that said attitude is reminiscent of Scarlet doesn't escape my notice, but I don't comment on it. "Yeah, yeah. Whatever you say."

His lips thin as he pins me with a serious look. "I'm guessing you still haven't heard from your dad?"

"Not a word." I get wanting to be left alone; hell, other than Ellis—and occasionally Scarlet—I could probably go days without talking to another human being. There's a reason I work as a park ranger, after all.

However, if someone needed to talk to me, they could damn sure get a hold of me. In this day and age, it's not like you need a carrier pigeon. A text message would suffice.

"Try calling him."

I slide off my stool and pad back into my room to grab my phone. Once I rejoin Ellis in the kitchen, I swipe my thumb across the screen to send the call.

"Put it on speaker."

Nodding, I tap the button and place my phone down on the island. As expected, it rings a few times before going to voicemail.

"Try again." The worry reflected at me in his eyes mirrors my own. Something sure as shit isn't right, and I can't seem to stop my brain from zeroing in on one hypothetical disaster after another.

Even though I know he won't pick up, I send the call again, my heart lodged in my throat as I wait for it to connect.

This is insane—I don't even get along with my old man all that well. I just know in my gut that something's wrong, and no matter what I do, I can't shake the feeling.

This time, the voicemail picks up after only two rings.

"He declined your call," Ellis muses, a troubled look clouding his features as he drums his fingers on the countertop. "So, he has his phone on him."

"I don't know, man." I scrub my hands over my face. "Something's going on. I just don't know what."

His eyes light. "Have you tried calling Nora?"

It's not a bad idea, except... "I don't have her number." I slump back.

"Shit." He begins pacing back and forth in front of the sink. "Your dad's always been...*out there*...but he's never gone fully off the grid before, right?"

"Nah. Things were dicey for a while after Mom died, what with his drinking. But once your old man got him into AA, he was okay-ish."

"Maybe he's taking Grace's death hard?"

"Could be," I agree, even though I actually don't. Call it a gut feeling or instinct, I don't know, but something tells me it's more than him mourning the loss of his second wife.

Maybe it's my imagination running wild, but I have a bad feeling about all of this, and no matter what I do, I can't seem to shake it.

Ellis turns and stalks into what should be our dining room but is mostly a store-all space, heading for his safe in the corner. He punches in the code, swings open the heavy door, and grabs his duty belt, securing it around his waist.

"I've gotta go, but I'll stop by and check on him once I sign on."

"Appreciate it, man," I tell him, meaning it with every fiber of my being. We've been friends since we were in diapers, waded through thick and thin together, and I'd easily give my left nut to help him if he was ever in a pinch—the fact that I know he'd do the same is just icing on the cake.

He claps my back as he passes me on his way to the door. "I'll let you know if anything comes of it."

I tip my chin in acknowledgment, already worrying over

what he may or may not find.

Every part of me wants to continue scouring Nora's diary for some sort of clue. It feels like everything—my mom's death, Grace's death, Dad's radio silence, Nora's diary—is stacking up like a precariously balanced house of cards. All it would take is one strong blow to send it all crashing down. I just hope I'm able to pick up all of the pieces once they scatter.

Resigned, I force myself up off my stool for another cup of coffee, hoping maybe some more caffeine will kick my brain online.

DIARY ENTRY, AGE 14

Dear Diary,

Mom's seeing someone. She thinks she's sneaky and that I'm clueless, but it's like Dad used to say, I wasn't born yesterday. She's been happy and smiling and most telling of all-busy.

She went from only going to work and the grocery store to having plans. Friday night drinks, Saturday lunches, and Sunday brunches. We used to spend our weekends together, as a family, and now I spend them alone.

Which is fine, I guess. It's not like I'm great company. Maybe Mom doesn't like sad girls, either.

As much as I want to be mad at her, I'm not. It's nice to see her smile again. I just wish she'd be honest with me. I'm not a little kid, but she and Ms. Maggie think I'm "emotionally fragile," which is the freaking dumbest thing I've ever heard.

Am I supposed to be all happy and laughy and smiley less than a year after my dad died? It's funny how it went from "grief isn't logical" to me being "emotionally fragile."

But whatever.

I guess she'll tell me when she's ready.

Irritated, Nora

Dear Diary,

Mama's gone again. For the weekend this time. She asked if I could stay with a friend so she could go for a girls' weekend. I told her yes even though we both know I don't have any friends.

I guess she doesn't remember…or is choosing not to.

Luckily, I have a key to the house and the fridge is stocked, so I guess I have the place to myself all weekend.

If my life was a movie or a TV show, I'd throw a big party and everyone would come. It would be some big turning point, and I'd either end up in the cool crowd or a whole heap of trouble.

But it's not, so I don't.

Plus, I don't even have social media to invite anyone anyway.

Looks like I'll spend the next two days reading the books I picked up after school when I was supposed to be heading to my imaginary sleepover.

It's getting harder not to be angry, though. How is it everyone's moving on but me? Why am I the only one still sad? Is this how I'll be forever? Angry and sad, with eyes that stay red from crying?

I want more for myself. I want friends and to be happy and to have a life of my own one day. But I just… I don't know how to get there. I don't know how to move on, and Ms. Maggie doesn't seem to know how to help me either.

Maybe I'm just broken. Maybe the part of me that knows how to smile died and was buried right alongside my dad.

I don't know. I don't know anything anymore.

Lost, Nora

Dear Diary,

It only took two months, but Mom finally came clean and admitted she's been seeing someone.

She also told me he's invited us over for dinner tonight. Way to give a girl some warning. I guess she thought the element of surprise was the way to go. It's like she doesn't know me at all anymore.

I'm like Dad—a planner. Always have been. And Mama knows this. She used to joke around and say our need to know and prepare kept her grounded, that without us she'd just float away.

I've gotta think a whole lot before I'm ready to do, and her springing this on me with less than an hour before show time is the worst thing she could've done.

Well, that's a lie. The worst would be her bringing him here with no warning. But this is a close second, and it makes me feel like she doesn't even care.

If Ms. Maggie were here, she'd tell me to make the best of it. Good thing she's not because I'd tell Ms. Maggie to shove it.

I guess I'll be back later with all of the gory details. Wish me luck.

Well, diary, I was right. Tonight was a total disaster. Well, not all of it. But most of it. Mostly because of me.

Mom and I argued the whole way there, which made me cry, because we haven't really fought about anything since before Dad died. Mainly because I've gotten so good at biting my tongue.

But tonight, when she asked me if I was excited to meet Rand and his son, I just couldn't.

I totally snapped and told her I wasn't excited and that she should be ashamed of herself for sneaking around the way she did. I told her it was obvious she didn't care how I felt about it all one way or the other, otherwise she wouldn't have hidden it from me.

Her eyes filled with tears, and she had to grip the steering wheel really hard to keep us from sliding all over the wet road. She said I wasn't being fair. I told her she wasn't either.

I feel bad for making her cry, but come on! Who does that to their kid?

Whatever. I wish I could say that was the worst part, but sadly, it wasn't.

We bickered all the way up until we got to his house-although it's more of a cabin, really. And way out in the woods. Like so far away that no one would hear you scream.

Rand, as Mama calls him, was waiting outside for us. I thought he looked mad, but when he came and opened Mama's door, he was all lovey-dovey and sweet. To her. He completely ignored me. Not that Mama noticed. She was too busy soaking up his affection to even think about me.

Rand's a big guy. Tall, with dark features and a little gray in his hair. His face looks mean anytime he's not looking at Mama. Whenever he focuses on her, his hard eyes go all soft and gooey.

I guess as long as he's nice to her, it doesn't much matter what he thinks of me. He doesn't have to like me, because I don't see myself ever liking him either.

The biggest surprise of the night was that Rand has a son. He's grown, though, and kind of looks like a superhero. He was nice enough, even if he did call me a pipsqueak.

I wasn't very nice to him, though, and now I feel awful. He made an effort to talk to me, and I ignored him. I was acting like a total snot. He even caught me when the weather scared me and I tripped. I didn't even say thanks. I just ran inside and did my best to ignore everyone for the rest of the night.

Atlas—that's his name, by the way—tried to include me in the dinner conversation, but I didn't want to talk.

Even worse, I cried over dessert. Rand served banana pudding, which was Dad's favorite. We used to make it together at least once a month. We tested hundreds of recipes before we found the perfect one.

It felt wrong to eat it at Rand's table. Mom sent me to the bathroom to "dry it up" and called me a brat on the way home, which really hurt. But I guess I deserved it.

If Dad would have been there, he would have said he taught me better than to be so rude. Guess I'm just a disappointment all around.

Any dreams of having a cool, older friend are out the window, too. I'm sure Atlas thinks I'm a little crybaby. I definitely came off like one. I guess the real question is which is worse—being a crybaby or being sad and socially inept?

Humiliated, Nora

The sound of my phone ringing pulls me out of Nora's despair. After two more cups of coffee, I retreated back to my room and fell face-first into her diary.

Reading our introduction, and the events that led up to it, leaves a hollow feeling in my chest. The kid's been through more shit than anyone her age should have.

Swiping my thumb over the screen, I blindly accept the call. "Hello."

"Atlas, man," Ellis's voice trickles through the line. "It's not good."

With those three words, he has all of my attention. "Tell me," I demand, jumping up from my desk chair, I begin pacing back and forth in front of my window. "Just… tell me." My voice breaks at the end, as I beg my oldest friend not to sugarcoat it.

"The place is totally trashed."

"Trashed how?" I ask, coming to an abrupt stop. My dad's a lot of things, but a slob isn't one of them. He was always damn near militant in his need for cleanliness.

"I don't know..." He pauses, and I can almost picture him surveying the space, his eyes narrowed and his feet planted wide. "Like someone tossed the place but didn't take anything."

"What do you mean?" My voice comes out steady, which is a small miracle given the Class VI rapids of conflicting emotions crashing against my insides.

"The furniture's all a mess, the dressers have been ransacked. But that's not all."

Icy dread crystallizes in my veins. Call it a premonition or something, but I know the next words out of his mouth aren't going to be good.

"You said Nora lived with your dad, right?"

"Yeah," I croak, a fresh wave of dread sending acid into my throat.

"You're sure?"

"Say what you're going to say," I snap, regretting it instantly. Ellis is doing me a favor and damn sure doesn't deserve my vitriol.

"There's hardly any food in the house. One of the spare bedrooms appears to be an office and the other is jam-packed with *junk*. Boxes of paper—newspapers and shit."

"What are you saying, Ellis?"

"I'm saying she doesn't have a bedroom here..."

"I sense a *but* coming." I swallow roughly, trying and failing to keep my cool.

A bead of sweat drips down my spine as I try to assemble the puzzle of my dad's disappearance with the pieces Ellis has given

me.

"You ever been down in the basement?"

"Not since I lived at home, why?"

"He's got a lock on the door." Ellis heaves out a breath. "A lock on the outside. He wasn't keeping someone out, man..."

"He was keeping someone in." My knees give out and the floor rushes up to meet me as my thoughts tumble and spiral, twisting and tangling together into an undistinguishable mess of anguish and disbelief. "Surely he wasn't keeping her—"

"There's a cot," Ellis whispers. "In the corner of the room. There's a cot."

"Fuck!" I shout, pounding my fist into the floor at my side. I knew he wasn't well, but I didn't think he'd lost his goddamn mind. *How long has he been locking her up? Was he feeding her? Was he hurting her?*

"I've gotta report this, you know that, right?"

I force myself up from the floor, shove my feet into my boots, grab my keys, and then head for the door. "I know."

"Shouldn't fucking be doing this," he mutters to himself, before speaking directly to me. "You can come by first if you promise not to flip out or mess with anything."

"I'm already on my way."

After holding my breath for damn near the whole drive, I let out a relieved exhale when Ellis's car is the only other vehicle in my dad's driveway. I know he has to file a report about what he finds here, but the thought of anyone other than him being here with me has my chest all kinds of tight.

I jump out of my truck and charge up the steps, only for Ellis to stop me with a hand pressed firmly to my chest.

"You gotta swear not to lose your shit, Atlas," he says gravely, causing the hair on the back of my neck to stand on end.

"I won't."

His lips twitch. "You won't swear or won't lose it?"

Fuck. I grip the back of my neck, digging my fingers into my flesh. He's asking a valid question, because I already want to flip out and I'm not even over the threshold. "I'm good. I'll *be* good."

He searches my eyes for a long moment before finally relenting and lowering his hand from my chest.

Once I'm inside, it's as though I'm a hound dog hot on a trail; I couldn't care less about the mess all around me—my focus is singular.

The basement. I need to see the basement. The lock. The cot. I need to make sense of this shit.

I take the steps two at a time, both trying and failing to rationalize the sight before me.

Ellis wasn't lying—not that I thought he was. But seeing the lock bolted to the frame and hearing about it are two different things.

What in the hell was he thinking? Is he really so far gone that he'd lock her away down here? Better yet, am I really so self-involved that I missed the signs? It's not like he lost the plot overnight.

I prod at the open lock with trembling fingers. It's sturdy; the kind when it's locked, nothing's getting past it. Especially not Nora. Last time I saw her she couldn't have been more than a buck-fifteen soaking wet.

A line of narrow windows near the ceiling let in just enough light for me to make out the shape of a cot along the wall, but not much else.

Part of me has seen enough—I mean, what else is there to see, really? It's pretty obvious what this room was for.

But the rest of me needs to know, conclusively.

"Where's it at?" I mumble, running my hand along the wall just inside the room, feeling for the light switch.

"It's out here," Ellis says, flicking the switch on. The tightness in his voice matches the uncomfortable pinch in my chest. *She had no control over the light switch.* There's a wrongness to this room, and it's fucking palpable. A living, breathing thing.

A single exposed bulb blinks to life, creating just enough light to cast shadows in the damp, rank room.

"Ellis," I exhale his name on a long sigh as I venture further into the hellhole below my father's house. Because that's what this is, plain and simple. *Hell.*

There's a cot shoved against the far wall, with a stained and threadbare blanket covering it. No pillow. No warmth. No cushioning or support of any kind.

To the right of the cot is a small, worn dresser with three crooked drawers. I don't want to open them, but at the same time, I have to.

Maybe this isn't what we think it is. Maybe he kept a rambunctious dog down here—

The thought dries up the second I tug open the first drawer, finding it full of unmistakably feminine items. The kind I'm not entirely comfortable touching, knowing they belong to Nora.

Moving on to the next drawer, I find a hairbrush, some hair ties, a handful of pens, and some crumpled papers with hauntingly familiar handwriting.

But it's the third drawer that's the final nail in the coffin.

Sitting all alone in the bottom is a well-worn Polaroid of a young Nora with a man I have to assume is her dad; they're both smiling wide, like they're in on a secret the rest of us just wished we knew.

The joy splashed across their faces reminds me of my mom. She always was the brightest light in any room—until she got sick, that is.

"Shit, man." I grab the image from the drawer and slide it into my back pocket. "My sick fuck of a father was keeping her locked up in here like a prisoner."

"I don't know what to say." Ellis takes a step closer to me. "Atlas—"

"There's nothing you can say." I laugh, but it's a dark and hollow sound.

I've had my suspicions about the kind of guy my dad was for years, since my mom died, but I always shrugged it off, always convinced myself my imagination was running wild, that I was reaching.

Clearly I wasn't, though, because the man's a monster.

"There's nothing anyone can say to make this better. He's..." I trail off and take one last look at the makeshift prison before turning for the door. "He needs to be found. He needs to be held accountable, to pay for this." A cold shiver works its way through my body. "More than that, *she* needs to be found. Fuck, man."

Ellis sighs, and I can tell he's just as worried as me. "Get out of here then, and I'll call it in."

"I mean it, Ellis. I don't care that he's my own flesh and blood, he's sick and I—if he did anything to hurt her, I'll kill him myself."

"Loud and clear, man," Ellis says, before I can pop off anymore. "We'll find him—*both of them*—and he'll have to answer for this. But I've gotta tell you, I'm not sure this'll stay quiet."

"What?"

"I'm just saying, if the press gets wind of your dad keeping Nora locked up like a dog, they'll be all over it."

"Let 'em. The world needs to know exactly what kind of man Randall Wallace is."

"And what kind is that?" my best friend asks.

"A spineless, nutless, no-good sack of shit who deserves every single thing coming his way," I say. Family or not, he's dead to me.

DIARY ENTRY, AGE 15

Dear Diary,

Yesterday was my birthday. I'm fifteen now.

There's no pretense of a party this year. At least not for me. In fact, Mom hasn't even acknowledged my birthday this year at all, because she's been far too busy preparing for her very own special day.

Her wedding day.

That's right, she's marrying Rand today, and while she's floating around like she doesn't have a care in the world, I feel like I'm slowly suffocating. Drowning. Dying.

How can she be walking down the aisle when Dad's only been gone a year? I mean, his grave dirt may as well still be fresh for all the time she waited.

She's really and truly marrying Randall Wallace.

It's like I'm trapped in a nightmare and can't wake up. God knows this abomination of a dress had to have been plucked straight from a nightmare-it's a lace and tulle monstrosity that no self-respecting girl over the age of seven would wear.

Yet here I am, doing just that. She even made me curl my hair in ringlets, too. I look like I'm five, not fifteen, and I hate it.

I'm so mad that I'm shaking.

In less than an hour, my mom will be Mrs. Grace Wallace. She mentioned changing my last name, too, and it was like I was possessed. I kicked and screamed and threw a fit worthy of the child they have me dressed like. I told her if she ever mentioned changing my name again, I'd hate her for the rest of forever.

I am my father's daughter, and I will keep his last name until the day I die.

I feel sick to my stomach. How could she do this? To me, to Dad, to us?

It's like she's got blinders on, and Rand is all she can see.

Did I tell you she quit her job to be with him? Rand says a woman's place is in the house, not the workforce, and she just listened like she didn't spend twelve years in school and another seven building her practice from the ground up.

I'm not sure if aliens are real or not, but if so, I think one might be controlling my mom. It's like I don't even know her anymore. Honestly, I'm not sure I want to.

Because what kind of mom marries a man who doesn't even like her daughter?

I have to go now. It's time to walk down the stupid, tainted aisle.

Crushed, Nora

Dear Diary,

You know the saying "what else could go wrong?"

Well, Dad used to always say phrases like that only served to tempt the universe into piling on more bad, and I guess I must have thrown it out there one too many times, because things have gone from bad to worse to absolutely awful.

This time last year, I thought the hardest thing I'd ever face was losing my dad, but I was wrong, because losing Mom while she's still living and breathing and under the same roof as me is twenty times harder.

They've only been married for a month, but I swear, it's like he lobotomized her or something. Mom has turned into some kind of Stepford Wife.

She makes him breakfast every morning, cleans the house all day, and has dinner on the table by the time he gets home each night.

At first, I ate dinner with them, but then Rand decided it should just be him and Mom at the table each night. He said my sullenness made the food taste bitter.

Stupidly, I thought my mom would stick up for me. But she just nodded and sent me into the kitchen to finish my roast.

You'd think that'd be the worst of it, but just wait, diary, because there's a freaking cherry dripping its nasty juice all over the top of the crap-sundae that is my life.

For some reason, Rand thinks that a "troubled young girl" should study at home.

That's right, he's making mom homeschool me-and she's just going along with it like a freaking zombie. I hate it here, and I hate him. Even worse, I'm scared I'm starting to hate her a little, too.

Helplessly, Nora

Dear Diary,

I'm a week deep into hell-and by that, I mean homeschool-and if I thought I was lonely at my old school... well, let's just say I'm to the point where I'd gladly listen to Kelsey and Eliza laugh at me if it meant I was around other people and outside of these four walls.

How pathetic am I, that I'd rather subject myself to my former friends making fun of me than to stay here one more minute?

I guess it doesn't really matter, though, because Rand has Mama convinced I'll end up pregnant or on drugs if I leave the house. It doesn't matter that I've never even kissed a boy, because his word is law, which means I'm on house arrest.

Does that make him my warden or my stepfather?

In the end it doesn't matter what he is to me, because he's made it more than clear I'm nothing to him. Which wouldn't be so bad if Mama didn't look at him like he hung the moon.

What does she even see in him anyway?

He's controlling, manipulative, and mean as a snake. I'm only fifteen, and I can clearly see that Rand's a walking red flag, so why can't Mama?

What's so good about him that she'd pick him over me?

She doesn't even teach me during our allotted homeschool hours! She says that Rand said the lessons are self-guided. It almost seems like he wants to drive a wedge between us.

I don't get it. Mama and I should be a packaged deal, but every day we're here, I feel more and more like the dented can they tossed in on sale.

I'm so annoyed I'm not even sure that made sense, but whatever. It doesn't matter. Maybe none of this matters…

Clearly, I don't matter.

Forgotten, Nora

Dear Diary,

I... He... He hit me. Rand hit me, and I haven't stopped crying since.

Mama cried, too, and then sent me to my room. Her not sticking up for me hurts worse than his palm stinging my cheek.

It used to be Rand just ignored me as long as I kept out of his way, but a few weeks ago he started saying mean things to me whenever Mama wasn't around. He started telling me I was worthless and unwanted, how he couldn't wait to get rid of me.

I did my best to ignore him, but tonight I overheard him calling Mama ugly names and I snapped. Honestly, I'm not even sure why it made me so mad. It's not like she stuck up for me.

But he was mad she burned the rolls. Like big mad. He threw the entire dish across the room so hard it rattled the walls. He told her if she was going to be a freeloading bitch, the least she could do is make his dinner right.

I stormed out of my room and told him to shut his nasty mouth because the only reason she doesn't work is because he won't let her.

He smacked me right across the face so hard he busted my lip.

I was just trying to protect her-to take up for her-since apparently she's lost her voice. But Mama sent me straight to bed without an ounce of concern for the blood pouring from my mouth like a freaking waterfall.

I know last week I said I was worried I might start hating her too... but tonight made me realize something. I can't hate my mom. Even if I want to-and I really, really want to-I can't.

I'm not trying to make excuses for her, but while waiting for the bleeding to stop, I realized something: losing Dad broke her.

Not in the same way it did me. Dad dying cracked me. It made me sad in a way I don't know how to bounce back from, but it shattered Mama, and even though her pieces are glued back together, she's weak now. Fragile.

So, no, I don't hate her. But I don't really like her either.

Why am I not enough for her? Why am I, her living and breathing daughter, not enough? I don't have an answer, and I'm not sure there's any reason she could give that would allow me to forgive her for essentially abandoning me.

Resentfully, Nora

My pulse pounds in my ears, keeping time with the frenetic rhythm of my heart, as I fly down my dad's long driveway.

Disbelief, disgust, and a heaping serving of guilt all sit heavy on my shoulders, pressing down on me, their combined weight impairing my ability to think rationally.

My focus is a pinprick. Finding Nora is the only thing that matters. But where is she? Did he take her with him when he went wherever he's at?

"His hunting cabin!" I jerk the wheel hard to the right, fishtailing out onto the main road. Tires screech and horns blare, but I can't stop.

There's a running loop in my brain saying, *find her, save her, fix this,* over and over again and I'm helpless but to listen.

Maybe if I'd have listened to that part of myself years ago this would've never happened. Maybe if I'd have voiced my concerns and suspicions when my mom died, Nora would be far, far away from the monster my dad is.

Denial has never served anyone well.

My thoughts spiral in a chaotic loop as I fly toward the cabin. *What if he's there? What if he has her there? What if she's hurt? Or worse?*

I'm not sure what to expect, much less how to prepare myself for the confrontation that may be to come, but there's one thing I know beyond a shadow of a doubt—if she's there with him and even a single hair on her head is harmed, I won't hesitate to put him down like the rabid dog he is.

What kind of man hurts a woman—a child? The question burns through me like acid in my veins.

But the one that follows is worse: *what kind of man keeps his suspicions to himself for years?*

Who's the real monster, him or me? Could I have prevented this if I'd have spoken up all those years ago?

"Fuck!" I pound my fist against the wheel, causing it to jerk in my grip. Briefly, my tires leave the road, but I'm able to get the truck back under my control before any real damage can be done.

"What-ifs won't solve anything," I mutter to myself as I turn down the unmarked road that leads to our hunting plot. "Just focus on the here and now. Figure out what needs to happen and handle that shit."

I hold my breath as the cabin comes into view, only to let out a disappointed exhale when his SUV's nowhere to be seen.

Still, I throw my truck into park and hop out to take a look around.

On silent feet, I creep around the rickety structure, listening and watching for any signs of life. But everything is silent and still.

If the layer of dust covering the windows is anything to go by, no one has been here in a while. But if I know anything, it's that looks can be deceiving.

Which means I won't be able to let this go until I check out the inside of the cabin—until I know beyond a shadow of a doubt that she's not here, chained up, or worse.

I try the front door first, but it's locked up tight. Defeat presses in on me from all sides. I don't know where my dad is, I don't know where Nora is, and because I spent the last three years with my head up my ass, I don't have the slightest idea of where to look.

"Oh, shit!" I hop down from the small porch and scramble around to the back of the cabin. To the best of my knowledge, the back door doesn't have a deadbolt. Or at least it didn't the last time I was here.

If that still holds true, it should be easy enough to get inside.

This time, I don't bother being quiet; I'm far too anxious for soft steps.

A quick jiggle of the knob tells me that I'm right—there's no deadbolt—and so, with a quick swipe of a card from my wallet, the door is open and I'm caught between hoping to find Nora and praying she's far, far away from here.

Stale air greets me as I step into the house. If it wasn't clear from the smell alone, the sheets still covering the sparse furniture tell me no one's been here in a long while.

I still do a quick walkthrough, finding each room as empty and untouched as the one before it.

They aren't here, which means I'm back at square one.

"Where else could they be?" I ask as I retrace my steps, making sure there's no sign of my visit as I head back for my truck.

Without knowing where else to look, I start for home, hoping like hell that Nora's diary has something—*anything*—that will point me in the right direction.

DIARY ENTRY, AGE 15

Dear Diary,

Something's wrong with Mama. I don't know what, but I know it like I know my own name. She's not right, but anytime I mention it, Mama and Rand act like I'm crazy.

I think they're gaslighting me, but it doesn't matter because I'm not crazy. There is something wrong with her, and I'm the only person who cares.

She's been going downhill ever since she and Rand got together. It's like his presence alone sucks the life out of her, and now her health is going, too.

It started off with a stomachache. "Just cramps," she said. But then the cramps turned to full-on nausea that hasn't let up. I'm talking weeks of feeling so sick and dizzy that she hasn't been able to eat.

But you better believe she still cooks and serves Rand a feast each and every night. He even makes her sit at the table with him while he prattles on and on about God knows what, not even caring that she's literally wasting away before our very eyes.

I know I sound dramatic, but she's lost enough weight that I've got more meat on my bones than she does—and that's saying something, seeing as Dad always called me his bean pole.

Things have changed a lot between us these last few months, and not for the better, but she's still my mom and I still love her... Even if it feels like she doesn't love me anymore.

Rand doesn't allow me out of my room any time after seven, so I had to sneak into the kitchen to confront her while she was cleaning up. She was swaying on her feet, struggling to load the dishwasher, so I took over doing it for her.

As I was scrubbing the pots and pans, I told her we should go to the doctor tomorrow to make sure she was okay, but she refused. She swore up and down that she was fine, that it was probably just a virus, and that she'd be better in no time.

When I insisted she at least call the doctor, she scoffed. I guess since she went to medical school, she knew everything about everything. I wanted to press the issue, but she waved away my concerns and said she'd ask Rand to bring her some meds from the pharmacy where he works.

I know I'm only fifteen, but I didn't know pharmacists could just bring home medicine. I thought they needed a prescription too, but maybe not.

Stupidly, I let her easy dismissal of my concern get the better of me, and I slammed the dishwasher closed. The next thing I know, Rand had me pinned to the fridge with a thick, meaty hand wrapped around my throat, squeezing tightly as he snarled like an angry dog.

He yelled and screamed and called me all sorts of names. He told me I was ungrateful and worthless and a spoiled little bitch. He ranted and raved about breaking my spirit.

I kept my eyes locked onto Mama the whole time, silent praying for her to make him stop, but she just sat there on her barstool with her head bowed and her eyes closed.

What kind of mother sits quietly while someone chokes and yells at her kid?

Sick or not, she's a coward, and I told her as much when Rand finally removed his hand from my throat.

Rand didn't like that, though. He backhanded me and told me not to speak unless spoken to.

I know he wanted a reaction from me, for me to cry and beg for forgiveness, but I refused, which made him big mad.

He roared like a lion and then grabbed me by my hair and dragged me back to my room. Before he slammed the door in my face, he said if he ever caught me out of my room after seven again, he'd lock me in the basement for a few days to teach me a lesson.

He's a monster, and I hate him.

I mean it-I really, really hate him.

My biggest regret is not telling Ms. Maggie how awful he is when I was still allowed to see her, because now I'm trapped here with no way out.

Worried, Nora

Dear Diary,

This entry might be hard to read, but I have to write it down.

Back when Mama first gave you to me, she told me to put my pain to paper, so maybe if I let it all out-and I mean all of it-the crack of Rand's palm and the heel of his boot won't hurt as bad.

I'm pretty sure he broke two of my fingers and cracked my ribs tonight. I was able to tape my fingers together pretty good, but I'm pretty sure my ribs are a lost cause.

I know from movies that I need to wrap them, but it hurts too much.

Moving in any kind of way hurts. Even breathing hurts.

I guess I should start at the beginning though, huh?

Mama's still sick. Sick-sick. This so-called virus has gone on for months now, but she and Rand keep acting like everything's fine and dandy.

You know, I never got the saying about "denial being more than a river in Egypt" until now. Mama talks like she's going to wake up better any day now, but she won't.

I'm starting to wonder if she'll ever get better. I've learned better than to ask, though. That lesson came courtesy of two black eyes, a busted nose, and a split lip.

But what hurt even more than that was Mama's indifference.

It sounds bad, but I think she doesn't speak up when he hurts me for fear of him hurting her instead.

If she wasn't sick, maybe we could leave. Maybe we could run away and never look back. But she is, and I can't leave her here alone with him. I won't.

Mama hasn't left her bed for almost two weeks now, which means it's now my job to keep the house clean and to make all of Rand's meals. Meals I'm still not allowed to enjoy.

Today was hard, though. He wanted a roast for dinner, and I don't know how to make it. I tried asking Mama, but she wouldn't wake up. I'm not allowed to use the internet, and Rand took my phone away months ago, so... I winged it.

Which was apparently the wrong thing to do, because Rand was furious when dinner was not only late but inedible.

I watched from the doorway as he took his first bite, and before he could even swallow it, the entire plate was flying at my head. It missed me by centimeters, shattering against the wall instead of my face.

I wanted to run back to the safety of my room, but my fear kept me rooted to the spot as Rand stomped his way across the room. "Stupid, useless bitch," he muttered before grabbing me by the back of my neck and shoving me down to my knees, hurting my fingers in the process.

He shouted for me to clean up the mess I made, and like the stupid girl I am, I asked him for the broom and dustpan.

"Use. Your. Fucking. Hands," he snarled, punctuating each word with a hard kick. Each time the toe of his boot met my body, pain like nothing I'd ever felt before exploded beneath my skin.

I sobbed and begged for him to stop, but he didn't care. It's like my suffering brings him joy. He's demented. Twisted in a way I thought was only in books and on television.

But I did it. With aching fingers and throbbing ribs, I picked up every last shard from the floor, and then I dragged myself into the kitchen to get a rag and some spray to clean up the food.

Once the dining room was spotless, Rand tossed me into my room with a cookbook and locked me in, telling me to read it front to back.

And I will. I'll read it cover to cover and memorize every recipe if it means a repeat of tonight never happens again.

Aching, Nora

SIX

Atlas

I slam the damn diary shut with an anguished roar as white-hot fury courses through my veins like molten lava, burning me up from the inside out.

Tremors rack my body as the weight of Nora's suffering threatens to crush me.

All these years, he's been hurting her—and yet, all these years, she's persevered.

Every single person in her life has let her down, which is why I won't stop until I find her; until I know she's safe. Ellis has asked me about bringing the diary into the station, but I can't do that until I read every word.

But at the same time, every part of me is terrified to read any more. Each entry is worse than the one before it, and I honestly don't know how much more I can take.

Which is bullshit. Nora fucking lived it, and I'm over here pussing out over reading about it?

"Get your shit together, man," I grumble out loud, trying to calm the beast raging inside of me.

Finding Nora is the only thing that will bring me peace.

If only I knew where to look. For now, my best bet is to keep searching for some kind of clue between the pages of her diary. She left it in my mailbox for a reason—I just need to figure out why, and fast.

And so, I read, pouring over her words, until it feels like I'm drowning in the pain she bled onto these pages.

I read until I physically can't take another entry without puking from the pure agony laid bare before me.

Nora might look small and unassuming, but I swear to God, she's the strongest person I've ever met.

After a quick break, I jump back in, trying all the while to prepare myself for the hurt. But it's a fruitless effort, because each new entry is like the slice of a sharpened razor blade across my skin—merciless and full of stinging anguish that lingers long after the cut's been made.

Hours pass, right along with the pages as I read about Grace's sickness—one that is eerily similar to my mother's—and about Nora's abysmal sixteenth and seventeenth birthdays and about the horrors she experienced at my father's hands.

By the time I'm a little over three-quarters in, it's dark outside and my stomach is rumbling. Though, I'm not sure if it's from hunger or the need for vengeance brewing inside of me...

The sheer amount of loathing I feel toward—fuck, calling him my dad at this point feels like another sin against Nora—*him* is unlike anything I've felt before.

It's this driving need that sends me back into her words, because if there's one thing I'm sure of, it's that I will find him, and he will pay.

DIARY ENTRY, AGE 17

Dear Diary,

She's gone.

Devastated, Nora

Dear Diary,

I knew it was coming. Deep down, I knew. But knowing doesn't ease the pain. Knowing doesn't fill the gaping hole in my chest, ease the burning in my eyes, or help me take a full breath.

I tried to write about it afterward but I couldn't-I wanted to hold onto the hurt for a little while longer.

It's weird, knowing that I'm truly alone now. I'm not sure there's anyone left that even remembers I exist, besides Rand. There's definitely not another soul on this earth that cares about me. Or maybe that's been the case for a while, because I'm pretty sure Mama stopped caring a long time ago.

But that doesn't mean I wouldn't give anything to have her back.

She was so sick for so long, and a small part of me is glad she isn't suffering any longer, but the rest of me-the most of me-wishes she was still here. That she was healthy and that we could escape the hell that is Rand's house together.

But instead, she left me here. All alone. And now it's me who can't eat or sleep, because every time I do, I see her lying there in her bed, completely unmoving-and that's not how I want to remember her.

At first, I thought she was just sleeping really hard. Rand said her new meds would do that-that they would make her tired. Well, more tired.

But when I turned on the overhead light, it was clear she wasn't sleeping. Her body was stiff, like all of her muscles were tensed up, and when I tried checking her pulse, her skin was as cold as ice.

If it weren't for her blue lips, she might have looked peaceful.

I feel like I should have cried, but I didn't. I can't. It's like Dad all over again. My eyes burn, but the tears refuse to fall.

Maybe Mama was right. Maybe there really is something wrong with me. Two parents dead and gone and I'm as dry-eyed as ever.

Up until my dad died, Mama was always the brightest light in any room. Losing my dad may have dimmed her glow, but Rand... He completely shattered the bulb, leaving me all alone in the dark without her.

It's the same with me. I was a little bent after losing Dad, but Rand broke me. I know I need to figure out some kind of plan-either to escape or to survive. I guess they're one and the same at this point.

Because whether he keeps me here or kicks me out, I'm screwed.

I'm nothing more than an unwanted orphan with a monster for a stepdad. Huh-maybe in another life I was a Disney princess...

Then again, Rand hasn't bothered me much since Mama passed. He hasn't even been home.

Or maybe he has and I just don't remember. Everything's been a blur. The only parts I remember clearly are finding Mama and then watching them wheel her bagged body out the front door.

I don't know if he's grieving or maybe he's working out a way to get rid of me too-God knows he's made it clear I'm not wanted-but the past few days have been this weird mixture of blessed peace and crippling agony all at once.

It's sort of like when you swim and you accidentally take a breath underwater-you know, the way your nose and chest both burn? That's how I feel without Mama. Like I can't take a full breath without sucking water deep into my lungs.

Yeah, that's how it feels. Like drowning, but on dry land.

I don't know what to do without her. What to think... how to feel.

For the past few years, things have just gone from bad to worse, and now, all I can think about is what horrible thing might be lurking around the corner.

When's the other shoe going to drop?

It's not like I have much left to lose.

Either way, it's tomorrow's problem, because today is Mama's funeral. Well, sort of. Rand had her cremated, even though I knew she wanted to be buried next to my dad.

But he did what he wanted, without a single care for me or her wishes. And now I have to make a dinner in her honor to serve Rand and whoever he invited to this sham of a service.

I wanted to say something to him about it, to scream and cry that she would want to be beside my dad, but I knew better. Rand likes it when I keep my eyes down and my mouth shut, so that's what I try to do.

It's better that way.

But now I don't know. I just don't know.

Anxiously, Nora

Dear Diary,

I told him no. I begged him to stop. I pleaded for him to let me go.

But my words fell on deaf ears as he feasted on my pain, savoring each and every cry and whimper.

He took and took and took, until there was no part of me left untouched, no part of me still whole, no part of me untainted by his wickedness.

There's this deep, pounding pressure in my chest, like the bone itself is caving in and piercing right through my heart every time I think of the cruel words he hissed at me. "Your mama's gone and I'm a man with needs. Without her here, someone has to step up and fill them, and that someone's you."

I didn't understand what he meant at first. I've been doing the cooking and cleaning for months now, even before Mama died. What else could he possibly need from me?

But then his hands dropped to his belt buckle and I knew—I knew exactly what he meant. I was torn between worry for myself and wondering how in the hell Mom was able to "fill his needs" when she couldn't even get out of bed.

It was in that moment I realized how truly evil Rand was.

I tried to reason with him by telling him I was too young and that I was a virgin—but both of these things only seemed to excite him more. I even threatened to call the cops and he just laughed and handed me his phone and told me to have at it—that his buddies down at the station would probably enjoy the show.

He stole from me the one thing I had left, and now I have nothing.

I am nothing.

Everything hurts. My heart, my soul, and body. I ache in unspeakable places, in unspeakable ways, and there's no one who can help me. I'm all alone and at his mercy.

I can't stay here. I can't! But I know I need a plan to make sure once I'm out, I never have to come back.

Painfully, Nora

Rage and horror coil together tightly inside of me, causing a crushing pressure to build beneath my sternum that pushes and presses and swells, until it feels like my heart and lungs might actually explode.

"How in the fuck—" My words stop as a tear falls from my cheek to the page, smearing some of her words.

Holy shit. I didn't realize I was crying, but how could I not be?

My dad—*he raped her.* And from the sounds of it, he was doing the same to Grace as well.

He's a fucking predator—the worst kind, too. The things he's done are unforgivable. The mere thought of sharing DNA with him makes me sick to my stomach.

Now more than ever, I have to find Nora and make things right. I'm not sure how, but I won't fucking rest until I do.

DIARY ENTRY, AGE 18

Dear Diary,

It's my birthday today. I'm officially eighteen-an adult. If my parents were still alive, they'd make a big fuss about today, with a special breakfast and gifts and cake, the works.

But they aren't. Instead, I'm all alone, locked in the basement again thanks to Rand catching me trying to take some cash he left on the kitchen counter last week. Luckily, he didn't find the sock full of money inside of my pillow.

After the night Rand-God, I still can't say it.

Anyway, I cracked open my piggy bank and hid all of the money in it just to be safe. Ever since then, I've been keeping all of the cash and change I find on the counter or in the laundry.

I know I'll need money for when I escape-and I will escape, because there's something wrong with me, Diary. Something very, very wrong, and I think I need help.

For the last few weeks, I've been off. At first I thought that whatever Mama had was hereditary, because I've been so tired and so nauseous.

But this morning, my boobs started hurting almost like they do before my period-oh my God! My period.

Oh, no. No, no, no.

This can't be happening. It just can't be.

I don't know what to do. I-oh, God, he's home.

Everything I know is about to change. So much change. Over

and over again. Because I was right. Typically, I like being right, but right now, I really wish I wasn't.

This is what happens when you tempt the universe. Or maybe this is all karma for a past life? I don't know. God. I can't stop crying.

Which is weird in and of itself. Lose both my parents, and not a tear-but in the last few hours, I think I've filled Lake Fortune ten times over.

I guess I need to backtrack, but it's hard. My thoughts-they're spiraling like they're caught in the middle of a cyclone, random words flying out like deadly pieces of debris.

Word soup, Mama used to call it.

Rand came home from work and let me out of the basement. Said he had to do some work in the yard and that he wanted the house spotless and dinner on the table before he came back in.

I was putting the toilet cleaner away in his bathroom when the box caught my eye.

I'm not sure why Mama had these-well, I guess I am, I'm not an idiot. I just don't want to think about it. Not now, not ever.

But anyway, I know I've gone on about being unlucky and the universe hating me, but in that moment, it felt like something was finally going my way.

That is, until I peed on the stick and two pink lines bled across the window faster than I could recap the stupid thing.

Then it felt like my entire life was ending. Or maybe it's just beginning.

I don't know. GOD! I just don't know. I'm not fit to be a mother. I'm barely grown. I have no real high school education, much less a diploma, no money other than what's in my sock, no job, and no prospects. I don't know anything about being an adult, much less raising a child.

I may as well be Rapunzel in her tower, only there's no prince coming to save me.

No. You know what, forget that. I don't need a stupid prince on a stupid horse. I'll be my own prince. I'll save myself, and the little life growing inside me.

I know it's not ideal, but I-I don't know how to describe it. I'm scared. Terrified, really. But at the same time, for the first time in a really long time, I feel hope.

Like I'm finally not alone.

But Rand can't know. Not ever. Which is why I have to get out of here, and fast.

Worried, Nora

Dear Diary,

I'm going to do it. I'm going to run.

I have to, because I finally have something to live for.

When I first saw those two pink lines, it was a blow that stung harder than any slap or punch ever could. I was devastated. I'm not sure I'm fit to be a mother, but I'm damn sure going to protect this child from the monster down the hall. He will never know it exists. He will never lay one finger on my baby. Not ever.

Some might think the life growing inside of me would be a reminder of all I've lost-of all of the pain I've endured, the hurt, and the terror. And in a way, they're right. But it also gives me hope. Now I have something-someone-to fight for. I have a family.

Anxiously, Nora

Dear Diary,

I hope this finds you in time-that you can help me, that you believe me. Please believe me...

I had to run sooner than planned... He's too unpredictable. I can't take any unnecessary risks, not anymore, not when I have so much to lose.

It's funny, I used to want to die, for him to hit me so hard I would never wake up, but now? Now I want to live. I have to live.

If you're reading this still, look for me in the place where the lake meets the shore. I'll wait for you as long as possible. I understand if you can't come, or if you don't want to...but I really hope you do.

Desperately, Nora

EIGHT

ATLAS

"Where the lake meets the shore—*oh, shit*!" I slam the diary shut and leap up from my chair, because not only do I believe her—I know exactly where to fucking find her.

I just hope I'm not too late.

SEVEN
Nora

"Checkout's tomorrow at eleven," Shirleen, the front desk manager of the motel I've been camped out in since last night, calls as I tiptoe through the lobby.

Her words stop me in my tracks. "Wh-what?" I ask, gnawing my lower lip as I wait for her reply, all the while hoping like crazy that I misheard her, even though I know I didn't.

She gives me a pitying look over the rim of her turquoise cat eyeglasses. "You only paid for two nights, hun."

"Oh, um." I shuffle my feet as I try to do a mental tally of how much money is left in my sock.

The two nights I paid for here cost me a hundred bucks and some change, and the snacks I bought from the vending machine were another ten dollars, so that only leaves me ninety dollars.

Dread drops like a stone in my belly, and bile burns the back of my throat as I clutch the ice bucket closer to my chest.

That's not a lot of money at all; certainly not enough to survive on, at least not for long.

I was really hoping Ellis would have found me by now. He investigates crimes, after all. But there's no guarantee he even read my diary, much less figured out my location.

Even worse, what if he's in Rand's pocket too? What if he finds me and takes me right back to him? He was there with the other cops when Mama died, after all...

Maybe I can use the money I have left for a bus ticket out of town—as far as it'll take me—and then sleep in a shelter or something until I can find work. Maybe I can—

"You okay?" Shirleen asks, leaning forward, like she might get out of her chair and come around the desk. She was hesitant to rent me a room to start with, and with my disheveled appearance combined with the fact that I don't have a credit card or ID, I can't say I blame her.

I promised her I wouldn't be any trouble, and I intend to keep that promise.

"Fine—I'm fine." I readjust my sunglasses and drop my gaze to the floor, letting my hair form a curtain around my face. The last thing I need is for her to see the black eye and split eyebrow I'm sporting. "S-sorry. I'll, uh, I'll be gone before checkout. Thanks."

She stares at me long and hard, like she can see straight past my lies and into my very soul. For a second, I worry she's going to call me on my crap, but eventually she settles back down into her seat and sends me off with a soft smile. "Okay then, hun. Sleep tight."

Her words loop in my brain as I exit the lobby—which is the heart of this tiny motel—and head for my room. *Sleep tight.* I don't know the last time I slept well. Most nights, I'm either too scared to truly sleep or I'm plagued with nightmares.

I'd hoped getting away from him would have helped, but I don't think I'll be able to actually sleep soundly until I'm far, far away from here—from him.

Even then, I can't help but feel like I'll be looking over my shoulder. Randall Wallace is like a dog—a vicious, rabid dog—with a bone. He's not the kind of man who gives up easily.

It sounds bad, but sometimes I worry the only way I'll truly feel at ease is to know he's dead and buried, where he can never hurt anyone else ever again.

I'm halfway to my room when the feeling of being watched causes every hair on my body to stand on end. My muscles tighten as my fight-or-flight kicks in, and my heart beats like a hummingbird's wings.

The biggest downside to the Lakeshore Motel is the open-air corridors. Anyone could be lurking in the parking lot, watching... waiting.

I suck in a deep breath and force myself to keep a steady pace. Only prey runs, and I will never allow myself to be anyone's victim again. Not ever.

Once I'm safely inside my room, though, all bets are off. I chuck the ice bucket down onto the dresser, lock the door—chain and all—and then shove the chair against it for good measure.

"You're safe," I say to myself, bracing myself against the arms of the chair as I will my hands to quit shaking and my heart to slow its racing. "You're completely and totally safe."

Bang! Bang! Bang!

The sound of something—*someone*—pounding on the door sends me into a tailspin, and I dive behind the full-sized bed, my entire body trembling in fear.

"Go away, just go away. Please go away," I whisper, clutching my knees to my chest as I rock back and forth.

"Nora, I know you're in there!" a deep, masculine voice booms.

Tears streak down my cheeks as silent sobs rack my body. I should've known better than to think I could escape.

Stupid, so stupid to think I could ever be free of him.

"Goddamn it," I mutter to myself, thumping my fist against the door in defeat. "Fucking idiot."

I just want to help her, and instead, all I've managed to do is terrify her.

"Nora…" I desperately need to regain control of the situation. "I-I'm not here to hurt you. I just want to help."

I strain my ears, listening for any sound from inside of the room, any clue to where she's at and what she's doing, but there's nothing.

"Please open the door," I plead, but I'm met with the same stark silence as before. "Nora, I'm begging you. At least talk to me—listen to what I have to say. You don't even have to let me in."

I'm about to give up and head to the lobby to beg whoever's

at the front desk to let me in when she speaks.

"I'm listening."

Hope and relief both explode inside of me. "I want to help you, Nora—"

"How did you find me?" she asks with an unsteady voice, cutting me off.

"Your diary."

"You read it?" The hope in her voice is powerful enough to make my knees weak. Even in the midst of her fear, she's strong. So. Fucking. Strong.

"Yeah," I start, but the sound of shuffling, followed by the lock disengaging, steals away anything else I might have said.

I'm frozen in place as she slowly opens the door. The last thing I want is to make a sudden move and scare her even more. Hell, the fact that she's even willing to open it after my colossal fuckup is nothing short of miraculous.

Except my plan to wait quietly all goes to shit the second we're face-to-face.

I suck in a sharp gasp at the mottled bruises covering her face and she screams at the sight of me, propelling herself backward.

But a chair stops her and she falls to the floor, landing hard on her ass.

"I won't go back!" she half screams, half sobs as she scrambles to put more distance between us. "You can't make me!"

The terror in her voice pierces my heart like poison-tipped arrows.

I don't think, I just act, crossing the threshold into the room.

"Please," she begs, curling in on herself, using one arm to cover her head and the other over her belly. "Please-please-please."

Her words devolve to whimpers as I shut the door and then

crouch down beside her.

"Hey, Nora, no." The urge to reach out and comfort her is so strong, I have to fist my hands at my sides. "C'mon, Pip, I'm not going to hurt you. I'd never hurt you."

I lower myself all the way to the floor, gently reassuring her that she's safe.

I'm not sure how long we sit like that, but eventually she stops shaking and dares to peek up at me with damp eyes.

"You're safe," I tell her, keeping my gaze locked on hers.

"Do you promise?" Her small, scared voice unleashes something deep within me. Something primal that I know won't rest until it's gotten its pound of flesh from my father in retribution for the sins he committed against her.

"I won't let anything happen to you." I swallow roughly. "Not ever again."

"What happens now?" she asks, sniffling as she uncurls and pushes herself into a seated position. "Is...is Ellis coming?"

Cocking my head to the side, I study her. *Why is she asking about Ellis?*

"I thought you were him." Her voice is soft and a little raspy, sandpaper wrapped in silk.

"Why would you think that?" I spear my fingers through my hair. "I can call him if you want..."

"It doesn't matter." She shakes her head. "I'm just really tired."

Her words settle between us like a weight. She doesn't just look tired—she looks exhausted. Bone-weary, like she hasn't slept in ages.

"Then let's get you out of here so you can sleep." All I want is to take her back to my place, where I know she'll be safe.

She flinches, and I instantly know I've said the wrong thing.

"I'm not—I can't—you..." She trips over her words as panic sinks its claws deeper into her, making me feel like the biggest asshole in the world. "You promised."

"Hey, no." I raise my hands in front of me. "I meant what I said. All I want to do is help you. I get it, you don't trust me, I haven't earned that yet. But mark my words, Nora, I will. I will earn your trust and prove to you that I'm on your side. No matter how long it takes."

When she doesn't reply, I haul myself up off the floor, relock the door, and position the chair back in front of it. Then, I lower myself into the chair, claiming it as my spot for the night.

"Wh-what are you doing?" she asks.

"You need sleep," I say, crossing my ankles as I sink deeper into the chair. "So, I'm going to sit here and keep watch."

She swipes furiously under her eyes as she uses the dresser to help herself up from the floor. I track her movements, half-expecting her to throw me out, but she doesn't.

Instead, she climbs onto the small bed and curls into herself on her side facing me. She keeps her eyes on me, distrust heavy in her stare.

"Sleep, Pip. You're safe."

"Thank you," she whispers, her eyes falling shut as sleep takes her.

NINE
Nora

"You really thought you could get away from me?" He punctuates each word with a painful slap. "You stupid, worthless bitch."

"Please," I beg as tears burn my eyes. "Please just let me go."

"Never." His already cruel gaze sharpens as he glances down at my swollen belly. "Now be a good little bitch and take care of me."

"No!" I shake my head as tears blur my vision. "Please, no!"

"You will do as I say!" he shouts, grabbing a thick chunk of my hair at the scalp while his other hand moves to his belt. "I swear to fucking God, if you don't shut your mouth and spread your legs, you'll never so much as see the baby growing in your belly."

I fight against his hold, trying to free myself from him. But he's bigger, stronger, and has no intentions of ever letting me go. He's never letting me go.

"Stay still," he snarls, as he wrenches my legs apart. *"And shut up."*

A heavy weight settles on top of me and a scream builds in my throat—

"Nora, shit, please open your eyes!"

I wake with a start, sitting up so fast my forehead knocks into Atlas's.

Why is Atlas in my bed?

"Why are you in my bed?" I croak, clutching the sheets to my chest, as if the scratchy polyester can somehow hide my fear.

"You were having a nightmare," he says, as if that explains everything. But it doesn't—not by a longshot.

First, because I rarely sleep deeply enough to have dreams. Second, why would my having a bad dream make him think climbing into bed with me was a good idea?

I can feel my cheeks burn at my wayward thoughts. As if a man like Atlas would ever want to be in my bed in *that* way.

Focus, Nora! "I'm not following."

Atlas pinches the bridge of his nose and mumbles something about the depths of hell before retreating back to his chair. "You were thrashing and screaming and I... I couldn't get you to stop. It was... *fuck, Nora.*"

He wraps his fingers around the arms of the chair, squeezing them with a white-knuckle grip. "It was killing me to see you like that, so scared, so I tried to wake you up. But once I sat on the edge of the bed and put my hand on your shoulder, you sort of, I don't know...settled."

His words sound honest, and I want to believe him, to believe his intentions were good, but how far did this apple really fall from the tree?

I feel bad even thinking it, but I can't help it. No matter how earnest Atlas seems, I can't seem to shake the thread of distrust weaving its way around my heart.

Trusting him could be the difference between life or death. I don't think I could survive going back to Rand—and I don't think he'd let me, either.

"Hey." Atlas snaps his fingers, startling me to attention. "Where'd you go?"

"Just thinking, sorry."

His eyes soften, and his lips turn down as he takes me in. "No need to apologize." I wouldn't quite call the look on his face pity—no, it's more like regret. But that doesn't make sense. *What could he possibly regret when it comes to me?*

"What time is it?" I stretch my arms over my head, feeling more rested than I've felt in days—years, even.

"Just after nine."

"In the morning?" My eyes must be the size of dinner plates. I can't remember the last time I was allowed to sleep this long. It was a long, long time ago, that's for sure.

"That's right." His lips twitch. "How do you feel? Any plans for today?"

"Oh, no!" I throw the covers off and jump out of the bed. I told Shirleen I'd be gone before checkout, and I really, *really* want to have time for a hot shower before I go. "Oh, God. Um—"

I'm so consumed with gathering my meager belongings that I don't notice Atlas's approach until he's right behind me, so close I can feel the heat of his body.

By then it's too late—my entire body is as taut as a bowstring. I want to move, to ask him to move, but I can't. My brain and body can't seem to get on the same wavelength, and the unfortunate result is me turning into a human statue, which leaves me far too vulnerable for my liking.

"Nora?" The sound of my name on his lips is so full of hurt it takes my breath away. "I need you to breathe, Pip. In through your nose."

He inhales deeply, and as if on autopilot, I draw air into my lungs, too.

"Now hold it." He speaks the words softly in my ear. "And now let it out slowly."

An unfamiliar and unexplainable sense of peace falls over me as we exhale together. Like some part of me knows he means me no harm. Or maybe it's just finally having someone in my corner after being on my own for so long.

"You better?" He takes a few steps back from me, giving me some much-needed space.

"Yes." I clutch my hands in front of me as I turn to face him. "Maybe. I don't know."

He lowers himself to sit on the foot of the bed. "Talk to me, tell me what's going through that pretty head of yours."

I part my lips to answer him, but no words come out. My brain is stuck on a merry-go-round, spinning over his words at breakneck speeds.

Logically, I know he's not calling *me* pretty, because come on, I've seen me—right now I look like someone's punching bag. An underfed one, at that.

But it's the closest I've ever come to anyone other than my parents calling me anything near pretty.

So, while *my brain* knows it wasn't really a compliment, *my stupid heart* didn't get the memo.

The silence stretches between us, but Atlas never once

pushes. He just sits and waits, everything about him the picture of patience.

"I have to check out today. Before eleven. And I'm not sure what to do or where I'm going. I think maybe to the bus station—"

"No!" Atlas is up and off the bed and in my space.

Instinctually, I drop to the floor, covering my head with my hands as I brace for impact.

"No." His voice is this strange mixture of honey and broken glass, almost like my reaction pains him but he's trying not to show it. "I'm—God, I'm sorry. I didn't mean to scare you."

I swallow roughly and push myself into an upright position, so I'm sitting with my back against the dresser. "It's okay."

"It's not." He looks so crushed, sitting there on the floor with his head in his hands, that I can't help but feel bad for him.

"No, really, it is. It's not your fault I'm scared of my own shadow." It sounds insincere, but I mean it; it's not his fault. *Just his dad's,* my subconscious bitterly supplies.

Atlas hangs his head even lower. "No, it's my dad's."

His words give voice to my unkind thoughts.

My dad always believed people should stand on their own merit, and that we shouldn't hold the faults of their loved ones against them. I'm trying to do that with Atlas, to give him the benefit of the doubt and not second-guess his words and motives.

It's already hard for me to let people in, but doubly so with him. I'm not sure why, but something inside of me feels like if I let my walls down for him and he double-crosses me, I would break clean in two.

And I can't let that happen. I can't survive Rand's abuse only to let his son take me out. *Walls up, Nora. Walls up.*

"He's not a good man."

"No," Atlas agrees, "he's not."

We both sit here on the floor, staring at one another, locked into some kind of silent standoff, until Atlas speaks.

"Please don't go."

Butterflies take flight inside of me, frantically flapping their wings until I'm dizzy with conflicting desires. But ultimately, it boils down to what I need, because until I'm free of Rand, my wants don't really matter.

"I don't have anywhere to go." My admission causes my cheeks to burn with embarrassment. "I can't afford to keep staying here and—"

"Stay with me," he says, his eagerness barely restrained. "And Ellis. Stay with us."

Those butterflies all drop as worry settles low into my belly. I couldn't possibly stay with them, could I?

On the other hand, where would I be safer than with a police officer? And I doubt Rand would ever think to look for me there.

"You'd have your own room," he adds. "And we have an alarm system and cameras. You'd be safe."

Those three words, they're my kryptonite, and judging from the small smile curling his lips, he knows it, too.

"Just until I figure something out." I know I need to get a job to earn some money. Maybe Atlas can help me figure out some kind of online work while I'm staying with him.

"As long as you need, Pip."

Please don't let me regret this...

TEN
Atlas

"What do you need to do before we head out?" I ask, knowing eleven will be here before we know it.

Glancing around the room, I look for something I can do to help her pack up, but aside from a small pile of clothes on the dresser, the space looks untouched.

A sweet blush spreads across Nora's cheeks as her gaze follows mine. "I, um—I wasn't able to bring much with me, so packing shouldn't take too long." She swallows roughly as she looks anywhere but at me. "I was hoping to take a quick shower, too."

I tug at my collar and then pull myself up from the floor. "I'll just, uh, step outside while you do that." I look toward the door as I try to wrangle the foreign discomfort swimming through me. "Give you some privacy."

"Are you sure?" She nibbles on her lower lip, and my

discomfort intensifies.

I'm not sure what in the hell is wrong with me, but I desperately need to get out of this room.

"A hundred percent." A hundred and ten, really, because for some reason, I feel hot all over and know the crisp fall air will do me good.

"Okay." She rises up to her knees and then stands. "Thanks, Atlas."

"No thanks needed," I murmur, heading for the door.

I slide my phone from my pocket as I step out of the room, hoping like hell it still has some battery left.

Ten percent; just enough to call Ellis.

My eyes bulge at the alarming number of notifications, but I guess that's what happens when you all but go off the grid and ignore everyone for a weekend. But they'll all have to wait.

I dial Ellis and he answers on the first ring.

"Where the hell have you been?" I don't miss the worry in his voice. We're both pretty good about letting the other know if we'll be out all night, but once I realized where Nora was, I was out of there like a bat out of hell.

"I found her, Ellis. I found her."

"Holy shit. Where? Is she okay? What's the plan?"

"Found her at the Lakeshore Motel. Depends on how you define okay. And... I'm bringing her back to our place." I answer his questions as rapidly as he fired them, hoping like hell he's on board with her coming home with me.

"I'll meet y'all there." He sighs, and I can just picture him pinching the bridge of his nose. "You know I'm going to have to question her though, right?"

"Delicately," I growl. Nora's already been through so much,

and I won't let anyone else hurt her, intentionally or not. "You will question her delicately."

"You don't even have to worry, man. I'll do it at the house with you there."

My entire body sags as I breathe a sigh of relief. "Thanks, Ellis."

"Don't mention it. I'll meet y'all at the house, okay?"

"Sounds good." I end the call and then check the time on my phone before sliding it back into my pocket. It's half past ten now—almost go time.

"Nora?" I call as I tap my knuckles against the door.

She opens it immediately, stepping back to let me in. She's still in the same clothes as before, despite her hair being wet, but I don't comment on it. Instead, I add it to my ever-growing list of future problems to solve.

"You just about ready?"

"Yeah, I just need to get my…" She trails off, and her cheeks fill with color.

"Your what?" My interest is definitely piqued now.

Nora mumbles something at her feet, and I step deeper into the room. "Whatever it is, I'm sure it's nothing to be embarrassed of."

"My sock. It's, um, it's where I keep my money."

I nod like that makes perfect sense. "Definitely better than what I used to use mine for."

"What does that mean?" Her eyes widen and her lips form a perfect O as she gets it. "Oh, gross!"

"I'm sorry," I say, trying to hold in my laughter. "That wasn't very appropriate."

"I'm not a child, you know?"

Now I'm the one looking at the floor. "Trust me, Pip, I know."

She pads into the bathroom and comes back seconds later with her sock clutched firmly in her grasp. "Okay, good to go."

"Let me grab your bag," I offer, only instead of a bag, she hands me a pillowcase that's so light I'm not entirely convinced there's anything in it.

My expression must give my thoughts away, because Nora drops her eyes to the floor. "It's all I had." Shame stains her cheeks, and I immediately feel like an ass for making her feel bad.

Nora's been to hell and back; the last thing she needs is me making her feel like anything less than the badass she is.

"You got out, Pip. That's all that matters."

"Yeah." Her lips lift in a weak smile. "I guess you're right."

"Let's go home." I cross the room and throw open the door, more than ready to get the hell out of here.

"I don't have a home, Atlas." She trudges past me and out into the hall. "I haven't in a long time."

ELEVEN
Nora

*I*was half expecting the drive to Atlas's house to be uncomfortable, but the second I climbed up into his behemoth of a truck and his scent wrapped around me, it was like a shot of dopamine straight to my heart.

As soon as I settled into the passenger seat, my limbs went limp and I practically melted against the butter-soft leather.

Atlas didn't push me to talk, either, which I appreciated. He just flipped on the radio and drove.

Now we're about a minute out, and suddenly my nerves are back in full force.

"Do you think Ellis is going to be mad?" I ask, fidgeting in my seat.

He turns down the music and glances my way over the rim of his sunglasses. "Mad about what?"

It seems like an obvious question to me. What young, single guy wouldn't be annoyed to have some random girl crashing at their place? Especially one like me. "About me staying there..."

Atlas sighs and instantly I worry that I'm right—that Ellis doesn't want me there.

"I-I can find somewhere—"

"You're coming home, Pip. With me. Where I know you'll be safe."

"But..."

"He's not mad." He turns down their long driveway.

"Promise?" I hate how small my voice sounds. I don't want to be weak and fragile. I want to be strong, an overcomer, a survivor. But right now, I'm just a scared girl with too many problems and not enough resources.

You could let them help, my brain supplies, *you reached out for a reason.*

"I promise." He throws the truck into park and pins me with a look. "Wait here, okay?"

It's on the tip of my tongue to argue, because I know he's going to come and help me down, but I swallow back the urge and nod.

I was stubborn on the way here and scraped my knee trying to climb in. I could tell Atlas wasn't impressed, but he didn't say anything about it either. It's hard, though, letting myself be at someone's mercy—even over something as simple as this.

But I need to try, otherwise I'll live my whole life in fear, and I refuse to let Rand control me like that. I want to be free of him in every way—physically, mentally, and emotionally.

Atlas swings my door open and extends a hand up to me.

It's no big deal, I tell myself. And to anyone else, it's not. But to me, it feels colossal.

I slide my hand into his, fully expecting his touch to make my skin crawl. But instead, the rough slide of his calloused palm against mine makes my skin tingle and my belly go all fizzy.

There's something about him that just sets me at ease.

"Down you go," he murmurs, reaching up to brace my waist with his other hand as I step down. It's over as fast as it starts, but I swear, I can still feel the ghost of his touch even as he grabs my dingy little pillowcase from the back seat.

"I'll get you a key made," Atlas says as we head toward the house. "That way you can come and go."

My breath catches at the thought of having such freedom—not that I have anywhere to go. But maybe one day...

I'm about to thank him when the sound of tires crunching on the driveway sends me into a panic. I dive behind Atlas, plastering myself to his back as I clutch his shirt between my shaking fingers.

"Nora?" Atlas tries to turn to see me, but I move with him, unwilling and unable to release my hold on him.

"Don't let him take me," I plead, burying my face in the soft flannel.

"Shit," he curses under his breath. I can feel him gesturing something, but I can't bring myself to look. "Pip, breathe, it's just Ellis."

His words penetrate my fear, and I peel myself back just enough to look past him. Sure enough, Ellis is standing in front of his Bronco, looking contrite.

Guilt swarms me like a hoard of angry bees, carrying shame on their stingers. He shouldn't feel bad just because I can't react like a normal person.

"Such an idiot," I mumble to myself, only Atlas hears me,

and if the fire in his eyes is anything to go by, he didn't like what he heard.

"I need you not only to listen to me, Nora, but to *hear me*, okay?"

He waits for my nod to continue.

"You are not an idiot. You are a fucking warrior who has gone through more than anyone should ever have to. You've survived unspeakable things. When so many would've given up, you. kept. going."

Atlas steps toward me, almost like he wants to hug me. It's been so long since anyone's hugged me, I almost wish he would. But my entire body flinches away on instinct, which makes him take a step back, shooting me an apologetic look.

How is it that I'm mourning something I never even had?

"So, no, you're not an idiot. You've experienced trauma, and you're going to need time to heal. Give yourself some grace, yeah?"

"Sorry." I sniffle, hating how out of control I feel. For once, I'd just like to be *normal* instead of a cowering or crying mess.

"Let's head inside." He gestures for Ellis to come on, and together the three of us head inside. "It's not much, but it's home."

I take in the space and immediately scoff at his words. What's *not much* to him is everything to me.

Their cabin has an open floor plan that allows me to see the living room, dining room, and kitchen all at once. Light floods the space, thanks to picture windows and a skylight. The wood accents, mixed with leather couches and plush rugs, all just scream *home*.

"You can see where everything is out here. You're welcome to anything in the kitchen, and the TV is one of those smart ones, so knock yourself out. Now let me show you to your room."

Ellis starts to speak but Atlas sends him a withering glare, effectively silencing whatever he was about to say.

Atlas guides me down the hall, pointing out Ellis's door before swinging open the one across from it. "You'll be staying in here. There's a connected bathroom and—"

He draws up short when he notices I'm frozen in the doorway.

"What's wrong?" he asks, looking around the room and then back to me.

"This is your room." His earthy scent hangs heavy in the room, wrapping around me like a warm blanket.

"It is." He speaks the words slowly, drawing each one out. "Don't worry, though, you'll have the space to yourself."

Knowing that he doesn't expect me to share the bed with him is a relief, and yet for some reason, I blurt out, "But where will you sleep?"

His lips twitch. "You worried about me, Pip?"

I dip my chin and nod. "Maybe a little."

"I'll be on the couch. It pulls out into a bed."

I'm torn between guilt and excitement. I feel bad he's being displaced—even if it's only temporarily—but I'm also so, *so* excited about sleeping in such a big, cozy-looking bed.

The cot Rand had for me was as hard as the floor, and the motel bed wasn't much better. But Atlas's bed has to be a king, and it's topped with loads of pillows and the fluffiest duvet I've ever seen.

It looks like heaven, really.

"I'm sure you're overwhelmed, but I need to talk to you about something," Atlas says, breaking my trance-like focus on his bed.

"What is it?" Nerves dance along my skin as I brace for

whatever blow he's about to deliver.

"Before I found you, I had Ellis go to my dad's house for a welfare check. He found the place wrecked and..." He swallows hard. "And the, um, basement. Anyway, he had to call it in, and he needs to talk to you about it all, officially."

"Oh." I pinch my eyes shut and force myself to breathe the same way Atlas did earlier. *Inhale, hold it, exhale.*

Atlas doesn't rush me; he just patiently waits while I get myself together. I don't know if reincarnation is real, but if it is, he must have been a saint in a past life, because the man is easily the most patient person I've ever known.

"Why does he need to question me? Am I in t-trouble?"

"No, Nora, no. Not at all. The things we found there were concerning enough for him to need to file a report, and since you lived there, he needs to ask you a few things about, well, all of it. He's also going to ask if you want to press charges against my—" His throat works. "Rand."

"Okay." I nod. "I can do that. But—will you...stay with me? You know, while he asks his questions."

Atlas flexes his hands at his sides, almost as if he's trying to keep himself from reaching for me. "I won't leave your side."

Back in the living room, Ellis is already seated in a comfy-looking recliner.

"You can take the couch or—"

"Please sit with me." I reach out and grab Atlas's wrist before I can think better of it.

He glances down at where my hand is gripping him, and I swear I see a grin tugging at his lips. "I told you I wouldn't leave your side."

I expect him to free himself from my hold once we're seated, but instead he wriggles his wrist until he can slide my hand into his, curling his fingers around my palm.

We're holding hands.

He's. Holding. My. Hand.

It's so totally innocent, and yet my heart is racing like I just ran the fastest mile. I feel light and giddy, nervous and secure, hopeful and so very naive.

Get it together, Nora. He's holding your hand to be nice.

Honestly, I don't care why he's doing it. I've been so starved of kind and positive touches that I can't help but relish the way his warm skin feels against mine.

Ellis clears his throat, effectively bringing me back down to earth.

"Glad you're here, Nora," he says.

"Thank you for letting me stay. Atlas said you needed to ask me some questions."

"I do, and I'm going to record our conversation—it's standard protocol, but Nora, please know, you're not in any trouble. You didn't do anything wrong. Do you understand?"

I nod, because I do. Sometimes my stupid brain gets the better of me and tricks me into thinking it's my fault Rand hurt me, but Ellis is right. I didn't do anything wrong.

"Okay, great." He slides out his phone and taps around on the screen before looking back toward me. "Please state your full name, date of birth, address, and phone number."

"Nora Leigh Morgan," I say, followed by my birthdate. "I'm, um, not sure what to say for my address. I guess I don't really have one right now. Or a phone number. Sorry."

Ellis nods like my answer is completely normal. "No worries. How do you know Randall Wallace?"

"My mom, she married him."

"And where is she now?"

Tears sting my eyes but I press on, knowing he's not asking to be cruel. "She's dead."

"How long ago did she pass?"

His questions seem endless—*did I ever see Rand hurt my mother, did he hurt me, when did it start, how long, how often.*

I answer every single one to the best of my ability, even the ones that hurt. *When did he first sexually assault you? How far along are you? Did he know about the baby?*

Atlas looks as tormented as I feel by the time we finish, and I can't help but feel bad for bringing all my issues to his doorstep.

But through it all, he never once let go of my hand. He held onto me like he was my anchor, keeping me moored in place despite the rolling waves.

"I just have one last question," Ellis says, leaning forward in his seat. "Do you have any idea as to where Rand might be?"

"I'm sorry, but I don't. I wish I did, but I don't."

"That's okay. Thank you for talking to me. If I think of any other questions or need to follow up on anything, I'll let you know."

"Okay. Is...is that all?"

"One more thing," Ellis says, ducking his head. "If it's all right with you, I'd like to photocopy your diary and also document any current injuries."

"That's, yeah, okay. Except I don't have my diary."

"Be right back," Atlas murmurs, releasing my hand and standing from the couch. He darts down the hall, returning seconds later with my diary in his hands.

He passes it to me, and I hug the worn leather book to my

chest as though greeting a long, lost friend. "I have so much to tell you," I whisper to the pages, completely uncaring of how strange I may seem.

This diary has been my only friend for so long that these few days without it have been like torture.

"I have an app on my phone that I can scan the pages with so you don't have to worry about me losing it or anything."

"Thank you. Both of you." I reluctantly pass my diary to Ellis, who sets it on the table beside his chair. "If it's okay, I think I'd like to lay down. Um. I mean, if you don't mind. Sorry." I trip over my words as old worries fight their way to the surface.

"Of course. Let me snap a few pics first and then you're good to go."

I stand and allow Ellis to document my black eyes, split eyebrow, healing ribs, along with a handful of mottled bruises on my legs.

By the time he's finished, both he and Atlas are breathing hard. For a split second, I worry they're mad at me. But I quickly realize they're mad *for* me, not at me.

"Go rest, Pip. I'll be right here if you need me."

He doesn't have to tell me twice—I take off down the hall and dive into his bed. It's every bit as amazing as I thought it would be, and with Atlas's scent all around me, I'm fast asleep before my head even hits the pillow.

TWELVE
Atlas

"Should we check on her?" Ellis cracks his neck and then his knuckles, something he's done over and over since questioning Nora.

Clearly, her answers pained him as much as they did me.

"No." I shake my head. "I don't think she's slept well in ages."

"She's so small, man. How could he—"

A knock at the front door interrupts him.

"Who in the hell is that?" I ask as Ellis grabs his phone, no doubt to pull the camera feed.

"Did you seriously invite Scarlet over tonight?" His voice drips with disapproval, as if I'd invite Scarlet over after ignoring her for two days while Nora sleeps in my bed.

"Fuck no." I stand from the couch and stalk to the door. "I haven't talked to her since Friday night."

"Guess she got tired of waiting." He pinches the bridge of his nose. "You need to get rid of her."

"Already on it." I throw the door open, intent on joining her outside, but she waltzes right past me, shoulder checking me as she invites herself into my house.

"Excuse you," I mutter before closing the door and following after her. "Why are you here?"

"We need to talk, Atlas." She glares from Ellis to me and back again, as though simply sitting in his own living room is somehow offensive to her. "And I'd like to do so without an audience."

Reaching behind me, I grip the back of my neck and squeeze. "Now's not really a good time," I say, hoping like hell those are the magic words to make her leave.

If the snarl curling her lips is anything to go by, they're not.

"No." She stomps her foot like a child. "Absolutely not. You *will* talk to me, and if *he* won't leave, we can talk in your room."

She darts around me and takes off down the hall before I can stop her.

"Atlas!" Ellis snaps, but he doesn't need to—I'm already giving chase.

"If you take one more step, Scarlet, I swear to God—" I'm panting by the time I catch up to her, not out of exhaustion but from worry. The last thing any of us needs is a confrontation between the woman in my hallway and the one in my bed.

"What?" She hisses the word like a cornered cat as she grips the doorknob. "What are you going to do, Atlas?"

I cover her hand with mine, forcing her hand away from the knob. "I'm begging you, please just stop. You don't understand what's going on—"

"Of course, I don't!" She throws her hands wide. "How

could I? I haven't heard a damn word from you since you left me at The Creek Friday night. Not a call or a text. Nothing. And God knows I've called you, so excuse the fuck out of me for wanting some answers."

The sound of the bed frame creaking followed by soft footsteps padding across the floor filters under the door, and despite praying for Scarlet not to hear, her eyes widen in accusation.

Fuck. Could this get any worse?

"It's not what you think."

"Isn't it?" Her eyes flash with hurt. "I swear to God if you've been ignoring me because you brought some whore home from the bar—"

"Shut. Up." I grit through clenched teeth. "There *is* someone in there, but it's not what you're thinking. Please, Scarlet, I am begging you, just be quiet."

"Then tell me. Right now. Tell me."

"It's Nora—"

"Your sister?" Her deadpan tone gives way to almost manic laughter. "You blew me off to play house with your sister? Wow, Atlas."

"Stepsister," I growl. "Nora is my step—"

My bedroom door opens, effectively shutting me up. Nora looks up at me with sad eyes before focusing her attention on Scarlet.

"What the fuck, Atlas?" Scarlet hisses.

"It's fine." Nora looks down at her bare feet. "I'll just, um. I'll go."

"What? Why?" I know I can't keep her here against her will, but the thought of her leaving sends icy dread pumping through my veins.

"I don't want to intrude…" Her voice breaks, and my heart shatters right along with it.

"You're not," I insist, shooting Scarlet a dark look telling her she better back me up.

"I'm trying really hard not to flip out right now," Scarlet says, a slight tremor to her voice. "But you look like someone went Mortal Kombat on your ass, and I need to understand. Did…" She swallows roughly. "Did Atlas—"

"No!" Nora shouts. The way she doesn't hesitate to rush to my defense has me feeling some kind of way. Like I'm the king of the fucking world. "No, he…he saved me."

"You saved yourself, Pip. I'm just helping you get back on your feet."

"Then who did this?" Scarlet fists her hands at her sides, as if it's taking all of her willpower not to reach for Nora.

Get in line, Scar. I know the feeling well.

Nora looks away, and I can't decide if it's out of shame or some misguided attempt at protecting my honor. I decide to rip the Band-Aid off for her.

"My dad." Venom infuses my tone, making it quite clear how I feel about the situation. "My fucking father did this to her."

Scarlet gulps as tears fill her eyes. "You weren't lying when you said you were worried, huh?"

"Nope." I wish I was lying. More than anything, I wish I was, because then none of this would be real. Nora wouldn't be hurt, and my dad wouldn't be a colossal piece of garbage. But that isn't how life works—wishes don't mean shit.

Scarlet wraps her arms around herself. "I-I'm sorry. God, I feel like such a rotten bitch."

It's on the tip of my tongue to tell her that's exactly how she should feel, but Nora speaks up before I have the chance.

"You didn't know." She offers us both a weak smile. "Now, if you'll excuse me…"

She tries to slip between us, but I block her path. "Where are you going?"

"I don't want to cause any more trouble for you. So, I'll just get my things and be on my way."

I cut my eyes at Scarlet, and she shrinks back under the weight of my glare.

"Where will you go?"

Nora's eyes flit up to Scarlet's in surprise. "Oh, um. I'm sure I'll think of somewhere."

"Of course, you will. You seem resourceful." Scarlet nods along, like what Nora's saying makes perfect sense. She better course correct, or I swear to God, I'll boot her out the front door without a shred of remorse.

"What about food, though? No offense, but you're pretty underweight." She pointedly lowers her eyes to Nora's midsection. "Especially for someone eating for two."

Nora's hands fly up, protectively cupping her small bump. "I-I, um, we'll be okay." She sniffles, and the sound cuts across my skin like the blade of a knife. "It's nothing you need to worry about."

"I told you I'd keep you safe, Pip. I can't do that if you're not here." I plead with my eyes for her to understand, to believe me, to stay. The mere thought of her leaving, of her being out there with no one, makes me gnash my molars together in frustration.

"Atlas, please. I don't want to be a burden." She sounds like she's on the verge of tears, and I hate it. *I. Fucking. Hate. It.*

"If you go, I go." I cross my arms over my chest.

"Have you seen a doctor?" Scarlet asks, reminding me that this isn't a private conversation.

Shame colors Nora's cheeks as she shakes her head.

"Do you know how far along you are?"

She squints one eye closed, her lips moving silently as she figures out her reply. "Um. Maybe two or three months. I'm not really sure."

Fuck. I don't know much about having kids, but even I know she should have seen a doctor by now.

Sensing my internal panic, Scarlet takes charge of the situation. "Sweetie, that's not good. I work for an OB, and most women have seen the doctor two or three times by this point. Why don't we all go talk in the living room, and we can figure this out together."

"Head on back to the living room," I say to Scarlet, needing a moment alone with Nora. "We'll be right there."

Wordlessly, she turns and heads down the hall, giving us some much-needed privacy.

"What're you thinking, Pip?" Despite standing still, my heart is racing as I wait for her reply.

Logically, I know I can't keep her here—that would make me as shitty as my father, to hold her against her will—but the thought of her leaving, being on her own and struggling, tears me up inside.

I meant it when I said if she goes that I'm packing a bag and tagging along. Her safety is my sole focus right now, and I have vacation days banked if I have to use them.

She shrugs. "I don't know, it just feels like I've turned your whole world upside down. You're fighting with your—" I don't miss her rough swallow or the way she balls her tiny hands into fists. "You and your girlfriend are fighting because of me. I'm not worth this kind of trouble."

"Wrong. So, fucking wrong." I hold up my index finger. "One, Scarlet's not my girlfriend—not really." I hold up another finger, mentally adding a talk with Scar to my mental to-do list. "Two, you're not trouble, and even if you were, you'd be worth every bit. None of what's happened is your fault. I know I can't make you stay, but I hope you believe me when I say I want you here with me."

My words hang between us as Nora mulls them over. I send up silent prayers to every deity I can think of, offering all kinds of deals for her to stay.

"Okay," she finally whispers, "I'll stay."

"Good. That's good." The evenness of my voice surprises me, because on the inside I'm doing a victory lap. "Why don't we go out there and talk with Scarlet now? It's probably not a good idea to leave those two unsupervised for long."

"What do you mean?"

"C'mon." I tip my head toward the hall. "You'll see."

"Overreact much?" Scarlet is saying as we enter the room.

"I'm not overreacting." Ellis glares at the feisty blonde who knows how to push all of his buttons so very well. "You're just insane."

"Me?" Her eyes narrow. "*I'm* insane?"

"Did I stutter?" He rises from his recliner and stomps over to where Scarlet's cozied up on the couch.

"Should we stop them?" Nora asks, looking truly alarmed.

"Nah. This is just what they do." Honestly, if I didn't know better, I'd think this was some weird kind of foreplay for them.

Nora and I watch, riveted as he kneels in front of her "Since your parents failed to teach you any kind of manners, I'll do it for them." He grabs her right ankle and pulls her shoe off.

"What are you doing?" she screeches, trying to kick his hands away, but Ellis's hold on her is solid.

He grabs her left ankle and repeats the motions before standing and dropping both of her shoes unceremoniously by the door. "It's fucking rude to wear dirty shoes into someone's home. It's even ruder to put said shoes on their furniture. Understand?"

She crosses her arms and kicks her sock-clad feet up onto the coffee table. "That you're a jackass? Yeah, that's coming through loud and clear."

He smirks as he drops back down into his chair. "That's Officer Jackass to you."

I give Nora a *told you so* look before clearing my throat. "If y'all are finished, we'd like to join you."

Scarlet's glacial glare softens as she turns her focus from Ellis to Nora. "Sit by me." She pats the spot next to her. "Regardless of what *some* might say, I don't bite."

Ellis snorts in a poor attempt to cover his laugh, but Nora remains rooted at my side.

"Go on, Pip. I'll sit with you." My voice is as soft as I step back and let her take the lead. If she wants to join Scar on the couch, then we will; if she doesn't, then we won't. It's as simple as that.

Hell, she can stand right here in this very spot all night for all I care. I'll be by her side like I'm glued there. She's one hundred percent in control, even if she doesn't realize it.

"Okay," she whispers, nodding to herself. She tries to hide the way her hands shake by balling them into fists, but I don't miss it.

I'm too tuned into all things her to miss much of anything.

She takes a hesitant step before pausing and glancing back at me, as if to make sure I'm following behind her. When she sees I am, she crosses the room quickly and perches herself on the edge of the center cushion.

I hate how apprehensive she feels, but I can't lie—something warms inside of me when the unsure look melts off her face at my reassurance.

Scarlet eyes me suspiciously as I claim the seat next to Nora, like she knows something I don't. It's unsettling. I'm not sure any of us can handle any more surprises this weekend.

"Do you know the date of your last period?" Scarlet asks, jumping right into things.

Ellis's eyes damn near bug out of his head. *Of course, the jackass gets grossed out by a little blood.*

"Um." Nora's cheeks are so red they rival a fire engine. "I'm not... I don't know."

Scarlet waves away her concern. "That's okay, an ultrasound will give us a clear idea as to when you're due. I'm guessing you don't have insurance, but my doctor offers private pay, so that shouldn't be an issue. I'll talk to her tomorrow, and we can figure out a time for you to come in—"

"That sounds expensive." Nora swallows hard. "I-I don't have a lot of money, but I'm going to get a job soon. I think. Hopefully..."

I can see the panic beginning to build as her breathing accelerates and the blush staining her cheeks works its way down her neck.

It's on the tip of my tongue to tell her not to worry about the cost, that I'll gladly pay it and more, but I grit my teeth and stay silent. The only thing I'd accomplish by offering to foot the bill is making Nora feel more uncomfortable than she already does.

I'll just arrange it with Scarlet later.

Ellis shoots me a look that says *fix this* and I nod, because one way or another, I intend to.

"I'm sure it won't be a problem," Scarlet says, her eyes pinging back and forth between Ellis and me before settling on Nora. "Do you want to give me your number so I can text you about everything?"

"Could you text Atlas instead?" She glances back at me over her shoulder. "I don't have a phone."

"Yup." Scarlet's eyes flare as she looks my way. "Not a problem."

Nora's relief is palpable, to the point where even my shoulders relax a little.

"There's just one more thing," I say, hoping it's something they can accommodate. "Her appointment needs to be completely private. I'm talking off the books and during lunch or something. I don't want anyone in that office other than you and your doc even knowing she was there."

Scarlet's looking at me like I've lost my mind, but I can't find it in me to care. "That's a big ask, but I'll do my best."

"Gonna need better than your best, Scar. I need to know that Nora's safe. Especially since we don't know where my dad is."

She runs her fingers through her long hair before flipping it behind her shoulder. "Got it." She turns her attention to Ellis. "Y'all are looking for him, right?"

"Yeah, we are." He nods, his eyes locked onto the woman at my side as he puzzles something out. "Hey, Nora, can I ask you something kind of random?"

She glances up at him with wide eyes and nods.

"When was the last time you ate?"

Shame immediately flares to life inside of me. I've been with her since last night and not once did it occur to me to feed her.

Some protector I am, I think bitterly.

"Today, I um, I had some chips while you stepped outside."

"Chips." I parrot the word back to her, feeling lower than low. "Fuck, Pip. You've got to be starving, why didn't you say anything?"

She shrugs, refusing to look my way.

"Nora." I brush my fingers against her knee, causing her to startle, her hazel eyes flying up to mine. "I meant it when I said you were safe with me, and part of being safe means your needs are being met. The thought of you being cold or hungry or without medical care—" My words halt as I suck in a deep breath, as I try to regain control of my emotions. "I can't stand it."

The room is quiet enough you could hear a pin drop. Maybe later I'll feel weird over my outburst, but for now I'm on a roll. "Anything in that kitchen is free game. I don't care if it's the last Oreo—you want it, eat it. You're cold? Turn up the heat. Tired? Take a nap. Anything you want, Nora, just tell me and I'll do my best to make it happen."

"I can't." She shakes her head as she wraps her arms around herself. "This is your house, and I—"

"What's mine is yours, Nora, for as long as you need."

Scarlet gasps, but I'm too focused on the trembling redhead at my side to pay her any mind.

Tears gather along Nora's lash line and her lower lip wobbles, but she doesn't actually cry. *So damn strong.*

"Honestly, I'm just really tired." She rubs her eyes. "It's been so long since I've been able to truly sleep. I think...if it's okay, I mean... I'd like to lie down for a bit."

"What did I tell you?" I ask, crossing my arms over my chest. "You don't need my permission, Pip. You want something—take it."

"Okay." She stands from the couch. "Maybe after I rest I can fix y'all some dinner?"

"Absolutely not," Ellis says, reading my mind. "We'll throw something together and wake you up when it's ready."

"Are you sure?" Her eyes flit back to mine, like it's *my* approval she's truly after.

"Positive." I can't wait for the day when she's bossing me around, all assertive and shit. It's going to be glorious.

"Do you think I could have my diary back?" She nibbles her lower lip as she looks over at Ellis. "You know, if you're finished with it."

"Yep." He hops from his chair and grabs it from the dining room, passing it to her on his way to his chair.

"Thank you." She clutches the leather book to her chest. "All of you."

We watch in silence as she retreats back to my room, waiting for the snick of the door closing behind her.

"Atlas." The way Scarlet sighs my name instantly sets my teeth on edge. "What's really going on?"

Ellis, the damn jackass, kicks back in his chair, pretending to toss popcorn into his mouth. He knows her cool and calm was all for Nora's benefit, and now that she's not here, all bets are off.

Still, I try for dumb, because at the very least I'd like to have this conversation privately. "I'm not sure what you mean."

"Cut the shit. You're treating her like she's this priceless treasure."

"She's been through a lot," I argue. *But that's not all it is,* the asshole part of my brain adds.

"Yeah, she has." Scarlet nods and I internally celebrate—she's seen reason. "But that doesn't change the fact that you have feelings for her."

I should have known better than to think she'd let it drop. But at the same time, is she right? Do I have feelings for her?

The realization hits me like a two-by-four to the face.

Shit... Oh, shit. She's right, I definitely have feelings for Nora.

"I can see from the dumbstruck look on your face that you're only now realizing it." She rolls her eyes. "Men are such idiots."

"It's not... I don't—"

Scarlet holds up a hand. "Save it. You're so gone over the girl it's sad."

"She's my stepsister." My whispered words hang between us until finally, Scarlet laughs. Hard.

I'm talking belly-clutching, tears-in-her-eyes guffaws.

Personally, I don't see what's so funny, because it feels like my entire life just imploded for the third time in as many days.

Maybe we're wrong. Maybe I'm just feeling really overprotective because of everything my dad did. Like some kind of misplaced guilt.

Fuck, man. Even as I try to rationalize it, the truth might as well be a flashing neon sign in front of my face.

I'm crushing hard on my stepsister. What in the hell is wrong with me?

"I don't see what's so funny." I cross my arms over my chest, feeling oddly defensive.

"There are people out there fucking their actual siblings, and you're worried about liking Nora—who you've spent virtually no time around?" She swipes beneath her eyes. "It's not like it's incest, Atlas."

"This feels weird to talk about with you," I mumble, my cheeks heating.

"Why?" She tilts her head to the side, like she truly doesn't get why this is weird. "Clearly we're over, and honestly, I think you'd be good for her. She needs someone like you."

I look to Ellis for—hell, I don't know, consolation? Backup, maybe? But he's too busy smiling like the cat who got the canary to be of any real help.

"What do you mean *someone like me?*" I'm not sure if her words are meant as a dig or not. Either way, they rankle, like I'm somehow not worthy of Nora.

Not that Nora's interested in me. God, how could she be? After everything she's been through, I'm sure I'm the ultimate reminder of all the hurt she's experienced. No, the best I can ever hope for with her is friendship—and that's if I'm lucky.

"Someone soft." Her lips quirk up into a semi-smile. "Someone gentle. Patient. Kind."

Ellis coughs, and I look his way to see him shifting in his seat, an unreadable look on his face.

"Scarlet," I say, stopping just as quickly as I start, because what is there to say? We were never really serious about each other, and our relationship wasn't going anywhere, but it's still weird to have her tell me that I have feelings for someone else. It makes me feel like a bad guy in her story, and that's the last thing I ever want to be.

"Don't worry about me, Atlas." She pushes herself up from the couch. "We both know we weren't working out. Plus, she needs you, and if I'm being real, I think you're the kind of guy who needs to be needed. Take care of her, okay?"

"I will," I say, standing to walk her to the door. "I appreciate you, Scar. And I mean that."

She rolls her eyes as she slips her boots back on. "I know you do."

"Just leave without saying bye then," Ellis calls from the living room. "Rude ass."

Without looking back, she pulls open the door with one hand while raising her middle finger in the air with the other. "Peace out, Officer Jackass."

DIARY ENTRY, PRESENT DAY

Dear Diary,

Is it weird to say I've missed you? Because I really have. These last few days without you have been unbearable. I have so much to tell you, but I don't even know where to start.

Wait, that's a lie. Yes, I do.

I did it—I escaped! It feels surreal to even say it, but I'm free, and that monster will never hurt me or the baby growing inside of me ever again.

It's crazy how it all worked out. Honestly, I keep thinking I'll wake up any minute back in the basement.

I took a chance and left you for Ellis, hoping he would be able to help me, but Atlas found you instead.

I was so scared when he showed up at the motel. I thought he was going to drag me kicking and screaming back to Rand, but he didn't. He says all he wants is to keep me safe, and even though it's hard, I believe him.

Atlas seems like a good man. Fingers crossed he doesn't prove me wrong.

Hopeful, Nora

FOURTEEN
Nora

You know that feeling you get when you wake up somewhere unfamiliar? That momentary burst of panic as you try to remember where you are and how you got there?

That feeling is completely absent as I blink myself awake in Atlas's bed. I take stock of my surroundings as I stretch my arms over my head and point my toes. I'm cozy and well-rested, which is odd in and of itself.

But it begs the question—*what woke me up?*

Dappled sunlight filters in through the blinds, but it's not overly bright. There are no birds chirping or anything. I'm not too hot or cold. And after the feast Atlas and Ellis served up last night, I'm certainly not hungry. I still can't get over *them* cooking for *me*.

If anything, the only discomfort I'm experiencing at the

moment is over how absolutely content I am in this cloud of a bed.

I'm not sure if it's the mattress topper, the thick duvet, or Atlas's scent clinging to all of it that settles me the most, but whatever it is—I love it. I feel safe and secure, neither of which I've felt in years.

"Nora?" a masculine voice calls from the other side of the closed door. The deep timbre of it sends shivers down my spine— the good kind.

"Yeah?" I say around a yawn.

"Can I come in?" Atlas asks.

I nod then immediately feel like an idiot since he can't see me. "Of course," I call back, "it's your room."

The door swings open and Atlas steps into the room. "We've been over this, Pip. While you're here, it's yours."

"It doesn't feel right." I push against the mattress so I'm sitting all the way up. "It feels like I'm pushing you out of your own space and—"

"Nora." Atlas is across the room and at the side of the bed in the blink of an eye. "I know it's hard, but I need you to let me take care of you."

"Why?" I whisper, struggling to understand the reason he cares as much as he does. Is it some kind of misplaced guilt over what his dad did to me, or is it something else entirely?

He lifts a hand, like maybe he's going to reach for me, before letting it drop again. "I know it doesn't make sense, but I... It's just something I need to do."

"Like a compulsion?" I don't know why I asked him that. I'm not sure I really want to know the answer. The thought of him thinking of me as some kind of obligation makes me feel about two inches tall.

It's probably dumb, but I want us to be equals, because if life with Rand taught me anything, it's that relationships—even friendships—with a power imbalance rarely work out.

And after being on my own for so long, I really want Atlas to be my friend.

"Sort of." He shrugs his broad shoulders. "But not in the way you're thinking."

I clutch the covers to my chest, uncertainty winding its way around my heart like thorny vines, pricking at me until tears fill my eyes. "Can you explain it to me?"

"Nora, no, don't cry." Atlas reaches out and brushes his thumbs under my eyes. "Please, Pip. Your tears kill me."

Something inside of me short circuits when he tries to pull his hand away from my face, and before I can think better of it, I reach out and grab his wrist, holding his hand in place.

I feel kind of like I'm losing it, but at the same time, the thought of him no longer touching my cheek is almost unbearable.

What is wrong with me?

Atlas glances down at where my fingers circle around his wrist. "Talk to me, Nora. What's going on?"

My cheeks heat as I ponder how to explain this to him without sounding a few cards shy of a full deck. He's always so careful around me, so how on earth do I tell him that his touch grounds me, that the feel of his skin against mine makes me feel safe? *How?*

"I like it when you touch me," I blurt out, my entire body heating in embarrassment. "Wait, no. That's not what I meant. I—"

"What did you mean then?" He glances down at me, an

amused smile playing on his lips as he brushes his thumb along the edge of my jaw.

I release my hold on him in favor of burying my face in my hands. He probably thinks I'm some kind of stage-five clinger.

"Hey." He peels my hands away from my face before cupping both of my cheeks. It takes my all not to melt into a puddle of goo at the soft look on his face. "Whatever you're thinking, stop it."

"I'm just humiliated because—"

"Why?" he scoffs. "Because you told me you liked it when I touched you? I'm fucking thrilled you told me. It's been hell holding myself back every time I wanted to reach out and comfort you. But now I know you're okay with it, because you spoke up and told me. Don't you get it? You ask, I deliver. You want me to touch you, Nora?"

It takes me a second, but when I realize he's waiting on a response, I nod.

"Good, because guess what, Pip"—he lowers himself down so that he's sitting on the edge of the bed—"I definitely like touching you, too."

Now my body feels hot for a totally different reason. His deep voice combined with his kind eyes—yeah, I'm feeling things I've never really felt before. Things I'm not even sure how to quantify. Almost like every bit of blood in my body is rushing to the space between my legs.

I'm tingling all over, and I think I like it. Which is wild.

I'm sure I'm just reading way into what he's saying. Way, way into it. He's just being a nice guy. *Get a grip, Nora!*

"It makes me feel safe," I whisper, dragging my lower lip between my teeth as I look down at my lap. "Like nothing can hurt me as long as you're near."

Acting braver than I feel, I peek up at Atlas from beneath my lashes. Much to my surprise, a wide, victorious smile curls his lips.

"Do you know how fucking good it feels to hear you say that? Pip, I feel like I'm on top of the world knowing that my presence does that for you." He places his hand on my knee over the top of the covers and squeezes once. "Like Superman."

"Would that make me your kryptonite?" I don't know where the question comes from, but it's out of my mouth before I can stop it. *What is it about this man that obliterates my filter?*

"Yeah." He drags his gaze up from his hand on my knee, over the length of my body, until we're eye to eye. Even with the blanket obscuring most of me from his view, his stare almost feels like a caress against my heated skin. It's terrifying and exhilarating all at once. "I think you just might be."

Silence falls around us, but it's not weird or uncomfortable. It's the welcoming kind of quiet. As if drawn by a magnet, Atlas leans forward, until he's crowding my space, and we're breathing the same air.

My entire body freezes, but Atlas mistakes my sudden stiffness as fear and pulls back, standing from the bed.

But I wasn't scared, not of him; no, I was frozen in anticipation because for a moment, for one stupid and glorious moment, I thought Atlas might kiss me.

And now, I'm not sure if I'm relieved or disappointed that he didn't. Or maybe he wasn't ever going to. Maybe I misread the situation altogether.

God, why can't I just be normal?

"I have to head to work now," he says, freeing me from my internal pity party. "Ellis does, too, so you'll have the house to yourself."

"Oh." All of the good feelings swimming around inside of me vanish, my old friend anxiety swiftly taking their place. "Okay."

I knew he had work today, but now that it's actually time for him to leave, I'm on edge. The thought of being alone is terrifying. At least at the motel, there were other patrons and the employees. Here, though, I'm completely alone...the only person for miles.

"I'm only working a half day today, so I won't be gone long. The door will be locked and the cameras on. You're perfectly safe, Pip."

"Okay," I say again when nothing better comes to mind. I've spent the last few years with only my diary to keep me company. What's one more? At least here, I'm safe. Here, I don't have to worry about when I'll eat next or whether or not I'll end the day with broken ribs or a black eye.

"If you need anything—" Atlas pauses abruptly, spearing his fingers through his slightly-too-long hair. "Shit. You don't have a phone, and you definitely need one," he rambles, pacing the length of the bed. "We're going to fix that today."

The thought of him spending that kind of money on me has my belly flipping. *I can't let him do that* is the only thought in my brain as I kick off the covers and spring out of the bed, positioning myself directly in his path.

"You're wearing my shirt," he says, seemingly dumbstruck by the sight of me. My cheeks heat under his scrutiny, but at least he's moved on from the idea of buying me a phone.

"I am." I dig my toes into the carpet as my entire body flushes. His shirt is the *only* thing I'm wearing, and even worse, I didn't ask first—like a heathen, I just helped myself. "I-I hope that's okay."

Atlas drops his eyes to my mouth, pausing there before continuing his slow perusal. "More than okay." He licks his lips, and I swear I feel it between my legs. *What is wrong with me?*

"Are you sure?" I don't know why I'm pushing the issue. He said it was fine, but for some reason, I can't let it go.

"Promise." He sways forward, tugging at the sleeve of the shirt. "It looks way better on you than it ever did on me."

My lips part on a shaky exhale. My legs tremble and my heart races as my belly flips like I'm caught in a freaking spin-cycle, 'round and 'round, tumbling in circles as I try not to make a fool of myself in front of this man.

"Fuck, Nora." Atlas sounds pained. "You can't look at me like that."

"Like what?" I ask, even though I'm pretty sure I know.

He pinches his eyes closed and balls his hands into fists, flexing his fingers until his knuckles flash white.

I know I shouldn't, but I take a step closer, pressing my palm to his chest.

His eyes fly open at the contact, his breathing choppy, like each inhale hurts. "Nora," he croaks as he brings his hand up to cup my cheek. The rough slide of his palm against my jaw nearly sends me to my knees. "God, you're so—"

I lean into him, desperately waiting for him to finish his sentence, but he doesn't. Instead, he presses a soft kiss to my forehead and steps back, putting a respectable distance between us.

"Have a good day, Pip. And if you need me for any reason, you can use the echo in the kitchen to drop in on my phone. I left instructions on how to use it on the fridge."

Atlas gives me one last lingering look and then he's gone, leaving me to obsess over exactly what he was going to say.

I pass the time doing things I wasn't allowed to do in Rand's house, starting with an hour-long bubble bath. If I thought the shower at the motel was luxurious, it's got nothing on soaking in Atlas's massive tub.

The bubbles I made using his soap are definitely a bonus. Knowing that his scent will cling to me all day soothes something inside of me.

Once the water grows cold, I drain the tub, dry off, and dress in my threadbare leggings and a hoodie I find in Atlas's closet. I also pilfer a pair of his socks, since the only pair I brought with me is so riddled with holes they're useless.

I make his bed and poke around his room a bit before finally giving in to my hunger, heading into the kitchen in search of food.

The pantry and fridge are both filled to the brim. Honestly, the sheer number of choices is overwhelming. With Rand, I was lucky to get scraps, and now, I'm looking at what feels like every food imaginable, and I'm allowed to eat *any* of it.

This is the kind of stuff I used to dream about when I was locked in the basement for days on end. And now it's my reality.

After much deliberation, I settle on a turkey sandwich with some chips before taking my plate into the living room to eat.

The remote taunts me from the coffee table as I tuck into my meal. It's been so long since I've watched TV. But Atlas said to make myself at home, so surely, he meant this, too, right?

My fingers itch to grab the remote, to press the power button and find something to watch. I used to love watching mindless reality shows.

"Just do it, Nora. Atlas said it was fine."

Okay, well, he didn't expressly say watching TV was okay, but he implied it.

"What's the worst that could happen?" I reason, wondering exactly when I reached the point of talking to myself out loud.

I polish off the last of my sandwich—which was absolutely the best thing I've ever eaten—and then lean forward, swapping my plate for the remote.

At first, I just hold it, silently hyping myself up to turn it on.

"Be normal, Nora." I rest my finger over the button. "Just. Be. Normal." I apply pressure and the screen blinks to life.

It takes me a minute or two of fumbling with the menus, but eventually, I get one of their recently watched shows playing.

It appears to be some kind of true crime thing—probably not the smartest choice—but I'm turning over a new leaf today. I'm being brave, normal Nora today.

Not sad Nora or broken Nora, just everyday normal Nora.

At least I'm trying to be, anyway.

The show starts out fairly benign. A missing girl and the frantic search to find her. But things take a turn once her body is found in the woods, and before I know it, I'm sitting on the couch, clutching my knees to my chest, jumping at every little thing.

A small part of me wants to turn the show off, but I don't. I can't. Even though I'm shaking like a leaf, the tragic mystery playing out on the screen has me completely enraptured.

This was definitely a bad idea.

"What was that?" The sound of tires crunching draws my attention away from the show. My entire body tenses as I mute the show, listening closely while hoping it's nothing more than my ears playing a trick on me.

A car door shuts outside.

Oh, God, someone's here.

Maybe it's Atlas. He said he was working a half day, but didn't give a time. But his truck is loud... I would have heard the rumbling engine if it was him.

My already rapid heartbeat speeds up, thump-thump-thumping against my rib cage like it's trying to break free.

Panic, fear, and paranoia press in on me from all angles, their oppressive weight leaving no room for logic.

"Nora," a deep voice calls from outside, causing the hair on the back of my neck to stand on end.

He's here. He found me.

I scramble off the couch right as the front door opens.

"Nora!" The voice shouts my name, but I'm already down the hall with no plans of stopping.

Get somewhere safe. Atlas. Atlas is safe.

I sprint toward his room, throwing the door shut and locking it before hiding in the back of his closet.

You have to be quiet. I slap my hands over my mouth, trying like hell not to make a sound. Maybe he'll give up. Maybe he'll—

"Nora, where are you?"

My ears ring and my entire body trembles as visions of Rand busting down the door and dragging me back to his house flash through my mind.

I can't go back there, I just can't. I won't.

Silent sobs rack my body and tears blur my vision as I cradle my belly, waiting for the inevitable...

FIFTEEN
Atlas

Only two more hours stand between me and Nora. I'd like to say I haven't been checking the time religiously, but I'd be lying. I'd also like to say I didn't send Ellis to check on her, but again, lies.

And now, to add to all of that, I'm obsessively checking my phone for messages, waiting to hear how she is.

Finally, my phone rings.

"How is—"

"You need to come home," Ellis says, cutting me off, his words rushed. "*Now.*"

"10-4." I put the call on speaker and fire off a text to my chief ranger letting him know I had to leave due to a family emergency and then hightail it to my truck. "But I need you to tell me what's going on."

"Well, I came to check on her like you asked, but I guess she didn't realize it was me and flipped out."

"Where. Is. She?" I grit out the words, trying to leash my temper. It's not his fault she got scared, but the urge to lash out is strong. I should have known better. I should have known she'd be scared.

"In your room. I think."

"What do you mean *you think*?" I crank the engine and gun it out of the parking lot.

"The door's locked."

"Fuck." I fly down the service road before turning out onto the main highway and punching it. "I'll be there in ten."

"It's at least a fifteen-minute drive."

"I'll be there in fucking ten. Tell your boys if you need to." I end the call and focus on the road, driving like a madman.

Thankfully, the lunch hour rush is over and there are no cops on my route, allowing me to make it home in record time.

I squeal to a stop in front of the house, throwing my truck into park and killing the engine before marching into the house.

Ellis meets me at the door. "Man, I'm sorry, I didn't mean—"

"I know you didn't." I wave away his concern as I stalk down the hallway, my sole focus on getting to Nora.

"Nora." I try my doorknob, but it's locked, like Ellis said. "It's me, Pip. It's Atlas."

I press my ear to the door, listening for any sign she's in there, but I don't hear much of anything.

Reaching overhead to the lip of the door frame, I feel around for the emergency pin lock key. It takes a few tries, but eventually my fingers brush against it. I grab it and shove it in the small hole on the knob, effectively disengaging the lock.

Everything in my room looks as it should—aside from the neatly made bed, which is clearly Nora's doing. The doors to the closet and bathroom are both shut, but before I can decide which to check first, the sound of muffled crying gives away her location.

Every part of me is screaming *get to her now*, but I approach the closet slowly. Rushing in would only scare her more. Patience is the name of the game, and I'm playing to win. How could I not be, when Nora's trust is the prize?

"Pip, it's me," I murmur, slowly pulling the door open to reveal Nora huddled in the corner, rocking back and forth as she cries.

No, *cries* isn't the right word. She's sobbing, her despair so tangible it's seeping out of her pores, hanging thick and heavy in the air around us.

I fall to my knees in front of her and scoop her into my arms. I'm expecting her to freak out, to fight, but she doesn't. No, she clings to me with her arms around my neck and her legs around my waist, like I'm the only thing standing between her and certain death.

"Shh, I've got you." I rub my hands over her back, trying to soothe her. "I'm here. You're safe, Pip. I'll never let anything happen to you."

She burrows into me, pressing her tear-soaked face into my neck as I continue whispering reassurances to her.

"Let's get you out of here," I say, attempting to stand.

But Nora flips out, digging her nails into the back of my neck as she tries to move impossibly closer. "Please don't leave me," she cries, and I swear to God, something irreparable inside of me breaks.

"I'm not, Pip. I'm not leaving you; I promise."

We sit here, on my closet floor, for what feels like hours, with me rocking and whispering and holding Nora. By the time she calms down, my back is cramping and my shirt is wet from her tears.

"Atlas." Her voice is hoarse when she whispers my name.

"I've got you, pretty girl." I press my lips to her temple. "I'm here."

She sniffles before pulling back ever so slightly. "I'm so sorry."

"For what?" I brush her matted hair away from her face. "You didn't do anything."

"I'm a freak." She buries her face in my neck again, trying to hide from me, but I'm not having it.

"No." I cup the nape of her neck, tipping her head back so that she's forced to look at me. "You're not a freak."

She shakes her head. "I am. I—"

I don't know what comes over me, but I lean in and press my lips to hers, effectively silencing whatever self-deprecating garbage she was about to spew.

Nora freezes against me, and I immediately pull away, wondering how to fix my colossal fuckup. "Shit, Pip. I'm so sorry. I don't know what I was—"

"Do it again." She raises her hands to my cheeks, before trailing her fingertips over my lips. "Kiss me again."

"Are you sure?" I ask, my muscles twitching under my skin from the restraint it takes not to dive headfirst into her. The last thing I want is to take advantage of her when she's already so, *so* vulnerable.

She nods, brushing her nose against mine. "Yes, I'm more sure than I've ever been about anything else in my whole life. Please kiss me, Atlas. Kiss me so all I can feel is you."

How am I supposed to deny her?

Simple—I don't.

Honestly, there's not much she could ask for that I wouldn't give her. The thought should worry me, and yet, as I lean in and once again touch my lips to hers, I can't help but think how right it feels having her in my arms.

The kiss is over as quick as it starts. Perfectly chaste, and yet, I know it's something I'll think of for years to come.

"We need to talk, Pip," I say, brushing my thumb over her cheek.

"I know." Her voice is still hoarse, and it fucking guts me.

"C'mon, let's get you out of here." She crawls out of my lap, allowing me to stand and help her up. "Is my room okay?"

"Yeah." She follows me back into my room, making herself at home in the middle of my bed.

I want nothing more than to crawl into it with her, but I think we both need some space, so I take the chair instead.

"Before we talk about what happened today, we need to talk about *what happened today*," I say, sounding like an absolute tool. "Did that even make sense?"

She shrugs, and I sigh. Of course, I'm fucking this all up.

"I shouldn't have kissed you, Pip. It was wrong of me, especially with how upset you were."

"Do...do you regret it?" she asks, running her index finger over the seam of her lips.

"Yes and no." I interlace my fingers behind my head and try to gather my thoughts. "I regret it because the timing was shit. You deserve so much more than an ill-timed kiss in a dark closet while you're terrified."

"And no because?" She's sitting with her back against the

headboard, knees pressed to her chest and her cheek resting on her knees as she waits for my reply.

The fact that I can still see tear tracks on her freckled cheeks makes me feel like an even bigger asshole than I already do.

"No, because you're you, Pip."

She lifts her head, sending a puzzled look my way. "I don't understand."

"I think that's a conversation for another day." Because how in the hell do I even begin to tell my stepsister, who's spent the last several years being abused by my dad, that I have feelings for her?

God, what is wrong with me?

"Well, I don't regret it." She straightens her spine, sitting up proudly. "I'm glad it was you."

"Glad what was me?" My heart climbs into my throat, because I'm pretty sure I know exactly what she's going to say, and I'm not sure if it's going to make me feel better or worse.

"You were my first kiss, and you're right, it wasn't ideal, but it was what I needed right then to bring me back. I trust you. I feel safe with you. So yeah, I don't regret it."

I scrub my hands over my face, trying to figure out how this day went so sideways.

"You deserve better, Nora. The best. I need you to promise me you'll never settle for anything less than that, okay? No matter who it's with. Promise me?"

Her eyes shine with unshed tears, and for a minute I think she might argue with me, but finally she nods. "Promise."

"Okay, good." I exhale a relieved breath, my guilt partially assuaged. "Now, can we talk about the *other* what happened today?"

"I feel so stupid." The self-loathing in her voice rivals my own.

I can't believe I fucking kissed her. She should hate me. God knows, she'd be well within her right.

"Why? Talk to me."

"I was watching TV, some true crime show one of you was watching earlier, and I got scared. So, when I heard the car in the driveway—"

"It was Ellis, I asked him to check on you."

She huffs out a humorless laugh. "I figured that out pretty quickly, but I was too wound up to do much about it."

"You wanna know what I think?" I ask, rolling my chair closer to the bed.

"What?" Her cheek's back on her knees again.

"I think you should give yourself a little more grace. You've lived through unspeakable things and moving on from them is not easy. Healing takes time, and everyone does it at their own pace. You're strong as hell, Pip—a fighter—and I'm fucking proud of you."

A pretty blush colors her cheeks as she ducks her head. "Thanks."

"And I know I've already said it, but I think it bears repeating—I'm sorry for taking advantage of you. I know you said you feel safe with me, and I hope that you still do. But..." I swallow roughly, lowering my focus to the floor. "I understand if you don't."

"I do, though."

My eyes snap up to meet hers. "You do what?"

"I do trust you, Atlas. With my life, and even though you're upset about it, I'm not mad you kissed me either. You're a good man. I know it like I know my own name."

I bow my head, relief rushing through me. "Thank you,

Nora."

I'm not sure I deserve her forgiveness, but like the selfish asshole I am, I'm going to claim it all the same.

"You don't need to thank me, weirdo." She shimmies her way to the edge of the bed before pressing her toes to the floor. "But if Ellis is home, could you take me to talk to him, and then maybe show me how to actually use the TV?"

A smile curls my lip as I stand. "Sounds like a plan."

DIARY ENTRY, PRESENT DAY

Dear Diary,

It's been nearly a week since my kiss with Atlas. Which means it's been nearly a week of me obsessing over it.

He says it was wrong of him to do it, and while I agree the timing was bad, I have a confession… I really liked it.

Honestly, I couldn't have imagined a better first kiss.

Maybe it's because I know he'd never hurt me or because I know he'd stop if I asked.

I want to talk to him about it, to maybe ask him to do it again, but he's acting like it never happened, and I'm not sure I could handle it if he turned me down.

I already have a learning curve compared to most girls my age.

Which is why I feel silly still thinking about it. I mean, gah! It was only a few seconds, which in the grand scheme of things shouldn't be a big deal. To a normal girl, it probably wouldn't be.

But, again, learning curve, so to me that stupid two-second kiss was everything.

Enough about that, for now anyway, because today's my first OB appointment, and while I'm trying not to be, I'm really nervous.

Everything I've read on the phone Atlas got me (that's a whole other issue because I told him a flip phone would be fine, but he insisted on adding me to his plan and getting me a smartphone like his) says that you don't really feel your baby move until somewhere between sixteen and twenty-four weeks, but I'm not sure how far along I am, so it doesn't really help me much.

I don't know. I guess I just want this baby so badly that it physically pains me to think of all the possible outcomes.

Atlas swears he won't leave my side the entire appointment, and I'm definitely holding him to that. I don't know how or when it happened, but over the last week, he's become my rock-my safe place-and I don't know that I'd be able to face any of this without him.

I'll update you after my appointment.

Apprehensive, Nora

"Are you nervous?" Atlas asks as I slide my boots onto my feet.

"Only a lot." Straightening, I tug up the waistband of my leggings. I've put on a little weight in the week I've been living with Atlas, but I'm still a lot smaller than all of the women I see online. "I'm excited, too, though. I'm pretty sure both emotions are battling it out inside of me."

"Which is winning?"

I shrug, not wanting to admit that my anxiety is at an all-time high.

Although, knowing Atlas, he's probably well aware that I'm stressed and wants us to try and talk it out. I can't, though, because what if talking about it gives life to all of the worries plaguing me?

Which brings me back to being nervous as heck. How could

I not be when thoughts like *What if I'm starving my baby, what if there's something wrong with it because of all of the things Rand did to me, what if there's no heartbeat?* keep knocking around in my brain.

This baby, this sweet innocent life growing inside of me, is what gave me the courage and the strength to get out, but I don't think I really had the brain space to worry about all of the things most first-time moms do when I was still locked away. Now that I'm free, the *what-ifs* have been raining down on me relentlessly.

It may seem strange, given the circumstances, but this little one is everything to me, and I *need* to know he's okay, to hear his heartbeat.

I need those things, because then it will be real. Then I'll know that I'll never be alone ever again. Then I'll know that my life truly has a purpose.

Atlas studies me for a long minute, tilting his head to one side and then to the other. I'm half-expecting him to call me on my sullen mood.

"Well, let's head out," he says instead, because that's the thing about Atlas—he knows when to push and when to let it go. "Scarlet said she'd let us in once they cleared the office out for lunch."

"That's nice of her." I try to focus on that, rather than her clearly complicated relationship with Atlas.

"Yeah." He chuffs out a laugh. "She has her moments."

"How did y'all meet?" I ask as we walk to his truck, clearly abandoning the idea of not thinking about *them*. "If you don't mind me asking."

"We met at The Creek. She was there with some guy, and he ended up being an asshole. Ellis and I found her crying outside, drunk as hell. So, we brought her back here to sleep it off on the couch. Then she sort of just...kept coming around."

"So, you have a hero complex then?"

"What?" He opens the passenger door for me and then lifts me up into the truck.

I wait for him to join me in the cab before replying. "You like saving people. Scarlet, and now me."

He scoffs as he starts the truck. "I'm not interested in saving anyone."

"Anyone else." I roll my lips inward to keep from smiling. He's getting all growly over this, and I'm not going to lie—I kind of love it.

"Pip." The single syllable holds a warning, but I know he's only joking.

"I'm just saying. One more helpless female and you've got yourself a pattern."

"First of all—" He cuts his eyes my way before checking the road and pulling out of the driveway. "You are *far* from helpless, so cut that shit out. You are the strongest person I know. Honestly, Nora, I'm in awe of you."

Emotion clogs my throat as I process his words. "That, uh, that got really serious, real fast."

"Sometimes I think you need the reminder." Atlas drums his fingers on the steering wheel as he waits for the light to change. "Not a reminder of what you've been through, but that you've made it to the other side."

I tuck my hands under my thighs to keep from fidgeting. "I guess you're right."

"And one more thing, Pip. You didn't need a knight or a prince to save you, because you did it your-own-damn-self. So anytime you're feeling down, just remember that you realized you had something to fight for and said *screw the prince, I'm saving myself.*"

This time, I don't try to stop my grin. "Man, it's almost like you've read my diary... Oh, wait!"

He flicks on the blinker and shoots me the cockiest smile known to mankind. "That's right, pretty girl, I got that insider knowledge."

I shake my head, but I'm smiling. This kind of light, playful banter is one of the things I missed the most. It's also one of the things I refused to let myself think much about. Out of sight, out of mind, and all that.

We fall quiet as Atlas navigates through town to the doctor's office, but with every turn, my anxiety climbs.

"Will you stay with me?" I ask as he expertly parks his beast of a truck near the back of the building. "During the appointment, I mean."

"Pip." He glances my way, his mouth frowning around his nickname for me.

"You don't have to," I rush to add, not wanting to make him uncomfortable. He's already done so much for me, so if this is his line, I'll be okay.

Reaching over the console, he takes my hand in his. "I won't leave your side, not just for this appointment, but for all of them. I'm with you every step of the way. Hell, I'll even hold your hand while you give birth if that's what you need from me." He brushes his thumb over my knuckles. "I mean it, Nora. Whatever you need, big or small, I'm there."

His words send a spike of relief through me. I lean over the console, intending to press a kiss to his cheek, only my aim is off and my lips meet the corner of his mouth instead.

Atlas and I both freeze, our faces pressed together as we just breathe one another in.

"Sorry," I whisper, my lips ghosting over his. But I don't mean it, not really.

He rakes his teeth over his bottom lip as he runs his knuckles under my chin, drawing me minutely closer. "Don't be."

"Atlas." His name is a prayer...an invitation. One he readily accepts.

"Need you to say it, Pip." His voice is thick and syrupy, and I swear I can feel it low in my belly. "Need to hear you say you want this."

"I want this." My heart pounds like a drum in my chest, the rhythm building and building as my anticipation grows. I want so badly to reach out and pull him closer that my fingers tingle.

I'm not sure why he has this effect on me, but I like it; I like him, and I most definitely want to feel his lips on mine. And this time not in a dark closet.

He tips my head back ever so slightly and then seals his mouth to mine, drawing my lower lip between his, sucking slightly.

It's like he has a direct line to my libido, and I gasp as prickles of pleasure fizz to life inside of me. Opportunist that he is, Atlas wastes no time deepening our kiss.

Time stops as our tongues swirl together, soft and teasing. Until this moment, I thought kissing was kind of weird, but now, with Atlas, I totally get it.

Feeling bold, I scrape my teeth over his lower lip. His answering groan has me clenching my thighs together in a way I'm not entirely sure I understand.

I mean, clearly I'm aroused. I'm not a complete idiot. I've

even touched myself a few times, but here and now, I'm so turned on that I want to climb over the center console and straddle his lap just so I can feel more of him.

The sound of someone tapping on the window brings our kiss to an abrupt halt. We break apart, eyes wild, lips swollen and chests heaving.

"Shit," Atlas hisses, tipping his head toward my window.

I glance over my shoulder to find Scarlet standing outside the truck with an indecipherable expression on her face.

She gives us a sharp look before pointing at her wrist and then the door, silently telling us to hurry up.

Atlas sighs and cuts the engine.

Meanwhile, I'm over here wishing I could disappear entirely. I mean, *come on*, I might not know the details of their relationship, but I know there was one. And that's enough for me to want to hide forever.

"You good, Pip?"

I choke out a laugh. "If by good you mean mortified and praying for the earth to open up and swallow me, yeah sure, I'm great."

He lowers his brows, giving me a curious look. "You embarrassed to be seen kissing me?" His voice holds a sliver of hurt, and I hate it.

"No!" I press my hands to my chest. "No, not at all. It's just weird because she's your—"

"She's not my anything," he interrupts with a growl. "But you... I'm starting to worry that you could be my everything." He says the last part so low I almost wonder if I misheard him.

I must have, right?

But before I can ask him to clarify, he's out of the truck and bounding around to open my door and help me down.

Scarlet gives us both a silent once-over before rolling her eyes and gesturing for us to follow her. She pauses at the door and whirls around to face us. "The next time y'all want to make out like teenagers, maybe do it on your own time, yeah?"

My entire body heats with shame. Not over kissing him, or even over being caught. It's the fact that Scarlet and her doctor are doing us—*doing me*—a huge favor, and the least we could do is respect their time.

I'm about to apologize, when Atlas grabs my hand and pulls me into him, wrapping a protective arm around my shoulders. "I get that we should've been more conscientious of the time, but don't you make her feel bad, Scar." He puffs out his chest. "I won't allow it."

"Right." Her lips twitch. "Got it."

She turns back to the door, which is wedged open with a wooden block, and pulls it open. "Right this way."

The inside of the building is no different than any other doctor's office I've ever been to, aside from the absence of other people. The hallway is so quiet you could hear a pin drop. Even our footsteps echo.

It sort of reminds me of the start of a zombie movie. I don't like it.

Noticing my discomfort, Atlas slows his steps and slides his hand into mine. "Everything's going to be fine."

His gentle reassurance prods at the worry wrapping itself around my heart, but it's not enough to vanquish it completely. "What if it's not?" I ask in a small voice.

He glances toward Scarlet, who is giving us as much privacy as the hallway allows, and then back to me. "Come hell or high water, I'm with you. No matter what happens, Pip, I've got you."

"Okay." I squeeze his hand and nod. "Let's do this."

"If you want to have a seat here," Scarlet says, gesturing toward a little alcove, "I'll take some vitals and get your chart started."

I know she's waiting on me, but my feet are rooted, my eyes pinging back and forth between the chair and Atlas.

She sighs dramatically before taking mercy on me. "You can take a seat, too."

Atlas presses a hand to the small of my back and we follow her into the recess, with me taking the chair closest to the desk.

"All right, you already told me you don't remember the first day of your last period." Scarlet wastes no time jumping right into everything. Her straightforwardness miraculously sets my mind at ease. "Which means we'll need to do an ultrasound to determine gestation. Before that, though, I'm going to check your blood pressure, iron, weight, and get a urine sample. These are things we'll do at most appointments."

My insides are rolling like a stormy sea, my nerves cresting higher and higher with each wave.

I look to Atlas for reassurance and he nods, his soft smile instantly calming me. It's wild to me, the way he's able to so effortlessly set me at ease.

"Okay, let's do it."

Scarlet flies through my work-up so quickly I hardly have time to think about all of the *what-ifs*. According to her, my urinalysis says I'm definitely pregnant, I need to gain some weight, my blood pressure is fine, and my iron is, unsurprisingly, low.

After mentioning a few foods to help with my iron, she stands and steps out into the hallway. "If y'all want to follow me, I'll be doing your ultrasound before you see the doctor. You should be far enough along for us to do a pelvic ultrasound."

She leads us into a dimly lit room two doors down. "If you'll hop up there, lift your shirt, and recline back that'd be great."

"Everything's going to be fine, Pip," Atlas says as he helps me get situated just right. "Promise." He presses a soft kiss to my temple before lowering himself into the chair next to me.

"This might be cold," Scarlet says apologetically before squirting a blob of gel onto my belly.

I brace, expecting the worst, but the goo is pleasantly warm.

As she uses some kind of wand to spread the goop around my lower stomach, the black screen flares to life. Well, sort of. Mostly it just looks like static to me.

"Okay, Nora, the first thing I'm going to do is look for the heartbeat." She rolls the wand over my belly, pressing harder in some spots than others.

The room is deathly still—the kind of silence that makes your ears ring. It's so quiet, I swear I can hear my own heart beating outside of my chest.

It feels like eons pass, though it's probably only seconds, before a whooshing sound fills the room.

My eyes flit from the screen to Scarlet and back again. "Is that—" My voice trembles with a mixture of hope and fear.

She nods. "That's your baby's heartbeat. Strong and steady at 150 beats per minute."

Tears fill my eyes as I listen to the sweetest sound I've ever heard.

"That's not too fast?" Atlas asks, interlacing his fingers with mine. The feeling of his palm pressing into mine grounds me in the moment.

I'm free. I'm safe. My baby is okay. This is all real.

Scarlet glances at our joined hands but—*thankfully*—doesn't comment on it. "Perfectly normal. As the pregnancy progresses, the heart rate will slow some. If you give me just a minute, I'll take some measurements, and we can narrow down your due date."

I watch with rapt attention as she clicks around on the screen, trying—and failing—to understand exactly what I'm looking at.

"According to my measurements, baby is right around thirteen weeks, so the end of the first trimester. We'll probably do a few additional scans to monitor baby's growth so we can be sure on the timing and progression." She rolls the wand over my belly again, pressing it firmly to the lower left side of my belly. "Now, for the fun part."

"The fun part?" I ask, wondering what on earth could be better than hearing my baby's heartbeat.

"See here." She nods toward the screen. "That's your baby's head, and here are the toes."

"How big is the baby?" Atlas asks, his voice filled with wonder.

"About the size of a peach."

"And you can see all of that?" The wonder quickly morphs into disbelief.

But Scarlet just smiles. "The wonders of science."

I know she's being sarcastic, but in a way, she's right. This is wonderful. Amazing, really, that my baby is the size of a piece of fruit but has fingers and toes and a heartbeat.

Talk about a perfect freaking day.

DIARY ENTRY, PRESENT DAY

Dear Diary,

I heard the most amazing sound in the world today… my baby's heartbeat. It was strong and steady and absolutely perfect. Honestly, if I could bottle the sound and keep it close by, I would.

Come to think of it, I might ask Scarlet if I can record it at my next appointment-which is only three weeks away! She said we might even be able to find out the sex of the baby.

Scarlet asked if I want a boy or a girl, like I have any say in the matter. I just want a healthy baby. Someone I can love and hold and care for…someone who will love me.

It sounds weird, but my arms literally ache to hold my baby. Only twenty-seven more weeks to go. It sounds far away, but everything I've read online says it will fly by.

I'm also nervous for what my baby's arrival means. I have no real education, no job, less than a hundred dollars to my name, and only a temporary living situation.

I need to make a plan, because my baby will not suffer or want for anything. I'll do whatever's necessary to provide for my child.

Talk to Atlas about finding a job

Get a job

Save money

Find somewhere permanent to live

Ugh! My to-do list is stacking up against me. Not to mention, the cost of actually having the baby and my prenatal appointments. I'm not stupid-I know Atlas paid for my appointment today. He didn't tell me because he didn't want me to feel bad, but I'm going to pay him back.

He says it's not taking advantage when it's something he's giving freely, but still, I feel beholden to him, and I don't like it.

Find a way to pay Atlas back for the phone, doctors' appointments, and clothes

Oh, God. It kind of feels like I can't breathe.

Somehow, I managed to free myself from one problem only to be pinned by another.

One step at a time... Dad used to say you can only take one step at a time. I just need to slow down and figure out my steps. I've survived worse than this, so I know I'll be okay.

No—we'll be okay.

Overwhelmed, Nora

SEVENTEEN
Atlas

I can't explain it, but I've been on cloud nine ever since hearing our little jellybean's heartbeat.

Fuck, man. I don't know when I started thinking of this baby as *ours*, because clearly, it's not my anything. Nora's not either, and while I'm not going to push her, I damn sure want her to be.

I want *both* of them to be mine.

It's wild; if someone would have asked me a few weeks ago if I ever wanted kids, I'd have laughed. But now I'm racking my brain, trying to think of where we can stick a nursery and how I can convince Nora to stay here with me.

Even if nothing more ever happens between us, I want to be in this kid's life, and while I'll gladly take on any role she'll allow me, I want to be a good example for him, to right my dad's wrongs.

Not that we know it's a boy—hence *jellybean*, because calling the baby *it* didn't feel right.

I'm so far ahead of myself it's not even funny. Forget putting the cart before the horse, I'm mashing the gas pedal to the floor, and there's not even an engine under the hood.

"What are you thinking so hard about over there?" Ellis asks, tossing a handful of chips at me.

"The fuck, man?" I jump back, trying to gather all of the crumbs. "Now the couch is going to be crunchy."

He rolls his eyes and digs another handful out of the bag. "Back to my question. You look like you're constipated or something."

"Just got a lot on my mind."

"Care to share with the class?"

I glance down the hall toward my room, where Nora's holed up, most likely writing in her diary. "About Nora and the baby and—"

"Dude, you're so sunk it's not even funny."

My first inclination is to deny it, but what's the point? There's something about the redhead down the hall that has me wearing my heart on my sleeve and acting like the sap I swore I'd never be.

"I know." I scrub my hands over my face before reclining back against the couch cushions. "I just wish I knew what to do about it."

"What"—Ellis blinks at me, clearly confused—"do you mean?"

"I'm not right for her." I lean my head against the back of the couch. "I wish like hell I was, but I'm not."

"I think you're full of shit." Ellis chuckles as he leans forward, bracing his elbows on his knees. "But I'll bite. Why aren't you right for her?"

"She needs someone..." My words dry up like the fucking Sahara relocated in my throat.

"Someone who'll love her and her baby, care for her, protect her, put her first, make her happy," Ellis lists with an eye roll.

"Yeah." I nod. "All of that."

"Hmm." He leans back, drumming his fingertips against his knees. "Seems like you already do most of that."

"None of that matters, though. Not when I'm directly related to the reason for all of her suffering. How could she ever want me, man? How could I ever hope to be more than a reminder of all she's suffered through?"

"One." Ellis holds up his index finger. "Self-pity doesn't look good on you." He adds a second finger. "Two, it's not your place to make these kinds of choices for her. She's had enough choices stripped away from her, Atlas."

My entire body melts into the couch as frustration and shame battle it out inside of me. "You're right. Fuck, man. You're right."

Ellis grins. "Usually am."

"Right about what?" Nora asks, stepping into the room, making my whole body jolt. *Sneaky little red-haired ninja.*

But before either of us can answer her, the front door flies open, and Nora drops to the floor, curling into a fetal position.

"Shit!" I growl, cutting my eyes at the rude-as-hell blonde darkening our doorway before rushing over to Nora. "It's okay, Pip. You're safe. It's just Scarlet."

She's shaking like a leaf but doesn't object when I wrap my arms around her, sliding her onto my lap.

"Listen to my heartbeat," I whisper to her, brushing her hair off her forehead. "You're here with me, and you're safe."

"I'm sorry." Scarlet sighs. "I wasn't thinking."

Ellis snorts. "You rarely do."

"Why are you here, Scar?" I ask, still rubbing soothing circles over Nora's back.

"I brought pizzas!" she says, as if that explains her presence inside of our home, uninvited.

Nora sniffles against my chest. "P-pizza?" she asks, pulling back from me and sniffing the air. "What kind?"

"Um, one pepperoni, one cheese, and one supreme."

Nora whimpers, and I want nothing more than to march Scarlet right back out the way she came in, but I'm not willing to let go of the woman on my lap to do it.

"I haven't had pizza in…" Nora glances up at me, her eyes wet and cheeks pink. "Years. It's been years." She sniffs the air again and shudders against me. "It smells *so* good."

"Then let's eat," Scarlet chirps, knowing she's off the hook.

Ellis tips his chin my way before following Scarlet into the kitchen, leaving me to make sure Nora's truly okay.

"You good?" I ask once it's just the two of us.

She tries to smile, but it comes off as more of a grimace. "Just embarrassed."

"Don't be." I slide her off of my lap so I can stand and help her up. "Scarlet should know better than to bust into someone's house without being invited. This is on her, Pip, not you."

"If you say so." It's clear she doesn't believe me, but I meant every word. Scarlet should know better than to just let herself into someone's house. Things were different when we were together, but we aren't now, and she damn sure needs to remember it.

"I do." I grab her hand and tug her into my side. "Now let's go grab some slices before those two eat them all."

The sound of Ellis and Scarlet bickering greet us as we make our way into the kitchen.

Just like the last time we stumbled upon the two of them going at it, we pause to listen.

"You want my mother's number?" Scarlet asks incredulously. Her back is to us, but I'd bet my entire paycheck that her eyes are narrowed into thin slits and her cheeks are every bit as red as her name implies.

"I do." Ellis is one hundred percent the calm to her storm, as he props one elbow on the island.

"Why?" The word sounds more like a snarl.

"I'd like to have a chat with her about your upbringing. Give her some feedback on the areas she failed you." He shrugs, looking her up and down. "I'm sure she did her best, given your natural predisposition."

"I swear to God," she growls. "You insufferable, pig-headed—"

"Yeah, no." He cuts her off. "You don't get to insult me in my own home, especially when you're not even an invited guest."

"Should we put a stop to this?" Nora asks, worrying the hem of her shirt between her fingers.

"Probably." I sigh and slide my palm against hers, interlocking our fingers. "C'mon, Pip, let's go settle the kids."

She gives me a goofy grin as we walk into the warzone formerly known as our kitchen.

"Sit by me," Scarlet says to Nora, suddenly calm and smiling. The girl's moods flip faster than a fair ride.

A burst of pride rockets through me when Nora releases my hand and claims the stool next to Scarlet. She may not realize it, but each day she's growing more confident in herself, and I'm fucking here for it.

Watching her come into herself is like watching a rare flower bloom. It sounds lame as hell, worded like that, but it's the truth. She's awe-inspiring.

I plate us each up a few slices before sliding onto the stool on her other side. Most of our meals together so far have been met with little fanfare, other than her thanking us—despite being told no thanks are necessary.

But her first bite of pizza—it's something I'll remember for the rest of my life. The little happy squirm she does after each bite is the cutest thing I've ever seen.

In this moment, she's pure and unbridled joy, and I'm the lucky fucker getting to bask in the glow of her smile.

"So, tell me, Nora," Scarlet says around a mouthful of pizza, ever the lady. "What did you think of Dr. Snider?"

Nora chews and swallows before answering. "She seemed really nice."

Scarlet swipes her tongue over her teeth and then leans a little closer. "Did you give any thought to what she asked?"

My heart slows in my chest as my entire body tenses; I'm a predator about to pounce and rip the throat out of my prey, because I know exactly what Scarlet's asking.

But Nora beats me to it. "I've already made up my mind, thanks."

"Are you sure?" Scarlet presses, never knowing when to leave well enough alone. "You have options, Nora. You don't have to keep—"

"I know you're coming from a good place," Nora cuts her off, leaning back into me.

I press a hand to the small of her back in a silent display of support, letting her know I'm here for her.

"I'm sure it probably seems strange, but I love my baby, and I'm keeping it. Just like I would never judge another woman for choosing differently, I hope you can find it in you to respect me and my decision."

Scarlet flushes but nods all the same. "Got it."

"Thanks." Nora twists in her stool so that she can look my way. "But I have been thinking about something…"

"What's up?" I already know whatever she says, I'll do my best to make it happen.

"I think I'd like to speak with someone. A professional. I-I used to see a lady named Maggie, but it's been years."

"Do you know her last name?" Ellis asks. He's been so quiet, I almost forgot he was with us.

"Tyler." She tips her head to the side. "I think."

Ellis nods, before giving voice to what I'm already thinking. "I'll find her."

And we will, because if there's one thing I know—if Nora needs it, we'll work tirelessly to make sure she has it.

EIGHTEEN
Nora

"I think talking to Atlas about finding some type of online job is a great idea," Maggie says, smiling at me through the screen. "The first step of many toward taking back your independence."

"I do, too." I glance away from the screen. "I just worry I'm not really qualified for anything."

Maggie takes a sip from her mug, regarding me over the rim. "There are plenty of positions you're qualified for, Nora. Don't make problems where they don't exist."

My shoulders slump in defeat. "You're right. I know you are. It's just hard not to look for all the ways something can go wrong." *Especially when so much in my life already has,* I add bitterly in my head.

"I know, which is why I want you to start a gratitude journal.

That way, whenever life feels overwhelming or it feels like everything's going wrong, you can look back and reflect on all that's going right."

"Okay, yeah. I can do that."

"Good. We'll talk again at the same time next week, but if you need me before then, I'm only a call away."

"Thanks, Maggie." I lower my eyes and scrape my teeth over my lower lip before refocusing on the screen. "I really missed you—talking to you, I mean."

Maggie smiles, her eyes crinkling in the corner. "I missed you, too, Nora," she says, before ending our session.

Tears blur my vision as I stare at the blank screen. Maggie kept our talk pretty surface-level, but just hearing her voice again after so long has a whole mess of emotions writhing inside of me, fighting to break free.

I'm still sitting at his desk, silently crying, when Atlas finds me.

"Shit, Pip." He rushes into the room, scooping me into his arms. "Are you okay? Talk to me, pretty girl."

"I just..." I shake my head, unable to give voice to thoughts swirling around in my head like a tornado.

"Shh." Atlas pulls me closer, and I nestle my head in the crook of his neck. "It's okay. I've got you."

He holds me, whispering softly, as I cry out all of my hurt. By the time I pull back, his neck and shirt are damp from my tears, though if he notices, he mercifully doesn't comment on it.

"You with me?" he asks, smoothing my hair back from my face.

"Yeah." I try to wriggle out of his hold, but he only pulls me closer, not giving an inch. If he was anyone else, I know I would lose myself to fear, but just like I know the sun will rise each morning, I know Atlas would never hurt me. "I'm with you."

He leans in, pressing his forehead to mine. "How can I help?"

"Distract me." I shrug, looking up at him. "Take my mind off everything."

"I know just the thing." He brushes his lips over my forehead before sliding out from under me. "Hop up on the bed. We're going to have a movie day."

I snuggle down into my spot, fluffing my pillow and pulling the covers up to my chin as he queues up some random comedy on his laptop.

"Is this okay?" He lifts the blanket, signaling he wants to join me under the covers.

My insides flip, but I nod. "Yeah, it's okay."

He doesn't waste a second before sliding into bed beside me.

The warmth of his body next to mine is the best kind of comfort, and when he slips his arm around my shoulders and pulls me into his side, it feels like coming home.

My eyelids grow heavy as the movie plays, and before I know it, I'm fast asleep.

NINETEEN
Atlas

Clarity teases the edge of my consciousness, leaving me somewhere between awake and asleep.

My bladder is telling me I need to get up, but my body is content to stay in this bed, with Nora curled around me, forever.

Her head is nestled perfectly into the crook of my neck with her arm thrown over my chest, her palm resting right over my heart. But it's her legs all tangled up with mine that has me reluctant to leave.

Nora's body molds to mine like we're two halves of the same whole. It sounds sappy as fuck, but it's true, and I love it.

The problem is, I'm hard as a rock, and she's dangerously close to being woken up by my *very hard* dick.

It feels wrong, being turned on while she sleeps in my arms. I could play it off as simple biology, but it's more than that. I've jerked off to thoughts of Nora more times than I can count in the short amount of time she's been here.

Maybe that makes me a pervert, I don't know. My feelings for her are so tangled up. To an outsider, our relationship—if we had one—seems wrong, but I know in my soul that she and I are so fucking right it's not even funny.

I don't know how I went from *content to stay single* to *ready to put down roots* in the blink of an eye, but somewhere along the way, I caught feelings.

She shifts against me, hitching her leg higher around my hips. She's damn near straddling my thigh, and her pussy is way too close for comfort.

"Pip," I whisper, brushing my fingertips over her shoulder. "You gotta roll over."

Instead of rolling over, Nora ratchets up my torture by *a lot* as she slides her hand down from my chest to the waistband of my sweats. Her pinky finger is dangerously close to my dick, and I swear to God, it's straining to rise up and meet her.

I know I could slip out of the bed. I could and I should. Unfortunately, my brain and body aren't on the same page. Hell, they're not even reading the same book.

My brain is shouting for me to be a gentleman, to hightail it out of the bed before something bad happens.

But my stupid, selfish body is warm and content and totally at peace.

Get your shit together, I scold myself, finally finding the willpower to move away from the little redheaded siren wrapped around me.

Only before I can, her hand slips down lower, and just like that, she's palming my cock.

Fuck. Me.

"Nora," I croak her name, trying with all my might to keep my body still. "You've gotta let me go."

I should have bounced the second I woke up, but now she's wrapped around me like an octopus, and I'm stuck.

She squeezes my dick, and even through my clothes, it sets me on fire. My hips buck involuntarily as a groan slips past my lips.

"Atlas?" she asks, her voice still thick with sleep.

"Yeah, Pip?" My voice sounds hoarse even to my own ears.

"I'm…touching you…" Her fingers give a little flex, as if to emphasize her words.

My throat bobs as I swallow. "You are." *Please don't hate me… please don't ever stop…*

"You're hard." She scrapes her teeth over her lower lip as she looks up at me from beneath her long lashes.

"I am." My cock pulses beneath her touch, as if it has a mind of its own.

Holy hell, how could I not be with Nora's lithe little body pressed so snugly against mine?

"Does…does it hurt?" Her voice is this odd combination of curiosity and embarrassment. But she doesn't need to be; she can ask me anything, any time.

"Nothing about your hand wrapped around my dick hurts, Nora." I pinch my eyes shut and take a calming breath before looking at her. "If anything, it feels too good."

"Are you sure? That face you just made looked pained." She pouts, and all I want to do is kiss her pretty mouth.

"Pained because I like it." *Pained because I want you to slip your hands into my sweatpants so I can feel your skin on mine.* I keep my answer short; Nora doesn't need to know all of the filthy things tumbling around in my head.

"Can I see it?" Her cheeks go atomic as soon as the words leave her mouth. "OhmyGod, never mind. I-I can't believe I just asked you that! What is wrong with me? Oh, God—"

"Pip." Something in the way I say her name has her lips snapping together like a rubber band. "There's no part of me that you can't see or touch anytime you want."

"Really?" The word is nothing more than a breathy whisper.

"Really." I hook my thumbs into the waistband of my sweats and drag them down, allowing my erection to spring free.

Her eyes bulge at the sight of it, causing a swell of masculine pride to rush through me.

"It's so..." She gulps. "Big."

I grin, and Nora rolls her eyes before looking her fill.

She lifts her hand from it resting on my abs, as if she's going to reach for me, but yanks it back at the last second.

"You can touch it," I say, silently praying I don't nut the second she makes contact.

"I can?" She licks her lips, and I nod. "Okay."

"Oh!" Nora sucks in a sharp breath as she gently squeezes the tip between her index finger and thumb. "It's softer than I thought it'd be."

I grunt, unable to form any kind of intelligent reply because I'm doing three-digit multiplication in my head.

Sliding her hand down, she fists my dick, jerking me once from tip to root.

That single motion has me seeing stars. *Fuck, how can this not-even-a-hand-job feel this good?* It's like I'm having some kind of out-of-body experience as Nora explores my body.

Precum leaks from my tip, drawing Nora's eyes. She looks

from it to me, and back again. "Can I taste it...taste you?"

Fuuuuuck. Who even is this woman? This innocent little spitfire of a vixen.

"Yes! God, please, yes." Every single muscle in my body tenses in anticipation. Jesus, the thought of her mouth on me is like my birthday, Halloween, and Christmas all rolled into one.

She wiggles out of my hold and pushes up to her knees, staring down at my dick like it's an equation that needs solving.

Leaning forward, she wraps one hand around my base. Anticipation thrums like electrical currents through a battery. My entire body is amped up, primed and waiting for whatever delicious torture she's about to unleash.

"Like this?" She slowly drags her fist up my length.

"Grip it harder." My voice sounds rough, even to my own ears, but I can't help it. I'm a man on the edge, and Nora's either going to be my savior or my damnation.

"Like this?" She tightens her fist a little bit.

"A little more."

She shoots me a worried look. "I-I don't want to hurt you."

"Nora, I promise, any time your hands are on me, the only thing I'm feeling is pleasure." I cover her hand with mine, adjusting her grip. "Now you're going to do it just like this."

I help guide her motions, loving the way her confidence grows with each pass.

"I'm ready," she says after a few strokes. "Ready to taste it."

That's all the warning I get before she swipes her tongue over the head of my cock, lapping up my precum like it's the tastiest treat.

"Salty." She wraps her lips around the crown and sucks softly.

"Fuck, Pip." I have to fist my hands at my sides to keep from reaching for her. "You feel so good."

My reaction is extreme, but her mouth on my dick—hell, on any part of me—is like finding water in the desert when you've been walking for days.

She's my oasis.

"Can you take any more?" I ask, actively pressing my hips back into the mattress to keep myself from fucking her mouth.

"Maybe a little." She speaks the words around my dick before sucking me deeper into her mouth.

"Hollow out your cheeks and just swallow down as much as you can."

She gags a little, and I try to pull back, but she follows me with her whole body, her lips never leaving me.

I feel like a fucking teenager getting his first ever BJ—it's sloppy, and Nora has literally no technique—and yet I'm still trying my hardest not to bust a nut two minutes in.

It's her, though; it's Nora. She's everything I never knew I wanted. Her skill level is irrelevant, simply because *it's her.*

"Pip," I groan her name. "You gotta stop."

She releases me with a wet pop. "Why?"

"I'm gonna—" My whole body tenses as my release rockets through me, rope after rope of cum jetting out onto my abs. "—come," I sigh, once I can speak again.

For the second time today, Nora studies me like I'm a problem to be solved. But this time, it's my jizz that holds her focus.

She leans forward and drags one finger through the milky substance, smearing it around a bit. "So warm," she murmurs, before bringing her finger to her lips, tasting my release. The face she makes has me grinning big. "Still salty, though."

Jesus Christ. That's it, lights out, I'm finished—this woman is too damn much for me. Somehow innocent and sexy all at once, she's got me tied up in knots.

"Pip." I rasp her name, and she whips her head up to look at me.

But instead of the desire I expect to see reflected back at me in her gaze, I find fear.

"I-I'm sorry," she starts, trying to scramble away from me.

"Hey, no." I hold my hands up, showing her I'm not a threat despite wanting nothing more than to yank her back into my arms. "You're fine. Nothing to apologize for."

Tears fill her eyes, and I feel like the biggest asshole on the planet. I should have slipped out of the bed when I had the chance.

"What's wrong, pretty girl? Talk to me." I tug my shirt over my head and use it to wipe up my stomach before sliding my sweats back up. "I hate seeing you cry. Hate it even more when it's my fault. Did I push you too far?"

I spear my fingers through my hair. Of course, I did, because I'm a selfish bastard. She showed a modicum of interest, and I lost my composure. *God.*

"No!" She all but shouts the word. "It's not you. I—it's me. I took advantage of you, Atlas, and that was wrong, and I'm sorry. I'm so, so sorry." She wails the last word, crumpling into a heap on my chest.

My heart beats erratically in my chest as she cries tears of misplaced guilt.

"Nora, I need you to listen to me." I thread my fingers through her messy hair so that I can see her eyes. "Can you do that?"

She sits up and then nods.

"Nothing about what just happened between us wasn't enthusiastically consensual on my part. I meant it when I said you can touch or taste any part of me, any time. As far as I'm concerned, you have carte blanche when it comes to me. Do you understand?"

"D-do you mean that?" She tucks her hair behind her ear, searching my face for any hint of deception.

"Wholeheartedly, Pip." I stroke my fingers over her lightly freckled cheek. "As long as you're okay with what just happened between us, I am, too. And if nothing else ever happens, that is fine, too. You set the pace, and I'll gladly follow, okay?"

"I don't deserve you, Atlas Wallace."

"That's where you're wrong." I lean forward and press a soft kiss to her lips. "You deserve every good thing there is, and then some. And if I happen to fit into that somewhere, then I'm the luckiest motherfucker on the whole planet."

DIARY ENTRY, PRESENT DAY

Dear Diary,

It's been three days since Atlas let me make him come.

Oh my God, just writing that has me blushing.

After our…encounter… I texted Maggie for an emergency ap-pointment.

Luckily, she was able to chat with me the next day. It was a little-okay, a lot-awkward telling her why I needed to talk to her so urgently when we had just talked the day before, but I'm so glad I did.

I also confessed to her, and now to you, Diary, that while I don't know that I'm ready to be touched, touching Atlas like that made me feel powerful. The fact that I was able to make someone so big and strong tremble with need was… gratifying.

Not to mention, he was respectful of me every step of the way. But a small part of me felt like it was all too fast.

Thankfully, Maggie was able to give me the perspective I was lacking. She told me the only person who can decide what I'm ready for is me, and that there's no right or wrong pace.

Which brings me to my new predicament…

I want more. More of Atlas, more of his pleasure, more of the power that comes with making his knees shake.

I'm just not sure how to go about asking him. I know he said I could put my hands and mouth on him any time, but I can't very well just walk up and grab his junk, now can I?

But I think asking out loud might be even worse. I don't know.

I remember one time Mama said if someone wasn't mature enough to talk about it, then they weren't mature enough to do it.

So, I guess I better practice in the mirror or something, because my body is so keyed up with need I'm liable to jump him if I don't.

Frustrated, Nora

TWENTY
Nora

"You really think I qualify for all of these jobs?" I swivel on my barstool to look at Atlas, shocked at the list of possible jobs he and Ellis compiled for me.

"None of the ones on this list require a degree," Ellis says, scrambling some eggs at the stove.

"And all of them offer in-house training," Atlas adds. "So, they're all perfect for you."

"Huh, who knew?" Certainly not me. I figured I'd be out of luck trying to find work, but not according to this list. Now the question is: Which one do I apply for? Do I apply for more than one? I'm not entirely sure how all of this works...

"Do any of them sound like something you'd like?"

I flick my eyes up to look at Atlas, unsure on how to reply. None of the jobs sound interesting, but I can't afford to be picky, either. "Which one do you think pays the best and has the best benefits?"

Both men level me with a befuddled stare. "Pip, you don't need to worry—"

"I do need to worry, Atlas." Frustrated tears burn the back of my eyes. "Having a baby is expensive, and so is raising one. Outside of the medical costs, which I'm sure will be astronomical, I need a crib, bottles, clothes, diapers, wipes. And then, I need somewhere for all that to go—somewhere to live, to raise my baby, to call home. All of that takes money, lots and lots of money."

By the time I'm finished, I'm full-on crying, and I hate it. I hate feeling this way, weak and small and so very unequipped for motherhood.

This baby saved me, and one way or another, I'm going to find a way to be the mother it deserves.

Ellis sets a plate in front of me, and I dig into the egg sandwich, grateful for the distraction.

"You know..." Ellis says around a mouthful of food, "you could always live here." He swallows. "Like permanently."

"What?" I choke on my bite, trying to make sense of his words and swallow at the same time. Atlas passes me his glass and I chug it down, shooting him a grateful smile.

It takes a minute, but once I'm able to speak, I try again. "I know you didn't just suggest me living here, like forever. I-I can't do that!"

"Why not?" Ellis asks, sliding his eyes from me to Atlas.

Atlas quirks a brow at his friend, who in turn nods.

"Yeah, Ellis is right." He turns to fully face me. "You should stay here."

"Is there a gas leak?" I sniff the air, despite it being odorless, because what else can explain Atlas and Ellis both suggesting I stay and raise my baby here. "Y'all can't be serious."

They trade looks again.

"We are," Ellis starts.

"Completely serious," Atlas finishes.

I throw my hands in the air. "Right, gas leak it is."

"Pip, of course we want you here." He reaches across the island and takes my hand in his. "Why wouldn't we?"

A bitter laugh breaks free before I can reply. "Yes, why wouldn't two bachelors want a young mom and her baby living with them? Nothing quite like bringing home a date only to get woken up in the middle of the night by a crying baby. Sounds like a dream come true, am I right?"

The kitchen is so quiet it's almost as if it exists in a vacuum. So quiet that my pulse roars in my ears like a waterfall.

"I don't think you get it," Atlas says, his voice low and still. "Having you here, watching you become a mother, being a part of that jellybean's life... Every single bit of that sounds like a dream come true—my dream, Nora. I want to be in your life in any capacity you'll allow it, and I'm a selfish bastard, because I want to keep you all to myself, to keep you in my room and by my side. But I'm not going to clip your wings. You wanna fly and find somewhere new, I'll help you every step of the way." He brushes the back of his knuckles over my cheekbone. "But I really, really hope you'll stay."

I'm too stunned to reply right away, my emotions rising and swelling inside of me like waves in a storm.

"Plus," Ellis adds helpfully, "I don't bring dates home. Best not to fuck where you eat, or however that goes."

I bust out laughing as some of the tension leaves my body.

"I've heard it both ways," I murmur.

"Did you just quote *Psych* to me?" Ellis asks, causing Atlas to groan.

A soft smile curls my lips. "I used to watch it with my dad."

"Of course. It's a classic." Ellis nods. "Definitely in my top five."

"Don't do it, don't do it, don't do it," Atlas whisper-chants.

So, naturally, I have to. "What's your top five?"

Atlas groans again, this one far more dramatic, but Ellis grins like a madman.

"In no particular order—*Psych*, *Gossip Girl*, *Outer Banks*, *New Girl*, and *The Mindy Project*."

"I've never heard of Outer Banks, but the rest are pretty good. *Psych* is my favorite, though."

"You know what we should do?" Ellis asks, not waiting for an answer. "*Psych* marathon!"

My grin morphs into a cheek-splitting smile. "Can we?" I ask Atlas.

He boops my nose. "How can I say no to you, pretty girl?"

"Y'all are on snack duty. Show's on in five!" He takes all of our plates and chucks them in the sink before dashing into the living room.

I take it upon myself to actually rinse the plates and load them into the dishwasher while Atlas tosses a bag of popcorn into the microwave.

"You know we meant it, right?" he asks softly. "We really do want you here."

"Are you sure?" *Please say yes, please, please, please.*

"More than sure." The timer sounds and he grabs the piping hot bag and yanks it open with his fingertips before dumping it into a bowl. "Having you here makes this house feel like a home."

"Okay, I'll stay," I whisper, hope settling into my belly like a seed taking root. Because if I'm not ready to admit it out loud, Atlas is right. Being here, with them, feels like home.

TWENTY-ONE
Atlas

Work's been hell lately—or maybe it's just me and my damn near obsessive need to be at Nora's side twenty-four-seven.

Either way, I put in for some of my vacation days at work, and now the next two weeks are all mine.

Well, actually, they're all Nora's—even if she doesn't know it yet.

Our talk the other night got me thinking... We have a lot to do before our little jellybean gets here, and I figured now's as good a time as any to get some things in order and maybe even set the nursery up.

Assuming Nora wants to, that is.

"Pip?" I knock before stepping into my room.

She looks up at me and right away, I can tell something's

wrong.

"What is it?"

"Shouldn't you be at work?" she asks, pointedly ignoring my question.

But her red cheeks, watery eyes, and wobbling chin aren't things I can ignore. "That's not important." I cross the room and drop to my knees in front of my desk chair, swiveling her to face me. "Talk to me."

"Am I even a person?" she asks, sounding so helpless and so frustrated, that I can't help but want to find a way to fix it, even if I don't really understand the issue.

"Of course, you are. What does that even mean?"

"All of these job applications want my social security number and a copy of my ID. I..." Her lips quiver as big, fat tears spill over. "I don't have any of those things. I don't even have a birth certificate!"

Shit. How can I fix this? Think, Atlas, think!

"Don't cry, Pip. I'll figure something out." My words are meant to reassure her, but all they do is make her cry harder.

"How?" she wails, clutching my shirt as she seeks comfort in my embrace. "How can you? This isn't even your problem, Atlas."

I wrap my arms around her and hold her close. "First of all, anything that upsets you is one-hundred-and-ten percent my problem. As for the *how*, you leave that to me, okay?"

Nora shakes her head, or she tries to anyway, but with her head tucked under my chin, she really just manages to rub her cheek against my chest. "You can't just swoop in and solve all of my problems."

The fuck I can't, is what I want to tell her, but instead I say,

"It's a joint effort, Pip. A give and take."

She huffs out an unamused laugh. "So far, all I do is take."

I tug her forward as I settle back into a seated position on the floor, pulling her completely onto my lap, silently delighting in her shocked squeals. "You've given me far more than you know, Nora."

"Like what?" It's clear from her tone of voice she thinks I'm blowing smoke up her ass. But I'm not. Nora's given me so, *so* much.

"A purpose, for starters. Before you, I was content to just float from one thing to the next, but now I know what I want in life. And that's thanks to you."

"And what is it you want?" she asks, her voice soft and small.

Well, shit. Sort of backed myself into a corner, haven't I? Here's to hoping I don't send her running...

"You, Nora. I want you." She pulls back and looks up at me, clearly perplexed by my confession. I cup her cheek, intent on setting her at ease. "I know it's a lot to take in and probably seems sudden, but I mean it."

"But you barely even know me." Her whispered argument holds no water, though.

"I'd argue to say I know you better than just about anyone else. I know every high and low point of your life. I know your hurts and your fears. I know your dreams, and if you'll let me, I'll do my level best to make them all come true. It's only been weeks, but in my heart, Pip, it feels like years."

"I..." she starts, but nothing follows.

My chest grows tight as disappointment swells inside of me. I pushed for too much, too soon. But that is on me, not her, and I need to make sure she knows that.

"Hey, it's okay." I let my hand drop from her cheek, curling my fingers inward to keep from reaching for her again. "Nothing has to change, Nora. You're still welcome here, and you're certainly still wanted here. This arrangement isn't dependent on you being with me. No matter how things turn out, this will always be your home, do you hear me?"

"What?" She blinks up at me, confusion swirling in her hazel eyes. "I don't understand."

Clearly I'm doing a shit job of explaining myself. "What I'm trying to say is—if you want me, I'm yours. Hell, I think I'm yours either way. But whether or not you feel the same doesn't change your status here. This is your home, too, Nora, no matter what."

"You're mine?" she asks.

Something about the way she says those two words has hope popping off inside of me like bottle rockets on the Fourth of July.

"Yeah, Pip. I'm yours."

"Good." She launches herself at me, looping her arms around my neck as she all but tackles me to the floor. "Because I'm yours, too, Atlas Wallace. Every single part of me."

"You mean that?" I ask, skimming my nose over hers.

"Yeah." She nods before ghosting her lips over mine. "I mean it."

And then, she's kissing me.

Her warm lips dance over mine before she boldly licks her way into my mouth. I groan as our tongues slide together, happy to sit back and let her take the lead.

Because I know—for now, at least—that's what she needs. Control makes Nora feel secure, and I always want to be a safe space for her, especially when we're intimate.

She tunnels her fingers into my hair, tugging me closer as

she sucks on my lower lip. The motion puts her center right over mine, and I know from her sharp gasp that she feels the steel rod that is currently my dick.

"Shh, it's fine," I murmur against her lips. "Just ignore it."

Nora flicks her tongue against mine and then rolls her hips. "What if I don't want to?"

With a willpower I didn't know I possessed, I grip Nora's hips and still her movements. "Talk to me, Pip. Check in. Where's your head?"

Her kiss-swollen lips turn down in the most adorable pout as she glares down at me. Once she sees I'm not budging, she plants one hand on my chest and pushes herself into an upright position.

I groan at the pressure, but we both ignore it.

"This is weird," she mumbles under her breath before clearing her throat and addressing me. "I like the way you make me feel— you're the perfect mix of gentle and assertive. You're always aware of what I need, even before I am sometimes. I feel safe with you, like I can explore the things you make me feel..."

"And how do I make you feel?" I ask, my heart nearly thumping out of my chest as I wait for her reply.

"Protected. Cherished. Desired. Powerful." She licks her lips before giving me a wicked grin and rolling her hips again.

"Nora," I groan, wanting nothing more than to thrust against her, to show her exactly how powerful she truly is. "You're all of those things, and so much more."

She rolls off of me so she's sitting on the floor beside me. "Don't think I didn't notice you ignored my question." Her tone is teasing, and everything in me aches to sit up and kiss her smiling lips.

It takes me a few seconds to realize she said something—my

body is too busy mourning the loss of her heat to fully focus. "I'm sorry, say that again?" I ask, reaching down to rearrange myself.

Nora giggles and repeats her question. "Why aren't you at work?"

"Oh, uh." I didn't plan on telling her my plans while flat on my back with a raging erection, but here we are. "I took some time off, figured we could work on a nursery for the jellybean and—"

That's all the explanation I manage before Nora's back on top of me, kissing the hell out of me, instantly reigniting my need for her.

"You're so good to me." She speaks the words against my mouth before teasing the seam of my lips with her tongue.

I open for her instantly, greedily swallowing her small moans as our bodies move together. "Fuck, Nora, I—" I suck her lower lip into my mouth before my next two words can escape.

Jesus, Atlas. It's way too soon for that.

"You what?" she asks, breaking our kiss, panting.

"I want you." Same number of words, same number of letters, but only half the truth.

Because I do want her—but not just her body, I want her heart, her mind, her laughs, her smiles, her dreams. Hell, I want her whole ass her future. All of it, every single thing she has to offer. I want it all.

And I'm damn sure willing to put in the time, work, and effort to get it. Nora deserves the world, and I'm going to be the one to give it to her.

"You have me," she says, pressing one last lingering kiss to my lips before once again rolling off me. "But I still don't have a way to apply for a job."

Back full circle, I think, sitting up. "Let me check on

something and see if I can find a solution, okay?"

"On what?"

"I've got an idea," I tell her, not wanting to dive into the details of it, because she'll only worry. "You think you can hold down the fort for a bit while I see what I can do?"

"Yeah." Nora nibbles her lip and then nods. "I can do that."

I stand and then help her up, pulling her small body into mine for a hug. "I'll be back soon, Pip. Maybe I can pick up dinner on my way home."

She pats her ever-growing belly. "I'll never say no to food."

"I'm thinking Chinese?"

"Lo mein?" she asks excitedly.

"Anything you want, Pip." I drop a kiss to her forehead. "Just text me your order."

The drive out to my dad's place is uneventful, but I'm on high alert as the house comes into view.

A part of me is expecting to find his truck parked in the driveway, but just like him, it's nowhere to be seen.

However, the empty yard doesn't ease the knot in my stomach even a little, because while he might not be here now, the fucker has to be somewhere, and I can't help but worry about when he's going to pop back up.

I kill the engine and head for the front door. It's locked, but I still have my key, so I let myself in.

The house smells stale, like no one's been here in a while, probably not since the day I asked Ellis to stop by.

But still, I keep my steps light and my guard up—if anyone

shows up here, they're damn sure not going to get the drop on me. Not when I have so much goodness waiting on me at home.

Growing up, I remember my dad having a safe in his closet. I make my way to his bedroom, hoping that it's still there and—more importantly—that I can get into it.

"Please be there," I mutter as I enter the closet, breathing a sigh of relief when I see the big, black box in the far corner.

Dropping to my knees in front of it, I try the first set of numbers I can think of—my mom's birthday—but the lock doesn't budge. I try my dad's birthday next, and then mine, but still nothing.

I turn the dial this way and that, trying to think of another set of numbers to try. "What if it's—surely it's not..." But I try the numbers all the same.

Sure enough, the lock disengages, sending chills down my spine. The sick fucker's lock code is my mom's date of death.

Dread pools in my gut as I retrieve a stack of papers from inside the safe, and it only grows as I shuffle through them.

I sift through a pile of seemingly random newspaper clippings before setting them to the side and opening the manilla folder I grabbed with them.

Inside it, I hit the jackpot, finding not only Nora's social security card, but also her birth certificate. Having these should make getting her a state ID a helluva lot easier.

I slide those documents into my back pocket before turning my attention back to the safe. I have what I came here for, but for some reason, I feel the need to dig a little deeper.

What I find in the next folder knocks the breath out of me—Mom's death certificate. *Fuck.* Even though I know what it's going to say, I read over it, line by line.

Nothing jumps out at me, until I read the cause of death. *Heart attack, and acute toxicity.* What in the hell does that mean?

I flip to the next page and find a toxicology report. There's a whole slew of positive findings, and even though I was fairly young when she died, I know for damn sure she didn't take as many meds as they have listed.

Shuffling those papers to the side, I see another death certificate... this one is Grace's. It reads damn near identical to my mom's. *Heart attack, and acute toxicity,* followed by an almost perfectly mirrored list of meds.

Does this mean what I think it does?

Something isn't adding up here. Hell, a lot of things aren't. I set the reports aside, intent on taking them home with me so I can dissect them later, before returning my attention to the safe.

I pull out the remaining contents, a well-worn brown paper bag, some pill bottles, and a passport.

Inside the bag I find a random assortment of things: a blue hair tie, a glittery barrette, a cross necklace, and so on. Weird but harmless, I suppose.

There's nothing else useful, so I shove everything other than the documents I'm keeping back into the safe, close the door, spin the lock, and then haul ass out of this house of horrors.

Any time spent here is too long, plus Nora's at home waiting on me, and I can't wait to give her the good news.

TWENTY-TWO
Nora

I'm sprawled out on the couch watching *Outer Banks*—at Ellis's insistence—while he provides a running commentary on the show from his recliner when the sound of Atlas's truck barreling down the driveway snags my attention.

"Got it!" Atlas hollers, stomping into the living room.

"Got what?" Ellis asks, pausing our show.

Hope flutters in my chest as he walks into the room. I want so badly to run and greet him with a hug and a kiss, but I force myself to remain seated in fear of rejection. I know he's told me he's mine, but deep-seated fears keep me firmly in place.

"I found your birth certificate and social security card." He cuts his eyes toward Ellis. "I also found Mom and Grace's death certificates. They're... interesting."

"How so?" Once again, Ellis speaks up before I can.

"They might as well be carbon copies of one another. It's…" Atlas shakes his head. "Something's not right."

Ellis stands, crossing the room to Atlas. "Mind if I take a look?"

This time, Ellis is on his own; I've never seen Mom's death certificate and I don't particularly want to.

Which is silly, because logically, I know she's dead. She has been for close to a year now, but still, the thought of seeing it in black and white somehow makes it even more real.

"Knock yourself out." He passes him a folder with a loaded look and then joins me on the couch, wrapping me in the hug I so desperately wanted. "Missed you."

"You weren't even gone long," I protest, even though hearing it secretly makes me giddy. I'm not sure anyone's ever missed me before, not really.

"Long enough," he counters, putting an end to my objections. After all, who am I to tell someone else how to feel?

A sobering thought pops my bliss bubble. "I still need an ID though."

Atlas wraps an arm around my shoulders, tucking me securely into his side. "Now that we have these…" He tugs another envelope from his pocket and places it on my lap. "There shouldn't be any problem getting one. We can go tomorrow if you want?"

"Really?"

"Yeah." Atlas drops a soft kiss on my temple. "Really."

"If y'all are done being mush balls," Ellis drawls, plopping back down onto his recliner, "my boy John B has got some shit to get up to."

"He sucked you in?" Atlas asks, toeing off his boots before kicking his feet up onto the coffee table.

"Oh, yeah." I snuggle in closer to his side, resting my cheek on his chest. "Totally."

With a smile on his face, Atlas grabs the blanket from the back of the couch, covers us both, and settles in for the rest of our binge-watch.

It's a simple thing, just the three of us camped out in front of the television as we devour our takeout, but at the same time, it's one of the best days I've had in a long, *long* time.

TWENTY-THREE
Nora

"That wasn't so bad, was it?" Atlas asks as we step out onto the sidewalk.

The sun is so bright overhead, I have to squint my eyes to look up at him. "I don't know. There were *so* many people in there. It was... kind of awful." I pretend to shake off my disgust.

Atlas laughs and I swear the rich sound warms me more than the sun. "Welcome to the DMV, pretty girl. It's one of the worst parts of adulthood. Just wait until you have to renew your tag."

I don't mean to, but I scoff. "That would require me to know how to drive." Dad used to always talk about teaching me. He drove an old Jeep named Mavis, and he swore up and down if you could handle Mavis, you could drive anything.

"You don't—" He clamps his lips together and then slips his hand into mine as we walk back to his truck. "Of course, you don't. I'll teach you."

"Really?" I pivot my entire body to face him, throwing my arms around his neck.

Miraculously, he catches me, and smoothly swings me around to his other side. "Hell yeah." Atlas once again laces our fingers together. "It'll be fun."

"I don't know about that." I roll my eyes to disguise the excitement rushing through me. Driving is something I thought I'd never get to do. "But I'm grateful all the same."

He unlocks his truck once and opens the passenger door, scooping me up and setting me on the seat before running around to his side. "I'd be hard pressed to think of a single thing you could ask me for that I'd say no to, Pip."

My laughter bubbles up from my belly. "Be careful now, you might live to regret saying that."

"Nah." Atlas starts the truck, checks his mirrors, and pulls smoothly into traffic. "There's no regrets when it comes to you."

Contentment swells within me, leaving no room for doubt. "Thank you, Atlas," I whisper, even though those three words aren't the ones I really want to say.

I love you has been stuck on the tip of my tongue for days now. But that's crazy, right? Is it even possible to fall in love this fast? I mean, sure, technically I've known Atlas for years, but only in the loosest sense of the word.

Maybe love is like grief—maybe it's not logical either. Maybe trying to justify or quantify my feelings isn't the answer. Because the reality of it is, no matter which way I slice it, I love Atlas Wallace.

The question is, could he ever truly love someone as broken as me?

"Did you hear me?" Atlas asks, alerting me to the fact that he asked an actual question.

"No, I'm sorry." I tuck my hair behind my ear and focus all of my attention on him. "Say it again."

"Do you want to grab something to eat?"

"Like from a restaurant?" I drum my fingers over my well-worn leggings. "Sure."

"Are you?" He glances my way before flicking on the turn signal. "We can hit a drive-thru if you want."

"No, I'm good. It's just… been a long time since I've been out to eat."

"Gonna kill that rotten motherfucker," Atlas mutters viciously under his breath. "What sounds good to you?"

"Take me somewhere you love." He knows so much about me, it's only fair for me to learn all about him. "Your favorite place."

He shoots me a wicked grin. "Hope you don't mind getting a little messy."

Before I have a chance to really think about what he meant, he turns into a familiar parking lot.

"Cluckers?" I ask, bouncing slightly in my seat.

"You know it?" He parks and cuts the engine.

"Yeah. My dad used to bring me here all the time when I was a kid." Memories of our many meals here flash through my mind, leaving me as excited as I am sad. "One time he even won the Clucker Challenge. He gave me the shirt, and I slept in it every day for a week."

"Maybe next time we come, I can compete and win you a shirt." He hops down and jogs around to my side, opening my door.

"You'd do that for me?" I ask, once I'm on my own two feet beside him.

He gives me a *duh* look. "I'd offer to do it today, but I have something else in mind."

"Oh, yeah, what's that?" Butterfly wings flutter low in my belly as possibilities race through my mind.

He presses a hand to the small of my back, ushering me toward the entrance. "You'll have to wait and see."

"That was so good," I mutter for the hundredth time since polishing off the last of my six wings. Growing up, I always got honey barbecue, but Atlas convinced me to try the mango pineapple habanero, and I have zero regrets.

Ugh. Is it possible to have a real baby and a food baby?

"We can come anytime you want, Pip." He smiles over at me from the driver's seat. "You just gotta say the word."

"I'll hold you to that. Where to now?"

His kissable lips curl into a mischievous grin. "You'll see."

"Atlas." I whine his name, not caring one single bit how childish I sound. "I don't like surprises."

Surprises have rarely ever turned out well for me. Instead of *surprise, we're going on vacation*, I got *surprise, your dad is dead,* and it really just snowballed from there.

"Okay, fine." He pauses a beat. "I was thinking we could go shopping."

"Shopping?" I ask. "Like for groceries?"

"No." He draws out the word. "Like for you."

"For me?" My brows dip in confusion. "What for me?"

"Clothes for one."

"I have clothes," I argue, knowing full well that's a lie. I've been living in the same two pairs of leggings and borrowed shirts and socks for weeks now.

"C'mon, Nora," he pleads, turning into the Target parking lot. "That bump of yours is growing every day and as much as I love seeing you in my clothes, I know you need some of your own."

"You know I don't have any money." Guilt over the money he's already spent on me pricks at me like tiny needles. "And you've already done so much for me—"

"So let me do one more thing."

On one hand, he's right, having my own clothes sounds like a dream, but my debts owed to him are racking up faster than I can tally.

"Atlas." Tears fill my eyes as I whisper his name.

"Please?" He has the audacity to pout at me, puppy dog eyes and all.

Damn him. I can feel my resolve weakening... bending to his will. At least he uses his powers for good and not evil.

"Fine." I heave the word out on a sigh. His answering smile is one of pure victory. "But my agreeance comes with terms."

"Name 'em."

"Okay, well, it's actually only one term." I can feel my cheeks heating under his scrutiny, but I press on because this is important to me. "You can't spend more than a hundred bucks on me."

"Pip," he pleads, but I cross my arms over my chest and shake my head. His eyes momentarily dip to my breasts, but I don't mention it.

We sit, locked in our stare down, until finally he relents.

"Fine, but that one hundred doesn't include food or anything for the jellybean, because if you think I'm not spoiling the shit out of our baby, you're damn wrong."

My brain trips over his use of the words *our baby*. How is it possible for him to be so all in with someone like me? Still, I find myself nodding as I unbuckle my seat belt.

Pick your battles, I suppose.

Before I can even blink, Atlas is out of the truck and opening my door. "C'mon, pretty girl. It's time to shop."

He slips his hand into mine as we cut across the parking lot, and even though we've held hands more times than I count now, it still feels like electricity skittering over me every time.

"Where to first?" He grabs a buggy and quirks a brow my way.

"Um…" I look around the brightly lit store, unsure of where to go.

"You sort of look like a deer in the headlights, Pip. How about I take the lead until you feel comfortable?"

I nod as a relieved sigh rushes out of me.

He steers us toward the women's section and tells me to go crazy, and I try to, really I do…

But I can't. It's been so long since I've picked out clothes for myself, I don't even know what I like anymore, much less what looks good on me.

My shoulders slump in defeat, the brightly colored clothes mocking me from the racks. Everything either looks small and tight or boxy and bland. Isn't there an *in-between* section?

Noticing my rising panic, Atlas abandons the cart and tugs me into his chest. "Hey, take a breath, you've got this."

"Do I?" I look up at him with watery eyes. "There are so

many choices and nothing over here seems quite right and—"

He leans down and presses his lips to mine, silencing my ramblings with the softest, sweetest kiss ever. The fact that we're in public isn't lost on me either.

"Let's start with the basics. I know Scarlet likes..." He trails off and scratches his chin. "Yoga pants? Leggings? I don't know. I think they're back this way. They're stretchy and should be comfy over your belly. Then we can grab some shirts to go with them, okay?"

I suck in a deep, calming breath. "Okay."

Atlas guides me back toward the activewear section. It's much smaller than the women's section, and I instantly feel more at ease.

"Do you want black ones or color?" he asks, pointing toward a display of neatly folded pants.

"Um." I know it's not a quiz, but I still feel like my answer will decide if I pass or fail. "Maybe both. A black pair and a green pair?"

He nods encouragingly. "That's a good start."

I grab a pair of each color in what I think is my size and toss them into the buggy. "What now?"

"It's like pulling teeth with you, huh?" he asks, but the smile on his face tells me he's only joking.

Smiling, I shrug and make my way over to a pile of folded sweatshirts, grabbing two to coordinate with my bottoms.

"Probably should grab a jacket, too," he murmurs, tipping his head toward the other side of the aisle where there is an entire wall of outerwear. "Go pick one you like, I'll wait here."

I cut my eyes his way, but he's the picture of innocence, resting his forearms on the handle of the cart while scrolling on his phone.

The sheer amount of jacket options is wild to me, and I know I should probably pick something basic, but my gaze keeps sliding back to a hot pink puffer with a fur-lined hood.

It's gaudy and bright, and for some reason, I love it.

I grab it one size too big so that it will fit over my belly before heading back to Atlas.

He intercepts me in the aisle. "Why don't you head over to the intimate apparel section next and get some underwear, bras, and socks?"

My cheeks burn so hotly, they must be redder than the store's trademark bullseye, but still, I do as he says and head over to pick out some new undies.

I grab ten pairs of boyshort-cut panties, two bras, and a pack of socks before making my way back to Atlas, who shockingly is right where I left him.

"Now, we can get you some pajamas or you can keep right on sleeping in my shirts. The choice is yours."

The words Atlas spoke to me when he caught me in his shirt my first morning at his house echo in my brain. *'It looks way better on you than it ever did me.'*

Just like that, my decision is made. "Your shirts, please."

He smiles, big and proud, like he's picturing me wearing one right now... and nothing else.

"Now, we can either check out the maternity section or the shoe section next. Your call, Pip."

I glance down at my small bump and then back up at him. "Do you think I need maternity clothes?" There's a vulnerable edge to my voice that I hate, because it's that very same voice that whispers mean things in my ear.

Things that make me doubt my worth.

Atlas once again steps away from the shopping cart and into my space. He pulls me in close, wrapping his strong arms around me as he rests his chin on the top of my head.

"You're perfect as you are, Pip." He leans down, bringing his lips to my temple. "And you'll be just as perfect when you're big and swollen with our baby." He kisses his way down my jaw. "And once our jellybean is in our arms instead of your belly… you'll be perfect then, too."

"Atlas." I hiccup his name, but he shushes me with another kiss—this one on my lips.

He licks into my mouth, tangling our tongues briefly before pulling away. "Your body is working miracles right now, Nora, and no matter how it changes, you're you, and that's all that matters to me."

"You really mean that?" I ask, cradling my belly. This baby is my everything, and the way Atlas so easily accepts us both makes me want to melt into a puddle at his boot-covered feet.

"With every ounce of my being." He boops my nose, and I grin. "Now, where are we going next?"

"I think shoes… it might be a while before I need maternity clothes."

"Lead the way, pretty girl."

Two pairs of shoes later, and we're on our way to the baby section—at Atlas's insistence.

He's like a kid in a candy store, *oohing* and *aahing* over every little thing.

"We don't need that," I murmur for the hundredth time, as he holds up the tiniest beanie I've ever seen.

"It'll be chilly when our jellybean makes its debut," he argues, clutching the hat to his chest, much like he did the pack of onesies, the blanket, and the mittens.

"Atlas." I drag his name out and he grins, already knowing what I'm going to say.

"It's a neutral color," he says, before I have a chance to argue. "Which means into the cart it goes."

My eyes follow the beanie as it lands on the top of the pile. "That's enough. Seriously, Atlas. There's not even room for anything else."

"We could always grab a second cart." He waggles his brows, and I can't help but laugh at his antics.

"Absolutely not." I nudge him with my elbow. "To checkout we go."

"Fine." He sighs dramatically, and together, we head toward the front of the store.

Once we're at the register, I realize what a sneaky-sneak he is. For every item I added to the cart, he tossed in two more.

"Atlas!" I hiss his name like an angry cat. "This is *way* more than the hundred dollars we agreed on."

"She's already scanning," he says, nodding toward the cashier. "You don't want her to have to stop and take things off and then put them back, right? That would be a lot of extra work for her."

I narrow my eyes at him, forcing myself to ignore the stupid way my heart pitter-patters in my chest. "You are sneaky, and you play dirty."

"Damn straight." The corners of his eyes crinkle as he smiles. "I'm playing to win, Pip, and you're a stubborn little thing, so I'll gladly take a mile for every inch you give."

"To win, huh?" I cross my arms over my chest and pretend to glare. "What's the prize, then?"

"You are, Nora." He gives me a thorough once-over before turning away and tapping his card to the reader. "You're the prize."

TWENTY-FOUR
Atlas

"Thank you," Nora whispers as we walk into the house. "Again."

I glance back at her, my arms loaded down with Target bags. "Anything for you, Pip," I reply, meaning every word.

There's just something about spoiling Nora that sets my damn soul on fire. I don't know if it's the way her cheeks turn the prettiest shade of pink or the way she pouts her full, kissable lips at me, but I fucking love it.

She's selfless to a fault, willing to go without so she won't feel like a burden or an inconvenience. Too bad I'm dead set and determined to give her the world.

"You know you don't have to buy me things though, right?" She follows behind me, down the hall, and into her—my—room.

"I know." I drop the bags unceremoniously onto the floor. "I didn't do it because I had to, I did it because I wanted to."

She tries to scowl at me, but the way her lips keep shaking tells me she's fighting a smile.

Honestly, it was a no-brainer to fill the cart with the things she liked at Target, and once she's a little farther along in her pregnancy, I'll gladly do it all over again.

I'm not wealthy by any stretch of the word, but I have some savings from my mom's side of the family along with a nice nest egg, money I've just been squirreling away for a rainy day. Money I'm more than happy to spend on Nora, our baby, and the life I hope we can one day build together.

She sighs and flops down onto the bed. "Who knew shopping was so exhausting?"

Laughing, I motion for her to scooch over so I can join her, lying on my back with one arm tucked behind my head.

Nora wastes no time snuggling into me, with her head on my chest. I wrap an arm around her waist, and before I know it, we're both out cold.

Minutes, or maybe hours later, I wake to the smell of bacon wafting through the house.

Ellis must be home.

I try to fish my phone out of my pocket without waking Nora, but she's wrapped around me like a damn octopus again, making it an impossible task.

There's no sunlight shining through the window, though, so we clearly snoozed for a few hours at the very least.

"Nora, you gotta wake up," I murmur, running my fingers

through her sleep-tangled hair. "Ellis is making dinner."

She throws her leg over mine, mumbling some kind of unintelligible reply as she buries her face into the crook of my neck.

"C'mon, Pip." I drag my fingers over her ribs, softly tickling her. "Up and at 'em."

"But I'm *so* cozy." She curls her fingers into the fabric of my shirt. "You're so warm and soft and smell nice."

I snort a laugh. If she were to slide her leg a little lower, she'd find out how *not soft* I am for her.

"Don't laugh at me."

"You can snuggle me any time, you know that, right? Day or night, you want me to be your living, breathing pillow, all you gotta do is say the word and I'm here."

"Fine." She releases my shirt and pushes herself into a seated position. "I'm up, are you happy?"

I lean up and steal a kiss. "With you? Always. Now, let's go see what Ellis's got going on in the kitchen."

But before we can get out of bed, Ellis bangs on the door. "BLTs in five. Wake up or finish boning—either way, this shit isn't good cold."

Nora gasps, slapping her palm over her mouth. "He thinks we're... we're... having sex!"

I shrug. "He also said wake up, so maybe he thinks we're sleeping."

"We were sleeping!" Her wide eyes and pink cheeks are a sight to behold.

"So, then, nothing to worry about, right?" I force myself out of the bed and then extend a hand her way to help her out, too.

She glares but takes my hand all the same.

"Good evening, love birds," Ellis says as we enter the kitchen. "For your dining pleasure, I've prepared BLTs on wheatberry with a side of Lay's finest potato chips." He slides two plates our way with all the flourish of a three-star chef. "Bon appétit."

Nora laughs at Ellis's antics as she eagerly bites into her sandwich, her earlier embarrassment long forgotten. "Oh, wow. This is good."

"It's my secret sauce." Ellis winks.

I make a pfft sound. "It's garlic aioli."

"Which I made myself!" he shouts, sending a glare my way. "From scratch!"

"Whatever it is, it's delicious." Nora emphasizes her declaration with another big bite, moaning happily as she chews.

"Thank you, Nora. You're my new favorite."

She grins at him and then sticks her tongue out at me. *Little brat.* "Yeah, yeah. Whatever."

"Are we watching anything tonight?" Ellis asks, smoothly—and wisely—changing the subject.

I shrug, content to let Nora decide.

"We can, but nothing too long. Atlas wore me out today and I'm tired."

"Did he now?" Ellis grins, holding his hand my way for a high-five.

"At Target," I clarify, pointedly ignoring his outstretched palm.

"Right." He snickers to himself. "Before we watch whatever, do y'all mind if I check the news? There's something I want to see."

"I don't mind," I say, turning to Nora. "Do you?"

"Go for it." She stands from her barstool. "Why don't y'all go on and I'll load our plates into the dishwasher."

"Are you sure?" For some reason, I hate the thought of her doing any kind of housework. Probably because my dad all but forced her into servitude.

She rolls her eyes and kisses me on my cheek. "I'm sure. Go on."

Ellis and I retreat to the living room. "I've been wanting to talk to you more about Rand," he says, settling into his recliner, "but my schedule's been so nuts I haven't had a chance."

My whole body tenses. "Okay, what's up?"

"I've been thinking about those death certificates. I agree, something isn't right with them, and I'd like to look into it more."

"With the department?" I give him my full attention. "Do you think it's enough for a warrant?"

He shrugs, looking toward me, but not quite meeting my eyes. "I'd like to look into it, regardless. Nora... she deserves it."

"Fucking right," I agree. Then a thought occurs. "Won't you get in trouble?"

"Don't borrow problems, Atlas. God knows we already have enough of them." He powers on the TV, effectively ending our conversation. "Should be on channel five."

"The victim was found just behind where I'm standing," an on-location correspondent says, speaking into the microphone, "marking the third homicide this month."

"Do the police have any leads?" The station anchor, Chelle, appears almost bored.

"As this is an active investigation, the authorities are not releasing a lot of information. So, we don't currently know for sure if it's an individual working alone or if multiple people are involved."

"We could potentially have a serial killer on our hands?" Chelle interrupts, staring dramatically into the camera.

The correspondent winces and then nods. "At this time, the police aren't ruling anything out. We heard today that several local law enforcement agencies are teaming up in an effort to solve these cases. Unfortunately, for now, we have more questions than answers."

"What can we do in the meantime?" Chelle asks.

"The authorities are asking everyone to stay alert and report any suspicious activity in hopes of finding whoever is responsible for these crimes."

"Here's to hoping they're able to get a lead. I know I'll sleep easier once justice has been served."

"Three murders?" I ask, incredulous.

"That's not counting the four from last month. All the same MO."

"Fuck." I scrub a hand over my face. "Are you working on it?"

"Yeah. It's why I've been so busy. Fucking sicko." The pure revulsion in his voice tells me all I need to know—the man behind these murders is a monster.

"All clean," Nora says, joining me on the couch. "What did I miss?"

But before either of us can answer, the news anchor drops a bombshell none of us were expecting.

"And in other news, local pharmacist, Randall Wallace, is still missing." A picture of him flashes across the screen. "The police are asking for the public's assistance in locating him..." She drones on, but my focus is locked on Nora, who is stock-still at my side.

"Pip." I keep my tone soft, much like our first night at the motel. "You're okay. You're safe." I reach for her hand, but the second my fingers brush hers, she's off like a shot, sprinting down the hall toward my room.

"Fuck, Atlas, I didn't know they had released that!" The worry on his face is as plain as day. I know he's being truthful.

"It's not your fault," I tell him, taking off after her.

The door to my bedroom is closed—I test the knob—but not locked. "Nora." I rap my knuckles against the frame. "I'm coming in."

I'm half expecting to find her hiding in my closet again, but I don't. Instead, she's curled into a ball in the center of my bed. Her shoulders shake with silent sobs, and I swear to God my heart breaks right in two as I watch her cry.

"Can I hold you, Pip?" I ask, not wanting to cause her more distress.

She lifts her head, piercing me with her tear-filled eyes. "P-please?" Her chin wobbles and so do my knees. Her pain and fear are palpable, flooding every bit of space in the room.

I fucking hate it—I hate that she's hurting and that I'm helpless to fix it. If I could, I'd take every ounce of her suffering and claim it as my own, if only to take the weight of it off her shoulders. But the universe is a cruel bitch, and all I can do is try my best to help her heal, one day at a time.

For the second time today, I crawl into the bed beside her. Once again, she wraps herself around me, this time pressing her face into my neck. I wrap my arms around her, rubbing my hands up and down her back in what I hope is a soothing way.

"I've got you, Pip. I'm here. You're safe."

She sniffles and burrows in deeper into my side.

"I won't let anything happen to you." I press a kiss to the top of her head. "Just rest. I've got you."

I keep whispering reassurances in her ear, until finally, her tears dry, her muscles relax, and sleep claims her.

I'm torn between retreating to the couch and staying here with her. I don't know which would freak her out more—waking up alone or with me in bed with her.

I waffle back and forth before finally deciding to stay. She needs me, said she feels safe with me.

Sleeping in jeans sounds terrible, but she whimpers when I try to wiggle out from under her, further cementing my plan to sleep in here with her.

"Stay," she murmurs, clutching at my shirt.

"I'm not leaving you," I whisper back, gently prying her fingers open. "Never leaving you."

I shuck off my jeans and pull on a pair of sweats before climbing back into the bed, tugging the comforter up and over both of us.

It's way too early to go to bed, but Nora's exhausted, so I settle in for the night, content to hold her until sleep claims me, too.

DIARY ENTRY, PRESENT DAY

Dear Diary,

For almost two whole weeks, my personal monster wasn't at the forefront of my mind.

For almost two whole weeks, my life felt normal.

For almost two whole weeks, I felt safe.

And then, with one measly news bulletin, it all came crashing down around me.

The safety I've been clinging to is nothing more than an illusion, because as long as Rand Wallace is out there, he's a threat.

Before that stupid report, I was looking forward to telling you all about my day out with Atlas, but now, here I am acting like the same scared girl I was two weeks ago.

God, has it really only been two weeks? Somehow it feels like a lifetime since I made a run for it. Maybe that's because of how at peace Atlas makes me feel.

Any time I'm around him, I just feel this overwhelming sense of calm-like no matter what happens, I'll be okay.

I'm sure it seems fast, and maybe a little crazy, but I really do love him, Diary. He's a good man, with a good heart. He's the complete opposite of his father.

I want so badly to give in to my feelings for him, but at the same time, I'm scared. He's my stepbrother and the son of my abuser! We don't make sense together on paper, but in my heart, I know he's it for me.

Almost everything in my brain is all mixed up... except my feelings for him. My love for him is almost like my very own North Star, guiding me back to the present when my thoughts stray too far into my past.

I'm so, so angry. That's what I am. I'm furious. The last two weeks here with Atlas have been the best two weeks of my life, and I refuse to let anything take that away from me.

So (excuse my language, Diary) fuck Randall Wallace. He doesn't get to control me any longer. He doesn't get to make me cower in fear.

I'm free of him, and I'm going to live like it.

Determined, Nora

TWENTY-FIVE
Atlas

Rolling over, I reach for Nora, intent on getting in some early morning cuddles, but my fingers only find cold sheets.

I bolt upright, frantically patting the sheets as if she's hiding under them. "Nora?"

"Atlas…"

I snap my eyes toward the sound of her voice, relief instantly filling me when I find her sitting at my desk, clutching her diary to her chest.

"Fuck, Pip." I spear my fingers through my hair, making it stand on end. "You weren't in the bed and I just… panicked."

"I'm here." She places her diary down on the desk and joins me in the bed. "I'm okay."

As soon as she's within reach, I tug her body into mine so that she's basically sprawled out on top of me with my arms wrapped snugly around her waist.

"Are you?" I keep my tone light, not wanting to upset her after how last night ended.

She nods, rubbing her cheek against my chest. "I am."

"Do you want to talk about it?"

Sighing, she rolls off me and into an upright position. "There's not much to talk about."

I heft myself up, resting my back against the headboard. "I think there is, but only if you're comfortable with it."

She twines our fingers together before continuing. "I've spent enough time letting *him* control me. I'm done with that. I knew he was still out there, but hearing the news talk about him made it real, if that makes sense. But I refuse to live my life in fear of him. He's a monster, and I have to believe he'll get what he deserves."

I study her a moment before responding. Her face is open and honest. She truly means what she's saying. "Okay then."

"Okay?" Her brows dip as she scrunches her nose. "Just like that?"

The confused look on her face is too damn cute. "Yeah, just like that. I trust you, Nora, so if you say you're good, then I'm inclined to believe you."

"You're a good man, Atlas." She leans forward and kisses my cheek.

Those words right there, they're at the top of the list of things I'll never get tired of hearing her say. "You make me want to be the best."

"You already are." This time she kisses my lips, soft and slow. The kind of kiss that's over too soon and leaves me wanting more. "So, what's on the agenda for today?"

"I don't know, you tell me." Because if it were up to me, we'd stay right here in my bed, wrapped up in one another, all damn day.

But the sparkle in her hazel eyes tells me she has something in mind. "I think I recall something about you teaching me to drive…"

"Hell yeah, Pip. Let me grab a shower and it's on."

"This is hopeless!" Nora pouts, banging her tiny fist against the steering wheel in defeat.

"No, it's not," I murmur, hiding my smile behind my hand. "You're doing great."

"I'm pretty sure little old grannies drive better than me."

"Well," I drawl, "to be fair, they've been driving a lot longer than you."

She growls, and I can't help it, I laugh. She's just too damn cute.

"Atlas! It's not funny." She crosses her arms over her chest and glares at me.

"Okay, but it kind of is." I lean over and shift my truck into park. "You've been behind the wheel for all of two hours, Pip. These things take time, so cut yourself some slack."

"How long did it take you?" she asks.

"About a week—and I failed my driver's test the first time I took it."

"Really?"

"Really, really. In fact, I still suck at parallel parking, so you might have to get Ellis to teach you that."

The way Nora's so hard on herself kills me. She's got the mechanics of driving down; she just needs some finesse.

"I guarantee that if you keep practicing, you'll be driving like a pro in no time."

"If you say so." Her shoulders droop as she turns away from me.

"I do say so, and I'm always right—just ask Ellis. But I also think we should call it for today and maybe grab a bite to eat."

She slides her gaze back my way. "Food does sound good."

"Perfect. Why don't we swap places, and I'll drive? Mexican sound good?"

"Oh." She sighs dreamily. "Cheese dip sounds divine."

"Your wish is my command, Pip."

I expect her to unbuckle and walk around to trade places, but Nora's full of surprises and instead twists on the bench seat and climbs over me.

Or she starts to, at least, but decides to pause straddling my lap.

"You sound pretty good right now, too, though." A sensuous smile curls her lips as she stares down at me.

"Do I?" God, I love this bold side of her. It speaks to her growth and comfort with me.

"Mmhmm." She licks her lips and settles her weight fully onto me. My dick rises to attention as she squirms on my lap, her body already seeking friction.

"What are you going to do about that?" I ask, bringing my hands down on her hips, stilling her restless movements.

She pouts for a millisecond before lunging for my mouth.

This kiss is nothing like any of our others. It's sloppy and hungry and loud. Our teeth scrape and our tongues mash together as we devour one another.

"Fuck, Pip," I grunt as she rocks against me. I'm a twenty-six-year-old man and about to come in my pants, dry humping in my truck. "We gotta stop."

"Why?" She sucks on my lower lip, and I swear I feel it in my cock.

"Because you deserve better than a truck seat bench." I nudge her with my nose, gently breaking our kiss. "Because when we take things further than kissing, it's going to be in my bed, where I can worship you the way you deserve."

Nora melts against me, pressing her forehead to mine. "Well, when you put it like that, I guess I can wait."

"Good." I kiss the tip of her nose. "Because what we have, what we're building, it's worth doing it right. You're worth doing it right. I love you, Pip, and I'm damn sure going to do right by you."

A surprised gasp escapes her. "You—you love me?"

I swallow thickly, bracing myself for her reaction. No matter what it is, my feelings stand. She's it for me. "Yeah, I do."

"But I-I'm broken, Atlas, and you deserve someone—"

"Shh." I bring my index finger to her lips. "First of all, you're not broken. But even if you were, I'd love every single piece. And it's okay if you don't feel the same. I'm willing to wait. And if loving me isn't something you can ever see happening, then I'm willing to step back. All I want is the best for you, Nora, no matter how that looks."

"It's you." She whispers the words, but they seem to echo in the cab of my truck. "You're the best for me. For us."

It wasn't an *I love you,* but I'll gladly take what she's offering because it's coming. I know it is, and I'm patient enough to wait.

TWENTY-SIX
Nora

"Sixteen weeks today, Pip," Atlas says as I walk into the kitchen.

"You keeping track?" I sass back, even though I know he is. In fact, just the other day, I saw a baby-tracking app on his phone that tells him little facts about not only the baby but my pregnancy as well.

"Abso-fucking-lutely." He slides a plate of avocado toast across the bar. "Seems fitting since our jellybean is the size of a small avocado."

I glance down at my ever-growing belly. "Hard to believe I'm this big when he's still so small."

"First of all, there's nothing wrong with your size. You're perfect." He stalks around to my side of the bar, claiming the stool next to me. "Secondly, *he* huh?"

"Well, it's a fifty-fifty chance, right?"

"You got a preference?" He's asked me this before, but my answer's still the same.

"No." I shrug and take another bite of my toast. It's surprisingly tasty. "Just a gut feeling."

"Well, in just under an hour, we'll know for sure." He jumps up from his stool and rushes around the island to the fridge. "Almost forgot your OJ. Scarlet said to drink a glass before your appointment to make sure baby is active."

Internally, I swoon. Atlas is so thoughtful. And not just when it comes to the baby—but me, too. He hasn't said those three little words to me again, but he *shows* me daily how he feels...

The night we saw *him* on the news and he held me while I slept was the best sleep of my life. And I told him so, and he's slept next to me every night since.

I keep expecting him to push for more—physically—but he's held true to his word about doing things right.

After our front seat make out session, he told me he wanted to take me on a real date. I told him it wasn't necessary; he insisted it was, and now, finally, today is the day.

Well, tonight is anyway. First up is my ultrasound appointment.

I'm not sure which one I'm more excited for. Or nervous.

Gah! It's like my emotions are a tangled-up ball of yarn, fraying and lopping, and hopelessly intertwined.

"Thank you," I say once I down the entire glass.

"Are you okay?" Sometimes he's so perceptive it hurts. There's no sneaking anything past him.

"I'm..." I pause to really think on how I'm feeling, but that stupid ball of yarn is so jumbled, I can't seem to differentiate the threads. I'm excited for my ultrasound, I'm eager about our date—and maybe a little apprehensive about what may come afterward, I'm anxious over Rand still being out there somewhere, but mostly, I think I'm good. "Overwhelmed."

"In a good way or a bad way?" He sips his coffee, studying me over the rim of his mug.

Again, I mull over my answer before replying. "I think good. Things are definitely better than they've ever been."

He gives me his best, most heartwarming smile. "The best is yet to come, Pip."

"I'll take your word for it."

"Didn't I already tell you I'm always right?" Atlas grabs both of our plates and deposits them in the sink. "Now, c'mon or we'll be late."

The drive to Dr. Snider's office is uneventful, and sadly, there's no parking lot make out session this time either, because Scarlet is at the door waiting on us.

"Are you ready to see baby again?" she asks, stepping back so we can enter ahead of her.

"Yes!" Atlas and I answer in unison, causing Scarlet to roll her eyes.

"Never took you for a dad-type, Atlas." Her tone is sour, but she's smiling. I'm typically pretty good at reading people, but Scarlet is one tough cookie.

"I'm full of surprises," Atlas deadpans as we step into the triage alcove.

"That you are," she replies before focusing her attention back on me. "Same as last time, Nora. Urine, weight, blood pressure, and since your iron was low at your last visit, I'd like to check it again today."

She quickly moves through my work-up—I've gained weight and my iron is looking better—and before I know it, it's ultrasound time.

"Again, Nora on the table, Atlas in the chair, goo may be cold."

"Anyone ever tell you have great bedside manner?" Atlas asks, helping me up onto the table.

Scarlet screws up her face as she mocks him.

All I can do is giggle at them both. This dynamic we have is so totally weird, and yet I can't help but feel right at home with Atlas and Scarlet.

"Okay, here we go." She squirts some of the gel onto my stomach and begins moving it around with the wand. "Going to take some measurements and then we'll get to the good stuff."

Despite not understanding much of what is happening on the screen, I watch with a laser-like focus as she clicks around.

"And here's baby's—"

The door to the room flings open and Ellis barges in, fully in uniform.

"What in the actual hell?" Scarlet shrieks as Atlas asks, "Is everything okay?"

"Did I miss it?" he asks, frantically looking from my bare belly to the screen to Scarlet. "Am I an uncle or an aunt?"

"An idiot, that's what you are. An absolute idiot." If looks could kill, Scarlet would have eviscerated Ellis on the spot.

"Didn't know you were joining us," Atlas says mildly, once it's clear nothing is wrong.

"I invited him." I duck my head. "I guess I forgot to mention it. Sorry."

Atlas grins. "Should've known. You two are like peanut

butter and jelly.”

"No," Ellis scoffs. "We're popcorn and movie theater butter."

"Oh my God, I'm surrounded by morons." Scarlet rolls her eyes. "Can we please get on with it? We do have other patients…"

My cheeks burn with embarrassment. She's right, I'm not her only patient, and both she and Dr. Snider are giving up their lunch hour for me. The least I could do—again—is be respectful of their time.

"Sorry, Scarlet." I recline back against the paper-covered pillow. "We'll be good."

She gives me a tight smile. "As I was saying, here's baby's heartbeat."

A gentle whooshing sound fills the room, bringing tears to my eyes. Seriously, that is the best sound I've ever heard.

"Hey, Scar," Atlas whispers. "You think I can record that?"

Maybe it's a trick of the light, but I swear, her eyes get a little bit misty. "Go for it."

With the hand that isn't holding mine, Atlas slides his phone out of his pocket and begins recording the sound of our baby's heartbeat.

"Damn, that's my favorite sound." His voice is thick with emotion, which only feeds into how I'm feeling, and before I know it, tears are rolling down my cheeks.

"Don't cry, Pip." Atlas slides his phone back into his pocket and then wipes away my tears.

"I'm not sad." Truly, I'm not. If anything, I'm the happiest I've ever been. "Promise."

"If you're done crying, we can check and see if baby will give us a peek at the goods."

"Anyone ever tell you that you're kind of a bitch?" Ellis asks, steepling his hands beneath his chin.

"Anyone ever tell you that only guys with small dicks call women bitches?" she fires back.

"We playing two truths and a lie or something?" He leans back in his chair, crossing his legs so that his right ankle rests on his left knee. "If so, let me think of something else true, because everything you just said was a damn lie."

"I swear to God—"

"Children!" Atlas growls, cutting her off. "I'd like to know if I'm about to have a son or a daughter, so if y'all could just save your fucking foreplay for later, that'd be great."

I lean over and grab Atlas's hand, pressing a soft kiss to his knuckles.

He mouths my three favorite words—*I love you*—and then turns his attention back toward the screen.

"It's not foreplay," Ellis mumbles, but Scarlet just glares.

The room falls quiet as she rolls the wand over my belly. "Sure is active. Wiggling and rolling all around in there."

Atlas beams. "I made her drink some OJ with breakfast."

"Aren't you just a peach—oh hey, look!" She snaps a still image and freezes the screen. "Looks like y'all are having a baby boy!"

"I'm going to be an uncle!" Ellis claps his hands as he springs up from his chair. "Congrats, you two, I gotta bounce."

"You won't be missed, Officer Jackass," Scarlet says, but he's already out the door.

"Really?" I ask, even though the evidence is plain as day. "A boy?"

"Yup." Scarlet's lips curl in the most genuine smile I've ever seen from her. "Congrats, Nora."

"Hot damn," Atlas murmurs. "We're having a boy, Pip. Guess we need to start talking about names, huh?" His cheeks turn a deep pink color. "I mean, uh, if you want my input, that is."

"Of course, I do." I squeeze his hand. "We're in this together, right?"

He grins, and I swear, I feel it all the way down to my toes. "Damn straight we are."

DIARY ENTRY, PRESENT DAY

Dear Diary,

A boy. We're having a boy. A sweet baby boy. A sweet, healthy, baby boy.

Scarlet said everything is measuring just right and his heart-beat sounded strong and steady. I need to remember to ask Atlas to send me the recording.

Our baby boy needs a name besides jellybean. I want to ask Atlas to help me come up with something. Maybe I will tonight... on our date.

Is it weird that I'm nervous? I'm eighteen, pregnant, and going on my first date. I'd say a therapist would have a field day with me, but Maggie's never been anything but professional. Still, I bet I'm one heck of a case.

Some days, it feels like my life is the plot of one of those Lifetime movies Mama liked so much.

Got sidetracked there, Diary, so let's get back to the point. I'm as anxious as I am excited for tonight, because I think I want to go all the way with Atlas.

I want us to have sex. For him to be my real first. He's a man worthy of it, and I know he'll take care of me—and more important-ly, I know he'll stop if I say so.

But what if I'm... bad at it? What if he doesn't enjoy being with me? What if I flip out, and he realizes how broken I really am? What if he decides I'm not worth the trouble?

NO! STOP IT, NORA!

Atlas is a good man. The best kind of man. He is everything I've ever wanted and never thought I would have—and then some.

He is kind and caring and patient and has the gentlest heart out of anyone I know.

He's the kind of man my parents would have loved. He's worked tirelessly to earn my trust, and deep down in my soul, I know he loves me.

No matter how things go between us tonight, I know it won't change the way he feels about me.

Flustered, Nora

TWENTY-SEVEN

Getting ready for a first date is hard enough as it is—at least, according to the shows and movies I've seen—but it's even harder without anyone around to guide you.

I don't have my mom to help with my hair and she never taught me to put makeup on—not that I own any anyway. I don't have a best friend to help me pick out an outfit. Here's to hoping leggings and a sweater are appropriate for whatever Atlas has planned, because even with him spoiling me, I don't have any date-worthy outfits.

I'm half-tempted to call Scarlet and beg for her help. But even I know asking your boyfriend's ex to help you get ready for a date is weird.

Is he even my boyfriend? We've done everything so out of order, I'm not sure I know up from down when it comes to explaining our relationship.

I'm pregnant, we live together, and share a bed, but haven't had sex. He told me he loves me, and his actions more than back up his words, but his dad abused me for years on end.

It's safe to say we're *complicated*. But if I'm being completely honest, Atlas Wallace is by far the best complication to ever come into my life.

He's caring, observant, intuitive, and kind... he's just... *every good thing*. So much so that the word *boyfriend* doesn't feel big enough to encompass all he is to me.

I flop down onto the bed, throwing one arm over my head and the other over my eyes. *This is hopeless.* Atlas is going to all of this trouble to do something nice for me and I—

A knock on the door derails my pity party. "Nora..."

Why is Ellis outside of my door? "Yeah?"

"Can I come in?"

I roll my eyes from the ceiling to the door. "I guess."

"You all ready for your big da—" He eyes me sprawled on the bed, dressed in a pair of my old leggings and one of Atlas's hoodies. "Clearly not, what gives?"

"Ellis." I sigh his name. "Are you here for girl talk?" It's not fair for me to take my frustrations out on him, especially when he's always so kind to me. "That was rude, I'm sorry. What's up?"

"Just wanted to check on you." He shrugs and crosses the room, claiming Atlas's desk chair. "Figured you might need some assistance getting ready, and while I know I'm not a chick, I *am* your best friend—right?" He shakes his head. "Of course, I am, so *voilà*, here I am."

"Riiiight." I force myself into a seated position. "And how do you plan to help?"

"Listen, I am a man of many talents." He springs up from the chair and stalks over to my closet—well, Atlas's closet.

I watch as he flips through the hangers, trying to figure out what exactly he's up to.

"Perfect!" He grabs a hanger and tosses it my way. "Put this on with your green leggings and boots."

"That's... Atlas's sweater..."

He rolls his eyes and grabs my green leggings. "Clearly." He drops them onto my lap.

"It's—are you sure?" I love wearing Atlas's clothes, so I'm all for it, I just can't imagine it being date appropriate.

"You don't watch as much *Gossip Girl* as I do without picking up a thing or two. Now, go into the bathroom and get dressed."

Reluctantly, I get to my feet and head into the bathroom. Shucking off my current pair of leggings is harder than I'd like to admit, but with this little bump disrupting my center of gravity, simple tasks like taking off and putting on pants have become a freaking chore.

I tug off my hoodie next, and then appraise myself in the mirror. My boobs have definitely grown and my belly is perfectly curved. I can't help but wonder what Atlas sees when he looks at me.

He's forever telling me I'm beautiful and perfect just as I am, but with an ex like Scarlet, it's hard to believe.

She's the kind of woman who probably wears matching lingerie, whereas my underwear is made of cotton and comes in a multipack.

Will Atlas think I'm desirable when he sees me stripped bare?

"Stop it." I clench my fists at my sides, willing myself to calm down; I refuse to let my own self-doubts ruin such a special night.

Grabbing my green leggings, I sit on the closed toilet seat and tug them on, followed by his sweater, and then assess myself in the mirror once again.

Even with my growing baby bump, the thick cable knit material is still oversized. And the creamy-white color pairs really well with my leggings.

Apparently, Ellis knows his stuff—*never would have guessed it.*

I may not be a supermodel, but I look nice... and that's good enough.

"Well?" he asks expectantly.

I swing the door open. "You were right."

He swivels the desk chair around to face me. "Of course, I was." He pretends to dust his shoulder off. "I always am."

"Oh, God," I groan. "You sound like Atlas."

"I think you mean Atlas sounds like me." He lifts his brows and smirks as he heads for the bedroom door. "Now, I won't be home until tomorrow afternoon, so you kids be good and don't do anything I wouldn't do."

"Ellis!" Embarrassment stains my cheeks, but he just grins.

"I'd say don't get pregnant..." He lowers his eyes to my belly. "But, you know..."

"You're... you're..." My words fail me. Ellis sort of reminds me of Maria from *The Sound of Music,* when all of the nuns are singing about her. *How do you solve a problem like Ellis?*

"The best? I know."

"Yeah." I smile, because he really is a good guy... one of the absolute best. "You are."

He closes the door behind him, leaving me to finish getting ready on my own.

I keep my hair simple, letting it hang around my shoulders before slipping on my boots. It's nothing fancy, but it's the best I can do; I just hope it's enough...

That I'm enough...

Twenty minutes later, another knock sounds on the bedroom door. "You ready, Pip?"

I force myself out of the bed, take one last glance in the mirror, and then open the door. "As ready as I'm going to be."

I'm not sure what kind of reaction I was expecting from him, but the look of pure desire wasn't it.

"Nora, you look..." His words taper off as he drags his teeth over his lower lip.

I've never felt more alive, or more desirable than I do now as he eats me up with a hungry gaze.

"I look what?" I rasp, fighting tooth and nail against the negative thoughts trying to weasel their way in.

"Perfect." He steps into me, wrapping an arm around my waist. "You look fucking perfect."

"Thank you." I rest my head on his chest, listening to the sound of his heart beating strong and true beneath his ribs.

"Got something for you," he murmurs.

"You do?"

"Of course." As he steps back from me, I notice the small bouquet of sunflowers in his other hand. "For you."

I take the bouquet from his outstretched hand and clutch it to my chest. No one's ever given me flowers before and I... I think I love it. "Thank you." I bury my nose in the blooms and inhale deeply. "They're beautiful. I... do you have a vase?"

He ducks his head. "I've got a cup. Will that work?"

"It'll work just fine," I murmur as I practically float into the kitchen to grab a cup from the cabinet.

Atlas swoops in and steals the cup from me, filling it with water before arranging the flowers inside of it. "There you go."

He sets it on the island and I beam. "Thank you, Atlas. I love them."

His thoughtfulness is unparalleled. When I was a kid, my dad would always find something for Mom any time he and I did something just the two of us. Whether it was a flower, a trinket, a candy, or a card—she was always at the forefront of his mind. I remember one time I asked him why, and he said *"it's the little things that matter the most,"* and Atlas is proving to me day in and day out just how right my dad was.

"Hopefully you love the rest of what I have planned just as much."

"I know I will." I rise up onto my tippy-toes to kiss his lips. "But I wouldn't be mad if you wanted to give me a hint."

"No can do, pretty girl. But grab your jacket and we can head out."

Anticipation flares to life inside of me as I follow his instructions. I may not be sure what he has planned, but Atlas is easily the most attentive and thoughtful person I know—which means no matter what, tonight will be perfect.

TWENTY-EIGHT
Atlas

I help Nora into her coat, and then into my truck. "Sit by me." I pat the middle section of the bench seat. "We're not going far."

She raises her brows in suspicion. "How far is not far?"

Smirking, I shrug and crank the engine, driving us toward the tree line at the back of the property.

"The road's the other way."

"Oh, is it?" I ask, feigning confusion. "I didn't notice."

"Smart aleck." She knocks her knee into mine, smiling.

I bring my hand down onto her leg, curling my fingers around her thigh, squeezing softly. "I was going to take you out somewhere fancy, dinner and a movie and all of that."

A small, and I mean microscopic, part of me is still worried she'll be disappointed by what I have planned.

"What made you change your mind?" There's a softness in her voice though, and it tells me she doesn't mind one bit.

"This is our first date—*your* first date. I don't want to share this with anyone." I come to a stop a few feet away from where I have everything all set up and shift my truck into park. "Want you all to myself tonight, Pip."

"Well." She twists around to face me. "You have me."

"Damn straight." I skim my knuckles along her jawline, just barely resisting the urge to kiss her. "Now, wait here."

I jump down from the truck and make quick work of a few last-minute details before returning to my truck for Nora. "You ready?"

She bounces in her seat and then scooches toward me, allowing me to help her down. "Yes."

A small gasp slips past her lips as we round the back of the truck. "Atlas!"

I glance her way, pleased to see her eyes are wide with wonder.

"You did all of this for me?" she asks, taking in the set-up. Her pretty hazel eyes bounce around, not knowing where to look first.

There's a fire going in the pit, with a pile of soft blankets a safe distance away. All the fixings for s'mores are in a basket, and there's a full-on picnic set up buffet style along my truck's tailgate, complete with a few bottles of water to wash everything down.

Her voice is tinged with a mixture of awe and disbelief as she takes it all in. She deserves all of this and more, and knowing that I'm the man who's going to give it to her? It makes me feel like I'm on top of the world.

It also makes me want to keep this up for eternity—to constantly find little ways to show her how much she means to me, so that she never forgets just what she means to me.

"Of course, I did." I tug on her hand, pulling her into my chest. "I love you."

"Thank you," she whispers into my shirt before looking up at me from beneath her lashes. "I love you, too."

My heart freezes in my chest before kicking into overtime. *Holy fuck—my girl loves me.*

"Sweetest words I've ever heard, Pip," I murmur before pressing a kiss to the top of her head. I mean it, too, because with those three words, I know all the way to my damn soul that she's mine every bit as much as I'm hers.

"What do we do first?" She steps out of my embrace, but not completely away from me. "I honestly don't know where to start."

"Anywhere you want." I reach down and interlace our fingers. "Are you hungry?"

Her stomach rumbles before she can reply.

"I'll take that as a yes." I guide her toward the tailgate. "It's not exactly gourmet, but we've got all the stuff to make sandwiches, fruit, chips, and a few bottles of water..."

"It's perfect." She pops up onto her toes and presses a kiss to my scruffy cheek. "I mean it. I couldn't think of anything better than this."

I can't help the grin that splits my cheeks. For a second, as I was listing our choices, a thread of doubt tried to worm its way in, but here Nora is, effortlessly reassuring me and setting me at ease.

We're far from conventional, but it's times like these that I can't help but think she was made just for me.

"This is just the start." I pass her a paper plate and nudge her closer to the truck so that she can make her sandwich the way she likes.

"What does that even mean?" she asks, slathering a generous serving of mayo across both slices of bread.

I shrug and then set to work on my own sandwich.

"Atlas!" She huffs in annoyance as she adds ham and muenster cheese. "That's not fair. Friends don't keep secrets."

"Good thing you're not my friend." It's a shit response, but I'm banking on her reaction.

"What?" Outwardly, she's calm but I hear the slight crack in her voice. "I'm not?"

"Hell no, Pip." I set my plate on the tailgate, lean into her space, and cup her cheek. "You're so much more. You're my everything. My entire reason for being."

She nibbles her lower lip and I brush my thumb over the apple of her cheek. With anyone else, this would be too much, too soon, but with Nora, it's perfect. *She's perfect.*

"You're mine, too." She glances down at her belly. "Well, you and the baby."

"Can't forget our jellybean," I agree.

"But so help me God, if you ever scare me like that again, I'll... I'll..." She pauses and glares. "Well, I don't know what I'll do, but you won't like it!"

I press a kiss to her temple, using my affection to hide my smile. She's about as scary as a field mouse, but honestly, it's part of her charm.

"Let's eat and then we can have s'mores."

She sighs dreamily and then resumes loading up her plate.

I watch like a hawk, noting her every choice. When she first came to stay with us, eating was hard for her after her meals being so scarce. I know I don't need to worry, because she seems to be doing really well—Scarlet even complimented her weight gain at her last prenatal appointment—but I can't help it.

The thought of anything taking her or our baby from me is unbearable. If Ellis realized the extent of my fixation with Nora, he'd undoubtedly call me an obsessive son-of-a-bitch, and that's okay, because I am.

I am absolutely and entirely obsessed with Nora Leigh Morgan.

Once my plate is made, I join her in the center of the blankets.

Nora wastes no time in taking a huge bite of her sandwich. "Oh my God. This is the best thing I've ever tasted."

"Didn't know ham and cheese did it for you like that, Pip."

Her eyes widen and her throat works as she swallows. "Atlas!"

"I'm just saying." I grin and raise my brows. "Over there moaning like that for Black Forest ham."

"I can't help it," she mumbles, her cheeks turning my favorite shade of pink. "I was really hungry."

"I'm just teasing, Nora. It's cute."

"Cute?" She frowns, tipping my grin into a full-blown smile.

I don't know what it is about her, but somehow, she manages to be the cutest damn thing I've ever seen *and* the sexiest. Which is why I keep on goading her.

"Yeah, that's right. Cute."

"Babies are cute." She shifts her plate to rest on the blanket and then crosses her arms over her chest, glaring at me. She looks about as fierce as a kitten. *A cute kitten.*

"They are," I agree, "and ours is going to be the cutest."

Her hazel eyes flare. "You mean that?"

"Wholeheartedly. How could our boy be anything but perfect?"

She nods before narrowing her eyes at me. "I know you're

trying to change the subject, and I'll allow it *this time*."

"Will you now?" I roll my lips inward to keep from smiling. "How kind."

"I will, but only because you went to all this trouble to plan such a perfect first date."

"Speaking of, I have something for you."

"Really?" I don't miss the spark of excitement in her tone. Nora's not used to receiving gifts, and it's something I damn sure plan to rectify. "What? Why?"

"Because I wanted to. Because I love you. Because it's Friday. Do I need a reason, Pip?"

"I guess not." The uncertainty in her voice is like a poison tipped arrow to my heart. "What... what is it?"

"Eat up and then I'll give it to you."

Nora sighs, and I swear it comes all the way from the bottom of her gut it's so longsuffering. "Fine."

Three bites later, she primly wipes her mouth and then sets her plate down near the edge of the blanket. "I'm ready."

I stack my plate on top of hers and then gesture for her to come closer. She doesn't hesitate, crawling right onto my lap.

"In one of your diary entries you mentioned your dad used to bring you a new book every week, and while I'm most certainly not your daddy, I thought you might like this..."

I reach behind me, feeling blindly for the slim package I tucked under the edge of the outermost blanket. My fingers finally make purchase and I bring my arm back around Nora with her prize in my hand.

"What is it?" Her voice is feather-soft as she rubs her index finger over the seam in the wrapping paper. "It's so pretty..." I'm a shit wrapper, but Ellis is like Martha-Stewart-level good at it and took care of it for me.

"Open it, Pip."

Her fingers tremble as she pulls the paper apart at the seam.

"What is it?" she asks again, glancing from the orange box up to me.

I wrap my arm around her middle, resting my palm on the swell of her belly. "A Kindle—part eReader and part tablet. So, you can go online and—"

"An eReader? Like for... books?"

Fuck, she's perfect. "Yeah, Pip. Books. Any book you want, as long as it's available in an eBook format." I rest my chin on the top of her head. "Hell, who am I kidding, if it's not, we'll hunt down the paperback."

"Atlas..." She rasps my name, twisting her head to look up at me. Her eyes are glassy with unspoken emotion. "This is... you are... I—"

"I know, pretty girl." I lean forward and kiss her temple. "Sometimes I rob myself of the ability to speak, too."

Just like that, she giggles, and the tension is lifted.

"Will you show me how to use it?"

"Yup." I bring my other arm around and slide the box out of her grasp. "I kind of took some liberties and linked it to my account," I say, powering the device on. "You can buy books, clothes, anything you need. Tap the Kindle icon for books and the little globe to browse online."

I tap the globe—thank God for hotspots—and just as planned, a popular online baby store loads onto the screen.

"Atlas..." She sighs, but it's the happy kind, not the sad. "What are you up to?"

"Definitely something." I smirk, guiding her attention to the upper right corner. "I was thinking we could register. You know, for the baby."

I'm not sure what kind of response I expected, but never at any point did I anticipate crying. But that's what I get—big, sobbing, fat tears rolling down her pink cheeks.

"Hey, whoa, Nora," I call helplessly as she scrambles off my lap. "What's wrong?"

"You are so kind and so thoughtful." She sniffles and the tears keep falling. "But, Atlas, there's no point in registering for anything. I don't have anyone to throw me a shower or any of that. I don't even have health insurance, and I have no idea how I'm going to pay for my medical stuff, much less all of the things our baby will need..." She trails off, wiping her tears on the sleeve of my borrowed sweater.

Damn, I'm an idiot. In my head, this was all sorted—I'm footing the bill, no questions asked, but it never once occurred to me to talk to Nora about all of it. Not in depth, anyway.

"Pip, hey, shh." I set the Kindle down next to me and drag her back onto my lap.

"You don't understand," she argues, while simultaneously melting into me.

"Let me ask you a question." I wait, and she nods. "Whose baby did you say it was?"

"I don't... what?"

"Whose baby?" I spread my fingers wide and palm her belly.

She blinks up at me, looking as sad and confused as ever. "Ours..."

I lean in and press a soft kiss to her tear-soaked lips. "That's right. *Our* baby. Say it again."

"It's our baby." She twists around so that she's straddling me, looping her arms around my neck. "Ours."

"Which means I'm going to—willingly and happily—take care of you and our jellybean. I'm going to provide for y'all, and before you even try to argue, it's not you taking advantage of me and you don't owe me. We're in this *together*. This baby is ours, and, Nora, you're mine. I take care of what's mine, and that means taking care of you, too."

"I just feel so useless." She slumps against me, resting her head on my shoulder.

"I'll say this as many times as it takes—you're a fighter, a survivor. You've lived through things no one should have to, and on top of that, you're not dwelling—not that anyone would blame you if you were—but nope. You're actively working toward securing your future, and if that means letting me hold you up while you're getting back on your feet, then so be it. I love you, Nora, and taking care of you is always an honor, never a chore. Okay?"

I wait with bated breath for her to reply, but finally she nods and whispers, "Okay."

TWENTY-NINE
Nora

While I may not have anything to compare it to, as far as first dates go, I think tonight has been pretty spectacular—and it's not even over.

Atlas truly went all out to make it special, and aside from me crying all over him like a baby, it has been.

"You ready for some s'mores?" he asks, nuzzling his face into the crook of my neck.

"Mm, yeah." I drag my lips over his temple and down his cheek. He pulls back and turns into me, meeting my mouth with his in a kiss that's over too soon.

"You test me like no other, Pip," he groans, moving me off his lap.

I'm ninety percent positive he means that sexually, and if so, then I'm not sure I see the problem. "And?" I emphasize my question with what I hope is a cheeky grin.

I don't know if it's pregnancy hormones, anticipation of knowing how tonight will end, or a combination of both—but I'm turned on like never before.

My brain and body almost feel like a dang roller coaster with how fast they both go from one extreme to the other. Happy to sad to crying to horny all in the blink of an eye.

Honestly, it's exhausting, going from one extreme to the other. But like the good guy he is, Atlas takes it all in stride.

"Nora, hey." Atlas waves a marshmallow in front of my face, effectively snapping me out of my wandering thoughts. "You didn't hear anything I said, did you?"

I can feel my cheeks heat as I nod. "Sorry. Say it again?"

"I asked how toasted you want your marshmallow."

"Oh." I glance away from him to the fire. "I'm not sure. It's been... at least ten years since I've..." I trail off, not wanting to bring the mood down any more than it already is. "How do you like yours?"

"Totally charred on the outside."

I wrinkle my nose, but nod anyway. "Okay, I'll take mine like that, too." It doesn't really sound good, but I won't know unless I try it.

Atlas chuckles under his breath as he spears two marshmallows.

I watch intently as he pulls them from the flame, and then sandwiches the gooey marshmallows between two graham crackers, along with a square of chocolate.

"What do you think?" he asks, a hopeful gleam in his eyes.

I bring the s'more to my mouth, but the smell alone makes me hesitate. It's this weird combination of bitter and sweet.

But still, Atlas says it's good, so I force an exhale and bite into it.

I try to school my reaction, but it's no use.

"Not a fan, huh?" he asks, amusement evident in both his tone and the crinkles at the corners of his eyes.

"It's..." I frown and set the s'more down. "Interesting." And by that I mean gross. It's like ash-crusted sugar goo mixed with chocolate.

"Let me try again?" he asks.

"Last chance," I whisper, shooting him what I hope is a teasing smile.

He assembles another s'more for me, but instead of handing it over like I expect, he beckons me closer. "C'mere, Pip."

I scoot closer, so our knees are touching, but Atlas simply pats his thigh.

"What are you up to?" I murmur, narrowing my eyes.

"Come find out." Those three words are somehow a promise and a dare, and before I know it, I'm rising to meet it, scrambling onto his lap. "Good girl."

I don't know why, but his softly spoken praise has me feeling all kinds of squirmy.

"Now, open." He taps my bottom lip with his index finger.

Wordlessly, I do as he says. As I wait for him to make his next move, I realize just how much I trust him. I know he has my best interest at heart and that even if he pushes my boundaries a little, he'll never, *ever* hurt me.

I startle as he slides the s'more between my parted lips. It's cooled now, but I don't care. It's perfect.

"Good?" he asks, his eyes blazing hotter than the fire behind us.

"So good." I lick my lips, chasing after any errant crumbs.

"You missed some." He swipes his thumb over the corner of my mouth, coming away with a smudge of melted chocolate. I watch, enraptured, as he licks it clean.

"Atlas." His name is a breathy whisper, as I press my forehead to his. "Kiss me."

Desire pricks my skin as he skims his calloused fingers over my heated cheeks until he's cradling my jaw and tipping my head just so.

For a long moment, we just exist, our bodies fused together as we share the same air. He's never teased me like this before, and as much as it shocks me, I can't say I hate it.

Not with how my entire body feels like a live wire, anticipation, desire, and a mustard-seed-sized grain of fear all mingling together inside of me, setting me on edge.

I'm restless and aching. "I need you."

Those three words break his resolve, and he *finally* traces his tongue ever so slightly over my lips. "Open for me, Pip," he growls, wrapping one arm around my waist to haul me closer.

He's every bit as affected as I am, if the hardness pressing into my thigh is anything to go by.

I can't tell if it's the fire or the way Atlas is kissing me like his life depends on it that has me feeling so hot, but either way, I welcome the burn. I relish every brush of his tongue against mine.

But something deep inside me wants more. *I need more.*

"Touch me," I beg, rolling my hips against him.

Atlas drags his lips away from mine, kissing down my jaw to my neck. "Where?" he asks, his voice cool silk against my fevered flesh.

"Everywhere."

"Here?" He slides both of his hands beneath the thick

material of my sweater, palming my belly.

I nod, roll my neck, and then shake my head back and forth. I want to feel him everywhere, all at once. *I can't just say that, though, can I?*

He grins. "Giving me mixed signals, Pip. You're the one in charge here. You want more, then you have to tell me. Want me to stop—tell me. You're calling the shots."

"I..." I swallow roughly, trying with all my might to banish my embarrassment. *This is Atlas. He loves me, he's safe, and he's never once laughed at me.* "I want you to... I want to feel you everywhere."

"Everywhere, huh?" Humor paints his words as he reaches one hand around to cup my butt and the other up to my breast.

I shiver as he drags his thumb over my sensitive nipple, burying my face in his neck.

"Like this?" He brings his lips to my neck, licking and sucking, making my eyes roll back in my head.

Who knew something so simple could feel so... good?

"More, Atlas."

He pinches my nipple, and then soothes away the sting with the pad of his thumb. It's the perfect mix of pleasure and pain—which shocks me, because I've never associated the two together before now.

I arch into him, desperate for more. I want his mouth on me, and mine on him. I want to taste the salt of his skin and make him shudder and quake with pleasure.

"I still need more. I want to feel you. With nothing between us."

"Fuck, Nora." He slants his lips back over mine, pushing his tongue into my mouth, tangling it with mine.

But then, just as quick as it started, he's pulling away. I whimper at the loss of his touch, but he just grins.

"We gotta take this inside." He shifts me off his lap, readjusts himself, and then stands.

I scramble up to follow after him.

"You go on to the truck and I'll get the fire put out."

Even in the heat of the moment, he's worried about safety. Another reminder of exactly what kind of man Atlas Wallace is.

He sets to work gathering up the blankets and our trash, stashing them all in the bed of his truck before dousing the fire pit with a bucket of water.

"What are you waiting for?" he asks, noticing I'm rooted in place watching him.

"You're just... you're a good man."

Atlas saunters my way, reaching out to cup my cheek once he's within reach. "I love you, Nora. And right now, if it's okay with you, I'd like to take you home and show you just how much."

"God, yes, please." I look up at him and lick my lips, my heart nearly beating out of my chest. "It's very much okay."

Atlas drives like a man on a mission, and I guess in a way he is—a mission to get me naked. Can't particularly say I'm mad about it, because I'm every bit as excited as he is, if not a little nervous.

He throws the truck into park, cuts the engine, throws open his door, and rushes around to open my door and haul me into his arms.

"I'm gonna make you feel so damn good, Pip." He skims his nose along my jaw. "Promise. Gonna take care of you. Love you right."

"I know you will."

He sets me down once we're safely inside the house. "But I meant what I said. You're in charge. I need your words, because knowing you're in this as much as me, that you feel safe, that's important. You hear me?"

"Yeah, I hear you." I can also hear my heart beating like a drum in my chest, wild and out of control—but in the best possible way.

"Good." He locks the front door and then turns to me with a wolfish grin. "Now, if you want this, if you want me, I need you to head on back to our room and strip."

"Strip?" I echo him, my voice shaking ever so slightly.

"Yeah, that's right." He toys with the ends of my hair. "I want to see all of you. But, Nora..." He takes a step back, and immediately, I miss his warmth. "If you don't want this, if at any point you want to stop, tell me and we will. This only goes as far as you want it to."

"Okay." I nod, silently hyping myself up for what I'm about to do.

I pivot on my heel and take off down the hall toward our room, shucking my sweater off about halfway there.

Footsteps sound behind me, but I don't look. If I do, I might lose my nerve.

Instead, I unhook my bra and let it fall to the floor as I enter our room. *Hearing him call this* our *room sent tingles all through me.*

Once inside, I kick off my boots, socks, and leggings. Standing in nothing but my underwear, apprehension wraps itself around me like a dark cloud. *What if he doesn't like the way my body looks? What if I'm not good at any of this? What if...*

A low groan snaps me back to the here and now, and I turn to face Atlas, boldly letting him look his fill, even if I am shaking so hard my knees are knocking together.

"Fucking hell, Nora." He steps fully into the room, his eyes devouring me. "You're... perfection."

"Really?" I glance down at my belly, at the stretch marks running across my skin and then back to him, nibbling my lip.

Atlas tugs his shirt over his head and then drops to his knees in front of me, pressing a tender kiss right above the edge of my panties. "Yes, a million times yes."

He flexes his hands before trailing the back of his fingers up the outside of my calves, up to my knees.

My entire body feels like it's on fire, and as he presses a soft kiss to the inside of my right thigh, and then another one to the left, the flames only grow higher.

It's almost like my body is at war with itself. I'm burning up with need, yet covered in chill bumps. I want to spread my legs wider for him and clamp them shut. I want him to move his mouth higher and—

"Eyes on me, Nora," he says, licking a strip up my thigh, causing my core to clench. "I want you to watch me while I make you feel good. I want you to know it's me, and when you come, I want you to scream my name. Can you do that for me?"

"Yes." My breathing is already ragged in anticipation of what's to come. He hasn't *really* even touched me yet, and I can feel my wetness coating my panties and the insides of my thighs.

"Good girl, but let's lose these, yeah?" He fingers the edge of my underwear before helping me out of them. Once I'm completely bare before him, he brings his mouth back to my skin, peppering my inner thighs with soft kisses, until his nose brushes against my neatly trimmed curls. "Fuck, you smell divine."

My cheeks burn, both with embarrassment and arousal. The thought of him sniffing me *there* is so strange, but at the same time, it's kind of hot, too. In a primal sort of way.

"Can I taste you now, Nora?" He looks up at me, watching my face carefully as he waits for my answer.

I nod.

But that's not enough for him. "Words. I need you to *tell* me. So, I'll ask again—can I put my mouth on your pretty pussy?"

Oh, wow. *Wow, wow, wow.* I've never understood the appeal of dirty talk, but now, I totally freaking get it.

"I-I think I might die if you don't," I tell him honestly.

He licks his lips and then grips my thighs, pushing softly outward. "Widen your stance a little."

"Wouldn't a bed—"

"I want to be on my knees for you." He parts my lips with his thumbs. "That way you're in control. If I do something you don't like or don't want, you can shove me away, knee me in the face, anything you need to do to get away. This. Is. About. You." He emphasizes each word with a kiss to my... *pussy.*

It's on the tip of my tongue to ask him where to put my hands when he spears me with his tongue. My hands fly to his hair on their own accord, holding onto the thick strands for dear life as he feasts on me like I'm the most decadent meal he's ever eaten.

There's no room for awkwardness with him on his knees before me, not where he's doing his level best to wring every ounce of pleasure from my touch-starved body.

"Oh-oh, God," I whimper, rocking my hips as he alternates between kissing, sucking, and licking me. Everything he's doing feels so, *so* good, but I still need more. "Touch... touch me... please."

"With pleasure," he growls, pressing his index finger against my slick center.

He takes his time, rubbing it up and down my slit, slowly

working the digit inside of me. The intrusion stings a bit at first, causing my entire body to tense up, but in the blink of an eye, euphoria unlike anything I've ever known before surges through me, making my muscles go practically liquid.

"Tastes so good," he murmurs before sealing his lips around my bundle of nerves, sucking in time with the pumping of his finger. "Want you to come all over my face."

I tug on his hair as I rock my hips, totally wanton, loving the way his slight scruff feels between my thighs.

"Atlas!" I cry out, as my entire body draws taut like a bowstring. "I..." Words fail me, but he knows.

"I've got you, Pip," he whispers, crooking his finger inside of me, rubbing against the sweetest spot as he doubles down on my clit.

And just like that, all of the pressure building inside of me blows. Blinding, white hot pleasure explodes inside of me. It's almost like I'm floating...

No, I'm flying, and I'm not sure I ever want to come down.

But eventually, I do, and it's to find Atlas still kneeling before me, looking all too pleased with himself.

"I..." It takes a few tries to get my words to work. "I want to make you feel just as good." I trail my fingers over his forehead and down his cheek. "Can I?"

He stands so fast that *I* get whiplash. "You damn well know you can. Just tell me where you want me."

I don't know if it's the way he's looking at me like I'm the best thing he's ever seen, or my orgasm loosened my tongue, but before I can think it through I blurt out, "In my mouth."

He groans, reaching down and cupping himself through his jeans. "I meant here, the chair, the bed..."

"Oh." I duck my head, but Atlas is right there, crowding my space and laying his lips on mine before I have the chance to feel embarrassed.

"Just tell me where you want me, and that's where I'll be," he says, breaking our kiss.

"Well." I take a small step away from him. "Before you go anywhere, I want you to…" *Is it hot in here? Man, saying this stuff is harder than I thought it would be.*

"Tell me." His voice is soft—just the encouragement I need.

"I want you naked, too."

Instantly, he grips his belt buckle, somehow undoing it with only one hand. I watch, utterly entranced, as he pops the button on his jeans before shucking them, and his boxers, down and kicking them off.

Atlas makes it look effortless, like stripping for me is second nature. Then again, with a body like his, maybe it is. He's a big guy with wide shoulders and a broad chest that tapers into a narrow waist. His abs are a work of art, but right now it's the space between his legs that has my attention.

He's rock-hard, and there's a small bead of liquid sitting right at the tip. I remember the taste of it on my tongue, the saltiness of it, and while I didn't particularly enjoy it, I loved knowing that it was me who made him feel that way.

"Get on the bed, Atlas." My voice is soft, wrapping around the two of us like silk.

Wordlessly, he obeys, positioning himself on his back in the center of the bed, with his arms behind his head.

I should probably be more nervous than I am, but as I join him on the bed, I can't find even a hint of anxiety rolling around inside of me.

Instead, I'm eager, because I know exactly how he likes to be touched. I know just what to do to make him lose his mind. That knowledge... it's intoxicating.

"You gonna stare at it?" Atlas asks, reaching down to stroke himself with one hand. "Or touch it?"

"Neither." I push his legs apart, making room for me to kneel between them. "I'm going to taste you just like you did me."

He groans, still stroking himself from root to tip.

I lean in and swipe my tongue over the head of his dick, barely even wincing at the taste before sucking the entire crown into my mouth.

"Fuck, Pip. Your mouth is perfect." His hips thrust ever so slightly, like he's desperately trying to keep himself from coming undone. Which is the exact opposite of what I want.

I want him wild with need for me. Feral even, because deep down, I know even if he's crazed with desire, he won't hurt me. It took my brain a while to get it, but now, I know unequivocally, he will never hurt me.

He's still working his hand up and down his shaft as I focus all of my attention on the tip, but I want to play with all of him. To touch and taste all he has to offer.

I push his hand away, replacing it with my own, fisting his length while sucking him like he's my own personal lollipop.

"Feels so good." His voice is a barely audible rasp, and I love it. "Bet your pussy will feel even better."

I gasp, and he slides deeper into my mouth. Tears fill my eyes and he tries to retreat, but I don't let him. He's so scared of pushing me too far, but what he doesn't realize—what I'm only now realizing—is there is no such thing as too far with him.

I want everything he has to give me. I want him to test my

boundaries and to help me be brave and bold. Because every time we're together, even if it's only kissing, he's helping me gain back what his father took away.

"Pip, baby." He fists the sheets between his strong fingers. "You gotta stop or—"

"Or what?" I ask, releasing him with a wet pop.

"Or I'll come in your mouth."

"And that's a bad thing why?" Well, other than the taste. But it's a win for him.

"Because I'd rather come deep inside your tight little pussy." His cheeks go crimson, and I love it. I love knowing I did this to him. "If you still want that, I mean."

"I very much want it."

"Are you sure?" He pushes himself up so he's sitting and takes my hands in both of his. "I don't—it's just this is your first time and—"

"I'm not exactly a virgin, you know?" I glance down to my rounded belly.

"I know." He swallows roughly, releasing my hands in favor of cupping my stomach instead. "Before, you didn't have a choice, but now you do. With me, you always do. And every time you choose me, I'm going to fucking cherish it, Nora."

I was already fully committed to going all the way with him, and this only reaffirms my decision.

"I love you," I tell him, resting my hands on top of his. "And I want this, with you and only you."

"I love you, too, Pip. I—"

"Then show me. Show me with your body just how much you love me."

I expect him to take charge, to lay me down and for him to fit himself between my legs so he can make love to me.

But that isn't what happens—at all.

Instead, he reclines back against the mound of pillows, a teasing sort of smile curling his lips. "Straddle me."

"What?" I nearly choke on the word. Isn't basic missionary the go-to as far as first times go?

Me being on top sort of feels like skipping training wheels in favor of a trick bike. Which is worrisome, seeing as I don't know how to ride anything—*a bike or a dick.*

"You heard me. We'll take this one step at a time." He taps his lower abdomen. "Now, come sit right here and kiss me."

One step at a time. I can do this.

I straddle him, sliding over his still-hard dick as I make my way to where he wants me. We both hiss at the contact. He's so big, I'm honestly not sure how he'll freaking fit.

"Good girl, Pip. You're doing so fucking good," he says, once I'm sitting on top of him. "Now brace your hands on my shoulders and put your mouth on mine."

This time, I don't hesitate. And neither does he. Our kiss goes from smoldering embers to a raging inferno just like that. We're a flurry of lips and teeth and tongues, feeding off one another's desire.

We kiss and kiss and kiss, until finally, the need to breathe causes us to break apart.

"I... I want you inside of me." Flames lick my cheeks, burning me from the inside out. *I literally can't believe I just said that.*

But Atlas's answering grin chases any doubts away. "What am I going to do with you? I don't know what's hotter—your lips wrapped around my cock or hearing you tell me exactly what you want."

"I just want you, Atlas." I rock forward and cover his lips with mine, speaking my next words directly against them. "I want you, all of you, any and every way I can have you."

It might be my imagination, but I swear, I feel his dick sort of jump against my thigh.

"I'm yours, Pip. In every way." He reaches between us, taking himself into his hand. "I'm completely clean, but if you want me to wear a condom, I will."

Oh, God. Protection never even crossed my mind. Not even once.

"Um." I swallow and look down to where he's poised nearly at my entrance. "No, we're, well—you're good." I shrug. "It's not like I can get pregnant."

The mood lightens as we both laugh.

"You're something else, Pip." Atlas darts forward, stealing a kiss. But once we lock eyes again, he's all business. "I'm going to use lube because it's your first time. If you reach over and open the nightstand drawer, you'll find a bottle. It has a gold cap."

My insides feel like they're in a blender, sloshing and mixing all around as I reach to retrieve the lube.

"Open it and squirt a little into the palm of my hand."

With shaking hands, I do as he says. My mouth feels like it's full of cotton as I watch him coat himself with the clear liquid.

"Now, I want you to spread yourself and then lower down onto me. It's probably going to hurt at first, Pip, but I'll do everything I can to ease the pain."

My heart is thrashing in my chest, slamming violently against my ribs, as if it's trying to break out of its cage and flee. It's fight or flight on steroids. Luckily, my trust in Atlas is stronger than my fear.

I'm safe, I'm safe, I'm safe. I chant the words inside of my head like a mantra as I spread my lips and line myself up with the head of his dick.

"You're doing so good," Atlas praises, his free hand roaming all over my body, offering soft touches that help ease some of my worry. "When you're ready, sink down onto me. Go as slow or fast as you want. We have all night, pretty girl."

For several long minutes, I'm a statue, barely even breathing I'm so still. Even my heart rate slows as I hover above him, fighting off memories of the last time someone was inside of me.

This is different, I reason with myself. *He's different. He loves you and even if you got up and walked away now, he'd be okay with it.*

"You're so perfect, Pip. Perfect for me. Whether we do this now or a year from now, I'll love you."

God, it's almost like he has a direct line to my insecurities. Which is fine by me, because he's also the balm, soothing away my worries and easing my pain.

He keeps whispering sweet words to me, all the while skimming his hands up and down my thighs, over my hips and belly, almost like he can't help himself, like he *has* to touch me.

I'm not sure if it's his gentle encouragement or the look of complete adoration in his eyes, but I know it like I know my own name: I'm ready for this. I'm ready to be completely and wholly his.

"Ah, oh, God." I exhale sharply, trying with all of my might to keep the tears stinging the back of my eyes from falling. The last thing I want is to cry and ruin what should be a special moment between us.

"Are you okay?" Atlas asks through clenched teeth. He sounds like he's in more pain than I am, which is alarming.

"Just really…" I wiggle my hips ever so slightly, noting the way he tangles his fingers in the sheets with a white-knuckle grip. "Full."

He nods, his entire body shaking.

"Are you?" I move one hand from his shoulder down to his chest, placing my palm right over his heart. Strangely enough, the staccato rhythm soothes something deep within me. "Okay, I mean."

"Pip, you feel so fucking good that it's taking every bit of willpower I possess not to fuck you like a madman. The way your sweet little pussy is squeezing my cock is… *fuuuuuck*. Best thing I've ever felt in my whole damn life."

"So, you're not in pain?" I tip my head to the side, my hair falling around my face like a curtain. "Because it kind of looks like you are."

"Jesus, Nora." His eyes crinkle in the corners as he grins up at me. "No, definitely not hurting. I should be asking you that, though."

I shake my head. "No. It's… snug."

"You're telling me," he mutters under his breath.

"And it was a little uncomfortable at first, but now, I'm just… full."

He releases the sheets and moves his hands to my waist. "Do you think you're ready to move?"

"Um." How is it even possible to be turned on and embarrassed at the same time? Shouldn't one cancel the other out or something? "Move how?"

"Just like when we kiss. Roll your hips, rub yourself against me, take some time and figure out what feels good to you." He pulls me forward, and I gasp at the sensation that zips through me, immediately repeating the motion. "Yeah, just like that, Pip."

"What about you?" I pant, finding a rhythm that works for me.

"Pretty girl, if it feels good for you, I can just about guarantee it does for me, too."

I keep rocking against him, loving the way my body slips and slides against his, the way I can feel him deep inside of me, like we're completely connected.

No, it's more than that.

It's like he's a part of me, and I'm a part of him. Intertwined down to our very souls.

Or maybe I'm just delirious with pleasure. Anything's possible with the way he's making me feel.

"Talk to me, Pip," Atlas urges. "Tell me how you're feeling."

I part my lips to answer him, but all that comes out is a soft moan.

"Good then?" he asks, his lips curling up in a lopsided, self-assured grin.

"So, so good," I say, lifting my hips ever so slightly before sliding back down his length.

He hisses, almost as if he's in pain—but I know better. He liked it. *A lot.*

If anything, he's holding himself back, so as not to scare me. It only makes me love him that much more.

And so, I do it again, lifting myself further this time, before grinding down onto him.

"Keep telling me." He feathers his fingers over my hips in a barely-there touch. "I need your words."

"Better than anything."

Atlas continues with his sweet torture, running his hands all over me while barely touching me at the same time. It's a delicious tease, turning my fevered, sweat-soaked skin to goose flesh.

"I never knew it could feel like this. Oh my God. It's so good. So. Good." I murmur those two words over and over as I rock against him, loving the feel of his skin against mine, enthralled by the way my clit rubs against him.

"That's right, pretty girl. Make yourself feel good, take what you need from me. I'm here for you, for your pleasure."

I lean down and kiss him, stroking my tongue against his. It feels like I'm teetering on the edge, but I need... "More," I whisper, ghosting my lips over his jaw.

"Can I touch you?" he asks. "Like really touch you."

I nod and he immediately palms both of my hips, helping guide my movements before sliding one hand up over my bump to cup my breast.

His deft fingers pluck and pull at my nipple, and I swear, it's like I feel it all the way down to my core.

"Your pussy's squeezing me so tight." He leans up, drawing my nipple into his mouth, sucking hard. "Feels so fucking good."

My thighs shake as I continue impaling myself on him. I truly never knew sex could be like this, that it could feel like this.

"You look so beautiful riding me. Like a fucking queen. You own me, Nora. My heart, my soul, all of it—all of me. Do you hear me? Everything I have is yours."

His sweet words wrap themselves around me, grounding me as his body brings me bliss unlike anything I've ever known before.

And yet I still need something more.

"Atlas." I whine his name, forcing my pelvis against his harder, desperately in search of whatever it is I need.

Somehow, though, he knows. "I've got you, Pip. I've always got you." He licks his thumb and then presses it to my clit, rubbing small, tight circles keeping a perfect rhythm with my hips.

"Atlas." His name is a prayer, a plea. "I think... I'm going to—"

My entire body short circuits, my muscles tense as my back arches, and my mouth falls open in a silent scream. My skin tingles and my body hums, like someone's pumping electricity straight into my veins.

He keeps rubbing my clit and thrusting up into me in search of his own release, now that I've found mine.

"I love you," I whisper, slumping against his chest, utterly exhausted.

"Fuck, Pip." He thrusts once... twice more before spilling into me. "I love you, too. So damn much."

THIRTY-ONE
Atlas

Watching Nora come back down from the high of her orgasm is fascinating. It's almost like I'm seeing her for the first time, all doe-eyed and breathless, with a look of total ecstasy painting her features.

I fucking love it—I love seeing her like this.

"You okay, Pip?" I ask, stroking my fingers up and down her spine, causing her to shiver.

"Mmhmm." She nods as she moves herself to an upright position, causing my half-hard dick to twitch inside of her. "Tired." She reaches between her thighs, experimentally touching where we're joined. "Sticky."

"Yeah." I chuckle. "Let's get you cleaned up."

I attempt to disentangle myself from her to stand, but her soft whimper stops me in my tracks.

"Sorry," she says, blushing so pretty. "It's dumb, but I... I don't want to let you go."

I grin up at her, not wanting to let her go either. "You're in luck then, because you don't have to. I'm yours forever." I press a quick kiss on her forehead. "Now, wrap your arms around my neck."

She does, and I jackknife myself into a seated position, sliding my arms beneath her legs so that I can stand, cradling her to my chest.

It's wild to me how small she is, even in her second trimester, but I know she's eating well and that the baby's fine. They're both healthy and safe, and really, that's all anyone can ask for.

I carry her into the bathroom and set her down on the mat outside of the shower. She wraps her arms around herself and watches me with a soft look in her eyes as I start the shower.

Once the water's warm I turn back to her, only to find her sort of in a trance-like state, staring off at nothing. She's so totally still, she reminds me of a statue. If it wasn't for the shallow rise and fall of her chest, I'd be truly worried.

"Pip." I skim the back of my knuckles along her freckled cheekbone. "You with me?"

Nora jolts, snapping her wide hazel eyes up to mine. "Yeah. Sorry, I'm, um..."

"Can I hold you?" I ask, hoping like hell she lets me.

She nods and I don't hesitate, wrapping her in my arms and pulling her close. "I love you, Nora, so much. You know that, right?"

"Yeah." She sniffles and nods. "I love you, too." I can tell from the sound of her voice that she's crying, and it absolutely guts me.

"In you go," I murmur, lifting her into the shower before

joining her. I walk her back into the spray, letting her shivering body warm as I squirt some shampoo into the palm of my hand.

"Can you talk to me? Tell me what's going through that pretty little head of yours?"

"I just..." She shudders and once again wraps her arms around herself. "I didn't know sex could be like that. Before tonight, it's always been something I feared. Something used against me, to hurt me. But you..."

Fuck, fuck, fuck. If she says I hurt her, I don't know what I'll do. Kick my own ass, for starters.

"You were so soft, and kind, and just perfect." She blinks up at me, her tears mingling with the water falling from the showerhead. "I was scared, you know? That it would hurt, or that I wouldn't like it, that I'd disappoint you, I don't know."

She shrugs, trying to downplay her emotions, but that doesn't fly with me.

"Nora, you could never disappoint me."

"But what if I freaked out or had a flashback or—"

I tunnel my sudsy fingers into her hair, massaging her scalp. "You survived unspeakable trauma, Pip. Tonight was... amazing, but also a lot, I'm sure. And while you handled everything really well, there may be times you don't. And when and if that happens, I'll be there, at your side, doing everything I can to help you through it."

She tips her head back, rinsing the shampoo from her hair. "I don't deserve you."

Her voice is quiet, and yet it echoes like a gunshot. Fitting, since it feels like a bullet's tearing through the muscle and sinew of my chest.

I grip her chin softly and tilt her gaze back to mine. "That's bullshit."

She gasps. "It's not. You... you deserve someone who isn't broken—"

"I mean this as kindly as possible, but fuck what you think I deserve. I *want* you and I *love* you and I want to be with you for as long as you'll have me. If you don't feel the same, if we're moving too fast or tonight was too much for you, tell me and I'll step back. I'm willing to wait, no matter how long it takes. You're my endgame, Nora. My priority, my forever."

"What if..." She swallows and then locks her eyes with mine. "What if being with me is to your detriment?"

"Even then. Always. As. Long. As. You'll. Have. Me. Do you get that? Do you understand what I'm saying? I love you, broken pieces and all. You're fucking strong. A fighter. The ball is in your court, Nora. It always has been."

She sucks in a quivering breath, holds it for a beat and then nods. "I'm sorry. I'm such a mess. I... I just..."

"It's okay. You're okay. *We're okay.*"

"Promise?" she asks, sucking her lower lip between her teeth.

"Cross my heart." I free it with my thumb and then lean down to kiss her. It's soft and short, my way of sealing my promise to her—that no matter what happens, we'll always be okay in the end. "Now let me finish cleaning you and then we can go to bed."

"It's too early to sleep." But even as she says the words, her eyelids droop.

"Then we can cuddle and put on a movie."

She nods, pacified, and I get to work running conditioner through her hair, letting it sit while I soap her up with *my* body wash instead of the fancy stuff I bought for her. There's something about her smelling like me that just does it for me.

Caveman mode: activated.

Once she's all rinsed, I grab the towel from the hook and wrap it around her before helping her out of the shower.

I speed through getting myself clean and dried off, eager to have her back in my arms. But by the time I get out, she's already back in the bedroom, dressed in one of my shirts—and only that, judging from the flash of skin I see as she crawls into the bed.

Down boy, I tell myself, because goddamn does she look perfect.

"What do you want to watch?" I ask, tugging on a pair of sweats.

"Anything." She yawns, snuggling down deeper into her pillow. And then, "Something funny."

"You got it." I grab the remote and join her in the bed. She immediately curls into me, resting her head on my chest.

I hit the power button and turn on some mindless comedy flick, but she's sound asleep before the opening credits play.

Sunlight fills the room, casting a warm, hazy glow over the space as I blink my eyes open.

Nora stirs beside me, groaning softly in her sleep as she nestles her head beneath my chin, clinging to me for dear life.

It's funny, because before her, I was never much for cuddling. But with her—*fuck,* I never want to stop.

I bury my nose in her sleep-wild hair and tighten my hold around her waist, content to breathe her in as memories from last night dance behind my eyelids.

For a split second, when sleep gave way to consciousness,

I feared it was only a dream. But as I look down at her, I know everything that happened between us last night was real.

We're real, and she's truly mine.

She mumbles in her sleep, and I swear to God, it's the cutest fucking thing. I want this with her every day, forever, for the rest of our lives.

While staying here, wrapped up in the sheets with her all morning, preferably between Nora's sweet thighs, sounds like my version of fucking heaven, I know both she and the jellybean need some breakfast. Which means I need to drag my ass out of bed so I can take care of her.

Not to mention, she's probably sore from last night. Which means round two is off the table until she asks for it. Because while I'd love nothing more than to fuck Nora straight through my mattress, her comfort is what matters the most.

Unfortunately, my still-hard dick hasn't gotten the memo.

I quickly readjust myself, barely suppressing a groan, before tiptoeing out of the bedroom and down the hall.

After starting a pot of coffee, I grab eggs and bacon from the fridge and get to work frying them up on the stove.

"Plates. I need plates." I turn off the burner and shove the pan off it before turning to the cabinet to grab some down.

But before I can, the front door swings open. "Knock, knock, lovebirds. Hope nobody's naked."

"Sure didn't give us much warning if we were," I growl, shooting a glare his way. Best friend or not, the thought of him seeing Nora without any clothes makes me want to beat his ass.

He holds his hands up in surrender, but he's smiling. The jackass baited me, and I let him.

"Mmm, something smells good."

I whip around to see Nora standing at the end of the hall, still wearing only my shirt.

The urge to rush to her and hide her from his view is strong, but I manage to cross the room at a normal pace, wrapping her in my arms. "Good morning, pretty girl."

She rubs her cheek against my bare chest as she wraps her arms around my waist. "'Morning."

"Did you sleep okay? Are you hungry? Sore?"

"One question at a time." She snickers, wiggling out of my hold. "And yes, I slept great. Missed waking up next to you though."

Ellis coughs in the kitchen, and we both turn to him. "Sorry, just wondering when the wedding is and if I can be the best man?"

Nora stiffens in my arms, and for the second time in less than five minutes, I glare at my best friend.

"Don't both agree at once. I guess I can settle for flower girl, but honestly, this is kind of bullshit." He thumps his chest. "I'm definitely best man material."

"What?" Nora finally asks, flicking her wide-eyed gaze back and forth between the two of us. "We're not getting married…"

"The hell we aren't." The words are out of my mouth before I can stop them.

"What?" she asks again, confusion painting her every word. "But…" She blinks and shakes her head. "I don't know what's going on. Maybe I'm still asleep, or… I don't know. But we are not getting married."

I grunt my disapproval while Ellis laughs under his breath.

"Mark my words, Nora Morgan, one day my ring will be on your finger, you will be my wife, and the dumbass in the kitchen will stand by my side as we exchange vows." I lean down and press my lips to hers, kissing her softly. "But that's in the future. Right now, we're going to go eat the breakfast I made, okay?"

She squints up at me, a semi-dazed look on her face. "I still think I might be dreaming, but yeah, okay."

Ellis laughs. "Look at me, making dreams come true."

"More like writing checks your ass can't cash," I say, rolling my eyes before turning back to Nora. "Why don't you go put on something a little warmer while I fix you a plate."

She glances down between us and gasps, as if only realizing she's only wearing my shirt. "Oh my God, be right back!"

I watch with a soft grin as she scurries back toward the bedroom, waiting until I hear the door shut before heading into the kitchen to plate up her food.

"Shit, toast," I mutter to myself.

"On it," Ellis says, grabbing the bread from the pantry, redeeming himself. He loads the toaster and pushes the lever before turning to me. "So, did you mean it?"

"Mean what?"

He rolls his eyes like I'm dumb and starts humming the wedding march. "About marrying Nora."

I don't answer him immediately, instead focusing on Nora's breakfast, arranging everything on her plate until it's just so. Once I'm satisfied, I turn my attention back to Ellis.

"Dead serious." I grab three forks from the drawer, since this apparently is a family breakfast now. "I know it's soon, but she's it for me. Full stop, for-fucking-ever."

The corners of his mouth kick up into a grin. "You don't have to convince me, man. It's obvious to everyone who sees y'all together. Just wanted to make sure *you* knew." He nudges my shoulder with his. "You've been known to be a bit dense from time to time."

"Shut up."

He nudges me again. "You love me. C'mon, just admit it. You'll feel better if you do."

"Whatever." I try to keep a straight face, but a smile breaks free. "Fucker."

Ellis whoops victoriously. "Hopefully you're better at talking about your feelings with Nora than you are with me."

"Oh, he is," she says, laughing as she climbs up onto a barstool. "Very emotionally aware, that one."

"You want jelly?" I ask, pointedly ignoring them both as I slide her plate across the bar.

She scrunches her nose and then nods. "Yes, please."

Ellis grabs it before I can, passing it directly to her with a small frown.

"Got something against strawberry jelly?" she asks.

He shrugs. "Prefer blackberry, but I'll survive."

Nora laughs, and I swear to God, the sound lights me up from the inside out. "How brave of you."

"Not to change the subject or anything," I say around a bite of eggs, cutting my eyes from Ellis to Nora, "but have you had a chance to look into that thing we talked about?"

Ellis sighs and then shakes his head. "Been meaning to, but work has me going nonstop. I'll make some time this weekend."

"I'd appreciate it. The more I think about it, the more off shit feels and I... I don't like it."

"Wanna know what I don't like?" Nora says, her tone frosty as she pushes her mostly empty plate away.

"What's that?" I tug at my collar, feeling like I'm about to be scolded.

"I don't like when people have conversations in front of me, that are most likely about me, but don't include me."

"Pip," I start, trying to figure this out. Because technically, she's right. We are talking about something that concerns her. And she does deserve to be in the loop. It's just... the thought of potentially upsetting her damn near kills me.

"Y'all either need to speak privately or speak freely." She shrugs and then wraps her arms around herself, making me feel lower than low.

I look to Ellis for assistance, but he's firmly on Team-Keep-Nora-In-The-Loop and has been from the start.

"Atlas." Something about the way she whispers my name tugs on my heart. They're both right—she's been in the dark for so long, she sure as shit doesn't deserve for me to try to keep her there, even if it is out of some misplaced sense of protection.

"Ellis is looking into our mothers' death certificates."

She props her elbow on the bar, resting her cheek against her palm as she looks at me. "You said they were similar, right?"

"Identical is more like it," Ellis says, his voice gruff. "I'm honestly not sure how it didn't raise any red flags with the ME."

Nora lifts her head, her gaze snapping toward Ellis. "How are you looking into it? Like, what does that mean?"

Ellis and I exchange looks, each of us wanting the other to explain. But he's out of luck—this part falls on him.

"I'm... looking into it..." He trails off, carefully choosing his words. I know he doesn't want to lie to her, but seeing as what he's doing isn't fully legal, he doesn't want to implicate her either. "In an unofficial capacity."

Nora draws her bottom lip between her teeth as she contemplates Ellis's confession.

There's a pit in my stomach as I wait for her reply. The thought of upsetting her—especially after our night together—has me waiting on pins and needles.

I'm sure that makes me sound weak, but I don't really give a fuck either, because I am weak when it comes to the little spitfire sitting on the stool next to me.

She is hands down the best thing to ever happen to me. She stumbled into my life in the strangest fucking way and now I can't bear to imagine a single day without her by my side.

So yeah, she's my weak spot, but only because she's carved a permanent place for herself right in the middle of my still-beating heart.

"Okay," she finally says, nodding once. "Just promise me one thing."

"Anything," Ellis says without a lick of hesitation. "Just name it."

"Be safe."

Ellis exhales slowly as a smile unfurls until it takes up his entire face. "I didn't realize you cared so much."

"Of course, I do, you big idiot," Nora huffs and rolls her eyes at him. "Just because you're built like a bear masquerading as a linebacker doesn't mean you're invincible."

Ellis puffs up his chest. "You hear that, man? Your girl thinks I'm stacked." He flexes, causing his bicep to swell.

Nora's cheeks bloom the prettiest shade of pink as she turns toward me. "I, you're—"

I lean in and silence her with a kiss. "I don't need you to pander to my ego, Pip. I'm completely secure in how you feel about me."

She breathes out a sigh of relief. "Good, because I love you more than I could possibly ever put into words."

I peck her lips again. "Love you, too, pretty girl. So damn much."

"What are you two lovebirds doing today?" Ellis asks, his eyes volleying back and forth between Nora and me.

She licks her lips and looks at me.

"I was thinking we could work on the nursery." I clear my throat. "You know, if you want to."

"Really?" She bounces on her barstool and then launches herself at me. "Thank you, Atlas."

"Don't thank me for providing for our son, Pip. It's my honor and one day, if I'm lucky, we'll have a whole house of 'em."

"You want more than one kid?" she asks in this soft, breathless voice I'm not sure I've ever heard her use before.

"Nora." I cup her cheeks with both hands. "I want any and everything you'll give me. Be it one kid or ten, as long as it's with you, I'm golden."

She bites her lips and sighs happily, all but melting into me.

"Why don't you go relax for a bit while Ellis and I clean up and then we can head out?"

"Sounds good." She slides down from my lap, tossing a cheeky finger wave Ellis's way before retreating back to our room.

"Sunk, my man," Ellis murmurs, once we hear the door close. "You are so fucking sunk."

I tip my chin and nod. "One-hundred and ten percent."

He grins. "I'm not saying I called it or anything, but I totally did."

"Yeah." I exhale a laugh. "I guess you did."

DIARY ENTRY, PRESENT DAY

Dear Diary,

If I didn't already know Atlas is the best kind of man, last night would have cemented it. He's every single thing I've ever wanted and more.

I'm pretty sure he checks every box on the list I made so many years ago, and even better is I know for certain my dad would have loved him. Atlas is the epitome of the kind of man any father would want for his daughter.

But back to last night... I got a little off track there. The date he planned was nothing short of perfect. From the picnic to the s'mores to the sex. It was all so amazing.

But it's the sex that really threw me. Being with him was... wow. I honestly didn't know it could be like that, that it could feel like that.

For so long, I equated sex with pain and punishment. There was no pleasure, just misery and suffering, self-loathing and regret.

But with Atlas...

With Atlas, not only did my body light up with pleasure, but my heart did, too. He made sure, every single step of the way, that I knew that I was safe and loved and cherished-and completely in control.

It's a surreal feeling-not being afraid of intimacy. But in a good way... in an I can't wait to do it again way. Assuming I can convince Atlas. I know he's worried about me being sore and taking things too fast.

God, I love that man and his heart of gold... he's so, so good to me.

But now that I've had a taste of what it's really like, with him anyway, I can't help but want more.

He wants to work on the nursery today, and I'm as excited as I am nervous. Well, maybe nervous isn't the right word. But with every step we take to prepare for our jellybean's arrival, my impending motherhood feels even more real.

I guess we need to figure out a name for him, but I'll let that be a problem for another day.

I'll update you again soon.

Smitten (and maybe a little sore), Nora

THIRTY-TWO
Nora

I close my diary and tuck it into the nightstand drawer before flopping back onto the bed.

Atlas told me to rest, but my mind and body seem to be at odds. Maybe a shower to split the difference, and if I can convince Atlas to join me, even better.

Rolling to my side, I huff and push myself into an upright position. It's wild how simple things, like getting out of bed or squatting down, are getting harder by the day, thanks to my ever-growing belly. But if it means my little man is healthy, then so be it.

With one last lingering look at the bed, I stand and strip out of Atlas's shirt leaving it on top of the covers for him to find, before heading into the bathroom.

I start the water and then move to the sink to brush my teeth and run a brush through my snarled locks—I'm guessing this is what the term *sex hair* means.

By the time it's knot-free, steam hangs heavy in the air and the mirror is starting to fog.

Hot showers are still somewhat of a luxury for me, and I'm often torn between flying through it and indulging myself.

Today though, I absolutely plan on taking my time. After all, Atlas can't join me if I'm already finished.

I step under the spray, letting the scalding water soak me from head to toe.

Once my hair is thoroughly wet, I grab the fancy shampoo Atlas bought me and flip the cap, squirting a dollop into my palm before massaging it into my scalp.

As the soap lathers, my thoughts return to last night, to the way Atlas was singularly focused on me. On my wants and my needs. It sounds cheesy, but it's almost as if he knows my body as well as I do. Maybe better...

I release a contented sigh as I tip my head back to rinse the suds.

"Nora?" Atlas calls my name as he enters the bedroom, but I don't reply. I want him to come find me.

He knocks on the bathroom door and I have to bite my lower lip to stay quiet. It's silly—I want him to join me, but I'm too scared to come right out and ask.

"You good, Pip?"

Maggie and I have been working on me being more assertive—on not being afraid to ask for what I want. And so, I suck in a calming breath and then say, "Actually, I need your help..."

The seconds creep by as I wait for him to open the door, but finally he does. "What do you need?" he asks, his voice deliciously low. I swear, just the sound of it sends a rush of warmth through me.

"You," I whisper, halfway wondering if he can even hear me over the water. Or maybe it's the sound of my own heartbeat whooshing in my ears.

"What was that?"

I flex my fingers at my side, debating whether or not I can go through with this.

No. I refuse to allow fear to win. He wants me, and I want him. It's as simple as that.

I reach out and grip the edge of the shower curtain, tugging it open, baring myself to him, wet and naked. "I said I needed you."

He swallows hard as he takes me in. His pupils are blown wide with desire and his jaw tics. "And how exactly do you need me, Nora?" He takes a step closer, and then another, until his feet are flush with the tub wall. "Tell me."

The cold air causes me to shiver and I try to cover myself, but Atlas is right there, stopping me. "Don't hide from me."

"I'm not." I duck my head, knowing that a part of me is. "It's cold."

He smirks. "The sooner you tell me what you need, the quicker we can warm you up."

"I want you to join me," I say, knowing full and well my entire body is glowing red with embarrassment. "I can't stop thinking about last night..."

Atlas looks torn, but at the sight of my pouting lower lip, his resolve breaks.

He shucks off his sweats and steps into the shower, tugging the curtain closed before crowding me against the cool tile wall.

"What about last night?" he asks, skimming his nose along

the sensitive skin of my throat.

I shiver against him—this time with need. "All of it. The way you made me feel."

"How did I make you feel?" He scrapes his teeth lightly over my collarbone before kissing away the sting. "Tell me. You know how much I love your words."

"Like I was floating... and flying... and falling..." I sigh as he presses an open-mouthed kiss to my neck. "All at once."

He moves his mouth lower, sliding his lips over my sternum.

My back arches involuntarily, thrusting my chest into his face, but Atlas just rolls with it, skating his hands up and over my belly until he's cupping my breasts. "Such perfect fucking tits." He jiggles them ever so slightly before sealing his lips around my right nipple.

He sucks hard and I gasp, a desperate moan lodged in my throat.

"Oh, God, Atlas..."

"You like that?" he asks, his lips brush my nipple with every word.

"So much, but..." I trail off as he moves to my other breast, flicking his tongue against the tip before drawing the hardened bud into his mouth.

"But what?" he asks. His ability to multitask sure is something.

"More," I beg shamelessly. "I still want more."

"Are you sore, pretty girl?"

"Only a little." I twine my arms around his neck and pull him closer. "Please, Atlas. Touch me and make me feel good."

He brings his mouth up to mine, ghosting his lips over my own before sinking to his knees in front of me. "Stand under the spray," he orders.

"What are you doing?" I ask, moving directly under the stream of water. My body warms instantly, but I feel bad. He has to be freezing.

"I'm going to eat your pussy…" He leans forward and presses a kiss to the top of my mound. "Until you're delirious with pleasure and screaming my name."

"Atlas," I exhale his name as anticipation zips through me.

"Put your hands on my shoulders, Pip."

The second my palms make contact, he's on me, licking a long stripe up my center.

Instinctually, I try to clamp my thighs shut, but Atlas isn't having it. He growls and positions my left foot to rest on the lip of the tub. "I wanna taste you, Nora. Wanna drown in your flavor."

His filthy words send fire racing through me, and the rapid swipes of his tongue may as well be kerosene.

He licks and sucks at me, focusing on everything *except* where I need him the most. He's teasing me, driving my need for him higher and higher, until finally, I can't take it anymore.

"Atlas, please!" I cry, threading my fingers through his hair, holding his face to my slick center. "Please."

His shoulders shake with silent laughter, but he gives me what I need, alternating between flicking the tip of his tongue against my clit and sucking on the ultra-sensitive nub.

My legs shake as pressure builds low in my belly. I'm teetering right on the edge, and more than anything, I want to topple over it and freefall into bliss.

Ever in tune with my body, Atlas knows I'm close and secures one hand around my left ankle, as if to brace me, while dragging the other one up my right leg, letting his fingers tease and explore until they're poised at my entrance.

His eyes flash up to mine, seeking permission, and I nod eagerly.

He slides one finger into my tight channel, rubbing it against my inner walls in perfect time with his ministrations. The combination of his hands and his mouth is exactly what I need, and as he adds a second finger, my orgasm barrels through me, and I come, screaming his name—just like he said I would.

I come back down to earth to find Atlas still kneeling between my legs, smirking up at me. "You with me, pretty girl?"

A soft sigh escapes me as I nod. "Yeah, I'm with you."

"Good." He presses a soft kiss to the inside of my left thigh before helping me plant my foot back onto the bathtub floor. "Now let's get you all cleaned up."

As he stands, his erection brushes against me. He's hard enough to pound nails. "What about you?" I ask, glancing down between us, where his dick is pointing at me like a heat-seeking missile.

He shakes his head and presses a soft kiss to my lips. "This was about you."

My heart flutters at his words, but a frown tugs at my lips. "You make everything about me."

A surprised laugh rumbles out of him as he grabs the shampoo and flips the cap, squirting some into his palm. "Turn around," he murmurs, and I do, allowing him to lather up my hair for a second time. "You say that like it's a bad thing?"

"Not bad," I say on a sigh. I swear, his fingers are magic as he massages my scalp. My whole body tingles with his efforts. "I just... I don't want things unbalanced between us. You're always looking out for me and taking care of me and... well, I want to take care of you sometimes, too."

Atlas hums and then withdraws his fingers from my hair.

I turn and tilt my head back, letting the now cooling spray rinse away the soap as I wait for his reply.

"I guess I never thought of it like that. When it comes to you, it's like some baser sense takes over, and all I think of is taking care of you. But I can see how that could create an imbalance." He grabs the conditioner and begins working it through my ends. "I don't want any kind of scoreboard or disparity between us. Not ever."

"I know you don't. But maybe try to let me spoil you sometimes too?"

"Consider it done. But, Pip, I've gotta be real with you—just to be able to call you mine spoils me."

I roll my eyes and grab his body wash. "Let me clean you up and then we can finish getting ready and head out."

He throws his arms wide—well, as wide as he can in the shower. "Have at it, pretty girl. Have at it."

Nerves tickle my belly as I squeeze a dollop of the masculine-scented soap into my palm. It's silly—the man literally just had his mouth between my thighs, he's been inside of me, and we tell each other we love each other regularly, but something about washing him feels intimate on a whole other level.

Get out of your head and wash the man, Nora!

I rub my hands together, working up a rich lather, but still can't bring myself to make contact. It's times like these I wish I wasn't so... *defective.*

"Hey." Atlas nudges my gaze up to his. "What's going on, Pip?"

"It's dumb," I mumble, focusing on the wet tile behind him.

Unfortunately, he's not having it. "Nothing you think

is dumb." He pries my soapy hands apart, placing them on his shoulders, and then bands his arms around my waist, drawing me as close as my belly will allow. "Now talk to me."

A soft sigh escapes me. "It's just... this feels so... what if I do it wrong?"

His lips quirk up into a grin. "Is there a wrong way to wash someone?"

Blood rushes to my cheeks, and I just know they're strawberry red. "See—it's totally dumb."

"I don't know... I kind of like that you're nervous. It's endearing. How about we do it together?"

I hesitate, not because I don't want his help, but because I feel like an idiot for needing it. I mean, he's right, it's not like there's a wrong way to do this. "Okay."

"Good girl," he whispers, placing his hands over mine.

Something about those two words on his lips sends the most delicious kind of shiver through me.

"Take your time," he says, guiding my hands down from his shoulders to his chest, "and work the soap in. You can rub in circles or massage with your fingertips. As long as your hands are on my body, I'm good."

I knead the body wash into his pecs. I'm mostly just touching him at this point, rather than cleaning him, but he doesn't seem to mind.

"Perfect, Pip." He tips his head back as I trail my fingers down the valley of his abs, his muscles constricting under my touch. "Just like that."

His easy praise spurs me on, and while his eyes are closed, I lower myself to my knees to wash his legs. Only, once my hands find purchase on his powerful thighs and my eyes land on his rock-hard erection, I can't help but think of all the other things I could do while I'm down here.

I glance up at him, startling when I find he's staring down at me, his eyes blazing hotter than I've ever seen them. It's almost like twin flames of desire are flickering in his pupils, and I can't help but want to turn those flames into a full-blown inferno.

"Nora..." I reach up and grip the base of his shaft, ghosting my lips over the mushroom head. "Wha—" he groans as I suck him fully into my mouth. "What are you doing?"

I pull back from him and smile. "Making you feel good."

"You don't—"

"Shh." I kiss the tip, lapping up the bead of precum with my tongue. "I know I don't *have* to. I *want* to."

"I'm definitely not gonna say no," he murmurs, low and husky as he threads his fingers through my damp hair.

It's weird, the way I feel more confident on my knees for him than I did washing him. Maybe it's the power dynamic, and how I know what this does for him, how good it makes him feel—how good *I* make him feel. Or maybe I'm just broken beyond repair.

All I know is Atlas treats me so dang good, he puts me first in all things. I'm his priority, me and our jellybean. And so, with that in mind, I wrap my lips back around the head of his dick, sucking the crown as though he's my favorite flavored lollipop.

His fingers tighten in my hair, not to the point of pain, but enough that I know he likes what I'm doing.

I slide my tongue over the veins on the underside of his shaft before swallowing him down to the back of my throat.

"Fucking shit, Pip," he hisses, thighs quivering as he fights off the urge to rut into my mouth. "God, you feel so good, your mouth is fucking heaven. Made for me."

My eyes water and my throat contracts as I suck him. I'm a slobbering mess, but the look of pure adoration in his eyes when I glance up at him is enough to keep me going.

I begin working the hand wrapped around his base in tandem with my mouth, sucking and jerking him as I bring my free hand up to cup his balls.

Which is apparently the right move, because Atlas loses it, pistoning his hips as he full-on fucks my face. The thought is so unlike me, but I can't think of any other way to describe it.

Animalistic groans fall from his lips, but I'm not scared. Even now, I know he'd never hurt me. If anything, the way he's falling apart from my touch turns me on. It makes me feel powerful to know that someone like me can bring a god-of-a-man like him such pleasure.

"Gonna come," he grunts, trying to pull out of my mouth, which further proves my point. Even on the brink of orgasm, he's thinking of me, and how I didn't love the salty taste of his release.

I slide my hand from his balls around to grip his backside, holding him in place as I double down my efforts, more determined than ever to drive him wild. I want him to see stars and have galaxies form behind his eyelids as he shouts my name and comes down my throat.

The thought is so out there, so strange, and yet *so hot*, that an ache forms between my thighs.

I swirl my tongue around the head and swallow down as much of his length as I can before releasing the base of his shaft to touch myself. It's foreign, but the insistent throb between my legs has me acting on autopilot.

With the first swipe of my index finger over my clit, I moan, and like a chain reaction, Atlas's entire body draws tighter than a bowstring as he comes, with my name on his lips.

"Fuck, Nora…" Atlas steps back and I turn my head, spitting his come out onto the shower floor, where it quickly rinses down the drain. "You're perfect, you know that?"

"I'm not." I look up at him, still kneeling. Being on my knees before him no longer feels like a power pose. Now I feel silly and vulnerable, and I hate it.

I hate that I can't just enjoy the afterglow of our time together. But like always, Atlas knows. He turns off the water and scoops me up, cradling me against his chest as if it's as easy as breathing.

"You're perfect *for me.*" He nudges my nose with his own before pressing his lips to mine. The kiss is sweet and chaste—exactly enough to ground me in the here and now. "Never doubt that."

"I promise I'm trying," I whisper, as he sets me down on the bathmat. I immediately nestle my head in the space between his chin and chest, plastering my body to his in search of warmth.

"I know you are, pretty girl." He grabs a towel from the rack and wraps it around my shoulders. "Now wrap those legs around my waist and hang on."

"Huh?" I don't know if the cool air and orgasm fried my brain or what, but what exactly am I hanging on for?

He sends me a wicked grin and once again picks me up like I'm as light as a feather. I do as he asks, gripping his hips with my thighs while clasping my hands behind his neck as he brings us back into the bedroom.

Anticipation buzzes beneath my skin like an electrical current. For the first time in practically ever, I'm excited—physically and mentally—for what's to come. Because if there's one thing I know with certainty, it's that Atlas's touch will always deliver pleasure, never pain.

Once we cross the threshold, he lowers me back down to my feet. "If you don't want this to go any farther, it won't. Just say the word."

This man, this gentle giant of mine. He's giving me an out, but there's no way in hell I'm taking it.

"I do," I whisper, my heart pounding like a jackhammer as I glance up at him from beneath my lashes.

THIRTY-THREE
Atlas

I do.

I nearly groan at the sound of those sweet words coming out of Nora's even sweeter mouth. Swear to God, one day—and hopefully soon—she'll say those exact words to me with my ring on her finger.

"Did you hear me?" Nora pops up onto her toes and presses her lips to mine. "I said I do…"

"You do what?" I ask, grinning down at Nora. *Goddamn, she's beautiful.*

"I do want this to go farther," she whispers, her soft voice going straight to my dick.

"How far?" I demand, stepping into her space and dragging my hand over her stomach, loving the curve of it and how it fills my palm.

Her tongue darts out to wet her lips as she places her small hands on my stomach, causing my ab muscles to contract, before sliding them up to my chest, pressing one hand directly over my heart.

"I..." Her words dry up as doubt clouds her features. "Um..."

But I just wait her out, knowing she's got this. My girl is strong as fuck, and has come so far in such a small amount of time.

My patience pays off when she speaks. "I want you to make love to me." She hurls the words out and immediately lowers her eyes.

Well, she tries to anyway, but I'm not having any of that.

"Hey," I murmur, catching her chin between my thumb and index finger, gently bringing her focus back to me. "You know I love you, right?"

Her response is immediate. "Yes."

"Good." I lean down and capture her lips in a soft kiss. "And you know I only want to bring you pleasure, right?"

Another immediate yes.

"You're completely in control here. The minute you want things to stop, all you have to do is say the word, and they stop. You know that, right?"

She starts to nod, but then adds a verbal *yes*.

"Good." I press another kiss to her full lips. "Now get your sweet ass on the bed and spread those legs for me."

Nora releases a shuddering breath before turning and crawling into the bed. I watch with rapt attention as she settles herself smack dab in the middle.

Her thighs glisten in the morning light with her arousal, and it takes my all not to pounce on her and bury my face between her legs all over again.

Instead, I fist my cock, giving it a slow tug as I look her up and down. She's exquisite. Fucking perfection. And by some twist of fate, all mine.

A part of me expects her to shy away from my stare, but my girl's feeling bold and instead slides one hand up to cup her breast while moving the other between her legs.

The whole fucking house could collapse around us and I still wouldn't be able to wrench my focus away from her, from the way she's teasing her slit with her index finger.

She plucks at her pebbled nipple and dips the tip of her finger into her dripping core. A growl builds low in my throat at the erotic sight before me. My entire body's burning up as I watch the show Nora's putting on for me.

A soft whimper falls from her lips as she writhes on the bed before me. "Atlas," she moans. "I need you."

"I know exactly what you need, Pip." I stroke myself twice more before joining her on the bed. "And you better believe I'm gonna give it to you."

"You're sure you're not too sore?" I ask, situating myself between her legs.

Nora huffs out a laugh. "Positive." She arches up off the bed and tunnels her fingers into my hair, pulling my face down to hers.

Our lips meet, and she sighs. "Now please make love to me?" she begs, our lips brushing with every word.

"Fuck, Nora." I lick into her mouth, our tongues tangling as I reach between us, lining my cock up with her entrance.

We both tense as I push into her. *Fucking fuck.* She feels like heaven as she clenches around my cock. *Don't blow before you even get started.*

"You feel so damn good, you know that?" I pepper kisses along her jawline, giving both her and me time to adjust.

Sweat gathers along my hairline as I gaze down at her. *What in the hell have I ever done in my life to deserve the love of this woman?* "You know why that is—why you feel like heaven?" I ask, my arms shaking as I force myself to remain still.

She shakes her head, her eyes never leaving mine.

"Because." I drag my teeth over my lower lip as I cradle her cheek with one hand. "You were made for me, Pip."

Her eyes fill with tears, and I curse myself for making things too intense. *Dammit.* "Hey, no, don't cry," I plead. "It's okay, we can stop, Nora. Just breathe."

I shift my hips back, trying to give her some space, but Nora locks her legs around my waist, holding me in place.

"No, wait!" She sniffles and shoots me a watery smile. "These are the good kind of tears. Happy ones."

I arch my brow.

"I promise I want this," she whispers, twining her arms around my neck. "I promise I want *you.* I love you."

"I love you, too, so goddamn much." I sink fully back into her, and I swear, my soul leaves my body with how tight and hot she is around me. But, still, I have to know... "You're sure you want this?"

"So much." She drags her fingers through my hair. "Now, move, *please?*"

It might just be me, but I swear my girl sounds a little frustrated—and I can't even lie—I love it.

Smirking, I inch back ever so slightly before snapping my hips forward, fucking into her with shallow thrusts.

"Atlas," she whines my name.

"Feels so good. Gotta go slow, Pip. Your pussy's wrapped around me like a vise grip."

"Is that a bad thing?" She trails her fingers from my nape and over my shoulders.

"Fuck no. Just don't wanna come before I get you off."

Despite the crimson glow infusing her cheeks, Nora licks her lips and gives voice to what she needs—*what we need*. "I'm so close. I... faster, p-please?"

Every molecule of my being wants to pound into her, but I hold back. She already admitted to being sore, and the last thing I want is to hurt her. *Fuck. Talk about a rock and a hard place.*

"I'm new to all of this, but I know my body, Atlas."

"I know you do, Pip," I reply through gritted teeth.

Nora pulls my face down to hers. "Then trust me to know what I need." She seals her lips to mine, darting her tongue into my mouth for a taste.

And that's all it takes for my control to snap.

Each thrust, every creak of the bedframe, spurs my need, giving fuel to the inferno burning between us. God, this fucking woman...

"Atlas, I—I'm almost there."

Covering her hand with mine, I guide it between her legs. "Touch yourself, Pip. Help me get you there."

She hesitates for only a moment before following my command.

I push myself up, bracing my hands on either side of her head, my eyes zeroed in on her as she begins to circle her clit with her middle finger.

"Fuck!" I spit the word as we both watch where our bodies merge together.

"Oh, God, Atlas, I'm—" And just like that, she shoots off like a rocket, clenching around me, engulfing my cock with white-hot pleasure.

"Ah, Pip." I thrust into her heat a few more times, my gaze bouncing from where we're joined to her pretty hazel eyes as I come.

Nora melts into the mattress, gasping for breath as I pull out of her. "That was…"

"Amazing," I finish for her. "You're amazing. How do you feel?"

She smiles up at me, trailing her fingertips over my jawline. "Like this is too good to be true. I've never felt better, more loved or cherished, than I do in your arms." She swallows hard. "I love you, so much."

"I love you, too, Pip." I roll off of her, my body already mourning the loss of hers. But this nursery won't set itself up, and the jellybean will be here sooner rather than later. "Ready to shop?"

She laughs. "I'm pretty sure I need another shower after that. And food."

DIARY ENTRY, PRESENT DAY

Dear Diary,

In true Atlas fashion, he went all-out on the nursery. And in true Ellis fashion, he insisted on tagging along. For muscle, he said. As if Atlas doesn't have enough. Then again, I have none, so I'm certainly not complaining.

We hit up the hardware store and got paint-the prettiest shade of pale, barely there blue. Then we grabbed lumber so Atlas could build a crib and shelves to store all of the so-called essentials. He's. Building. Them. Like, by hand.

I even let him talk me into going online and registering for things. At this point, I'm treating it as more of a personal shopping list, because let's be real, other than Atlas and Ellis, who's going to buy anything from it?

Speaking of buying things, Ellis mentioned he's on foot patrol at the Lake Fortune Fall Festival tomorrow until two and said we should meet up with him there after to do a little more shopping. I think they like shopping more than I do. One too many episodes of Gossip Girl, if you ask me.

Either way, I'm ridiculously excited to go. Dad and I used to go every year up until he died. Five years may not seem like that long, but it feels like a lifetime.

Anyway, that's all for now.

Stupidly happy, Nora

THIRTY-FOUR
Atlas

"Pip?" Atlas calls from the front of the house, the sound of the front door closing echoes behind him.

"Back here," I call back, my eyes glued to the space we've designated for our jellybean.

Atlas and I decided that since we're in the primary bedroom, we'd section off the little sitting area for our guy. He even went ahead and painted the walls in his space last night and I can't stop staring at it.

The space still smells slightly of wet paint, but the color is perfect. I can see it all so clearly—his crib will go right beneath the window, with floating shelves on the wall above it, and a rocking chair off to the side in the corner.

I can see myself rocking him and feeding him in the middle of the night.

It's small—no, that's not right—it's cozy and perfect and keeps him close to me, which is exactly where I want him.

I keep picturing white fluffy clouds painted over the blue on the walls—a nod to Atlas's mom, who loved the sky, thick white curtains over the window to filter the light, and a whole shelf of sweet little books for us to read to him as he grows.

"There you are," he murmurs, stepping up behind me, lifting my hair off my neck and pressing his lips to the sensitive skin there. "You about ready to go?"

"Just gotta put my boots on."

"And your coat." He pins me with a look, but I can't help but give him a little sass.

"It's not that cold." I wrinkle my nose as I plop down onto the bed to slip on my boots.

He opens his mouth, undoubtedly to argue his point further, but I beat him to it.

"But sure, I'll bring it. Just know if I get hot, you're carrying it."

"Pip, I'll carry *you* if need be." He kneels in front of me and helps me into my boots. "Now c'mon. Ellis has texted me like six times."

A small laugh escapes me as I force myself back up to my feet to grab my jacket. "I like him. He makes me feel less needy."

Atlas grins, and I swear, the sight of it alone sends a rush of warmth through me. "Yeah, yeah." His brows furrow. "He mentioned inviting Scarlet, too. You cool with that?"

"Yeah, why wouldn't I be?" Sure, our initial meeting was beyond uncomfortable, but the more time I spend around her, the more I like her. And I'm pretty positive she likes me, too.

"Just making sure." He leans down and captures my lips in a

kiss that has my toes curling in my boots. "Now let's go."

Like the gentleman he is, Atlas has the truck running so it's nice and toasty inside. The fall chill is setting in fast, but I think I'd rather be big and pregnant when it's cool outside versus when it's hot, so I have no complaints.

"You ready to pumpkin chuck?" Atlas asks as we pass through the gates marking off the festival grounds.

I link my arm with his, holding him as close as possible while also trying my best to keep my anxiety at bay. Logically, I know I'm safe with Atlas, but being around *this* many people out in the open is... *unnerving*.

I refuse to let my trauma ruin our day out together though. And so, with a wobbly smile, I reply, "I'm ready to *watch* you do it. What I'm excited for is donuts and cider."

He clutches at his heart with his free hand, kindly not remarking on the mini freakout I know he's aware I'm having. The man is more tuned into me and my emotions than I am sometimes. "Donuts? You like the donuts? What about the funnel cake?"

I shake my head. "Nope. My dad and I used to come every year, and the donuts were always our favorite part. Cinnamon sugar is superior to powdered sugar. It's just science."

"She's right, you know," a deep, masculine voice says out of nowhere, sending me into a blind panic.

My heart gallops in my chest, thundering in my ears louder than an entire herd of wild horses as my head swivels side-to-side, looking for anything out of place.

But there's nothing. Just normal people strolling about, not paying me a lick of attention.

"It's just me, Nora," Ellis says, his hands out in front of him as he slowly moves closer.

Of course, it's just Ellis. Safe, trusty Ellis, who we planned to meet in this very spot.

I turn into Atlas, burying my face in his chest as a generous dose of mortification and shame burns my cheeks. If not for his bulk supporting me, I'm not sure I'd be able to stand.

"I'm sorry," I whisper.

"Nothing to be sorry about, Pip," Atlas says, kissing the top of my head. "This jackass knows better than to sneak up on you."

"Sneak?" Ellis raises a brow. "I did *not* sneak up on anyone. Hell, I was waving my arms like a damn car dealership inflatable."

The visual is enough to put a small smile on my face. "Gonna put a freaking bell around your neck," I mutter, spinning to face him.

"Like a cat?" He tips his head to the side. "Kinky. I like it."

"What? No!" I giggle. "Well, kind of. But just so I can hear you. It's unnatural for someone of your size to be so stealthy."

He rolls his eyes before dropping down to his knees. "From here on out, I will loudly announce my arrival. Please forgive me, Nora."

The smile on his face tells me he's kidding, but oh my God, my embarrassment is real. "Get up! Get up right now and I'll forgive you—this time." I point my finger at him in faux warning. "But only because you agree with me about the donuts."

"Noted." His eyes crinkle in the corners as he looks between Atlas and me.

"You're really okay, Pip?" he asks, looking down at me with

the most tender look.

"Promise." He stares at me for a beat before nodding and turning his focus to Ellis.

"Where's Scar?"

"I was just about to ask if either of you have seen the she-devil."

"Don't call her that!" I scold, which only serves to make both of them laugh.

"I love it when you give us sass, Pip," Atlas murmurs, wrapping both of his arms around me so he can rest his chin on the top of my head. "I love the little spitfire you're turning into. Want more of it."

"Y'all gonna kiss?" Ellis asks, wagging his brows, erasing any lingering tension from my episode. "Lemme know first so I can look away. Gotta protect my innocence, ya know?"

I huff out a small laugh while Atlas only glares.

"Geez, tough crowd." He checks his watch. "Seriously, where is she? I told her to meet us by the gate ten minutes ago."

"You weren't even here ten minutes ago," Atlas says.

Ellis shrugs, his face looking like he sucked on a lemon. "When is she ever on time? I should've told her twenty minutes early."

I sigh and snuggle deeper into Atlas's embrace, content to leave the conversation to them while we wait for Scarlet to join us.

Which she does, after about ten more minutes.

"Sorry! Had to stop and get gas. And coffee." She thrusts her paper cup in the air toward us.

"Didn't you learn as a kid that if you're going to bring something, you need to bring enough for the class?" Ellis crosses his arms, glowering at Scarlet.

"Oh, get over yourself, you big baby." She cradles the cup to her chest before raising it to her mouth for a long sip. "So good."

Ellis strikes like a cobra, snatching it from her and stealing a sip for himself, only to promptly spit the coffee out. "The fuck is this? Warmed ice cream?"

Atlas and I both chuckle under our breath as Scarlet throws her arms out to either side. "First of all, you don't get to steal my drink and then complain about not liking it. So sorry I don't drink bitter bean juice like you. I prefer my coffee on the sweet side."

He spits again and then wipes his mouth with the back of his hand. "This coffee is the only thing sweet about you."

"Whatever you say, Officer Jackass." She turns to where Atlas and I are standing. "Hey there, you two. What are we doing first?"

"Hi," I murmur, turning my gaze toward Atlas. "I-I was thinking donuts and cider, but you already have coffee, so we can totally do—"

Scarlet grins. "A donut sounds perfect. Let's go."

"Am I the only one who prefers the funnel cake?" Atlas sputters.

All three of us answer in tandem. "Yes."

As we walk toward the food area, Scarlet sidles up next to me. "How do you deal with all of this testosterone twenty-four-seven?"

Atlas grunts his displeasure while I merely shrug. "It doesn't bother me."

"That's because you're a saint, clearly."

"It's not like I know any differently." It pains me to admit that out loud to her, but it's true. I kind of like being around Atlas and Ellis all the time though. Knowing they're always near offers me more than a sense of security—which I crave—but their presence also offers me companionship. It means I'm no longer alone.

Scarlet gasps and jerks to a halt directly in front of us. "Oh my God, you don't, do you!" She claps her hands together in a way that has trepidation slithering through me. "I know just the thing you need."

"Scarlet, no..." Atlas hedges, his discomfort evident by his now rigid posture.

"Yes!" She nods her head, even as he shakes his.

"I don't know what's about to come out of your mouth, but I already know I'm not gonna like it."

His edginess is causing my unease to coil around my heart, tightening and squeezing to the point where drawing in a full breath is impossible.

"Atlas," I whisper, desperate to ease the tension settling over our little group.

Up ahead, Ellis finally notices we're no longer trailing behind him. Turning back, he jogs over to join us. "What are y'all doing? I turned around and *poof*, y'all were gone."

"Scarlet here's about to—"

"I can speak for myself, Atlas Wallace." She cuts her eyes at him in a frosty glare before turning back to me. "I was about to suggest a girls' day for Nora and me."

"No." Atlas's growled monosyllabic reply is so cold, I can't help but shiver.

Atlas notices, too. Of course he does, and he immediately presses his chest to my back and wraps his arms around me, cocooning me in his warmth.

Unfortunately, this isn't the kind of cold body heat can help.

"Please don't fight," I whisper, but none of them seem to hear me.

"It's not happening, Scarlet." Atlas's tone is resolute—as if his say is final.

Usually, I don't mind him taking charge, but much like at breakfast the other morning, the conversation is merely *about* me. Then again, it would include me, if I'd just speak up.

"Your girlfriend can speak for herself, too." Scarlet's tone matches Atlas's as she crosses her arms over her chest.

My stomach churns as I try to work up the nerve to intervene. I don't want them to fight—especially not because of me.

Luckily, Scarlet's words seem to knock some sense into Atlas.

"Fuck, Pip," he murmurs, twirling me around to face him. "I'm sorry. Scarlet's right. You can think and speak for yourself. The idea of you being out somewhere in public without me has me feeling some kind of way. But that's on me. That's my shit to own, not yours. So, if you want to go, I'll support that decision."

"You mean that?" I blink up at him, wondering how it's possible for him to be real.

"Yeah, I mean it." He inhales deeply before adding, "I'll support you in anything you want to do. But be patient with me, too, Pip. Knowing he's still out there somewhere makes me want to never let you leave my side."

The thought of Rand has my spine snapping straight as paranoia and fear go to war inside of me. A small part of me wants to burrow into Atlas's side and never leave. After all, he is my safe space. But a larger part of me knows that if I ever want to truly be free from him, I have to be strong... brave.

I take a few deep breaths, counting down slowly from five in my head, before forcing my muscles to unclench. "I-I think a girls' day sounds fun. I... I've never really done that before."

I can tell Scarlet wants to comment on that, but Ellis

intervenes before she can.

"Rude." He looks me up and down. "We've had many a girls' day, Nora."

Just like that, the tension breaks and a laugh slips past my lips. "I'm not sure binge-watching girly shows with you counts, but..."

"It so does," he insists.

But Scarlet's not having it. "It absolutely does not. I'll get your number from Atlas, and we can set something up."

Atlas rolls his eyes and leans down to whisper in my ear. "You sure you don't wanna ditch these two and just do us?"

"I'm sure." I pop up onto my toes and press a quick kiss to his lips.

"If you're really sure..."

"I am."

THIRTY-FIVE

Nora

"How does it feel to be off your leash?" Scarlet asks.

I raise my brows and shoot her an unimpressed glare. "Really?"

She sighs. "Yeah, that was bitchy. Sorry. Sometimes my brain to mouth filter doesn't work."

"Sometimes?"

She flicks on her blinker and shrugs. "Fine, most of the time."

"Sooo, what exactly are we doing?" I speak slowly, trying my hardest to keep my voice neutral—to not let my fear bleed through. When we initially made our plans, I was excited. But in the two weeks that have passed since, my nerves have gotten the better of me, and now I'm an anxious mess.

I'm safe with Scarlet. Atlas wouldn't have agreed to this otherwise. But it's hard to get my brain on the same page, especially when this is my first outing without him at my side.

Maggie says this is a good first step to regaining my independence though, so I've just gotta power through it. Even if it makes my skin crawl.

"I'm guessing you don't like surprises, huh?" Scarlet glances at me and then back to the road.

"You could say that," I reply, knowing she doesn't really mean anything by it. Scarlet's just... *Scarlet*. She's brash and outspoken and definitely doesn't think before she speaks. But in the grand scheme of things, she's harmless. *A total b-word, but harmless.*

"Okay, fine, I'll tell you." She pauses, giving my brain ample time to come up with every possible worst-case scenario. "We're starting at the salon; I'm guessing it's been a long time since you've had a haircut. Then we're getting mani-pedis, followed by lunch. You don't have any food allergies, right?"

"Nope, none."

"Great. I figured we could go to The Smoke Shack. It's nothing fancy, but their ribs are to die for."

"If you say so," I murmur, drumming my fingertips against my thighs as I work through one of Maggie's many exercises to keep me calm.

I screw my eyes shut and start counting. *Inhale... one... exhale. Inhale... two... exhale.* By the time I make it to ten, my heart rate is almost normal and my hands are steady, well steady-ish, anyway.

"So, how long has it been?" she asks, parking in front of what looks like some kind of fancy spa that's way outside of my budget.

Well, my pre-Atlas budget. The man spares no expense, regardless of how awkward it makes me feel. He's big on taking care of what's his—and even though it's a little caveman of him, it also feels kind of good to be... taken care of.

"Um..." I gnaw on my bottom lip as I run the numbers. "I think my last real haircut was when I was fifteen or sixteen. Before Mom got really sick."

I dare a glance toward Scarlet, expecting to see pity shining in her gaze. But I don't. Instead, I see her eyes wide and her lips curled in a look of mild horror. "Holy. Shit. Nora. Your split ends probably have split ends."

Something about her unexpected shock sends me into a fit of laughter. What utterly different lives we've led. "Haircuts are inconsequential when you're trying to survive."

She scoffs and throws open her door. "Okay, Daisy-Downer. Let's go get you checked in."

With only a little reluctance, I follow after her.

The inside of the salon is every bit as nice as the outside. Nicer even—it's all gleaming white marble mixed with ashy woods and matte gold finishes; it's a modern marvel unlike anything I've ever seen.

"Welcome to Bliss," a melodic voice says, drawing my attention to the front desk. The woman seated behind it is the living embodiment of ethereal grace, with her pale skin, blood-red lips, and nearly white hair. "How can we make you feel beautiful today?"

I shoot Scarlet an apprehensive look, because I don't have a clue. Luckily, she takes the lead.

"I have a ten o'clock with Rochelle and Nora here is booked for the same time with Mira."

"Great, let me get you both checked in." She clicks around on the computer for a few seconds. "Oh, and I see you're both booked for nails after. Perf. Your stylists should be ready shortly. In the meantime, would either of you like anything to drink while you wait?"

I shake my head no, right as Scarlet says, "A mimosa would be great." She tips her head toward me. "And my friend here will take a water."

It's stupid, so absurdly stupid, but something inside me warms at hearing her call me her friend.

For years, my entire world was narrowed to only one person… no, not a person; a monster. But now, I have three people in my life that I care about and that care about me. Four, really, if I count my jellybean. Although, if I'm being honest, the latter is the most important, because this baby gave me the push I needed to escape the hell I had all but resigned myself to.

My son may have been conceived through horrific circumstances, but he… he saved me, too.

"Do you know how you want it cut?" Scarlet asks, drawing me out of my thoughts.

"Um." I flex my fingers in my lap. "What do you think?"

Scarlet regards me carefully. "Well, I think you're so used to deferring to other people that you have no idea what you want."

I swallow roughly as tears burn the back of my eyes. *Do not cry, do not cry, do not cry.* I repeat the words like a mantra to myself, over and over. Scarlet clearly already thinks I'm pathetic—the last thing I need to do is break down in the middle of this fancy spa and prove her right.

But my best efforts aren't enough and a sniffle breaks free, alerting Scarlet to my distress.

"Hey, Nora, whoa. Clearly that came out wrong." She reaches for me and, instinctively, I flinch away from her touch. "Jesus Christ, I'm fucking this up left and right. Atlas is never going to let me take you anywhere ever again at this rate."

"I'm sorry," I whisper.

"No, don't be. I guess decision making isn't something you're used to anymore. But, babe, it's time to reclaim that shit. You are free. You are your own boss. You're a fucking queen. Own that shit."

"I know. Kind of. At least, I want to... you know... own my shit." I whisper the last word, my cheeks burning. "But I wouldn't be opposed to some guidance."

Scarlet rubs her hands together in a way that should probably worry me. "Well, I'd say you could stand to lose like five or so inches. Your hair is long and will still be long."

I run my fingers through the ends. She's right. My hair is long, and I have absolutely no idea how to style it. Mama bought me a flat iron when I was in middle school, but outside of that, I'm clueless.

"Okay, that sounds good."

"How do you feel about color?"

My *no* is both instant and emphatic. "My dad... his hair was the same color as mine. It's probably stupid, but it's all I have left of him now."

"No color, got it." She claps her hands together. "A gloss then. It will just make it, like, really shiny."

Before I can reply, two women step into the waiting room. "Scarlet, Nora, we're ready for y'all."

I once again let Scarlet take the lead as she warmly greets both women, before relaying to one of them what I want. *Here's to hoping she knows her stuff...*

Ninety minutes later, I'm a well-styled puddle of goo. Seriously, I'm pretty sure my stylist has magic fingers or something.

"Wow," I whisper, for probably the hundredth time as I run my fingers through my perfectly waved hair. It's seriously perfect. Bouncy and healthy and shiny and... yeah, perfect.

"If you liked that, you'll love a pedicure," Scarlet says, grinning at me. "Now let's go pick our colors."

"What are you getting?" I ask, my heart already racing at the multitude of choices laid before me, in neat and tidy rainbow order. Bottle after bottle, as far as the eye can see, and I'm somehow supposed to narrow it down to one.

"Something bright and bold." She taps her index finger against her bottom lip. "Oh, this one!" She grabs a polish that I can only describe as neon red. It's pretty, if a little loud. *Perfect for Scarlet.*

"Hmm." I scan the wall until the colors all start to blend together before finally settling on a soft pearlescent blue. It's understated but pretty. Safe, but with a little sparkle, too.

"Oh, that's cute," Scarlet murmurs as she guides me over to the pedicure chairs. "Have you ever done this before?"

I smile, as a bittersweet warmth fills my chest. "A few times with my mom before..." I swallow roughly but push through. The past is just that, and I have to learn to be able to talk about it. I have to own my trauma so it doesn't own me. "Before she met R-Rand." I hate the way I struggle to say his name, like it somehow will summon him to me.

When I read Harry Potter as a kid, I always thought it was so stupid how everyone was scared to say Voldemort›s name. But now, I get it. There is a power in a name, and whether I like it or not, his still holds power over me.

But the stronger I grow, the weaker his hold on me becomes, and one day, he'll be nothing more than a bad memory. *A really freaking awful memory.*

"How in the hell did Atlas come from a man like that?" Scarlet says, snapping me back into the present.

"I ask myself that all the time. He's such a good man, and his dad is, well, evil."

"It was really bad?" she asks, her voice barely above a whisper. "I mean, I saw how you looked, you know, but like..."

I sigh as a maelstrom of emotions race through me, before offering her a wobbly smile so she knows I'm not mad. After all, it's human nature to be curious, even when it's morbid. Or maybe especially when.

"Yeah, it was bad. Really bad." So bad I'm not sure how to discuss it conversationally while sitting in a massage chair with my feet in warm, bubbling water. "I still, um, have nightmares. But Atlas, he helps." I lower my eyes to my lap in an effort to hide my flaming cheeks—I bet they're just about the same color as the nail polish she picked. I mean, I'm talking to her about her ex, who I'm currently dating. Talk about awkward. Then again, nothing about my life has been very orthodox, so why start now?

"It's fine, you know," she says, reaching over and laying her hand over the top of mine. By some miracle, instead of flinching, I find comfort in her touch.

"What is?"

"You and Atlas." She flits her eyes toward the ceiling and laughs under her breath before focusing back on me. "Don't get me wrong, I was mad at first, but real talk, he and I weren't all that serious, and the two of you are clearly meant to be together. I may be a bitch, but I'm not a *raging* bitch. I›d never stand in the way of true love."

"True love?" Butterflies take flight within me, their wings flapping wildly in my belly. "You really think so?"

"Girl." Scarlet draws out the word. "That man would burn the whole world to the ground to save you. So, yeah, true love."

She sounds almost wistful as she says it, and I can't help but wonder if she's ever been in love. But before I can ask, my nail technician drops down onto the stool in front of me, effectively stealing all of my attention.

"Are you still cool with The Smoke Shack for lunch?" Scarlet asks once we're back in her car. "It's a little out of the way, so if you're hungry, we can go somewhere closer."

I shrug. "I'm good with anything." It's not like I'm going to make a fuss when she's doing all of this for me. As sad as it sounds, I'm just happy to be along for the ride.

"Okay then, buckle up and let's go."

Scarlet cranks the radio and belts the lyrics at the top of her lungs, while I stare at her in wonder. How she manages to keep us on the road while singing and dancing like she's on stage is beyond me. I still hate driving—and I still suck at it, too.

"So, what gives?" she asks, when she mimes holding the mic my way and I shake my head. "Are you shy, or just a shower singer?"

"I don't... I don't know any of these." I slide my hands under my thighs to keep from fidgeting.

"Like, none of them?" Her eyes bug and her glossy lips make a perfect 'O.' Scarlet quickly schools her features, but I saw all I needed to—this is just one more way I'm an oddball.

For a split second, I worry she's going to laugh at me, but instead, she turns it into a game, where she plays a song and asks if I know it or not. I do pretty good with the older pop, awful with any and everything new, and absolutely kill it with the older rock my dad always listened to.

"Well, that was fun, but are you ready for the best bar-b-que of your life?" Scarlet asks as she whips the car into a parking space, sending gravel dust into the air all around us.

"I guess." My heart is still thumping hard against my breast-bone. Where Atlas is safe and steady, Scarlet drives like a mad-woman. Polar opposites.

"Oh, ye of little faith." She cuts the engine. "You'll see. C'mon."

I unbuckle my seat belt and open my door, only to instantly be surrounded by the mouthwatering aroma of smoked meats.

"Look at you." She laughs, nudging me with her elbow. "We're not even through the door and your mouth's watering."

I don't bother replying, because she's right. It smells amazing, like when I was little and my dad would barbecue for Labor Day. If it tastes even half as good as it smells, this might just become my newest pregnancy craving.

The outside of the building—smell notwithstanding—is nondescript, but the inside is like stepping back in time. String lights dangle overhead and vintage mementos and memorabilia line the wide-plank wooden walls. None of the tables and chairs match, but somehow, it works.

"Do you trust me?" Scarlet asks, quirking a brow.

"Um." Talk about a loaded question, but strangely enough... "Yes, I do." Saying the words feels as weird as thinking them, but it feels good, too.

"'Kay, great. Go make us drinks, Diet Coke for me, and then grab us a table while I order."

God, she's bossy. But it works for me; it took me a small eternity to choose a nail polish, so I can only imagine how long it'd take me to navigate the menu and make a decision. The thing is written on a giant chalkboard that takes up almost an entire wall.

After making our drinks and finding us a table near the door, I slide my phone out of my purse and check my notifications. Two texts from Atlas.

Atlas
You having fun, Pip?

Atlas
I told myself I'd let you enjoy your day and not hover and I meant it, but damn, I miss you. Check in with me, yeah? Love you.

My cheeks warm and something low in my belly flutters as I read his messages. He's totally overbearing and protective and I kind of love it.

I snap a pic of my nails and add it to our text thread.

Me
Surprisingly, I *AM* having fun.
We're getting lunch now. Love you, too.

Atlas
Pretty, Pip. Let me guess... ribs?

> **Me**
> How did you know?

> **Atlas**
> Scarlet is nothing if not predictable.

> **Me**
> That's not the word I'd use…

A thread of discomfort tries to weave its way through me, but I promptly shake it off. Atlas has proved over and over just how dedicated he is to not only me, but my—*our*—baby, too.

> **Atlas**
> Yeah, LOL. I can think of a few others. You ever watched The Sound of Music as a kid?

Where in the heck is he going with this?

> **Me**
> Yeah… My mom loved that movie.

> **Atlas**
> That one song the nuns all sing about the nanny…

"What's so funny?" Scarlet asks, placing an overflowing tray down on the table between us.

"Nothing!" I quickly text Atlas back, telling him our food is here. "There's no way we can eat all of this."

"Speak for yourself," Scarlet scoffs before slapping a paper plate down in front of me. "I got all of my favorites, plus some extra, that way we can figure out what you like."

It's totally overkill, but I'm also touched. From start to finish, she's put so much thought into our day out together. If this is what it's like having a friend, then I'm so totally down.

"You said the ribs, right?" I ask, grabbing a few for my plate.

"Yup. And the potato salad is insane."

We both fill our plates with a little bit of everything. My mouth waters as I taste my first bite of the fall-off-the-bone ribs. I can't help the happy little moan that slips past my lips. This is definitely my new pregnancy craving. I can feel it.

Scarlet chuckles. "Told you."

I smile at her, a sense of contentment like I've never known before washes over me. "Yup. One hundred percent right—but don't let it go to your head."

She taps her temple twice. "Too late."

A bubbling laugh escapes me, which makes Scarlet giggle, and before I know it, we're both cackling like hyenas, with barbecue sauce all over our faces.

I know I'm an absolute mess, but I can't find it in me to care. *Because you're happy,* a little voice in the back of my mind whispers, causing me to freeze.

"You good?" Scarlet asks.

"Yeah," I murmur. "I really, really am." I mean it, too. It's like everything is finally falling into place. Like my life is finally *mine.* It's a rush, and a little nerve-racking, but I love it and I can't wait to see what else the future has in store for me.

"Okay, wow." Scarlet wipes her mouth and then leans back against her side of the booth. "Are you as stuffed as I am?"

I pat my rounded belly. "More."

She laughs before leaning forward and passing me a napkin. "Wipe your face up and let's take a selfie before we head out."

I clean off my face and then we lean in together over the table, crushing our cheeks together for a few silly shots.

"Send those to me while I throw our trash away?" I ask, gathering everything and stacking it back on the tray.

"You got it."

THIRTY-SIX
Nora

"Oh, shit." Scarlet turns to me with wide eyes. "I think I left my phone on the table."

I glance from her toward the door and back again. "Okay…"

"Let me run and grab it and then we can head home. Will you—"

I already know what she's asking. *Will I be okay?* The honest answer is I don>t know, but I want to be. No, I need to be. *I have to be.*

"Yeah." I lick my lips and then force a smile. "Go grab it. I'll be fine."

I want so badly to be normal, and normal girls can wait alone in a car.

"Okay, be right back." She spares me a long glance before hopping out and dashing back into the restaurant.

It probably makes me pathetic, but I keep my back ramrod straight and my eyes laser-focused on Scarlet as she dashes toward the building, not blinking, barely even moving besides the slight trembling of my hands, until she's out of sight.

It's okay. I'm okay. Everything's okay.

I repeat the words over and over again, my fingers idly fidgeting with the compass charm of my necklace, all the while refusing to take my eyes off the door. I want to know the second she's on her way back to me.

It's deathly quiet in the car. So quiet, it amplifies the sound of my accelerated breathing—or maybe it's the sound of my thundering heart.

A car door slams somewhere in the parking lot, and I flinch.

"Get a grip," I mutter, curling both of my hands into white-knuckle fists. It feels like she's been gone for hours, when in reality, it's only been minutes. But it's fine. I'm fine. "Everything is f—"

Before I can finish the word, the passenger door flies open, bringing me face-to-face with my worst nightmare.

I try to scream for help, but he slaps his meaty hand over my mouth, digging his fingers in hard on either side of my jaw.

"I've got you now, you little bitch," he snarls, and then everything goes black.

THIRTY-SIX
RAND

Little bitch.

Stupid little bitch.

Predictable stupid little bitch.

She thought she was safe. That she was free of me. How could she be when she's mine? *My* property. *My* stupid little bitch, carrying *my* baby. But the apple didn't fall far from the tree, and she fell for the illusion of security, just like her mother.

Weak-minded women with soft hearts are only good for one thing, and since Nora's forgotten, I'll gladly remind her exactly what that is. And I'm going to make it hurt.

How dare she defy me... *leave me?* After I took her and her mother in, gave them a roof over their heads and food in their bellies, and this is the thanks I get? I think the fuck not. I'm practically a saint for putting up with her—especially after Grace kicked it. The whining and the crying and the pleading, when all she had to do was submit...

So, I let her escape, and I watched. I waited. I plotted and I planned.

I'll admit, her running to Atlas, my own flesh and blood, was a bit of a surprise. But in a way, it helped me find her. He made her feel safe, undoubtedly with promises of love and protection, but she's mine. Thankfully, Atlas has always been too trusting for his own good, and thanks to his own stupidity, she'll soon be back where she belongs—with me.

If she wants to play house, fine—but we'll do it *my* way. I won't be as lenient with this kid like I was with Atlas. He's useless. Weak. But I'll make sure this one's strong, make sure this one takes after me. Teach 'em everything I know. This one will be my protégé, if you will.

I keep my eyes on the back of their car, waiting for the brunette driving to put it into gear. I've waited far too long for this moment to let anything fuck it up.

The brunette she's with is a pretty little bitch. It's a shame she's the one standing between me and my prize, otherwise, she'd potentially be worth adding to my collection. At the very least, I'll take a moment to savor the way she bleeds when I put a bullet through her skull.

But then, she flings open the driver's side door and exits the vehicle, leaving Nora all alone and at my mercy—something I'm all out of where she's concerned.

Immediately, I'm out of my truck and ripping open the passenger side door of the little coupe.

Nora tries to scream for help, but I crush her mouth shut, silencing her cries.

"I've got you now, you little bitch," I growl, reveling in the way her eyes widen with fear. There's something so delicious about her terror. All of the ones before her pale in comparison.

The way her cheeks burn with the perfect mixture of shame and fear. The way she shakes and cries and begs, so beautifully. It could sustain me for days. Years, even. My perfect little pet.

She jerks against my hold, but she's no match for me, and with one solid hit to her temple, she's out cold.

THIRTY-SEVEN
Atlas

"You got a minute?" Ellis asks, dropping down onto the barstool next to me.

"What's up?" I'm already on edge with Nora being gone, and something about his tone tells me that whatever he's about to say isn't going to help.

"I've just been thinking about your dad…"

"What about him?" I ask, hating the way the mere mention of the asshole has tension creeping up my back and into my shoulders.

"His safe, your mom, and all that bullshit." Ellis drums his fingers against the countertop. "I don't really know how to say this, so I'm just gonna spit it out."

I raise my brows at him in lieu of an actual reply. At this point, I don't trust myself not to be a jackass given the topic at hand.

"I think your dad killed your mom." He swallows roughly. "And Nora's mom. And possibly many others."

"Like he's a... serial killer or some shit?" I ask, bewildered but also not. I've known for a long fucking time that my dad was a piece of shit, and deep down, a little part of me always thought he killed my mom, but hearing someone else confirm these thoughts is something else entirely.

"Exactly like that," Ellis says, nodding. "Hear me out."

I signal for him to continue—it's not like there's any love lost for my father. If anything, I want to see him pay for all the pain he's inflicted on the woman I love, and if whatever Ellis is about to tell me helps, then I'm all for it, even if it hurts to hear.

"You know that big case we've been working on?" he asks, seemingly shifting gears out of nowhere.

"Yeah..."

"Well, I can't help but wonder if this is all related."

"Related how?"

"Fuck, man." Ellis rubs the back of his neck. "I mean, we both know the death certificates are bullshit. The odds of him losing two wives to the same mystery illness... not buying it. But the paper bag you found full of random shit? Those are trophies, man."

"Trophies... like from..."

"Women he's killed."

"What the fuck?" I hiss the words on a ragged exhale.

"There's more."

"Of course there is."

"The passport—it's not under his name."

"Jesus, this is all so fucked." I pinch the bridge of my nose as a steady throb starts up behind my eyes. "So, what do we do now?"

The thought of him being out there somewhere—that he could still be a threat to Nora—sets my teeth on edge.

"Man, I don't even know," Ellis starts. "I think we need to hand this info over—"

The sound of my phone vibrating on the counter steals my attention. Maybe it's Nora. I've been trying not to blow up her phone checking in, but *fuck,* it's hard.

I lunge for my phone, causing Ellis to laugh as he mimes cracking a whip. Which is beyond accurate; my Pip has me wrapped around her little finger and then some.

But it's not Nora. It's Scarlet, which immediately sets off warning bells. Why in the hell is she calling me instead of Nora?

"Hel-"

"She's gone!" she screams. "Atlas, I don't know where she is."

My heart smashes into my ribs, slamming against the bone cage as if it's trying to break free. "What do you mean *gone*?" I ask, my voice shaking, right along with the rest of me.

"Put it on speaker," Ellis murmurs.

I tap the button and then lay my phone on the counter. Scarlet's incoherent nonsense immediately fills the space, as she tries to tell me where my girl is.

"Shut up, take a breath, and then explain to me how you lost her," I growl. This, right here, is my literal worst nightmare come to life. I vowed to protect Nora, and now she's God knows where. A million scenarios all flit through my mind, each one more horrific than the last.

The sound of Scarlet's ragged inhale fills the room, wrapping itself around me, squeezing all of the air out of my body, leaving only rage in its wake.

"I-I left my phone in The Smoke Shack and ran back in to get it, and when I came b-back, she was..." A sob rips out of her that sounds nearly as broken as I feel.

"She was what?" I demand, even though I already know what she's going to say.

"She was gone."

My heart catapults itself into my throat as I flex my fingers into white-knuckle fists to keep from smashing things.

Luckily, Ellis is able to keep a cool head and slips right into cop mode.

"Scarlet, I need you to tell me everything you remember leading up to her going missing, okay? No matter how insignificant it seems."

She sucks in another deep breath and then launches into a recount of their day, from the spa all the way up to lunch.

"I swear I was only gone a couple of minutes. We took a selfie, and I left my phone on the table. She... she said she would be okay and for me to go. And I hurried, I swear to God I did, but when I got back, her door was open and she was just... gone."

Ellis starts to ask her something else, but there's no point—not when I *know*.

"God fucking dammit!" I roar, snatching my phone off the counter. "He has her."

Scarlet whimpers, and Ellis tries to reason with me. "Atlas, you don't know for—"

"The fuck I don't." I open the app I prayed I'd never have to use, watching with bated breath as her location loads. "That piece of shit has my girl at his hunting cabin!" I roar, shoving my phone into his face.

She's at his cabin. The very same one I looked for him at not so long ago. He has her and is doing God knows what to her... to our baby.

A haze of red clouds my vision as anger unlike anything I've ever known pulses through my body like a tsunami headed for shore. "I'm going to fucking kill him," I hiss through gritted teeth as I grab my keys and shove them into my front pocket before grabbing my gun from the safe.

"Slow down, man," Ellis says, stepping into my space

"Move." I clench my jaw so tightly that my molars grind together as I press forward, but he stops me with a palm to my chest, pushing me back.

"Let me call it in, Atlas." His eyes beg me to see reason, but reason went out the window the second Scarlet told me Nora was gone. "Let's do this right."

"He. Has. Her." I shove him back, fully prepared to lay my best friend out on his ass if need be. "Now get the fuck out of my way or—"

"Go." He sighs, stepping back. "But, Atlas, I'm still calling it in."

I toss a hand up over my shoulder in acknowledgment as I race to my truck.

I crank the engine and slip my gun into the center console before tearing down the driveway like the devil himself is after me. But that's not right—it's me who's after the devil, and I'm going to send that miserable son of a bitch back to hell permanently.

I'm coming, Pip...

THIRTY-NINE
Nora

Oh my God, my head. I lift my arm, only to find I can't move it. I try again, jerking harder this time, but it's no use.

Why can't I move my arms?

My breathing grows ragged, each inhale like sucking in needles, as I try to take stock of my body. I'm upright—mostly—on something solid. A chair, maybe, and my arms seem to be bound behind me.

Question after question floods my brain. *Where am I? Why am I restrained? Why does my head feel like someone beat me with a bowling ball? Is my baby okay?*

I wince as I try to open my eyes, but it's no use. Between the ringing in my ears, the excruciating pain radiating from my forehead, the discomfort pulsing through my shoulders, and the bright light overhead, I can't seem to get my bearings.

Think, Nora! I was with Scarlet... hair, nails, barbecue, and—Rand!

Panic unlike anything I've ever felt before flares to life inside of me as reality sinks in, rendering me completely motionless as the memory of Rand taking me flashes behind the back of my eyelids like a highlight reel of horrors.

Just stay still and maybe he won't realize you're awake. I strain to listen out for him, but the only thing I hear is the faint dripping of a faucet.

How did this happen? What do I do? What do I do?

When I finally manage to pry my eyes open, my vision swims. I blink once... twice... three times before the small room I'm in comes into focus. It's sparsely furnished, with no windows that I can see. Most importantly, there's no sign of Rand.

I escaped this hell once already. I can do it again.

Footsteps sound behind me, and my entire body stiffens as I squeeze my eyes shut. Maybe if I'm still enough and quiet enough, he'll leave me be for a little longer.

"Wake up, little bitch," the voice from my nightmares growls moments before ice-cold water sprays me in the face. A scream lodges in my throat as the liquid fills my nose and mouth, making it impossible to breathe, much less speak.

Instinctively, I try to cover my face, but all I manage to do is send myself crashing to the floor. "Stop, please," I whimper, my wet hair clinging to my face.

Please let my son be okay. Please, please, please. I silently pray, my tears mingling with the water droplets already coating my cheeks, as I try my hardest to twist my body in such a way that offers my belly some protection.

"That's right," he snarls, the toes of his worn boots coming into view. "Keep begging. Scream, cry, *plead*, and maybe I'll let you hold the little bastard before I bleed you dry."

I wish I was strong enough not to give in to him, but I do exactly as he says—I scream and I cry, I beg and I plead. The noises spilling out of my mouth are far more animal than human. "Don't you touch my baby!"

"I believe you mean *our* baby." He nudges me gently with his boot before cocking his leg back and delivering a brutal kick to my ribs.

A guttural scream tears past my trembling lips, my eyes involuntarily pinching closed as seemingly endless pain steals the air from my lungs.

"Look at me," Rand demands, dragging his knuckles over my cheek, in a move so mockingly tender it sends shivers down my spine.

I peel my eyes open to find him kneeling before me, his lips curled in a malicious grin as he reaches toward my belly.

I try to stop him, but the only sound that comes out is a rasping, high-pitched wheeze as I struggle to inhale past the agonizing pain in my chest.

Please, please, please.

Tremors rack my body as I flail and kick, desperate to keep his hands away from my stomach but he presses forward completely undeterred.

"Stop fucking moving," he snaps, grabbing me by the hair with one hand, slamming my head into the floor, while cradling my belly with the other.

The juxtaposition between the two points of contact—his punishing grip on my hair and the gentle way he palms my bump—is sickening.

White spots dance in front of my eyes as I try to shrink in on myself and protect my stomach from his wrath.

But there's nowhere to go. There's no reprieve or safety to be found. I can't even escape into the shelter of my mind because all I can think of is protecting my son. I'm stuck. Stuck here in hell, with my own personal monster.

Let us go. Please just let us go.

A soft fluttering in my stomach breaks through the all-encompassing agony, and while I can't be sure, I tell myself it's my jellybean. That he's okay—*that we're both going to be okay.*

"Should've put a chip in you, like a damn dog. Wouldn't've had to wait so long to get you back," he mutters to himself. "But I've got you now, and I plan to have some fun before I... dispose of you." His thin lips curl into a grotesque mockery of a smile as he leans down further into my face.

He slides his hand over my protruding belly, up between the valley of my breasts, all the way to my throat, where he curls his fingers tight. His grip is like a vise, restricting my airflow until my vision goes hazy.

"Don't worry, though." He suddenly releases me, and I greedily suck down as much air as my burning lungs will allow. "I'll raise this one right."

"You won't touch my baby!" I rasp the words at him, my growing resolve steadily overriding my fear. "I'll die before I let you hurt him!"

"A boy!" He whistles, a look of twisted joy filling his usually dead eyes. "I'll raise him right, indeed."

"Fuck you, you monster!" I buck against his hold, barely even noticing my use of the f-word.

"You're right, you know," he says, his voice devoid of any

feeling at all. "You will die. I thought maybe you were the one. That I'd get to keep you, but clearly you're not worth the trouble. But first, you're going to apologize to me for running away."

"You're actually insane," I whisper brokenly, as I try to figure a way out of this.

But it's hopeless. I'm bound and completely at his mercy.

"I've been thinking of how to punish you." He leans forward and licks the side of my face, his rank breath warming my cheek. "Dreaming of it. And I think I know just the thing."

"Get off of me!" I shout, lurching violently in his hold. The rough wooden floor pulls and tears at my skin, but I barely notice it. Especially when he grips my jaw again, his other hand going to his belt.

"Thought I beat that smart mouth out of you," he mumbles under his breath. "Stubborn little bitch. Should've did you like your mom."

My entire body stills as the implication of his words sinks in.

"Wh-what about my... my m-mama?" I hate how weak my voice is... how weak I am in his presence. I foolishly thought I was finally free of this monster and let my guard down. Now I'm back in his clutches, and I'm starting to worry I won't make it out alive this time.

He pops the buckle of his belt and then the button on his jeans. "Doesn't matter, though. I'll still get to watch you die. To watch the life bleed out of your pretty little eyes. Even if it wasn't the long game, I still win in the end."

He's completely lost it. Oh, God.

"Thought you were the one, but you're nothing. Bitches like you are a dime a dozen." He reaches down, palming himself through his jeans. The knowledge that he's aroused right now is nauseating. "No matter, though. I'll find someone else. Maybe that bitch you were with today."

Scarlet. He means Scarlet. For the first time in my life, I have people in my corner—people who care. It doesn't matter that I barely know her, I can't let him hurt her.

"No!" I shout, my voice echoing all around us. "Please. Please just leave her alone."

"You dare to tell me what to do?" He once again grips my jaw, his grip so bruising, I'm shocked my bones don't turn to dust under the pressure.

"You're nothing." He forces my head back, my neck bending at an unnatural angle, so that the only thing I can see is him. "You're no one. A worthless whore who won't be mourned or missed by anyone."

"That's not true," I grit out, my words barely decipherable thanks to his hand covering my mouth.

"Sure it is." He makes a big show of looking around. "I bet no one's even noticed you're gone. And if they have, I bet they're glad to be rid of a needy bitch like you."

My scalp burns as I try to shake my head, his unrelenting grip on both my hair and jaw severely limiting my range of motion.

"You're nothing but a burden. A drain."

He's preying on my insecurities. Logically, I know this. But there's still this small, awful voice in the back of my head whispering to me that he's right. That Atlas—and Ellis and even Scarlet—are all better off without me. That they'll be relieved I'm gone.

No. Stop that. Stop it right now, Nora. Atlas loves you. You know he does.

"You're wrong." My denial sounds as pathetic as I'm sure I

look, restrained and sopping wet on the floor, but I mean it. I mean it with every ounce of my soul. Atlas Wallace loves me, and he loves our son, and if we make it through this, I'm going to tell him every day that it was his love for me that helped me survive.

"Stupid little bitch." Rand abruptly releases my jaw and shoves his hand into his pocket, retrieving a knife. Before I can fully process it, he's cut open the front of my shirt and has the tip of the blade poised over my belly, pushing ever-so-slightly against my taut skin.

My entire world narrows to the point of his blade. I want to thrash and kick and scream, but I don't. I can't. I'm a statue, for fear that any sudden movement will send the blade plunging into my stomach.

"Please," I beg as fat tears spill down my cheeks. "P-please don't do this. Y-you can d-do anything you w-want to me. Just don't hurt my baby."

"You're not in charge." He presses harder, dragging the blade down to my hip. "If I want to gut you like a fucking deer here and now, I'll damn sure do it."

My body trembles violently as a stinging pain radiates outward from the laceration. Warm liquid trickles from the cut—blood.

I open my mouth, ready to beg, to truly plead for my life, but I snap it shut again. There's not an ounce of humanity inside of Rand, pleading with him will go nowhere. How could it? He doesn't have a heart, much less a soul.

Don't make any sudden movements. Just breathe, Nora. It's going to be okay.

He watches the blood ooze from the wound he inflicted with a sick sense of glee for a moment, but then he shutters his face in a mask devoid of any emotion whatsoever.

Nausea swirls through me as he regards me coolly, as if I'm worth less than the dirt on his shoe before flicking the blade closed and repocketing it.

"Lucky for you, I don't want to." He presses his index and middle into the cut, smearing the blood around. "Yet."

My entire body heaves as he brings his bloodied fingers to his lips, licking away the crimson liquid.

"*Mmm*, just as good as your tears," he groans, as if savoring the taste. "But there's something else I want more."

This time when he reaches for me, his hand moving to the waistband of my leggings, I absolutely lose it, screaming like my life depends on it.

The drive to the cabin is a blur. I couldn't tell you how fast I drove, how many cars I passed, or if I even stopped at any lights.

My focus was singular—get to Nora.

And now that I'm here, I swear to God, if even one hair on her head is out of place, I'll gut that piece of shit like the pig he is. Nora's mine. Mine to love and to cherish. Mine to protect, and I've failed her.

As much as I want to punch it down the long, winding drive and come in guns blazing, I ditch my truck near the road and go in on foot.

I need to be stealthy, because he already has home field advantage, so to speak, and the last thing I want to give him is a leg up on me. Especially when he has the most precious person in my world in his hands.

So, while I want to run, I don't. I creep, gun drawn, eyes peeled, and ready for whatever he may have up his sleeve.

I pause at his truck, taking a quick peek through the windows, but nothing jumps out at me.

In fact, nothing seems amiss at all as the cabin comes into view—that is until I hear Nora's terrified screams bleeding through the walls.

All bets are off now as I flick the safety off and race toward the cabin. "I'm coming, Pip."

I burst through the front door, only to stop dead in my tracks at the sight before me.

Nora is on her side with her arms tied behind her, soaking wet, and bleeding. Rand is gripping her jaw so tightly I can see his fingers digging into her delicate, already bruised skin as he tries to pull her leggings down.

Hell. Fucking. No.

"Get the fuck away from her!" I shout, cocking the gun and aiming it straight at him.

Nora's wide, tearful eyes nearly gut me where I stand. She tries desperately to speak, but Rand's tight hold on her prevents any intelligible words from coming out.

"Well, look who's here," Rand murmurs, not remotely fazed by my appearance or the weapon pointed directly at his chest. "I was wondering if you'd show up. Nora here—" He yanks her by the hair, hard enough that her whole body slides toward him, her neck bent at an unnatural angle. "She was certain you'd swoop in and save her, but I had my doubts. That's a lot of trouble to go through for a used piece of ass carrying another man's child."

Nora whimpers, and something inside of me breaks as fury

unlike anything I've ever felt before sparks inside of me, racing through my veins like liquid fire.

"She may not be worth it to you," I say quietly, "but she's everything to me."

He laughs, but it's a dark sound, devoid of any humor. "Good. Then I'll make sure to let you watch while I fuck the life right out of her."

He shifts their position, maneuvering them so Nora's battered body blocks any chance I have at a clean shot.

Her pained sobs echo in the small space, and it's a sound that will haunt me for the rest of my life.

"I will end you," I vow, flexing the fingers on my left hand before once again steadying the weapon in my right.

One way or another, when we leave here, he *will* be bleeding out on this floor, but I refuse to risk her to make the shot. So, for now, I just need to keep his focus off of her and on me instead.

"You can try, son." His patronizing tone sets my teeth on edge, causing my anger to override the fear.

"I'm not your son. I'm not your anything." I look him up and down before glancing toward Nora. She's shivering and crying, and her lips are looking a little blue. I hate how fucking helpless I feel. "You disgust me."

Rand—because he's not my father—sighs, as if he's disappointed in me. "Soft," he murmurs, shaking his head. "Just like your mother."

His words hit their mark, striking me square in the chest.

"Leave her out of this." My focus is split between him and Nora. She's in bad shape, but I worry if I take my eyes off him for a single second, he'll take her from me for good.

He laughs, loudly, coldly. "How can I, when she's where it

all started?"

Is he saying what I think he is?

"Meaning..."

"I'll never forget the first time I saw her." He sighs wistfully, finally releasing his tight hold on Nora's hair.

Her entire body goes lax, save for her shoulders, which shake as she cries.

In this moment, everything about him is completely at odds with the actual hell playing out before me. He's walking down memory lane while simultaneously laying waste to everything I love.

"All I could think about was how pretty she'd look with my hands 'round her neck and her eyes rolled back in her head. She was the start of everything... my genesis. She showed me who I really am and led me down a path I could've never imagined."

He shakes his head, as if clearing away the cobwebs, bringing his focus back to me. "Made a lot of mistakes with her, but I fine-tuned my process before Grace."

A heart-wrenching sob slips past Nora's trembling lips, causing Rand to flick his eyes toward her, an evil smirk curling his lips as he clocks her reaction.

I don't let his words get to me, at least not outwardly. Outrage is exactly what he's looking for, and I refuse to give him the satisfaction.

"You're telling me you killed my mom, and Nora's?" My voice is calm, despite the inferno of rage and regret warring inside of me, burning every decent memory of the man in front of me to ash.

"That's exactly what I'm telling you. And countless other bitches." He has the sick audacity to sound proud. "Practice makes perfect, son."

"I'm not your son." My voice is low. Deadly. "I meant it when I said I'm not your anything." I spit the words at him, disgust dripping from every single syllable.

"Watch your tone, Atlas." He rakes his bloodied fingers through Nora's hair, yanking her head back.

She yelps, her back bowing under the pressure of his grip.

My eyes connect with hers, and for a moment I catalog every injury—from her black eye and split lip, to her bruised neck and bleeding stomach.

I'm going to kill him. I'm going to end his sad, miserable existence so he can never hurt Nora ever again.

"Atlas," she whispers my name, her hoarse voice barely audible.

"I've got you," I promise, meaning it. This has gone on long enough.

The man—no, the piece of shit on his knees before me, using the love of my life as a living shield—is reprehensible. He's hurt God knows how many people, and now, he needs to pay.

I just need to lure him away from my girl so I can make the shot.

"You're pathetic," I whisper, hoping to bait him.

"What was that?" Those three words take me back to my childhood, to the way he'd whisper them any time I did something to disappoint him. They were usually followed with the back of his hand striking hard against my cheek.

Which means my plan is working. He's getting pissed—at me. And if I'm lucky, he'll play right into my hand. He's an arrogant fuck. Here's to hoping pride really does come before the fall.

"You heard me." I stare down my nose at him, not masking an

ounce of my hatred for him. "Look at you, preying on defenseless women because you know going toe-to-toe with a real man would leave you on your ass."

He appraises me with a wicked glint in his eyes. "And I suppose you're a real man?"

"Why don't you get off your sorry ass and find out?"

His grip on Nora's hair tightens momentarily before he shoves her out of the way and climbs to his feet, immediately charging me.

I let him think he has the upper hand, allowing him to slam me against the wall. I even let him get a few licks in, knowing if I give him an inch, he'll shamelessly try for a mile, and that's when I'll fucking end him. His cockiness will be his downfall.

As we go toe-to-toe, trading and blocking blows, I maneuver us so that Nora's out of the line of fire.

I grunt as he drives his knee into my ribs. He's in decent shape for his age, but he's no match for me. Especially not with all I have on the line.

Playtime's over.

"Should've killed you when I did your mom," he growls, trying—and failing—to pry the gun out of my grip.

"Fuck. You." I spit in his face, shoving him away from me.

He roars like a man possessed, charging me once again.

But I'm ready, and I take a step back and then to the side at the last minute, faking him out.

His shout shakes the windowsills, but I just grin, because he's playing so perfectly into my hand.

Before he can charge me again, I move in from behind him, wrapping one arm around his neck while using the other to wrench his arm behind his back.

Nora whimpers at the sound, momentarily distracting me. It's the in he needs, and he grabs the gun from me.

I react with a mixture of fear, instinct, and adrenaline—punching him hard in the nose. Blood sprays as he staggers back, his eyes wide.

Sirens sound in the distance, and I know we're running out of time, the same way I know there's no justice for him inside the four walls of a courtroom, only death.

"They're coming for you," I sneer. "They're coming and they're going to lock you up in a cage for the rest of your life."

He waves the gun through the air, more animal than man, as panic washes over him.

"You know what happens in jail to men who hurt women, right?" I scoff. "What about what they do to pedophiles? They're going to put you through every ounce of torment you put Nora through. Over and over and over again."

"There's no fucking way," he mutters, the only thing shaking harder than his voice is his hand as he brings the gun to his own head.

"Do it," I hiss. "Fucking do it."

I wait with bated breath, but he's as much of a pussy now as he ever was and can't pull the trigger.

That's okay though, because I fucking can.

Moving slowly, I step into him, sliding my hand over his, I force the muzzle harder against his temple.

"Atlas..." he croaks, but I have no desire to listen to anything else he has to say.

"Who's soft now, you sad sack of shit?" I ask before I shove my finger over his and pull the trigger.

FORTY-ONE
Nora

I watch, almost as if in a daze, as Rand's lifeless body slumps to the floor.

It's over.

He's dead.

It's really, truly, finally over.

Atlas scrambles off him and rushes to me, hauling my trembling body against his.

"Fuck, Pip." He buries his nose into my hair. "Oh my God."

I'm so relieved to be in his arms that I don't care about the blood and gore covering him. He's real and he's here and he's mine. He came for me.

"You came," I whisper, my voice a barely audible rasp.

"Nora, baby, are you okay?" Atlas is nearly frantic as he checks me over, cataloging my injuries. "Fuck, of course you're not. Tell me, what can I do?"

"Just hold me." I snuggle into him—as much as I can with my arms tied behind my back—and bury my face in the crook of his neck.

My body aches, but I'm too tired, too relieved, too everything to care much about anything except that he's here and I'm safe, and our baby will be, too.

I cling to him as the sirens in the distance grow louder and louder, until finally flashing red and blue lights illuminate the trees surrounding the cabin, casting everything in an eerie glow.

"Atlas!" Ellis's familiar and welcome voice echoes around us as he storms into the cabin.

"Over here," Atlas calls back, never once taking his focus away from me.

"Oh, fuck," Ellis mutters, taking in the scene before him. His eyes sweep over everything, methodically cataloging every minute detail. "Are y'all okay—don't answer that, of course you're not."

He pinches the bridge of his nose and then slides a knife from his belt, flicking it open with a practiced ease that instantly has me burrowing into Atlas.

The sight of his blade sends my heart into overdrive. It's pristine and probably duty-issued, but all I can picture is it coated in my blood.

Deep down, I know Ellis is safe, but right now, I'm freaking out.

"Nora, baby," Atlas coos, his voice the very definition of calm. "You're safe. It's just you, me, and Ellis. Neither of us would ever hurt you."

"I-I... I..." I want to tell him I know they wouldn't, but I can't get my mouth to form the words.

"Easy, Nora," Ellis says, raising his hands and taking a step back. "I just want to cut your arms free. That rope's gotta hurt."

Atlas rubs soothing circles over my upper back. "He just wants to help. Your wrists are raw and bleeding. I'll hold you the whole time, okay? You're safe."

I'm shaking like a leaf, but I manage a small nod before turning my face into Atlas's chest, allowing his scent and his heat to ground me.

The sound of Ellis shuffling closer makes every hair on my body stand on end, but I clench my teeth and force myself—as best I can—to stay still.

I must paint a pretty pathetic picture as it is; no sense in adding fuel to that particular fire.

"Hold still, Nora," Ellis says from behind me.

I cry out as his knife pulls the rope taut against my tender wrists. Moments later, the rope falls away, and I fling my arms around Atlas's neck, clinging to him as another round of sobs rack my exhausted body.

"Thanks, man," Atlas says, now rubbing his hands up and down the entire length of my back.

There's a weighted pause, and then Ellis says, "I need to know exactly what happened here—"

"Take a breath," Atlas mutters. "He shot himself."

I risk a glance toward Ellis, and even through my endless tears, I can't help but notice the dubious look Ellis gives him.

"It's true," I slur, my body growing weaker as the adrenaline fades. "S-said he'd rather d-die than go to ja-jail."

"Good." He heaves out a relieved breath. "That's real good."

He fiddles with his radio. "Okay, I'm about to call this in. When they arrive, you need to tell them everything that happened in as much detail as possible."

Ellis squats down so we're at eye level. "I mean it, both of you, every detail, no matter how small, okay? He may be dead, but I don't want there to be room for even an inkling of doubt in anyone's mind about what went on here."

Atlas nods, and I think I do, too, until Ellis says, "Nora, are you with me?"

His voice is distorted, almost as if I'm underwater.

"She needs medical care, man." Atlas's voice is thick, almost like he's trying not to cry. "The baby..."

"I know, brother. I know." Ellis nods and grabs his radio. "Eight-two-five to Fortune County, requesting additional backup and ambulance to respond for a pregnant female with obvious assault injuries, unknown extent, and one unresponsive male on the ground, probable GSW. Requesting priority response, code three."

"You're okay, Pip." Atlas brushes his lips over my temple. "You're okay."

"The ba-baby," I mumble, my worry losing out to my exhaustion, my eyes slipping closed as I sink into blissful oblivion.

Atlas is here...

I'm safe...

"How's she doing?" Ellis asks, his posture rigid as he continuously surveys the scene. His eyes keep straying to Rand, as if he's worried he's still a threat.

"I don't know, man." I tighten my hold on my girl, trying like hell to let her know I'm here, even as she sleeps—at least I hope she's sleeping—fitfully in my arms.

"She's shaking like a leaf, and I'm pretty sure..."—my words dry up faster than the Sahara, and I have to force myself to swallow around the watermelon-sized lump in my throat—"...pretty sure he stabbed her. In the stomach."

I press my head to hers, temple to temple, relishing the feel of her soft breaths puffing against my cheek. As long as she's breathing, I know she'll be okay. "Fucking hell, I'm freaking out."

Please let her be okay.

"Deep breaths, man. Backup will be here soon." He pauses and then grins. "Between you and me, though, I'm glad you killed him. Sorry sack of shit."

"I just wish I'd have done it sooner." I sigh, guilt pressing in on me from all sides. The weight of it is damn near enough to crush me like a Coke can. If I'd have reported him as a kid, or hell, I don't even know—done anything, something, then maybe this could've been prevented.

Maybe I could've saved Nora a whole world of hurt.

But then you wouldn't have her, an insidious voice inside my mind whispers, amplifying my guilt to near nuclear levels.

Nora stirs in my arms, a weak, barely audible whimper slipping past her swollen lips as she presses herself impossibly closer to me.

"It's okay, pretty girl." I keep my voice soft, back like when I first found her at the Lakeshore Motel and she was more skittish than a doe. "You're safe."

"Any minute now," Ellis says, checking his watch, and sure enough, within seconds, the sound of sirens pierces the air.

I keep rubbing soothing circles on Nora's back, even as uniformed officers spill into the small cabin. Much like Ellis did, they scan the area, making sure the threat is neutralized before allowing paramedics to enter.

I'm desperate for her to be okay. For our baby to be okay. For us to be okay. The mere thought of losing either of them, of losing my family, is damn near—*No! Cut that shit out. They're both going to be just fine.*

And if they're not, I swear to God, I'll find a way to bring Rand back from the dead just so I can kill him again.

"Atlas," Nora croaks my name, her voice still so raspy and

weak.

"I'm here, Pip." I brush her matted hair away from her face. "You're okay."

She shudders against my chest, her small fingers curling into the fabric of my shirt as she clings to me. "St-stay."

"I'm not going anywhere." I nuzzle my nose into the top of her head, somehow still finding a hint of her sweet scent through the musty smell of the cabin and the coppery tang of blood permeating the air.

"Promise?" she asks, but it sounds like her mouth is full of cotton.

Before I can reply, a paramedic interrupts us, launching into a whole host of questions about Nora.

"Sh-she's been stabbed. In the belly. She's pregnant. Nineteen weeks." My voice is pleading, frantic even. Now that help is truly here, all of my calm and collected is gone. I need to know she's going to be okay more than I need my next breath. "Please help her."

"Sir, take a breath," one of the paramedics says, earning themselves a mean glare. "We just have a few quick questions."

I shake my head, nearly rabid with my need to get her out of here. "She needs help!"

"Atlas, man," Ellis cuts in, laying a hand on my shoulder. "They're just doing their jobs. Sooner you let 'em, the sooner she gets help."

I take a deep breath and hold it for a moment before slowly releasing it. "You're right. Fuck. Okay."

I answer all of their questions—from her medical history to whether or not she has allergies and everything in between—as they pry her from my arms and strap her to a board, all while someone else takes her vitals and covers the wound on her belly with gauze.

"What about you?" he asks once they have all of the info they need on Nora.

"I'm fine," I say, at the same time Ellis says, "Possible concussion."

I cut my eyes his way, silently promising retribution. But the smartass just shrugs.

"We need to get her loaded up," the one who took Nora's vitals says.

"I'm riding with." I narrow my eyes to slits, daring any one of them to try and stop me from tagging along. I'm not leaving her side until I absolutely have to.

The paramedics and Ellis exchange knowing looks, before the one with all the questions says, "Sounds good, let's go."

They lift the board and carry her out, promptly transferring her onto the stretcher outside.

I hang back helplessly as they load her into the back of the ambulance. I hate not being close enough to touch her, to see the rise and fall of her chest.

"You coming?" one of the paramedics asks, drumming his fingers on the outside of the door.

"Yes." I start to climb into the back of the ambulance, but Ellis calls my name, and I pause halfway in, waiting to hear what he has to say.

"Some officers are gonna follow and ask some questions once y'all are stable." He snuffs the toe of his boot against the ground. "She's strong, man. She'll... she'll be okay."

I tip my head at him in acknowledgment, unable to speak around the ball of emotion clogging my throat, before settling down beside Nora.

Once the doors are shut and we're on our way, I take her hand in mine, rubbing my thumb softly over her knuckles. "I promise I'll never leave you, Pip. I promise."

The second we're in the hospital, my promise to not leave her side goes out the window. They need to take her for scans and tests, and I'm not allowed to go with her.

Even worse, they insist I get looked at, too.

After a whole lot of hurrying to wait, I finally prove to them I'm no worse for wear. Which doesn't feel like much of a win when they relegate me to the waiting room.

Where I wait... and wait... and wait.

Eventually a shadow falls over me, making me jolt in the hard plastic chair.

Hope soars in my heart as I glance up, hoping for an update.

"Do you have an update?" I ask, only to slump back into my chair when I realize it's two uniformed officers standing before me, instead of someone with news about Nora. "Oh." The defeat and disappointment in my tone hang heavy in the air between us.

"Atlas Wallace?" the taller cop with a bushy mustache asks.

"That's me."

"I'm Officer Johansson," Mustache says before nodding toward the other guy. "And this is my partner, Officer Lewis. We're hoping to ask you a few questions and get a statement from you while it's fresh in your mind."

I heave out a deep, weary sigh. "Might as well get it over with."

They both nod, and then settle into the chairs on either side of me.

Officer Lewis flips open his leather folder and clicks his pen twice over the blank sheet in front of him. "We know it's been a long and stressful night, so we'll try to make it as brief as possible."

I lean back in my seat, tipping my head toward the ceiling. "Go for it."

And go for it they do, asking me question after question after question.

Why I was at the cabin, what's my relationship with Nora, what do I know of her history with Rand, what made him turn the gun on himself, did I try to stop him?

I answer each and every one with surety and not a stitch of guilt in my heart over how everything played out.

If anything, he got off easy.

It feels like hours have passed by the time they finally decide they have enough information from me, even though it's probably been thirty minutes tops.

"Thanks for your time," Officer Lewis says, standing and tucking his notepad away.

Officer Johansson also stands and produces a business card from his front pocket. "We'll want to talk to Nora as soon as she's feeling up to it." He extends the card toward me. "The sooner the better."

I take it and nod, not trusting myself to say anything else. I'm beyond exhausted, my head is pounding like someone took a jackhammer to my brain, and I feel like I'm about to crawl out of my skin with the need to lay eyes on Nora.

I've never considered myself an anxious person—until now. But there are just too many variables in play. The unknown of it all has my every muscle tensing with the desire to bolt out of this stupid plastic chair and demand answers—to do something, *anything.*

But there's no point. The only thing acting like an ass would do is get me kicked out—and possibly a criminal charge, which I've already miraculously avoided once tonight.

And so, with my elbows propped on my knees and my head in my hands, I settle in to wait.

And wait, and wait, and wait.

FORTY-THREE
Nora

"*I'll always love you, my sweet babies.*"

"*Moooom,*" *James whines in the way that only a young boy can as he crosses his arms over his chest. "I'm eight. I'm not a baby!"*

My lips tip up into a soft smile as I gaze down at him. "You'll always be my babies..."

The vision playing out before me wavers, giving way to darkness as a steady, incessant beeping rouses me from the deepest sleep I've ever experienced.

Wait...

No... that's not right. Is it?

Am I sleeping?

Where am I?

I try to open my eyes, only to get hit with a tidal wave of déjà vu so strong it steals the air from my lungs.

Scarlet.

Lunch.

Rand.

Dead.

Atlas.

Safe. *I'm safe.*

I try again, but it's too bright. Too loud. Too hard.
Too everything.

Someone somewhere murmurs my name—Atlas. He's here.

But before I can try for a third time, the darkness claims me
again.

FORTY-FOUR
Atlas

I haven't left Nora's side since they finally allowed me into her room. Hell, I couldn't even tell what else is in the room with us, because my eyes haven't looked anywhere except for at her.

I may have lied and said she was my fiancée in order to get back here, but it's hardly a lie when in reality she's so much more than that. She's my light, my air, my happiness. The tiny little spitfire of a woman is my entire reason for existing.

She's bruised and beat to hell and back, with a concussion, her arm in a splint and a few stitches in her belly. But she's going to make a full recovery, and our little jellybean is as healthy as ever.

The relief I felt when I heard those words nearly brought me to my knees. They're words I know I'll treasure until the end of time. Maybe longer.

Now, it's just a waiting game to see when she'll wake up. The doctor said something about her brain needing to recover from the trauma.

A knock sounds outside of her door, most likely a nurse coming to check her stats.

"Come in!" I holler, never once taking my eyes off Nora.

"How's she doing?" Ellis asks, moving into my line of sight.

I flick my eyes his way; he's still in uniform and looks damn near as wrung out as I feel.

"The doctor says she and the baby are both fine."

He drags a spare chair over so it's next to mine. "Any idea when she'll wake up?"

"I wish I knew." The uncertainty of it all has me on edge. They've told me over and over that she's fine—because God knows I've asked every single person who's walked into her room. But seeing is believing, and I know I'll be a damn mess until I see her pretty hazel eyes and hear her sweet voice.

"Not to be that guy, but..." I can already tell from the tone of his voice I'm not going to like what he has to say. "...have you heard anything else from Scarlet?"

My shoulders tense at the mention of her name. "She hasn't stopped blowing up my phone. I had to turn the damn thing off."

He sighs and leans back in his seat, the hard plastic creaking under his weight. "You gonna talk to her?"

"Fuck," I groan, running my hands through my hair and tugging on the ends. "I don't know, man."

"Talk about a rock and a hard place."

"I—I just... the rational part of my brain knows it's not her fault, but at the same time, I..." Tears burn the back of my eyes as I look over at Nora lying on the bed in front of me. She looks so small and fragile. "I could've lost them both."

"I know." He reaches over and squeezes my shoulder. "No matter what you decide there, I'm with you."

"Appreciate it." Those two words aren't nearly enough to convey how much his support means to me. Not just in dealing with Scarlet, but in how he's had my back from the start.

He never once gave me shit over her diary. He didn't balk at the idea of moving her into our house. He didn't say shit when things went from friendly to *more.* Hell, I put his entire job on the line today when I went after Nora, and he. Didn't. Say. Shit.

Ellis-fucking-Wilder is the living embodiment of loyalty, and if it takes the rest of my life to repay him in kind, then so be it.

"I mean it," I say, my voice a rough whisper. "I fucking appreciate you."

Ellis huffs, and I know that, like me, he's trying to keep his emotions at bay. "I know, man. I know."

Silence settles back over us as we both go back to watching Nora.

It feels like days have passed, even though according to the clock on the wall, it's only been an hour, when I feel the slightest twitch of her fingers against mine.

"Pip?" I jolt out of my chair as her fingers spasm again. "Open those pretty eyes, baby."

I wait with my heart in my throat, hope surging violently inside of me, but nothing happens.

"Come on, Nora," I whisper brokenly, desperate for her to wake up. "Come back to me."

The room falls silent once again, save for the steady beep of her heart monitor.

"Man, are you sure—" Ellis starts to say.

I cut him off. "Positive." I felt her move. She wants to wake up. She's trying. I know she is. My girl may look tiny, but she's a fighter. Hell, she's easily the toughest person I know.

"I'm here, Pip." I lean down and sweep my lips over her forehead in a barely-there kiss. "Come back to me."

I repeat those same four words, over and over, begging her—the universe, right along with anything or anyone that may be listening—for her to wake up.

Right as I lower myself back down into my chair, she gasps, her fingers clutching at mine.

"Nora?" I scramble back to my feet, trying my best to give her space as not to overwhelm her.

She opens her mouth as if she's going to speak, but nothing comes out. Panic flares behind her eyes as she clutches her throat.

She wants to say something, but the torment Rand put her through bruised her vocal cords. "Take your time, Pip." I brush my knuckles over her cheekbone. "Want some water?"

She nods fervently, wincing slightly as I grab the jug from Ellis's outstretched hand.

"Go slow," I murmur, bringing the straw to her lips.

I watch her throat work as she swallows down several sips, her eyes never once leaving mine, and the look of pain and worry never once lessening.

"Ja-James," she rasps. "How's James?"

My brows pinch together as I try to make sense of what she's asking me.

"Who... who's James, Pip?" I ask, proud as hell when my voice doesn't betray the confusion rushing through me. "Whoever he is, I'll find—"

"Our son," she cries, her eyes filling with tears. "He's our son. I—I met him."

Ellis clears his throat, undoubtedly asking me whether or not I think she's okay.

"You met him?" I ask, making sure to keep my tone even. "When?"

She tries to nod, her tear-soaked eyes begging me to believe her. "And our daughter—Lydie Grace—I met them both, Atlas, and they're perfect." Her entire body trembles as she tries to sit up. "Please tell me he's okay. Please?"

Every hair on my body stands on end as the full impact of her words hits me. James after her dad and Lydie Grace after both of our mothers, my God. They couldn't be any more perfect. *She couldn't be any more perfect.*

I've heard people can have all sorts of out-of-body experiences after trauma, so maybe that's what this is.

Either way, her comfort—both physical and mental—is all that matters right now.

"Our jellybean—James—he's fine. Perfectly healthy and perfectly safe."

"You mean it?" The fragile thread of hope weaving itself through her words is almost enough to break me. How she can sound so broken and so resilient all at once, is a mystery to me. One thing I do know is I'll do any and everything within my power to nurture that hope.

"Yeah, Pip. I mean it." I turn my attention to Ellis, and ask, "Why don't you step out and let them know she's awake so the doctor can come in and tell her herself?"

"On it." Ellis immediately stands and heads for the door,

pausing on the threshold. "Glad you're okay."

"Thank you," she whispers.

He gives her a long look and then nods once before stepping out into the hall, pulling the door closed behind him, giving us some much-needed privacy.

FORTY-FIVE
Nora

"You believe me, right?" I ask, trying my best to keep my lower lip from wobbling. I know how *out there* it sounds. I really do, but I also mean it with every ounce of my soul.

"Nora." Atlas's voice is softer than I've ever heard it, and perfectly neutral, giving absolutely nothing away. For all I know, he thinks this is all some kind of messed up trauma response.

But I've never been more certain about anything in my life. Not ever.

When I first woke up, sure, I was disoriented. I didn't understand the enormity of what I'd witnessed, but as I regained consciousness, I also gained clarity, and there's no convincing me that it was only a dream.

Because it was more. *So much more.*

It was a glimpse into our future.

A future I'm desperate to protect.

"It was so real, Atlas," I croak, clutching at my tender throat. There's not a single part of me that doesn't ache. From the tippy-top of my head, all the way down to my toes, I'm stiff and sore, like my body's been put through a meat grinder.

But I grin and bear it as I force myself into a seated position. I need to look him in the eye... I need him to understand just how serious I am.

"Nora, whoa." Atlas is up and at my side in a second, one hand at my back bracing me as I find a semi-comfortable position. "Go slow, Pip."

I allow him to fuss over me for a minute, knowing it's something he needs to reassure himself that I'm truly here and okay.

But my mind wanders as he fluffs my pillow and tucks the blankets around me, thinking of all the ways I can convince him to believe me.

My mama was never one to buy into this woo-woo kind of stuff, as she called it, but my dad—he *always* did. He said life was full of unexplained phenomena, and if we simply trusted our gut, we'd always end up where we're meant to be.

He never once steered me wrong. I believe him wholeheartedly, and now I need Atlas to believe me.

"They were so perfect." Tears fill my eyes, as I recount the details. But this time, they're happy tears. "They had your eyes and your golden skin, but with my hair and a smattering of freckles across the bridges of their noses."

He drags his fingertips over my cheek, swiping away the tears before taking my hand in his. "Tell me more, Pip." The deep but gentle rumble of his voice soothes my frayed nerves. "Tell me

everything."

I send up a silent prayer to any deity that might be listening for him to believe me. I don't know why it's so important to me that he does, but it is. It really, truly is.

"The sun was setting, and we were cuddled up on the back steps, watching the kids play. James was pushing Lydie Grace on a tire swing."

"What tree was it hanging from?" Atlas asks, his voice still neutral.

"You know the big one, to the left of the steps?" He nods and starts rubbing soothing circles over the back of my hand with his thumb. "That one, from the really big branch that points toward the house."

"Always thought that tree would be perfect for a swing—or even a treehouse."

"They were having so much fun. James was spinning Lydie Grace, and they were laughing and squealing and hollering."

"How old were they?" he murmurs, his eyes crinkling at the corners as he gazes down at me with a small smile curling his lips.

"James was eight and Lydie Grace was five." My lips tip up into a watery smile. "They were so perfect, Atlas. I told them how much I loved them, and it felt so right. So perfect and right."

My shoulders curl inward when he doesn't say anything. "I... I know how it sounds." I laugh, but it's a flat, dull sound. I thought he believed me, but maybe he was just indulging me. "Never... never mind... it was just a –"

"I-believe-you." The words explode out of him, all jumbled together into one long word rather than three.

"Really?" My heart swells in my chest, pressing against my ribs, as a sense of hope radiates within me, warming me from the inside out.

He huffs out a breath and then smiles down at me, with a look so tender it makes me melt. "Really." He leans forward and presses the softest kiss to my bruised lips. "I love you, and I've always got your back."

"Thank you," I whisper, uncaring of the crack in my voice. I don't know how I ended up lucky enough to have this man's unconditional love, but I'll spend the rest of my life not only basking in it, but loving him right back.

"There's something I've gotta know, though..."

"What's that?"

"Does our boy have a middle name?"

That was the absolute last question I expected, but also somehow the best.

"He does." I clasp my hands together in my lap, grinning mischievously up at him.

Atlas leans forward, bracing his arms on the railings of my bed. "You gonna tell me, Pip?"

"Wilder."

He whistles. "James Wilder—that's gonna go straight to Ellis's head."

"What is?" Ellis asks, walking back into the room.

"Speak of the devil," Atlas groans, and I giggle.

"Seriously." He crosses his arms over his chest and pretends to glare. "One of y'all better tell me."

Atlas leans back in his chair, crossing his ankle over his knee. "I think I'll let you handle this one, Pip."

"We were just talking about James's middle name."

"Riveting stuff." Ellis drops back down into his chair. "You gonna tell me what it is or..."

"Well, if it's okay with you, Wilder."

Silence blankets the room—so quiet you could hear a pin drop.

"You... you're naming your baby... after me?" he asks, thumping his fist against his chest.

"Hoping to," I tell him honestly.

"Fuck yes!" he shouts, jumping up and literally clicking his heels together. "Best day ever."

Atlas grunts, and Ellis has the good sense to tone down his celebration.

"I mean, worst day, too, getting kidnapped and whatnot, but I'm choosing to focus on the positive, okay?" He shoots a wink my way, and I can't help but smile.

Because in a way, he's right—it is a good day. Sure, I was taken and I'm pretty banged up, but knowing that Rand can never, ever hurt me or anyone else ever again? Best day ever.

FORTY-SIX
Atlas

"I swear to God," I mumble under my breath, wondering how in the hell the usually stoic six-foot-five man I call my best friend can transform into a sugared-up six-year-old in the blink of an eye. "We can't take you anywhere, can we?"

Nora laughs, and on my life, it's the sweetest sound in the whole world.

Ellis cuts his eyes at me. "Talk all the shit you want, brother, but a little positivity goes a long way."

I cross my arms over my chest. "I'm positive I'm gonna stick my foot up your ass if you don't sit down and shut up. I'm tired."

Ellis sobers and drops down into his chair. "I know, man. And in case I haven't said it, I'm glad you're okay—both of you."

A knock interrupts us, saving me from trying to form a reply around the ball of emotion lodged in my throat.

"Come in," Nora calls, her raspy voice sending chills down my spine. It's a good thing that asshole is dead, because every time I look at my girl, I have half a mind to find a way to resurrect him just so I can kill him again.

The door swings open revealing Dr. Duplantier. I met her earlier while Nora was sleeping, and just as I expected, my girl already seems at ease in her presence.

"So good to see you awake," she says, bustling into the room, marching straight to the computer next to Nora's bed. "I'm Dr. Duplantier, but you can call me Dr. D. So, tell me, how are you feeling, dear?"

I don't know what it is about her, but she radiates grandma energy, and it is exactly what Nora needs right now. Someone soft and caring.

Nora laughs, but this time, there's not a drop of humor to be found. "Like I got hit by a bus."

She smiles and pats Nora's shoulder. "But you lived."

Nora's lips lift ever-so-slightly as she brings both of her hands to rest on her belly. "That I did."

Dr. D's eyes track Nora's movements. "Worried about the baby, are you?"

She shrugs and then nods. "Atlas said he's fine, but..."

"But you want to see for yourself."

"If... if it's possible. Yes, please."

"Of course it is, my dear. I'll have them come by with a portable ultrasound machine before you're discharged. I know if I was in your shoes, I'd feel the same way."

"Discharged, like going home?" The spark of hope in Nora's voice has me sitting up straight in my chair.

"That's the plan. Assuming you have someone there who can

care for you." She cuts her eyes toward Ellis and me. "Concussion protocol and whatnot."

"She does," Ellis and I state in unison, no doubt confusing Dr. D. But like a true professional, she doesn't comment on it.

Then again, I'm sure she's witnessed far stranger things than the three of us.

"Okay," Nora whispers, before sucking in a shaky breath. "Thank you."

"Given the state you were brought to us in, you're quite fortunate. As I mentioned, you have a mild concussion, which means you'll need to limit not only your physical activity, but also your screen time—phones, computers, and television."

"So, no *Gossip Girl*." Ellis sighs, earning him a glare from Dr. D.

"Not for at least forty-eight hours," she says in a no-nonsense voice that leaves even me feeling scolded. "Your discharge paperwork will include a list of things to watch out for; if you experience any of them, you'll need to come back for further evaluation."

Nora nods and the good doctor continues. "You also have a fractured wrist, which as I'm sure you've noticed is already splinted. However, you will require a follow-up with an orthopedist, who will most likely want to place it in a hard cast."

"I call dibs on signing it first," Ellis blurts, clearly stuck in kid mode. Guy's going to be a helluva uncle, seeing as he'll be about as mature as our son.

Dr. D shakes her head and rolls her lips inward to suppress her smile. "You'll also want to follow up with your OB, just to be safe. And last, but not least, I highly suggest getting in with a therapist. You've been through quite an ordeal. If you don't have anyone in mind, your discharge paperwork will have a few options listed."

"I... I have someone," Nora says. "Thank you, though."

"Glad to hear it, dear. I'm going to let you rest while I get your paperwork sorted. Someone will be up soon for that ultrasound."

"Thanks," Nora murmurs, her eyelids already drooping.

The doctor steps out and quiet falls over the room, save for the beeping of the machine Nora's hooked up to.

"Poor thing." Ellis tips his head toward Nora, who's out cold. "She's gotta be exhausted."

"Strongest damn person I've ever met." Pride suffuses my every word as I watch the steady rise and fall of her chest as she sleeps.

"She really is," Ellis agrees. "Smallest person I know, too. What's that quote?"

"Small but mighty... I think it was Shakespeare."

He nods. "Yeah, that's your girl to a T."

"I think..." I trail off, fidgeting in my chair as I try to find the right words. "I think maybe I should make an appointment with someone to talk to about all of this, too."

Ellis scoots his chair to face me. "Glad you said it, because I've been trying to think about how to bring it up. I didn't care for the shrink the department uses, so I found my own. Happy to give you his info."

"Appreciate it, man."

"You should know I've always got your back." He crosses his arms over his chest and grins. "Especially after today."

All I can do is huff out a laugh, because he's got me there. Ellis-fucking-Wilder is as loyal as they come, and I'm damn lucky to have him in my life—as a friend and now my soon-to-be firstborn's namesake.

FORTY-SEVEN
Nora

The sound of knocking wakes me, and I blink my eyes open just in time to see a scrub-clad nurse roll a cart into my room.

"Hi, I'm Andrea, and I'm here to do your ultrasound."

"Thank you," I whisper, my voice still thick with sleep.

She smiles and wheels the machine to the far side of my bed. "I have to ask, do you want it to be just you, you and dad, or…" Her eyes ping back and forth between Atlas, Ellis, and me.

My reply is instantaneous. "We're all family here."

To Andrea's credit, her smile never falters. If anything, it grows when Ellis hops out of his chair, crowing like a kid on Christmas morning who just got everything he asked for.

"Family," he murmurs, dropping unceremoniously back down onto his chair. "I like the sound of that."

Andrea's lips tremble as she tries to hold in her laugh.

"Ignore him," I stage whisper. "He can't help it."

She sucks in a deep breath and then slowly exhales it. "Alrighty then, let's get this show on the road." With quick, methodical movements, she rolls down the blankets that Atlas tucked so tightly around me and lifts my gown, all while making sure to keep the important bits covered.

"Fair warning, this is going to be cold."

I try my best not to tense up, but I do, because she's right—it is cold. A sharp hiss escapes me as pain ricochets through my body.

Atlas interlaces his fingers through mine. "You've got this, Pip."

I force myself to unclench my muscles, my body sagging back against the pillow as I exhale.

"Easy now, Nora," she murmurs, pressing the wand into my abdomen.

Instantly the sweetest whooshing sound fills the room.

"Hear that? He's got a nice, strong heartbeat." Tears burn the back of my eyes as I watch James—our little jellybean—on the small screen. "He's doing just fine, dear."

"I don't think I've ever heard a better sound," Atlas whispers roughly, giving voice to my very thoughts.

"I love you," I tell him, meaning it with my entire being.

He squeezes my hand before leaning in and pressing a kiss to my forehead. "Love you, too, pretty girl."

"And I love you both," Ellis says, effectively lightening the moment.

"Well, that's my cue," Andrea says, handing me a towel to wipe the goo from my belly.

"Thank you. So much." I know she's just doing her job, but

the peace and reassurance she gave me is something I'll be forever grateful for.

Andrea offers me one last smile as she rolls her cart out the door, once again leaving the three of us alone.

"How are you feeling?" Atlas asks, stroking his thumb across the back of my hand.

"Better." I wince, a fact Atlas doesn't miss. Ellis either for that matter. "Better mentally," I amend. "Tired. Hungry. Sore. Thankful. Mostly, I just really, *really* want to go home."

Atlas brings my hand to his lips and brushes a kiss across my knuckles. "Let me go check on that discharge paperwork, yeah?"

I nod and he stands, heading for the nurses' station in search of answers.

"Alone at last." Ellis wags his brows as he leans forward, bracing both arms on his knees. "How are you really feeling?"

"I meant what I said. I feel all of those things. But also... relieved. Thankful. He can never hurt me again."

"Fucking right," Ellis growls.

"Guilty," I hiccup the word out on a sob.

Ellis rears back. "Why?"

"Atlas killed his own father because of me. What... what if he regrets it or resents me because of it?"

He snaps his fingers together. "Gonna stop you right there. That man loves you. Fucking adores you. Worships the ground you walk on. I was there when he found out you were missing, that his dad took you. The only regret he could possibly have is not ending that miserable son of a bitch sooner. He was a monster, Nora. You know it, I know it, and Atlas damn sure knows it. He was a threat to not only you, but women as a whole, and frankly, the world is better off without him. So cut that shit out, you hear me?"

I sniffle and nod. "I'll try."

He sighs. "I mean it. And if you can't, talk to Maggie about it, okay?"

"Okay."

"Promise?"

"Yeah, I promise."

"Promise what?" Atlas asks, walking back into the room.

"Your girl here was just promising to make me your son's godfather." He whistles and nods his head. "His namesake and his godfather. I must be a helluva man. A role model, even."

"Christ," Atlas groans. "This has all gone straight to your head, hasn't it?"

Ellis shrugs, his lips curled into a shit-eating grin.

"Anyway." Atlas pointedly turns away from Ellis. "Nurses' station said it's basically a waiting game for the paperwork at this point. So, good news, you definitely get to go home today. Bad news, I'm not super sure when."

"As long as I get to go home, I'm good."

Atlas leans over me and presses a kiss to my lips. "Just rest, Pip. We'll be out of here soon enough."

Soon enough just so happens to come three hours later.

"Now, don't forget," Dr. Duplantier says, "your follow-up appointment with the orthopedist has already been scheduled; you can find the date and time in your discharge paperwork. And, as I mentioned earlier, I strongly suggest following up with your OB and a mental health professional."

I nod, too exhausted to talk. I am so beyond ready to get out of here. All I want is to shower this godforsaken day off me, find something to eat, and snuggle up with Atlas. I'm desperate for the comfort only he can offer me.

"Well then, let's get you out of here." The doctor's words are punctuated by a nurse stepping into the room with a wheelchair in tow.

A groan escapes me as I cross my arms over my chest. "Is this really necessary?" I ask.

Atlas and Ellis both cross their arms over their chest and glare at me, saying *yes* in tandem. Dr. Duplantier just laughs. "Hospital policy, I'm afraid."

"Fine." I uncross my arms and push the blankets down, only to realize I'm wearing nothing more than a hospital gown. "Um..." I force myself to swallow as my cheeks burn crimson. "I need clothes."

"Wait!" Ellis jumps up. "I brought some from the house. They're in my car. Be right back!"

True to his word, Ellis is back in a flash. Atlas helps me hobble into the bathroom and takes great care dressing me in my favorite leggings and one of his sweaters. Unfortunately, Ellis forgot my shoes.

I could wear the ones from earlier today, but the thought of putting them on makes my skin crawl. The only thing I want to do with anything I was wearing today is burn it.

Good thing they brought the wheelchair, I guess.

"You ready, Pip?" Atlas asks.

"So ready."

"Let's get you home, then."

FORTY-EIGHT
Atlas

I'm damn near ready to crawl out of my skin by the time our mailbox comes into view. I have a single-track mind—the only thing I want is to get Nora comfy and cozy, so I can glue myself to her side until she begs me for space.

Because, *fucking hell*, how am I supposed to let her out of my sight after this?

She's safe, you eliminated the threat. He can never hurt her—or anyone else—ever again.

"You excited to be home?" I ask, shaking myself out of my funk as I turn toward my girl, only to freeze at the sight of big, fat tears rolling down her cheeks.

"Shit." I unbuckle my seat belt and slide across the back seat, tucking her into my side. "What's wrong?"

Heaving sobs rack her small body, as she completely breaks

down in the shelter of my arms.

Ellis catches my gaze in the rearview mirror as he turns down our long, winding drive, silently asking if she's okay.

I lift my brows and shrug, hoping like hell she is.

"I-I just... for a little bit, I didn't think I'd ever be here again. Home. This is my home." She blinks up at me, her hazel eyes glassy and her pink cheeks slick with tears. "You're my home."

"Damn right, I am," I say before wiping away her still-falling tears and pressing a kiss to the top of her head. Her hair is a matted mess, but I'm more than happy to help her comb through it once she's showered. "And I always will be. You're safe here, and I promise you, Nora, I'll do my level best to never let anything or anyone hurt you ever again."

Ellis is so silent behind the wheel, it's almost like it's just the two of us back here. It's a small thing, but I'm thankful for the illusion of privacy as he follows the tree lined path to our house.

"You... you know it's not your fault, right?" Nora asks, her voice so soft and small, and yet so strong.

God, this woman. Almost died today but she's trying to comfort me. I undoubtedly don't deserve her, but I'm damn sure going to spend the rest of my life showing her how much she means to me.

"Logically, yes." I suck in a breath through my teeth. "But a part of me can't help but run the what ifs."

"Let's just be happy you found me." Nora sighs and snuggles deeper into my side. "Talk about luck."

I turn to stone as our house finally comes into view. "About that..." I croak, knowing I have to tell her the truth—no matter what.

"Well..." Ellis throws the car into park, but keeps it running. "Why don't y'all head inside and I'll go pick up dinner." He shifts uncomfortably, unable to meet Nora's eyes. "Give y'all time to... get settled... and to talk."

"Because that's not ominous or anything," she mutters as I slide my arm from around her to undo her seat belt.

"Wait here, Pip." I climb out of the back seat before hauling ass to Nora's side to get the door for her. "Let's get you inside and comfy and then we can talk, okay?"

She crosses her arms as she regards me, her nose wrinkling as she stares me down. She's trying to look tough, but I see just how exhausted she is. "I guess."

"I love you, Nora. Truly." I offer her my hand and she takes it, allowing me to help her out of the car. "Just... do me a favor and keep an open mind."

"That's my cue," Ellis says, signaling for me to shut the door. I nudge it closed and then turn my attention to the slip of a woman who's single-handedly become my everything.

"Shower first and then we can talk?" I ask, as we both watch him drive away.

"No." She plants her hands on her hips. "You can talk while I shower."

God, I'm glad she still has her fire. My girl's strong as hell. "Deal."

I unlock the door and hold it open for Nora before following behind her into the house, pausing to resecure the lock. Every step feels like an eternity—like I'm stuck in some fucked-up limbo, waiting impatiently to learn my fate.

Beads of sweat dot my hairline, and my blood's fizzy in my veins as I run through all of the possible reactions Nora may have to learning the truth about how I found her—hurt, betrayal, anger, hatred...

Please, please, please don't let her hate me.

I enter the bathroom only moments after her, shocked to find her with the water already heating as she struggles to undress.

"Pip, let me help you."

She huffs an annoyed breath at me and narrows her eyes at me, like she wants to tell me no.

I'm not above begging, though. I'll do just about anything to make her life easier.

Thankfully, she relents and allows me to step in. "Fine." She braces her hands on my shoulders, sagging against me. "I'm huge and sore and tired—"

"You're perfect," I murmur, kneeling down so I can help her out of the leggings Ellis brought her. I push her borrowed sweater up as I stand, pausing to press a soft kiss to her rounded belly before gently tugging the garment over her head and tossing it to the floor, leaving her completely naked.

I hover like a mother hen as she steps into the shower, torn between wanting to spill my guts or take this shit to the grave for all eternity.

But my girl's not having it. Not by a long shot. And she deserves the truth—no matter how uncomfortable it is for me.

"I'm in the shower, Atlas." I hear the snick of a soap bottle opening. "Now talk."

I swallow roughly as I slide down the wall until I'm seated on my ass with my legs out in front of me. "You said it was luck that I found you—and the first time, at the motel, I guess you could say it was. But today..."

Fuck, why is this so hard?

"Today what?" she asks, her feather-soft words hitting me square in the gut like a boulder.

I drag my fingers through my hair, tugging on the ends. "It's because of your necklace."

My half-assed admission is met with silence. I can just picture the confusion written all over her face, and it's a struggle not to beg her to say something—anything.

But, eventually, she asks, "What about it?"

Here goes nothing...

"It has a GPS chip in it. I used it to track your location. And I know—I know that's fucked up, Pip. I know it's a breach of your trust, but I also know I don't regret it, not even a little, because you're here and safe and—"

She whips the curtain open, and my eyes fly up to hers, widening at the sight of her standing there, dripping wet, covered in soap bubbles and bruises, with the compass charm clutched between her trembling fingers.

"This has a tracker in it?" She looks down at the golden compass and then back to me. Confusion, hurt, and disbelief are flashing across her delicate features.

"Nora, baby—"

She stares down at me, but I don't think she's actually *seeing* me. "Like I'm... Like I'm a dog," she whispers brokenly.

Her fucking words more than gut me—they crack my ribs, tear me open, and steal my still-beating heart from my chest.

"Absolutely not." I bolt up from the floor and take a step toward her, only to draw up short when she flinches at my sudden movement.

God, I'm fucking this all up. Get it together, man.

"Like you're the single most precious thing to ever come into my life." My voice shakes, but I keep talking. I'm desperate for her to understand. "Like you're my sole reason for existing. Like you're the center of my whole world. Don't you realize that I'll do anything—and I mean *anything*—to keep you and our son safe?"

Her entire body trembles as she wraps her arms around herself, and I feel like the biggest asshole to ever walk the planet. All I want to do is climb in the shower with her and wrap her in my arms, to take every ounce of pain she's feeling away. To remind her just how much I love her.

Watching Nora struggle with my actions—well-intentioned or not—is nearly unbearable. I'd take her pain and make it my own in a heartbeat if I could.

"I love you, Nora." My voice cracks. "And I know I fucked up. But I meant what I said—I don't regret it. Not if it means you're alive. I know you're probably mad at me. Hell, I deserve it. And I get it if you need space—"

"Atlas, please stop talking." Her voice is deadly calm, almost devoid of any emotion whatsoever.

Despite my worry, my lips clamp together like they've been superglued, as I wait with my heart in my throat for whatever she says next.

But instead of speaking, she turns away from me, pulls the curtain closed, and finishes her shower.

I want to question her—to demand answers, for her to tell me she loves me. But I swallow down every word that tries to escape. Waiting her out is the least I can do.

I suck in a deep breath and force myself to relax back against the countertop as I exhale.

It feels like hours pass, though it's probably only minutes before she shuts off the water. I rush forward, and grab the towel, ready to help her over the edge of the tub in case she needs it.

"You're right," she whispers as she steps into me. I wrap a

towel around her shoulders and hold her against my chest. "You broke my trust, but I know firsthand how stupid fear can make us."

"I'm so sorry, Pip."

"I know." She pulls back and looks up at me. "I need you to do something for me."

"Anything. Name it." I mean it too—any-fucking-thing she says, I'll find a way to do it.

"Don't lie to me again, Atlas. Not to me, not ever again."

"Done." I draw an X over my heart with my fingertip and then seal my vow with a kiss on her forehead.

She smiles up at me, and it's the sweetest smile I've ever seen, even if she does look exhausted.

"Does that mean you forgive me?" I ask. I know the answer now, but I still need to hear her say it.

"Of course I do." She rubs her cheek against my now soaking wet shirt. "I love you. Now please can we get dressed, so we can eat right when Ellis gets back? I'm exhausted and want to sleep for like a year."

"I know, Pip." I run one hand up her back in a soothing motion. "C'mon, I've got you."

Nora sags against me before sighing and reluctantly stepping out of my embrace.

I strip off my wet shirt and splash my face and chest with cold water before dragging a towel over myself and following after her.

I glance toward the bed as I step out of the bathroom, half expecting Nora to be curled up asleep, but she's nowhere in sight.

A sniffle sounds from the closet, and I pivot, poking my head in to check on her.

The vision that greets me causes my heart to thump painfully against my ribs. My girl, who's fought so damn hard to overcome all of the shit she's gone through, looks absolutely pitiful.

She's ghostly pale, which only serves to make the bruises marring her skin stand out even more, and looks like she could fall asleep standing up.

"You need help, Pip?" I ask, making sure to keep my tone soft.

"Please," she whispers, her voice cracking as she curls her shoulders inward, the way she used to when she wanted to make herself seem smaller.

I fucking hate this. I hate that she's scared, that she's hurting. But most of all, I hate that I can't fix it, that I can't take her pain away. Because if I could, I would. In a fucking heartbeat.

"You look miserable," I murmur, as I riffle through the drawers for everything she needs.

"That's because I am." A drawn-out yawn punctuates her reply.

I set the pile of clothes on top of the dresser and then take a step closer to my girl, softly running my hands over the towel she's still wrapped up in, making sure she's good and dry. "C'mon, pretty girl. Let's get you bundled up."

Kneeling before her, I help her into a pair of simple cotton panties, followed by a pair of my sweats, which I have to fold the waistband on twice. Even halfway through her pregnancy, Nora's tiny.

I cradle her belly between my palms, and press a soft kiss to her taut skin, sending up a silent thanks that our little man is okay before standing and tugging one of my shirts over her head.

"Socks or no socks?"

Nora looks at her bare feet and wiggles her toes. "Socks," she croaks, and I smile, because we both know she will kick them off in the middle of the night.

I grab her favorite pair from the top drawer and drop down to my knees again, quickly tugging them onto her feet.

"Let me change really quick, okay?"

She nods sleepily, wrapping her arms around her waist as she rests her head against the wall.

I shuck off my jeans and pull on a pair of sweats to match hers and call it good. In all honesty, I'd kill for a shower, but for now, this'll have to do, because Nora needs me more, and if I'm being honest, the thought of leaving her side for even a second is a hard no at the moment.

"Now, come to the bed so I can help you brush out these knots. Ellis should be home by then, and we can eat, and then we can—"

"Sleep."

"That's right." I scoop Nora into my arms and carry her bridal style into our bedroom, depositing her gently onto the bed. "Let's get some food in you and then we can sleep."

FORTY-NINE
Nora

I suck in a deep breath and draw the blanket wrapped around my shoulders tighter as I wait for the video call with Maggie to connect.

The thought of talking to her about *everything* is unsettling to say the least. A part of me wants to pretend it never happened, but there's a small voice in the back of my mind—that sounds suspiciously like my mother—telling me that hiding from my trauma isn't the answer.

"Nora, how are you?" Maggie's voice filters out through my speaker moments before her face fills my screen. Seeing her kind eyes and welcoming smile instantly relieves some of the tension building inside of me.

"I've been better." I shrug. "I've also been worse."

"You're still here." She appraises me through the screen.

"You're here, and you have your whole life ahead of you. How do you feel about that?"

How do I feel? A million different possible answers surge forward, but only one really fits. "Grateful."

Maggie steeples her fingers beneath her chin. "What is it you're grateful for, Nora?"

"That I'm here. I survived." I swallow around the lump in my throat. "That Atlas found me. That our baby's okay." My hand strokes across my rounded belly as if it has a mind of its own. "But most of all, I'm grateful that he's dead. That he can never hurt anyone else ever again."

When Maggie doesn't immediately reply, I rush to fill the silence. "That makes me a horrible person, doesn't it?" Tears burst forth without any warning as the weight of my confession bears down on me. "It does—I'm happy someone's dead and I—I think that might make me a monster."

"Oh, Nora." Maggie sighs softly. "Monster is the last word anyone would ever use to describe you. It might be unprofessional of me to say this, but I can promise you, a lot of people are happy he's gone. The world is a better place without him."

"You... do you really mean that?" I whisper, clutching the blanket between my fingers in my lap.

"Yes, Nora." Maggie nods once. "I very much do. Now, let's talk about how you're coping with all of this."

I curl my shoulders inward, fully aware she's not going to like my reply. "I've been trying to pretend it didn't happen."

She arches one brow. "And how's that working out for you?"

I huff out an unamused laugh. "It's not."

"Have you tried writing about it?"

"I... want to." My eyes flit to my nightstand, where my diary sits, mocking me. "I've tried, but I just can't."

"You have writer's block." She says it like a statement, but it feels like a question. One I don't know how to answer.

"Something like that, I guess."

"Tell me about it."

"It's like... ugh." I run my fingers through my hair, tugging the ends in frustration. "It's like every time I try, I-I get lost."

"Lost how?" Maggie asks, her voice soft.

I rub at my wrists as they burn with phantom pains from the ropes Rand bound me with. "In the memories. They're so real... so vivid... it's almost like I'm back there."

My heart feels like it's being squeezed in an iron vise as I fight to stay in the present. "Like I'm still with him." I scrub away the fat tears rolling down my cheeks with the back of my hands. *I will not cry over him. Not ever again.*

"Nora—"

"I just want it all to stop!" I shout, my volume making both Maggie and I jump. "How do I make it stop?"

"Nora," Maggie says my name again, but firmer this time. "I need you to take a deep breath, close your eyes, and tell me five things you can see, four things you can touch, three things you can hear, two things you can smell, and one thing you can taste."

I try to do as she says, but it's almost as if I can feel his hands around my throat.

"In through your nose," she guides me. "That's right, Nora. Good. And out through your mouth. Again."

After several deep breaths, I begin counting. "I-I can see James's crib, his rocking chair, his dresser..." It takes an eternity, but as I work my way down the list, I can feel my panic lessening, as both my heart rate and my breathing return to normal. "I can taste my lip balm—it's vanilla."

"Good, Nora. Any time you're struggling with staying in the present, this is a great method to reground yourself. I also think it would be beneficial for you to confide in Atlas—he can't offer support for an issue he's not aware of."

"I... I don't want to burden him, though. He... he killed his dad for me, Maggie. What if he—"

"Want to know the best way to clear up those what-ifs?" She gives me a knowing look. "Talk to him."

"Yeah." I heave out a heavy sigh. "You're right."

"Another great method is vagus nerve stimulation."

"Vagus what now?"

"Basically, if you're in a panic state, try sipping some cold water slowly or rub an ice cube across your wrist. Even a bag of frozen peas to your chest. This temperature change activates your vagus nerve, which is a part of your autonomous nervous system. When you activate it by changing the temperature, your body naturally calms down."

"Huh." I pull the blanket tighter around me. "Probably a method I should tell Atlas and Ellis about."

Maggie smiles. "Probably. And, Nora, I definitely think you should give your diary another try."

"Yeah, you're right. I will try to write again and talk to Atlas. Thank you, Maggie."

"Any time, Nora. And as always, if you need me before our next session, I'm here."

I wait for the screen to go dark before disconnecting on my end and closing the laptop. Maggie's right—my diary is a part of me, and I'm not letting Rand take it from me. I refuse.

And so, with a new sense of confidence, I abandon the desk

in favor of James's rocker, determined and ready to put the pain Rand's caused me to paper, so that once and forever, I can give it away.

DIARY ENTRY, PRESENT DAY

Dear Diary,

It's been a whole week since everything went down. Seven whole days of Atlas and Ellis treating me like I'm made of the most fragile, handblown glass. 168 hours of the two of them micromanaging my every movement-down to when I eat and how much I sleep. 10,080 minutes of being torn between relief and dread.

I sound dramatic, but for the love of God, I can hardly even pee alone. They're driving me up the wall.

You'd think with Rand gone, I'd finally be truly free. But the guys barely want to leave the house. I haven't even gotten a new phone-which means I haven't talked to Scarlet either.

Somehow, I'm surrounded by love, but more alone than ever.

Now I sound selfish, but I just want everything to be normal again.

I want to claim the second chance at life -well, third chance, really-I've been given. I want to explore, go to school, find a job. I want to do it all, but every time I mention it, Atlas turns into a worried mother hen.

Don't get me wrong, I love his protectiveness, but there's a divide between us now. A disconnect. He's coddling me when all I want is to finally spread my wings and fly.

There's so much more I want to tell you, Diary. But I hear my keepers, as well-intentioned as they may be, calling for me, and if I don't respond, they very well may bust down the door.

Annoyed, Nora

"hat time was her appointment again?" Ellis asks, interrupting my nervous pacing.

"Ten."

"That was two hours ago," he mutters, slapping another slice of cheese onto the sandwich he's making.

"Well aware." My answers are short, but we've both been wound tighter than tight since bringing Nora home. And with us both on leave from work, we have all the time in the world to worry.

Worry about what? *Every-fucking-thing.* Is Nora eating enough? Is she sleeping well? Is she having nightmares? Does she blame me for her getting taken? Is James okay? Will I be a good dad? And on, and on, and on.

Honestly, I'm on my own nerves at this point, so it's a wonder

Nora hasn't told me to take a hike.

I post up against the bar and watch as Ellis fusses with our plates—positioning the perfectly cut sandwiches just so, with fresh fruit, and chips.

"Maybe we should check on her?" he asks, his eyes anxiously flicking my way before going back down at Nora's plate.

At this point, his worry is more than an echo of mine—hell, the other night, I caught him trying to poke his head into our room to check on her. If he was anyone else, I'd worry, but I know Ellis, and while he's *invested* in Nora, he's not *interested*.

If anything, knowing he has her back the way he does allows me to breathe a little easier.

"Roger that." I head for the hall. "Make us drinks and I'll see if she's done."

Despite my every instinct telling me to run, I force myself to walk back to our room, where I rap my knuckle against the door frame.

I hear Nora's muffled groan followed by the sound of a book—most likely her diary—snapping shut.

"Pip?" I ask, forcing my hands down to my sides so I don't knock again. "You okay?"

"Yup." Her monosyllabic reply is brimming with forced positivity. My girl's in a mood, and while I don't know who or what upset her, I'll damn sure do my level best to fix it.

"Lunch is ready..." I trail my fingers over the doorknob, but it swings open before I can actually turn it.

"Great." She slips past me, and stalks off toward the kitchen. "Let's eat."

"I have just the thing to turn that frown upside down," Ellis says as Nora and I both grab seats at the bar.

"I'm sure you think you do," Nora mutters, crossing her arms over her chest.

"Oh, someone's feeling big spicy, huh?" Ellis mimics her pose. It'd be comical if Nora didn't look ready to explode.

"I'm really not in the mood."

My eyes zero in on the way her lower lip quivers, as if she's holding back tears. *Fuck.*

"Are you okay, Pip?" I try to wrap my arm around her shoulders but she shrugs out of my hold. "Talk to me," I urge, feeling helpless. "What's wrong?"

"You're what's wrong!" she snaps. "Both of you!"

Ellis and I both rear back. Jesus, fuck. A bullet to the chest would've hurt less.

"Us?" Ellis asks with enough audacity for both of us. "Surely not."

"Surely yes." Nora shoves her stool away from the bar and hops to her feet.

"Gonna need you to take a breath and explain," Ellis says, while I just gape at her in shock.

I pride myself for being in tune with Nora, down to the point of almost anticipating her every need, but it's crystal-fucking-clear that I'm missing something. And I don't like the way it feels. Not one bit.

"Nora?" I croak, desperate to soothe whatever's bothering her.

"I'm sorry," she whispers, her hazel eyes filling with tears.

"It's okay. You've been through so much," I say, trying to comfort her.

"No." She steps away from me. "It's not that."

"Then what is it?" My head is spinning trying to figure her

out. "Please talk to me, Pip. How can I protect you—"

"That's just it!" she shouts, her face red with anger I never realized she was carrying.

"There's nothing left to protect me from. Rand is dead. He's gone. But I'm not." She thumps her small fist against her chest. "I'm still here. He. Didn't. Win."

Nora's trembling and crying as she lays into us, and all I want to do is take her in my arms. But I know damn well that's the wrong move.

"I'm not some broken little doll y'all need to super glue back together. I'm here and I'm whole and I'm healing. We..." She sniffles as she swipes angrily at the tears lining her cheeks. "We have our entire lives ahead of us—but how am I supposed to live mine if you two want to keep me under lock and key?"

"Fuck, Pip," I say, finally finding my voice. "I-I had no idea you felt like this." I take a step closer to her and then freeze. "I'm sorry."

Nora raises one delicate brow.

"I am." I flex my hands at my sides to keep from balling them into fists. "I'm not sorry for worrying about you or for wanting to protect you, but I am sorry my actions made you feel smothered. You're right, there is no imminent threat anymore with Rand gone."

Ellis remains silent, allowing the two of us to hash it out.

"I just want to experience life—all of it, the good and the bad—"

"Let's maybe take a long break from the bad, yeah?" Ellis says lightly.

"For a long time, I didn't think I'd ever see anything outside of the four walls of your dad's basement, but I'm finally, truly free and I want to live my life—with you by my side—to the absolute fullest. Even if it hurts sometimes, I know I'll make it with you there to catch me. I love you, Atlas."

Ellis huffs under his breath like a bear-sized toddler.

"And you, too, you big idiot. But y'all have to let me spread my wings, otherwise this house, which I love, will start to feel like a cage."

"You hear that, man?" Ellis asks, wagging his brows. "Your girl loves me."

"Like a brother," Nora and I say at the same time, effectively alleviating the last of the lingering tension. "But seriously, Pip. I'll do my best to take a step back. I love you—so much. But maybe be patient with me? I almost lost you."

"Deal." She grins, and I swear to God, she's glowing—Nora's the most beautiful woman on the planet, and she's all mine. "Baby steps. Now, let's eat so I can tell you two idiots about a new calming technique Maggie taught me."

FIFTY-ONE
Nora

It's not the chipper sound of birds singing or the soft dappled sunlight shining in between the crack in the curtains that wakes me up the next morning.

Nope.

It's the sound of someone knocking on our front door like they're seconds away from kicking it down and forcing their way inside.

"What the hell?" Atlas mutters, shoving the blankets off himself before stumbling out of bed.

"Atlas," I hiss, torn between tugging the covers closer and following after him.

Ultimately staying behind—where it's safe—wins out. Not because I'm necessarily afraid, but because Atlas would probably blow a gasket if I tried to follow him.

Baby steps and all that.

Another round of knocking starts up, followed by shouting, and while I can't make out exact words, the voice sounds feminine—but also sort of like a bear. You know, if bears sounded like they were preparing for war.

"The fuck?" I hear Ellis mumble as he, too, heads toward the front door.

Too intrigued to stay put, I rush to the bedroom door and peek my head out, hoping to figure out what's going on.

"Atlas Wallace, I swear to God, you better open this damn door or I'll find a way to rip it off its hinges!"

That's... Scarlet's here!

I poke my head out a little further when I hear the front door open.

"Why are you here?" Atlas growls, sounding every bit like a guard dog I neither want nor need.

"I'm here to see Nora—"

"You need to leave," Ellis says, his voice a menacing rumble as he stands shoulder to shoulder with Atlas, physically denying her entry.

"This is ridiculous." I can't see Scarlet, but I can picture her throwing her hands in the air in frustration. "You're both acting like—"

"Like you allowed the woman I love to get taken by a goddamn monster?"

"No, you're acting like Nora's a child, incapable of making her own choices. I don't know how she deals with y'all's macho bullshit, but she deserves—"

"Shut your mouth," Ellis says, cutting her off, "and leave."

"Not until I see Nora."

"Haven't you done enough?" Atlas asks.

Fury burns through me like lava—which is fitting, because I feel like I'm about to blow—as I tug on one of Atlas's hoodies and jam my feet into my slippers. I've had enough of their *macho bullshit*, as Scarlet called it, and one way or another, it ends here and now.

"Did either of you hear a single thing I said yesterday?" I ask, my voice barely above a whisper as I join them all in the foyer.

"Nora!" Atlas whips around to face me but refuses to make eye contact. "Pip, please."

"No." I cross my arms over my chest. "Don't you *Pip, please* me. We literally just talked about this last night. Y'all promised to take a step back, but here we are less than twenty-four hours later, and you're both out here making choices for me that you have no right to make."

"Fuck." Atlas scrubs his hands over his face and then through his hair. "You're right, Pip. I just want to keep you safe."

"I get that," I whisper, stepping closer to him and cradling his cheek with my palm as I smooth his furrowed brow with my thumb. "And I appreciate it. Your heart is in the right place, but, Atlas, I want a partner. Not a guard dog."

"Woof!" Scarlet barks before shouldering her way past Ellis. "Now, can we *please* talk?"

"That's up to Nora," Atlas mutters, finally getting on the same page as me.

"Yes, please," I say, linking arms with Scarlet. "But first, coffee."

"Well, I still think inviting Satan into our house is a mistake," Ellis says as he shuts the front door. "But no one cares what I think."

"Now you're getting it, Officer Jackass," Scarlet quips back at him. "Now be a good boy and make us some coffee. We have much to discuss."

I start for the kitchen, but Scarlet tugs me toward the living room. "Might as well be comfy for this conversation," she murmurs with a self-deprecating smile.

She plops down onto the couch, and I follow suit, scooting closer to her than either of us is probably comfortable with. I angle myself toward her and then tuck my feet beneath me before reaching for her hands.

It's a little weird, but something tells me we could both use the comfort.

"You know it wasn't your fault, right?" I ask, even as tears burn the back of my eyes. "I don't blame you."

"I... fuck." Scarlet swipes away her tears and then laughs. "You don't know how badly I needed to hear that. It's been hell since you were taken. Especially because Dumb and Dumber decided to ice me out."

I give her hand a squeeze. "I'm sorry about them. They're... struggling."

"If I can't internalize blame, you can't apologize on their behalf. They're grown-ass men."

"Oh, listen to you," I say right as Atlas and Ellis join us. "You almost sound like my therapist."

Atlas passes me a still-steaming mug of coffee before claiming the seat on the other side of me. "Thank you," I tell him before taking a long sip of the piping-hot liquid.

Ellis hands Scarlet hers with a scowl before retreating to his chair, where he crosses his arms over his chest and glares at us like a petulant child.

"You're not the only one in therapy here, babe," Scarlet says. "In fact, if you two idiots aren't talking to someone, I strongly suggest it."

"Ellis actually gave me the number of the guy he talks to." Atlas glances away as he scratches the back of his neck. "I, uh, plan to call him in the next few days to set up an appointment."

"Wait, wait, wait." Scarlet whips her head around to Ellis. "You mean to tell me Officer Jackass over there is actually emotionally mature?" She rubs her chin. "Color me surprised."

"Color you a bitch," Ellis mutters, his glare somehow both frostier and more heated than ever.

"My favorite shade of pink." Scarlet grins. "No, but in all seriousness, I'm glad y'all are *all* talking with someone about this. It's..." Her throat bobs as she swallows. "A lot."

FIFTY-TWO
Atlas

It's late afternoon by the time Scarlet finally leaves, and while Nora will never admit it out loud, I can tell my girl is running on fumes. She needs food and a nap, in that order.

Well, and another apology, because once again, she was right and I was wrong.

It's not that I want to control or micromanage her. Hell no. The fear of losing her seems to override every ounce of logic I possess. It's like the minute her safety is on the line, my rational brain checks the fuck out.

I know she's right, though—and now I have to make sure she knows that I know. Which means we need to talk, and it'll undoubtedly go smoother without an audience.

I nod my head toward the front door and lift my brows at Ellis. Luckily, we've known each other long enough that he knows

I'm silently asking him to scram.

"I've gotta head out for a bit," he says as he stands. "I'm sorry about this morning, Nora. I was a dick."

Asshole just had to beat me to apologizing.

"You were," Nora agrees.

"What can I say?" He shrugs his shoulders. "Scarlet brings out the worst in me."

Nora rolls her eyes. "There's a fine line between love—"

Ellis slams his hands over his ears. "Don't you dare finish that sentence. The only person who's ever loved that she-devil is her parents, and even that's questionable."

"Ellis Wilder, you better be nice, because there's no way I'm naming my son after an asshole!"

"Whoa!" My best friend clutches at his chest like he's been shot. "Okay, okay. I'll play nice—ish."

"I'll take what I can get." Nora sighs and shakes her head. "Be safe, okay?"

Ellis nods and then pulls the door closed behind him.

"So," I say, now that it is just the two of us, "I need to apologize. Again."

Nora simply quirks a brow at me, waiting for me to actually make good on my word.

"I'm so damn sorry, Pip. I heard everything you said last night, but I didn't listen." I scoot closer to her and take her hands in mine. "You deserve better than that. You hit the nail on the head this morning when you said you wanted a partner, not a guard dog. I promise—I fucking vow—to do better. To be the man you deserve."

"You really mean that?" she asks, her lower lip quivering as she takes me in with damp, wide eyes.

"From the bottom of my heart." I free one of my hands and draw an X over my chest.

She launches herself at me, peppering my face with sloppy, excited kisses as she climbs into my lap, her legs straddling mine. "I love you so much, Atlas. You may be flawed, but you're absolutely perfect for me."

"Love you, too," I bite out between kisses. "Love you—"

Nora nips at my lips, effectively silencing me. "Take me to bed."

"Are... are you sure?" Nora tenses in my arms, making me want to kick my own ass. "Never mind. Ignore me. You wouldn't have said it if you didn't mean it."

"Now you're getting it," she murmurs, relaxing back into my embrace.

"Hang on tight," I say as I band my arms beneath her ass and stand, holding her as close to me as her rounded belly will allow.

"So..." she draws out the word. "Would you consider this our first fight?"

"More of a disagreement, really." I breathe the words against her neck, breathing in her sweet scent as I fumble down the hall.

"Shame." She sticks out her tongue at me. "I was hoping we could make up."

"Nora Morgan, are you asking me for makeup sex?" Honest to God, my brain damn near short circuits. I fucking love this bold, playful side of her.

"Maybe." She tries burying her head in my chest, her cheeks undoubtedly strawberry red, but I'm not having it.

"You know what you need to do, Pip." I set her down at the foot of our bed. "Look me in the eye and ask for what you want, like a good girl."

"Yes, Atlas." A shiver works its way through her as she peers up at me from beneath her lashes, her pupils blown wide. "I am asking you for makeup sex. I want you to show me exactly how sorry you are—preferably with your body."

"Hot damn, Pip," I groan, tugging my shirt over my head and tossing it to the floor. "Strip for me?"

"Are you asking or telling?" she asks coyly. The minx knows just what to say to rile me up.

"Asking. Always asking. When it comes to the two of us, you're always in control, Pip. But you know that already, don't you?"

"Yes, I know." She grins and then captures her bottom lip between her teeth. "Sit down."

My ass hits the bed like there's a magnet in it, my eyes never once leaving her. She starts slow, toeing off her thick socks before letting her hair down and running her fingers through it. Her long, coppery locks remind me of fire with the way the sun's shining on her through the cracks in the blinds.

Then she pulls off my hoodie, leaving her in only a pair of my sweats. I have to clench my fists at my sides to keep from reaching for her, because while seeing her in my clothes is a sight I'll never grow tired of, seeing Nora naked is a damn near religious experience.

My girl's pale, freckled perfection, and I can't fucking wait to worship at her altar.

She hooks her thumbs beneath the waistband, tugging the fabric down ever so slightly, toying with me in the most delicious way.

"Take them off," I growl, desperate to see how wet she already is for me. Because if I know Nora even a little, she's dripping. Her pregnancy hormones have her libido in hyperdrive, and like the idiot I am, I've been denying her since everything went down with Rand. "Show me that pretty pussy, Pip."

Her cheeks burn my favorite shade of red as she tugs them down, baring herself to me. All I want is to lean forward and finish stripping her down.

Thankfully, she doesn't draw out her sweet, teasing torture for long.

As soon as she's bare before me, I give in to the temptation her naked body brings, dragging my lips over her lower belly as I breathe in the intoxicating scent of her arousal. "Fuck, you're already so wet for me," I moan, my mouth already watering at the thought of tasting her.

"Atlas," she whimpers, and it's hands down the single most erotic sound I've ever heard in my life. I'm helpless but to give her what she wants—what we both want.

I pull her into me and flip us around, laying her out in the middle of the bed. She looks like a damn siren, with her wild hair, rosy cheeks, and lust-blown eyes.

"Spread your legs for me, Pip," I command, leaning over her.

She complies with a breathy moan, parting her thighs for me and then hitching them up toward her chest, completely baring her slick pussy to me.

"Such a good girl," I say as I settle myself between her legs and shoulder them wider before licking a path right up her center. "Tastes like fucking heaven."

"Atlas." My name is nothing more than a whine as she writhes against the sheets. "Please."

"Tell me what you need." I already know, but like always, I crave her words.

"Make me…" She squirms beneath me, desperately trying to create friction. "Feel good."

I spread her lips with my thumbs, lick my way up her slit, and then draw her clit into my mouth, sucking hard on the sensitive bundle of nerves.

"Oh, God," she pants, twisting the sheets in her grasp as she bucks against me. "More!"

"You want more, Nora?" I sound more beast than man, but that's what she does to me. She brings every baser instinct roaring to life.

"Please." One word, and it's somehow both a taunt and a plea. But I'll never, ever leave my girl wanting, and I'll never not rise to the occasion.

"I've got you, Pip." Dipping my index finger inside of her, I tease her mercilessly before adding another, curling them inside her in the way I know drives her wild.

She tunnels her fingers into my hair, tugging hard as I work her over with my fingers and my tongue in tandem. "Oh, God, I'm so—"

"I know, Pip." I nip at her thigh. "Ride my face and let me hear you scream."

She tugs hard, guiding me back to where she wants me, and I dive in, licking and sucking and kissing and rubbing until her legs shake and her back bows up off the mattress as she screams my name.

"I still want more," Nora whispers as I pepper her slick thighs with soft kisses.

"Then I'll give you more." I kiss my way up her body, paying special attention to her hips, belly, breasts, and neck, before lining myself up and pushing into her tight, wet heat. "Fuck, you feel so good, Pip."

"So do you." She wraps her arms around my neck and pulls my face toward hers, meeting me halfway for a sloppy kiss.

I rock into her, over and over, keeping a slow, tantalizing pace. But my girl's not having it. "Harder, Atlas. Please, I... I want it harder."

God, I love hearing her vocalize what she needs. It's so fucking hot.

"You want it harder?" I ask, my lips curling in a pleasure-soaked smile.

She nods frantically as she reaches behind her head to grip the headboard.

I pull back, until just the tip of my cock is still inside of her, and then slam back into her hard enough to make her eyes roll back into her head.

"You feel so fucking good, Pip. Like heaven." I murmur sweet filth into her ear as I fill her over and over again. "So wet and tight and perfect and mine. You're mine, Nora. In this life and the next."

"Always," she vows, her chest heaving, her cheeks flush, and her pupils blown wide with pleasure. She's a sight to behold—a fucking goddess, my goddess.

I feel the telltale tingle at the base of my spine and slip my hand between us, pressing my thumb down onto her clit, massaging it in time with my stroke. "Need you to come, Pip. Be a good girl and come all over my cock."

Nora throws her head back, crying out my name as she crashes over the edge into oblivion.

Her pussy squeezes my dick like a fist, milking me for all I'm worth as I spill myself inside of her.

"So. Damn. Perfect." I rasp my praise against her neck, punctuating each word with a kiss as we both come back down to earth.

"I love you," she murmurs sweetly, exhaustion already settling in.

"I love you, Pip. So damn much."

FIFTY-THREE
Nora

I chew on the end of my pen and stretch my back from side to side as I read over my latest diary entry. This one is all about my last ultrasound—Scarlet convinced Dr. Snider to do a few extra, given the trauma I went through.

James is absolutely perfect—from his heart rate to his measurements. Scarlet says he's a wiggler and that I should feel him move any day now. Which is annoying, since my pregnancy book says most first-time moms feel their baby by twenty weeks, and here I am a whole two weeks past that, and haven't felt a thing.

Wait a minute...

I freeze in place, focusing all of my attention on my belly.

No way...

I toss my diary to the side and hold my breath, hoping like hell this isn't just wishful thinking.

Minutes that feel like hours pass, but then, sure enough, my belly ripples like someone's popping popcorn inside of it.

"Atlas!" I grab his hand and place it on my belly.

"What?" he asks, still halfway asleep.

"The baby!" Excitement and disbelief pulse through me in equal measure.

"What about the baby?" he asks, panic edging the sleep out of his voice.

"I can feel him!" I literally feel like I'm floating, I'm so happy. "He's moving."

His focus lasers in on where I placed his hand. "I don't..."

"Shh. Just wait."

We both sit in silence, holding our breath as we wait for James to move again.

"There!" I glance his way. "Did you feel it?"

"Holy shit!" His voice is tinged with awe. "That's—that's our baby?"

"Yeah." I nod as tears fill my eyes.

"Fuck." That single word somehow encompasses every single emotion rocketing through me.

"I know." I rub the space our sweet jellybean was just kicking. "It's so surreal to feel him... I can't even describe it."

Atlas abruptly rolls away from me, grabbing something from his nightstand. "I can."

He rolls back toward me with a small velvet ring box in his hand. "It feels like the start of forever. Like the rest of our lives. Like every good thing that ever was or ever will be. I love you, Nora. I love you more than I can put into words."

"Atlas," I whimper, already knowing but somehow not daring to believe where this is going.

"Shh, Pip. Let me try." He flips open the box revealing a sparkling oval cut diamond on a gold band. It's simple, yet perfect. "Marry me, Pip. Let's make this thing between us official."

I don't mean to laugh at him, but I do. "We're official no matter what. You know that, right?"

"Yeah." He grins as he plucks the ring from the box. "I know. Doesn't mean I don't wanna see this on your finger, though."

I hold my left hand out to him. "Then make it *official*."

"Are you saying yes?"

I roll my eyes.

"C'mon, Nora. Put me out of my misery. You know I need your words, pretty girl."

"Yes, Atlas. Yes. A million times over, in this life and the next. Yes. I'd be honored to be your wife and to spend forever with you by my side."

He slides the ring onto my finger, and we both take a minute to admire it. "You've made me the happiest man on this planet. You know that, right?"

"If you're the happiest man, I'm the happiest woman. You've given me a life I never thought I'd have. I'm... *God*." I use the sleeves of his hoodie to wipe away my tears. "I'm so thankful for you, for your persistence. Your patience. The way you love me is what dreams are made of."

He darts forward and presses his lips to mine, sealing his proposal with a kiss.

"I love you," he murmurs again before pulling away. "And now that you're wearing my ring, there's something else I want to talk to you about."

"Okay..." I hedge, suddenly unsure. *What could he possibly want to talk about? We should be celebrating.*

He suddenly looks nervous—like he's not sure how whatever he's about to say is going to go over. "I've just... I've been thinking about my last name."

I blink at him and then slowly nod. "What about it?"

Atlas reaches forward and takes both of my hands in his, his thumb absentmindedly rubbing over the band of my ring. "I don't want you to take my last name."

"What?" Surely I heard him wrong. Not that I think a woman has to take her partner's last name; I think people should do whatever works for them. But he's definitely thrown me for a loop. "I... I don't understand."

He sighs. "I guess this might fall into the me acting like an overbearing ass category, so please know if you're not into it, I won't mind."

"I can't tell you how I feel, because you still haven't actually told me anything."

His lips curve up into the smallest of smiles. "I think I should take your last name instead. The Wallace name isn't something I want to pass down to our son. My dad's legacy should end with him."

"I..." A fresh round of tears blurs my vision as I try to find the right words. "Do you mean that?"

"With all of my heart. My father put you through hell, and he doesn't deserve the honor of having any part of our family or our future, even in name. I know it's unorthodox, but..."

I launch myself at him. "I love you, Atlas *Morgan*."

He catches me easily, positioning us so we both lie on our sides, forehead to forehead. "Sounds good, am I right?"

"It sounds perfect. Like it was meant to be."

"Fitting." He darts forward and kisses the tip of my nose.

"Seeing as we're meant to be. You really are my whole heart, Nora. Without you, there is no me."

"Well, that's a little dramatic." I giggle, but Atlas is as serious as I've ever seen him.

"It's not dramatic, Pip. Before you, I wasn't living—I was merely existing. But you, you've given me a purpose. Now I know why I'm on this earth. Loving you is my entire reason for being. Do you believe me?"

I can feel my heart knocking against my ribs, a steady thump-thump-thump, as I take in the man before me. His face is open and honest—he truly means every word he's saying. And that's absolutely enough for me.

"I do."

He groans. "Can't wait to hear you say those two words for real. Maybe wearing a white dress, in front of our friends."

"Name the date and place, and I'll be there," I say with a wink.

"Depends. Do we want to get married before or after James is born?"

I tap my index finger against my chin as I mull it over. "Both."

He lifts his brows. "Both? What does that mean?"

"It means I want us to do the legal stuff before he's born so he can come into this world with us all sharing the same last name, but I want to hold off on the ceremony until he's born. I know it's dumb, but I want him to be a part of it, even if he'll only be a baby."

"It's not weird." Atlas cups my cheek, and I can't help but nuzzle into his warm calloused palm. "It's perfect."

"You mean it?" I ask, even though I already know he does. He's honest to a fault.

"Yeah, Pip. I mean it. Now, let's go tell Ellis the big news."

"Are you going to ask him to be your best man?"

"I was thinking flower girl."

Laughter explodes out of me. "He'd so do it. He's been showing me these videos of guys doing just that. Says they're called flower dudes."

"Oh, shit." Atlas releases a deep chuckle. "Maybe we better stick to best man then. You gonna ask Scarlet?"

"Yup." Who else would I ask?

"Here's to hoping those two can get along long enough for us to say our vows."

"I think they might surprise you." It's like I tried saying to Ellis the other day, the line between love and hate is razor thin, after all.

EPILOGUE ONE
Atlas

"Atlas," Nora calls from a few yards away.

"Almost done!" I holler back, assuming lunch is ready. "Just gotta tighten these straps."

Nora's due in two weeks, so I figure now's as good a time as any to get the car seat installed.

"Tighten them quickly."

The strain in her voice has me whipping around to face her. She has one hand on the top of her belly and the other cradling it from below. Her shoulders are tense, her eyes are pinched shut, and her lips are pursed.

Something's wrong.

"What's going on, Pip?" I ask, giving the strap one last tug before closing the car door.

"James—he's—now."

"What about James?"

"It's time," she says through clenched teeth.

"Time... time like—"

"We need to head to the hospital, Atlas." She sucks in a deep breath and then lets it out slowly. *"Now."*

"Fuck, now. Okay. Bags! We need your bags." I rush toward the house, but stop at the threshold. "Where are they again?"

"Our closet."

"Okay. Got it. You wait here. I'll grab everything and then help you into the truck."

She nods, and I take off like a shot, hollering Ellis's name as I rush down the hall.

"Yeah?" he calls back, poking his head out of his door.

"It's baby time."

"For real?" Leave it to him to somehow sound more nervous than me.

"Yeah. We're headed to the hospital. Do me a favor and let Scarlet know."

"You're lucky I love y'all, man." Maybe Nora's right and there is something there, because God knows, they fight like an old married couple. "Let me know when my nephew is born. I call dibs on holding him first."

"Yeah, yeah. You two better be on your best behavior or I swear to God, I'll kick you out of Nora's hospital room."

"It's not my fault you and your girl befriended Satan." Ellis mimes a halo over his head. "I'm a perfect angel."

I try not to grin at his antics, but it's a losing battle. "I don't have time for this. Text Scar and keep your phone nearby. I've gotta go."

He tips his head my way in acknowledgment, and then I'm

on my way. I make quick work of grabbing Nora's bag, pillow, and the gift I picked out for her, especially for this occasion—a push present, Scarlet called it.

I race back to the truck like I'm trying for Olympic gold, throw the bag in the back seat, and then help Nora into the cab.

"You ready, Pip?" I ask, stepping onto the running board to buckle her in.

She looks back at me with wide eyes. "What if I'm a bad mom?"

I rear back. "Not possible."

"Atlas, I mean it."

"Nora Morgan, you are everything good in this world, and there's absolutely zero possibility of that not carrying over to motherhood. I guarantee it."

She gasps and grabs my hand, squeezing it with a strength I didn't know she was capable of. "Okay."

"How far apart are your contractions?" I ask, because they seem to be coming pretty quickly.

"Um, like two or three minutes apart."

My eyes widen to the point where I'm sure I look like a cartoon character. "Okay." I suck in a deep breath of my own. "Okay, yup. Let's go."

I step down and race around the front of the truck before hopping behind the wheel and hitting the ignition. I'd like to say I drive calmly and follow all of the traffic laws, but that'd be a damn lie. I drive like a bat out of hell, bobbing and weaving between cars, my eyes anxiously flitting between the road and Nora.

In fact, the only other time I've ever driven anywhere near like this was the day Nora was taken, and coincidentally, both of those days ended up with us in the hospital. At least this visit is planned—mostly.

"How you doing over there?" I ask as I merge onto the highway.

"Peachy," Nora replies through gritted teeth. "Just freaking peachy."

I reach over and take her hand in mine, knowing damn well she's about to use it like a stress ball. "We're not too far out now."

She nods in my peripheral, too focused on her breathing to reply.

Please let us make it in time. Please don't let my son be born in my truck...

"Um, Atlas," Nora whispers as she grabs my hand, clutching it tight. "You m-might wanna hurry."

"Going as fast as I can, Pip." I rub the back of her hand with my thumb. "Traffic's—"

"You don't understand." She's nearly panting. "My wa-water just broke."

"Shit!" Every single part of me wants to panic, but I can't. Nora needs me to keep my cool. "Okay. Um. Fuck."

"Sums it up," she groans, her entire body tensing yet again. "I... I don't think we're gonna make it."

"Just breathe through it, Pip. I'll get us there, I promise."

If I could, I'd take every ounce of pain and worry she's feeling and pull it into my body so she wouldn't have to suffer, but life unfortunately doesn't work like that.

I spot a break in traffic and flick on my blinker before merging into the outside lane. "You're doing so good, Nora. We're almost there."

"Atlas... I'm not... oh, God."

"What?" I ask, panic clawing up the back of my throat.

"What is it?"

"There's so much pressure. It... I don't know. I think I need to..."

Horror dawns as her words truly sink in. "Push... you need to push."

She nods. "I think so. It's... oh, God. Pull over! Please, Atlas, pull over!"

Once again, I pop my blinker on, this time pulling onto the shoulder, where I throw it into park and flip on my hazards.

"Tell me what you need."

"To get this baby out of me!" she wails. She's a mess with glassy eyes, rosy cheeks, and wild hair—and yet, she's never looked more perfect to me. "What do we do, Atlas?"

"I'm gonna help you into the back seat and see if we can't get you at least somewhat comfortable. Then I'm going to call 911, okay?"

She sniffles and nods as she unbuckles her seat belt.

"Stay here and let me come around to help you."

It takes a second for a break in the relentless line of cars rushing past before I can safely hop out and make my way around to her side of the truck.

When I open her door, Nora practically throws herself into my arms. "I'm scared," she whispers, as I guide her to the back seat.

"I know you are, but I've got you. I won't let anything happen to you."

"You can't say that," she objects, but I silence her with a soft kiss.

"I can and I will. Now, I want you to prop your pillow against the door and try to get comfy. Can you do that for me?"

She nods and positions her pillow just so before reclining back against it.

"You good?"

She tenses as yet another contraction works its way through her. "Not really."

"I think I have a blanket in the bed from our last bonfire. I'm gonna run and check, okay?"

Nora nods and I take off toward the tailgate, sliding my phone from my pocket and firing off a text to Ellis as I go.

> **Me**
> It's GO time.
> Didn't make it to the hospital.
> On 27 just past mile marker 15.

Sure enough, there's a soft flannel blanket in the back of my truck, along with two bottles of water. I repocket my phone and grab my found supplies before rushing back to Nora.

My phone buzzes and I quickly scan Ellis's reply as I rush back to Nora.

> **Ellis**
> 10-4.

By the time I make it back to Nora, she's kicked off her leggings and is on her knees in the back seat, bracing herself on the center console, as she pants.

"How you doing, pretty girl?" I ask, keeping my voice low.

She glares in reply as a bead of sweat rolls down her temple, despite the frigid air.

"Got a blanket and some water," I offer lamely, setting my bundle down on the seat beside her. "Gonna call us some backup now, okay?"

Nora huffs and nods, a pained cry escaping her lips. "I need to push, Atlas. Oh, God."

I hit dial, put the call on speaker, and climb into the back seat with her.

"911. What's your emergency?"

"My wife is in labor. We're on the side of 27 and not going to make it to the hospital."

"How many weeks pregnant is she?"

"Thirty-eight."

"How far apart are her contractions?"

"It seems like they're relentless."

"Okay, sir. Has her water broken?"

"Yes. She's... she's pushing." A thread of panic bleeds into my voice as I think of all the ways this could go wrong.

"Stay calm for me, paramedics will be there soon. Do you have a blanket or anything—"

"Yes, I do."

"Good. If the baby's born before the ambulance gets there, I want you to wrap the baby in the blanket, okay? Then you'll need to wipe the baby's face. You may also need to clear the airway."

"I... how the fuck do I do that?"

The dispatcher rattles off instructions, and then says, "I'm going to stay on the phone with you until paramedics arrive."

I leave the call on speaker and drop my phone down onto the floorboard before I turn all of my focus to Nora, rubbing her lower back as I try to soothe her. "You're doing great, Pip. Deep breaths."

"Atlas," she growls my name in a tone I've never heard her use before. "I swear to God, if you tell me to breathe again I am going to lose my mind."

"Okay, okay." *Shit, man, get it together. Nora needs you to be strong for her.* "How can I help?"

"I-I don't know. It hurts. There's so much pressure. It... it feels like he's—"

Her words cut off mid-sentence as her entire body tenses. I swear, I can see her pulse pounding in her neck.

"Are you..." I force myself to swallow back my fear. "Do you need to push?"

"Already there," she clips out, her face as red as a tomato as she digs her fingers into the soft leather of my seat.

I watch on helplessly as the love of my life pushes and grunts and groans and wails, until finally—even though it's actually only been moments—she brings our son into this world all on her own.

"His head, Atlas. Get his—"

I fling myself out of the truck and lean in as far as I can, prepared to help guide him earthside.

His ear-piercing cry fills the truck cab in time with sirens in the distance, as I bundle him in the blanket.

"That's... that's our baby, Pip," I murmur, totally and completely awestruck. I use the tail of the blanket to wipe away the gunk smeared across his chubby little cheeks. "He's perfect."

She collapses back against the seat, bloody and exhausted— *oh, God, is that much blood normal? Fuck! Get. It. Together.*

"Lemme hold him, baby hog," she mutters, her eyelids drooping even as she holds out her arms.

I slide onto the seat next to her and place him on her chest. "James Wilder Morgan," she coos. "You're absolutely..." She looks up at me, and her eyes may as well be hearts.

"Perfect."

The sound of a vehicle pulling up behind draws my attention

momentarily away from Nora.

"It's just Ellis," I murmur softly.

"Look at my guy," he crows, crowding me at the back door. "He has all ten fingers and all ten toes?"

Nora rolls her eyes and then kisses his wrinkly forehead. "We'd love him even if he didn't."

"That's a good mama." He leans around me to get a better look at him, only to immediately blanch and back away.

"Do you get gifts when a baby's born?" he asks, looking a little green around the gills. "I mean, it is his birthday, right?"

"What are you even talking about, man?"

"Doesn't matter. Gonna get you a gift certificate to get your damn truck detailed. Looks like a crime scene in here."

Nora cuts her eyes at him, and I worry for a split second he's offended her, but then she laughs and calls him an idiot.

"I'd say takes one to know one, but you might just be the smartest person I know."

She scoffs. "Whatever."

"Well, you are with this guy." He nods his head toward me. "So maybe I'm onto something."

"Swear to God," I mutter under my breath, sounding put out even though I'm smiling. How could I not be? Nora's okay. Our son is here and seems healthy. Hell, today just might be the best day of my life.

EPILOGUE TWO
Nora

"Are you nervous?" Scarlet asks, peeking her head around the flowy curtain separating us from the ceremony space.

"Not even a little," I reply, meaning it with every ounce of my being. What's there to be nervous about? Atlas is, without a doubt, my other half. He's my forever. Not to mention, we're already official on paper, today is just to celebrate with friends.

Aside from Ellis and Scar, who are both standing with us as we exchange vows, we both invited a handful of other people.

"Mama," James babbles, reaching for one of the curls framing my face, but Scarlet redirects him in the nick of time.

"Yes, my love?" I coo, brushing my index finger over his cheek.

"Dada!" He wriggles in my arms, trying to get me to set him down.

"It's almost time to walk to Dada." I press a kiss to his

forehead, only for Scarlet to scold me.

"You're gonna ruin your lips." I shrug, and she throws her hands in the air. "I swear to God, Nora!"

"If my lip gloss getting smeared because I kiss my baby is the worst thing that happens to me today, it's still a pretty good day, Scar."

"Yeah, yeah," she snarks. "I know, your glass is always half full."

"Indeed, it is." I nod, trying my best not to smile. She's been crabbier than usual since the rehearsal dinner last night, and while I'm not saying it's because Ellis was dancing with a girl from my foundations of learning class, I'm also not *not* saying it either.

"Whatever. Hand him to me and go fix your face."

I pass James to her, not missing the way she melts when my toddler snuggles into her. "Ma'am, yes, ma'am," I say, complete with a mock salute.

"Such a smartass."

"Learned it from you," I fire back, swiping my index finger beneath my bottom lip to gather any stray gloss as I check my reflection one last time.

"Okay, my not-so-little jellybean, are you ready to go see Dada?"

"Dada!" He claps his hands together and squeals. You always hear the saying *mama's boy*, and while he was for the first ten or so months of his life, for the last two months James Wilder Morgan has been all about Atlas. Not that I don't see the appeal—I'm all about the man, too.

Scarlet sets him down, and he immediately tries to take off, but her hand on his shoulder holds him in place.

"Wait for the music," I murmur. "And then straight to Dada."

"Dada!" The song starts, and Scarlet lets him go. And go he does—like a rocket, screaming *Dada* over and over, until finally, he›s right in front of Atlas, with his arms straight in the air, waiting for his daddy to pick him up.

"He made it down the aisle before the chorus." Scarlet is doubled over, cackling.

"All the practice in the world wasn't slowing him down." I sigh and then laugh myself. He's the cutest kid on the planet, that's for sure.

"Should I go now or wait for the next song?"

"Um." I'm not sure what the right call is, but luckily, the DJ pivots and cues up Scarlet's song. "Well, there's your answer."

She reaches over and gives my hand a squeeze. "See you in a few!"

Before I know it, the opening notes of the song Atlas and I selected together fill the venue. I wait a beat, and then with my simple sunflower bouquet clutched to my chest, I step around the curtain and start down the aisle toward my forever.

The sight of Atlas standing at the altar, dressed in his brown and tan wool plaid suit, has me weak in the knees. He looks so handsome, and our son dressed to match on his hip only adds to his appeal.

Honestly, it's unfair how good-looking he is, but I guess I'm okay with it, since he's all mine.

We've technically been married—on paper—since before James was born, but there's something about the thought of committing ourselves to one another in front of all the people we love and who love us that just feels *different*. But in a good way. Like we're on the precipice of something truly epic.

"Mama!" James babbles as I get closer, pointing and waving

and clapping.

"Hi, baby," I whisper, glancing from him to the three empty chairs reserved in remembrance of my parents and Atlas's mother. I'd give anything to have them here with us as we exchange our vows.

I'm not quite sure what I believe happens after death, but it makes me feel better to think they're somewhere together looking down on us, so that's what I'm going with for now.

I shake off the melancholy and close the distance between me and my guys, pausing to press a kiss on James's mysteriously sticky cheek.

Paul—one of Atlas's co-workers and our officiant—kicks off the ceremony as I take my place across from my husband. "Welcome friends and loved ones. We're gathered here today to celebrate the wedding of Atlas and Nora Morgan, to share in the promise they are making to one another, to offer your love and support toward their union, and to help Atlas and Nora to start this new chapter of their lives surrounded by the people they love most."

My gaze settles on Atlas, his eyes meeting mine like a magnet to metal, watching him as he watches me. We're surrounded by everyone we love, and yet, everything falls away and it's like it's just the two of us.

I can hear Paul in the background saying something about our love being our strength, but I'm essentially on autopilot as I attempt to catalog every detail of Atlas holding our son as he stares at me like I'm the single most precious thing he's ever seen.

Day in and day out he *shows* me just how much he loves me—how much he loves us. And while it's been a hell of a ride to get here, I can't help but feel like I ended up exactly where I'm meant to be.

"As I understand it, the couple have prepared their own vows. Atlas?"

I snap back to the present as my groom slides a small index card from his pocket. "Nora, I can say with one-hundred-and-ten percent certainty that you're the best thing that's ever happened to me. Each and every single day with you is better than the last. Before you, I was drifting, content to spend each day just going through the motions—no offense, Scar."

My maid of honor and best friend crosses her arms over her chest and scoffs. "Plenty taken."

"Yeah, well." Atlas shrugs and resituates James on his hip before continuing. "But with you, Pip, it's like suddenly everything makes sense. You're the strongest person I've ever met. The bravest. You've walked through hell—*twice*—and somehow managed to come out the other side still soft, generous, and kind. All of the good in you brings out the best in me.

"And this is going to sound like a line, but I mean it... You're my reason for living, my entire purpose. You and James..." He trails off and presses a sweet kiss to our son's temple, who readily turns and snuggles into him.

"The two of you are my whole world, and I promise to always put our family first. I promise to cherish you and to never take you for granted. You're my heart, Pip, and I love you more than I can put into words. But know that even if I can't articulate it, I'll show you just how much you mean to me, every single day, for the rest of our lives."

"I know you will," I whisper as tears fill my eyes.

"Nora," Paul prompts as Atlas tucks his notecard back into his pocket before focusing all of his attention on me.

"My life didn't truly begin until you saved me." I pause, fully aware he's going to interject.

"You saved yourself, Pip." *Like freaking clockwork.*

Smiling, I shake my head and press on. "Trust me, you did the heavy lifting. You gave me a safe place to land. You helped me heal. You never gave up on me, and I promise, anyone else would have. But not you, never you, Atlas. You've set the bar so high, it's honestly unfair for other men."

"Tell me more, Pip. Keep going." He pretends to brush his shoulder off, making everyone laugh while I roll my eyes. *This man.*

"You're as patient as the day is long. You're kind and gentle and protective. You are every good thing, and I'm so beyond thankful to call you mine. To know I'll get to raise a family with you, to grow old with you by my side, it makes every minute of suffering before you worth it. You're the light that dispelled the darkness. I love you, Atlas Morgan. I love you—now, tomorrow, and forever."

"The couple will now exchange rings as a symbol of their undying love and commitment to one another."

Atlas passes James off to Ellis before plucking a velvet pouch from his pocket. A pouch that I know contains the band he has made for me—the band he's all but kept under lock and key. Apparently, it's a surprise.

My heart thumps like a jackrabbit in my chest as I give my bouquet to Scarlet for safekeeping. In turn, she gives me Atlas's ring, which was tied to her bouquet with twine.

"Please repeat after me as you exchange rings—I give you this ring as a symbol of my love for you. Let it be a reminder that every day, I choose you to be my lover, my partner, and my best friend, now and forever."

We repeat after him in tandem and then I slide Atlas's ring onto his left hand before offering mine for him to do the same. My breath stalls in my chest at the sight of the band—I expected something simple, maybe even understated. But in true Atlas fashion, he went all out.

The band is dainty, with a slight curve, but what makes it really special is instead of diamonds, it alternates our birthstones.

"Atlas," I whisper in complete awe as he slides the ring onto my finger. It nestles the diamond of my engagement ring perfectly. "I love it."

"And I love you." He boops my nose and then takes half a step back.

"Do you, Atlas, take Nora to be your lawfully wedded wife?" Paul asks, and despite us already being married on paper, I find myself waiting with bated breath.

"I do. Today and forever."

"Do you, Nora, take Atlas to be your lawfully wedded husband?"

"I do. Always."

"By the authority vested in me, it is with joy that I pronounce you married. Atlas, you may now kiss your bride."

Atlas closes the distance between us in the blink of an eye, banding his left arm around my waist while lightly cupping my cheek with his right hand.

"Love you, Pip." He presses his mouth to mine, in the softest of kisses. "So much."

I try to reply, but the second I part my lips, Atlas takes full advantage and deepens our kiss.

The crowd cheers as he takes us from zero to sixty, dipping

me backward as he devours me whole.

"Okay, lovebirds, break it up," Scarlet says, checking me with her hip.

My cheeks ignite as we break apart, both of our chests heaving.

"Way to kill the mood, Scar," Atlas grumbles, but the dopey grin on his face belies him.

"Save it for the honeymoon, Romeo." She rolls her eyes and struts past us, marching right up to Ellis to demand James. "Come see Aunt Scarlet?"

"Noooo. He doesn't want you." Ellis twists out of her reach, playing keep away with my son. "Do you, bud?"

"Scar!" James screeches, all but launching himself at her.

She plucks him from Ellis's arms, props him on her hip, and smirks before turning back toward us. "C'mon, y'all aren't out of here yet. We have toasts and dancing and cake, and *then* y'all can head out and"—she covers James's ears— "Fuck like rabbits."

"Scarlet!" I hiss her name, glaring. "What if people hear you?"

She snorts. "They all know what y'all are gonna be up to tonight—and tomorrow—and the next day. Y'all are literally that annoying couple that has to be touching in some way at all times." She pretends to gag. "It's gross."

"You sound jealous," Atlas says, goading her.

"As if." She rolls her eyes, but I don't miss the way she looks at Ellis when she thinks no one's watching. "We're gonna head inside. Y'all don't take too long."

I loop my arm through Atlas's as she and Ellis head into the main cabin, where we're holding the reception. "Let's not keep everyone waiting."

"Hold on a second." Atlas grins down at me, his eyes full of filthy promises that I'm all too eager for him to deliver on, as he steps into my space. "Can't wait for tonight, Pip," he whispers in my ear. "Have I told you how amazing you look in this dress? My jaw damn near came unhinged when you walked down the aisle."

"Thank you." I glance down at my feet, suddenly feeling shy under his heated stare.

But like always, Atlas doesn't let me linger in my self-doubt. "Now let me tell you how much better you're going to look when I strip it off you and fuck you later tonight." He groans as if he's in pain. "Can't wait to make you scream my name, to make you mine."

I don't mean to laugh, but a giggle breaks free, nonetheless. "I'm already yours, you caveman."

He puffs out his chest. "Damn right you are. Forever."

My lips curl into a private smile, because the rest of our forever officially starts right now.

THE END

WANT A LITTLE MORE ATLAS & NORA?
Sign up for my newsletter to receive an exclusive bonus scene!

BEFORE YOU GO

Stay up to date with all LK's bookish happenings—from new releases to sales to exclusive content, and more.

No spam, just good books, and that's a promise!

Join her Facebook group by scanning the QR code below

LK'S OTHER TITLES

All of LK's titles can be read as standalones & are available with Kindle Unlimited. An * beside a title denotes it is also available in audio.

Sweet Little Nothing * (an enemies-to-lovers/bully romance)

Dirty Little Secret * (an older brother's best friend/second chance romance)

Pretty Little Thing * (a single mom/forced proximity/mistaken identity romance)

Best Laid Plans * (an older brother's best friend/secret baby romance)

Best of Intentions * (a friends-to-lovers/little sister's best friend romance)

Best of Me * (a second chance at love/forbidden twin romance)

Rebel Heart (an enemies-to-lovers jock/tutor rom-com)

Rebel Soul (an arranged baby/friends-to-lovers rom-com)

Rebel Desire (an unrequited soulmates/surprise single dad rom-com)

Coming Up Roses (a small-town/single mom romance)

An Uphill Battle (a frenemies-to-lovers romance)

Weather the Storm (a second chance at love romantic suspense)

Come What May (an age gap/single dad romance)

ACKNOWLEDGMENTS

They say it takes a village to raise a child, but apparently it applies to writing a book too. So, let me take a minute to thank my village.

Heather, the bffoml, you are the wind beneath my wings and I am beyond thankful for you. Your steady presence in my life and our morning meetings keep me going. Thank you for letting me bounce ideas off of you and for the countless times I made you talk out the same plot points over and over.

Renee, your belief in me as I wrote this book is part of what kept me going, and trust me, there were times I really, really wanted to quit. Thank you for never giving up on me—and for not letting me give up on Atlas and Nora. Your friendship means more to me than you'll ever know.

Kris & Drea, my babes. I don't know what I would do without y'all, and hopefully I never have to find out. Thank you both for always being there for me, for always having a listening ear, and for never judging. Y'all are the calm to my storm. My sweet Bubbles and Buttercup.

Harloe, you've listened to me whine endless about this story—and a million other things—and never once made me feel like a burden. Your friendship soothes a part of my soul and I am so thankful you slid into my messages and demanded a spot in my life all those years ago.

Amie, thank you simply for being you. You're my person and I love you. I couldn't, for a single second, imagine doing this thing called life without you. It doesn't matter how busy you are, you always find time for me, and I am forever appreciative and in awe of you.

Jodie, my soul sister, simply put, this book would not exist without you. There aren't enough words in the English language to express my thankfulness for you. Love you always!

Rue, Samantha, Laura, JJ, and Malia, thank you ladies so much for lending me your knowledge and insight in areas where I lacked it. Y'all helped make sure Atlas and Nora's story shined in the best way possible, even if some of my questions were watchlist worthy.

Heather F., you get a special mention, because without you so graciously sharing your firsthand experience, the first epilogue wouldn't be nearly as epic as it is. You're a total badass, and I am so thankful for you.

Kiezha, you always go above and beyond for me and I so, super thankful. Even if you took away all of my emotional...support...ellipses.

Julie, this book wouldn't be complete with your eagle eyes. And your notes totally made me cry. Thank you so much.

Laura, your input on this book was detrimental. Seriously, thank you so much. Atlas and Nora would not be what they are now without you.

To my accountability chat, thank y'all for holding me...you guessed it...accountable day in and day out. Y'all's support truly helped me make it to the end.

Stacey, ILYSM! You are always there for me, and I hope you know the same is true for you—you need it, and I'm there.

Alyssa, Aundi, Amanda, Bailey, Brianna, Amy, & Laura, thank you ladies so much beta reading this story. Some of you read it in chunks and had to wait a small eternity for the ending. Y'all's notes, feedback, reactions, and encouragement means the world to me.

Helena, Lauren, Shain, Amanda, & KP, thank you ladies so much for always taking the time to chat with me, talk me down from the ledge, and through my millions of questions after such a long hiatus. People like y'all are what make this industry so amazing.

Kathy, thank you so much for putting the name Atlas in my ear. You rock!

To my family, your unending patience and support mean the world to me.

And most of all, to my amazing readers, THANK YOU FROM THE BOTTOM OF MY HEART. Whether you're an OG who's been with me from the start or a newbie who took a chance on this book, your support means everything to me. Thank you a million times over—and then some.

ABOUT LK FARLOW

Known by Kate to most, LK Farlow is an Amazon Top 40 bestselling author of over a dozen small town romances, ranging from sweet, to sexy, to rip your heart out, and everything in between.

Kate has a heart built for happily-ever-afters, which is lucky since she found hers at the young age of nineteen. Now, at thirty-something, she is the wife to one hunky man and the mother to four semi-feral humans, three lizards, and a handful of stray cats.

Kate often jokes that her life is all out chaos on most days, but she wouldn't trade it for the world.

facebook.com/authorlkfarlow
instagram.com/authorlkfarlow
tiktok.com/@lkfarlowwrites
amazon.com/author/lkfarlow
goodreads.com/lkfarlow